# GUARDIANS
# OF THE JESUS
# GENE

*Guardians of the Jesus Gene*

THAMES RIVER PRESS
An imprint of Wimbledon Publishing Company Limited (WPC)
Another imprint of WPC is Anthem Press (www.anthempress.com)
First published in the United Kingdom in 2013 by
THAMES RIVER PRESS
75–76 Blackfriars Road
London SE1 8HA

www.thamesriverpress.com

A CIP record for this book is available from the British Library.

ISBN 978-0-85728-133-3

This title is also available as an eBook

# GUARDIANS OF THE JESUS GENE

PETER R. HALL

THAMES RIVER PRESS

# Acknowledgements

To my wife, Wendy, who typed and retyped my endless handwritten drafts, and without whose help this story could not have been fashioned.

To my agent, Darin Jewell, managing director of The Inspira Group.

To my publisher, Mr K Sood, managing director of Thames River Press.

Men must commit evil, for without
evil there cannot be good.
Just as without dark there cannot be
light.
To accept the concept of a supreme
deity is an endorsement of evil,
since evil is his creation too.

—*Brahma*

# Historical Note

In a village outside Caesarea, Jesus asked his disciples, "Who do men say I am?"

Peter replied, "You are the Messiah, the Anointed One."

For 800 years the Jews had waited for the man whom the God of Israel would choose to establish His Kingdom on earth. Down the centuries his coming had been foretold by the greatest of the Judaean prophets and Jesus, as much as any other Jew, would have regarded as blasphemous any suggestion that he was a deity.

The very term 'Anointed One' signifies a call to office.

If Jesus had ever dared to claim to be divine, all Jews, including his disciples, would have instantly rejected it as an abhorrent and unforgivable blasphemy.

None of the Apostles regarded Jesus as being other than a man anointed by God, whom He had imbued with supernatural power.

We owe the deification of Jesus to the Roman emperor Constantine, who in the summer of 325AD personally summoned all Christian bishops and church leaders to the first ever Church Council, which he held at the lakeside town of Nicaea – today Isnik in north western Turkey.

The issue, which has caused bitter divisions within the Church and was the reason for Constantine summoning the bishops from every part of the empire, was an argument over whether Jesus was human. Was he a man who had been brought into existence to serve God's purpose and to act as God's messenger, or had he been with God for all eternity "of one substance with the father"?

In the Greek language used at the time of the New Testament, Messiah means 'messenger.'

For Constantine, who mixed Christianity with the pagan Sol-in-Victus cult, and only became baptised on his deathbed, deification wasn't anything special. He had had his father, Constantius, deified and would, in the tradition of all Caesars, be accorded the same honour after his own death.

Under pressure from Constantine, the Council of Nicaea declared Jesus to be, "Very God through all eternity." Worse still, they imposed a theology on all Christians that contained none of the ethical teachings Jesus had preached.

After the pronouncement of the Council of Nicaea, the gap between Christian and Jew became unbridgeable. For the Jews, the Roman practice of deification was an insupportable blasphemy.

In 431 at the Council of Ephesus it was declared that Mary should be called *Theotokus* – God bearing – and therefore Mother of God, ever virgin, in spite of the fact that, in addition to Jesus, she had borne two daughters and four sons. Mark 6:1–6, "This is the carpenter surely, the Son of Mary. The brother of James and Joset and Jude and Simon. His sisters too, are they not with us?"

St Paul corroborates the existence of James as the brother of Christ in Galatians 1:20, "I saw only James, the brother of the Lord."

**For further evidence, see the appendix at the back of this book.**

Jesus was a member of a family that, from the time of David, had produced a long line of priests, faith-healers, exorcists, magicians and prophets – an inheritance of the blood coded into the genes.

Judaism shares with Christianity a belief in a continuous divine relationship between man and God, and that God fills with supernatural grace the men and women He chooses to be His messengers.

Such a belief is as old as the belief in Satan. The mystery of opposition to the Creator, an adversary who cannot exist without His consent, Satan is the power that even Jesus acknowledged as ruler of the earth and all matter.

The Apocalypse of Moses and the Wisdom of Solomon identify Satan as "master of the world with the evil impulse in man" – a power that rules all matter and thus stands between the spirit of man and its eventual return to its maker.

Throughout the centuries – past and to come – there appears from the House of David an 'anointed one,' the defender of humanity against the coming of the Anti-Christ.

Among my sources I include material from the authorised version of the Bible, which clearly states that Jesus had brothers and sisters.

The War of the Jews was one of the bloodiest in history. Its legacy is with us to this day, as Arab and Jew continue to contest ownership of what was once Canaan, in an ongoing war that will be fought to the death, with both sides claiming their God is on their side.

To some problems there are no solutions – only consequences.

Peter R. Hall
Somerset
2013

1

The corpses bobbed and dipped in counterpoint to the rhythm of the lake's movement. A stiff early morning breeze funnelling down between the barren hills ploughed its surface with furrows of wavelets that banged and bumped across its length, each joust ending in a sullen collapse on its desolate shores.

The bodies mostly floated face down, only the tumescence of the backs of heads and buttocks breaking the lake's surface. Occasionally an aimlessly drifting figure would gently bump against its neighbours, its crow-picked eyes blindly accusing the huge carrion birds not yet sated with the abundance spread before them.

For the bloated hundreds that cobbled the lake's surface, in its depths shoals of thousands eddied in gentle communion, the dimpled white of their blanched and mutilated flesh a hazy gleam in the rosy liquor.

Those who had not been driven into the water had been cut down wherever they had finally given up their flight – in their fields, their orchards, their villages, their gardens. The dusty roads leading from the burning towns were avenues of agony. The Romans had planted crosses along their verges, nailing aloft the bodies of six thousand men and women who had begged in vain for death as they were forced to suffer the torture of the foulest method of execution man had yet devised.

The Judaean uprising had been defiant and widespread, but when it collapsed, the survivors were exterminated as perfunctorily as an infestation of lice. Only the fittest young males were spared, sent in chains to work themselves to death in the Empire's mines in Syria and Egypt. As these captives marched to their own living hell, their last view of the earth's surface was a landscape of death. As they trudged on, day after day, it was as though they and their captors were the only ones left alive in the whole land.

The dead populated every village. The women, stripped naked and used for the relief of the army, lay on their backs next to their dead children. The men lay where they had been cut down – in the byre next to the animals bawling to be milked, or in the hedge bottoms of the fields they had defended.

In the towns and villages of the mountains, rebel resistance had been organised and fierce. When they finally capitulated, the Romans took few prisoners. Instead, as an act of revenge, captives of both sexes had been nailed to trees or burned alive.

The uprising, which had resulted in the massacre in the foothills of the Dead Sea, was a serious setback for the Jews and greatly embarrassed the Romans. The last of the organised resistance had tried to retreat to the safety of the barren, rock strewn hills which were honeycombed with caves that could hide an army. But they had been overtaken on the lake's shore and, trapped by the low-lying land between the hills and the water, were cut to pieces in a single day. An abundance found by the vultures at first light.

As the sun rose higher in the sky, the breeze died away and the fretful movement of the lake's waters stilled. The only thing to disturb their calm was the occasional muted pop and hissing release of gas from a distended abdomen bursting in sudden relief. These minor explosions did not disturb the clouds of flies and insects with their incessant buzz and flashing iridescence, which had gathered with the birds of carrion. The latter were now so stuffed they were incapable of flight and were forced to waddle and wade obscenely from cadaver to cadaver in a fastidious search for dainties.

The few survivors who had escaped the legions fled to the wilderness where, in a vast and hostile wasteland, they eked out a miserable existence. To remain in Judaea or Galilee was to court certain death. Many Jews returned to the safety of the desert, to those barren lands where their forefathers had lived for forty years, as Moses tempered the spiritual steel of the nation he was forging.

Others remained in the mountain wilderness of Judaea, the harsh uncompromising land of John the Baptist. They stayed in spite of the scorchingly hot days and bitterly cold nights.

There were some that ventured into the corpse-strewn hills of the salt sea to cast nets across its stinking waters and reap a ghastly harvest. They did so without fear of encountering the Romans, who had long since left the killing ground. The scavengers who fished this foul sea had no fear of the pestilence, for they held every disease known to man in absolute contempt being already inflicted with the most hideous – leprosy.

What these fishers sought was meagre enough – a pair of sandals, a few coins, a brooch, a weapon, a useful farm tool – any items that could be sold, if a buyer could be found!

When the corpses were fresher and if they were young and female, they could be abused, as the sin of necrophilia did not carry much weight with human beings cast out of society and driven away by stones if they ventured near even the humblest dwelling.

In this society of pariahs, leadership went to the strong, and the length of office was determined by the speed at which that strength was literally eaten away by the living death of their disease. The end came when they were no longer capable of scavenging enough food or water to sustain life.

A victim could survive his face being eaten away, even an arm, a foot or a leg, but not both arms and both feet, for without them he could not even crawl on his belly with his face in the dust to compete with the dogs in the town's middens. So he wrapped his horror in rags, covered his head with cloth and lived as a pariah, the living dead as his only companions.

Every morning before crawling out of whatever crack he had found to hide in, he'd curse God and unwrap his mutilations. How far had the disease spread in the night? Would another finger, or foot, or hand, or arm, simply break off like the stem of a field mushroom to lie white and bloodless in his poor clouts, or would the sight of what he had seen yesterday be denied him today because he had woken up blind?

It was all a matter of chance. In some victims, the disease, once contracted, hardly advanced at all, and the sufferer dragged out a miserable existence that lasted for years. For others the disease reduced its victim down to a rotting, limbless grub within a matter of weeks. The best they could hope for was that one of their brethren would be merciful enough to kill them.

The leader of this particular band was a woman of indeterminate age. Beneath a wild mane of filthy, silver-streaked black hair was a ruined face, a parody of human features, the typical 'lion mask' of advanced leprosy. Only the eyes bespoke a human intelligence, a mind that burned with bitter resentment at her condition. Tall and big boned, years of physical effort had imbued her with a wiry strength that would have been equal to that of a Corinth wrestler.

During those same bitter years Clodia had learned everything there was to know about survival. She was quick to use anything at hand to gain the advantage, from the blade she kept in her sleeve to the bullwhip that girdled her waist, which she could uncoil and flip over a man's head with devastating speed.

If her victim was not a fellow leper, she delighted in kneeling on his chest, her crossed hands white to the knuckles as the iron hard plaited whip bit into the throat and finally crushed the larynx. Like some terrible incubus she would pin her helpless, choking victim to the ground and gleefully bend over him, the curtain of hair framing both their faces. The last thing on earth the dying man would see was the hideous lion mask inches from his own face and all-consuming hatred in its eyes.

It was she who found the man still alive. He lay in the cleft of a giant boulder, split by the volcano that had given it birth aeons before. From the way his left leg was doubled up it was obviously broken. He also had a badly bruised forehead and the side of his face and beard were matted with congealed blood.

When Clodia first saw him she thought him dead. It was only as she dragged him out of the crack into which he was wedged, to strip and search his body, that his eyes fluttered open.

With an expert stroke of her knife she cut his belt and outer garment. A second slash and a shake and she rolled his naked body into the dust. The man groaned softly from the pain of his shattered leg, but was too weak to move. The woman ignored him as she went through his clothes, noting that they were of good cloth.

As he stirred ineffectually she flashed him a hideous grin, devoid of all humour. When she found the purse she sought she growled softly in triumph and, as she swept his clothes up into a rough bundle, heard him moan again. Others had found her prize and like hyenas were scuttling in for a share of the pickings. Two were already fighting to get his sandals off, while a third was using a stick to try and force his jaws apart. Gold! Of course, she should have thought of it.

With a warning shout she freed the heavy whip and with a practised swing, cut the air above the leper's head. The ominous whirr of its heavy length ending in an explosive crack that reverberated and echoed off the surrounding hills caused the crouching figure to look up from his task.

The face that stared up at her had no nose or lips, the bare gums a mandrill's mask, a bray of permanently bared teeth. The hands that tried so clumsily to force the injured man's jaws apart were without fingers and had only thumbs and the pads of the palms to grip with. With a harsh bark of protest, the ruin let the injured man's head go. Fresh blood surrounded his lips, which were bruised and torn from his assailant's ineffectual poking.

With her competitors driven off the prize, Clodia made no effort to enquire of the injured man if there was any gold to be mined from his mouth. After all, when she had slit his throat an examination of his teeth would be as swift and as easy as knocking them out with a rock.

As she advanced on the prostrate figure, drawn knife at the ready, he spoke in a voice barely above a whisper. "Stay your blade and call off your wolves. Your reward will be a treasure beyond all the gold that exists on earth."

If the words had any effect on the advancing amazon it didn't show on the grotesque face, and the taloned hands that jerked the man's head back to lay his throat open to the butcher's stoke heralded death within seconds. With their faces only inches apart, it was the lack of revulsion that stayed Clodia's hand. The bloodshot eyes staring into what should have been her face, though they were filled with pain and sunken into a face grey with exhaustion, did not flinch from the living gargoyle that masqueraded as human flesh.

With the tip of the blade drawing blood from his throat, she spoke, "And what makes you think you can offer me anything of more value than the pleasure of your dying?"

To the leper's amazement, her battered captive managed the ghost of a smile before replying, "Bend closer sister so that only you may hear."

For a moment Clodia stared in disbelief into the exhausted face. For a few seconds she was mentally completely off balance – it had been a long time since she had been asked to approach another human being who was not a leper.

Before bending her ear to the man's lips she swivelled her head, eyes darting from side to side. With a circling sweep of her arm she scythed the air with her knife, the heavy blade carving a wide arc of space to keep back the curious among her followers. Those who had hopped and scrambled in a flap of loose bandages and frayed rags to form a circle of mummy-like figures that crouched and squatted, chirping like goblins, flies swarming over their filthy bandages in an effort to find a centimetre of uncovered flesh.

With a warning outstretched arm to keep them at bay, Clodia did as she was bidden and lowered her head to the whispering lips. What she heard held her frozen. "I am Simon, the brother of him they call the Christ. I am a magician of great powers. If you help me, I will cast out the devils that entered into you and make you clean."

As the import of the whispered words sank into her mind, Clodia sprang upright with a terrible scream – a raw sound compounded of shock and disbelief at what she had been promised. Hope burst like a supernova, filling her with a brilliance of joy that was expunged as quickly as it had been born. It was replaced by a wave of black despair; an overwhelming weight of what might have been that caused her to tear her hair out in handfuls as she screamed her frustration. Of all the things he could have promised, she had been offered the one she believed to be so impossible, so beyond belief, that not for a single second of her waking existence did she dare allow herself to think about it. Only in her dreams was she tormented by the unattainable.

Howling with fury, the demented woman scattered her followers as she sprang from the side of the injured man, her monstrous visage suffused with blood, eyes glittering with passion. In her rage she cracked her deadly flail and without any conscious thought whirled it around her head, its heavy four-metre tapered length just a blur in the bright sunlit air. Anybody caught by that deadly rotor would be as dead as if the sharpest sword had cut him or her down.

As suddenly as the explosion of passion had galvanised her into action, the tempest left her. In its place was an implacable ice-cold rage, "If you can cure lepers, then you can start with yourself, for that is what you shall become. Your food shall be that which has been chewed by lepers and your bed will be shared by the most afflicted among us – that is, if you survive this."

The snarling woman treading on his injured leg accompanied this last. To her and her companions' amazement, the injured man gave no outward sign of what should have been excruciating pain as Clodia malevolently bore down on the damaged limb with all her weight.

Instead he answered her in a surprisingly strong voice, "In Jerusalem there is a building with five porticoes, in front of which is a pool. There did he not make the crippled walk? Do you not know of the magician, the Nazarene who healed? I tell you his powers are in me for we are of the same blood, the same bone. Did we not suck the same milk?"

The woman removed her foot. "Then," she said slowly as though fearing to say the words, "show me." Without thinking she dropped to her knees to stare deep into Simon's eyes. "Cure me!"

Slowly the injured man levered himself onto his elbows, raised his right hand and placed it against her hideous cheek. "You have faith and so you will, I promise, be cured – but think what would happen if you and you alone were cured now, this minute, in this place." He saw the anger, the contempt of betrayal flare in the woman's eyes. He dropped his hand and fell back into the dust, staring straight into the sky. "They would kill us both." His voice was flat, final. He would debate no more.

The woman turned to stare across the crimson lake with its desperate fishers, their cries the different and discordant sounds of death trembling in the shimmering heat. Without moving her head she said, "Tell me what to do."

# 2

Under Simon's instructions they roughly splinted his leg and bound it to his good one, before placing him on a makeshift litter. Then, at Clodia's command, they bundled up the harvest they had scavenged from the dead and set out at a shambling march, the fitter lepers taking it in turns to help carry the litter. The rest hopped and scrambled on crutches and sticks, hampered by the booty crudely strapped to their backs.

The ground over which they travelled was rough and stony and rose steeply from the shores of the Dead Sea. Great salt cliffs, six hundred feet high at the southwest end of the lake, bounced the heat of the sun back across the valley. It heliographed a dazzling illusion of glacier cool to the ramparts of Herod's castle at Machaerus, where it topped the monstrous mass of rock that reared up for a thousand feet from the shore.

The track they toiled along was boulder strewn and wound tortuously through the desolate hills. This was the harsh barren land of Judaea, an irregular broken plateau of mountains, hills and valleys.

In the whole of its worn, grey, rocky ridges and narrow boulder-strewn valleys, there was not a single running stream whose waters flowed throughout the year, and very few springs of water. The winter rains rushed down these stony hillsides into the valleys where, for Jerusalem or Hebron, the other outstanding city of the area, the collection of this water in immense rock-hewn cisterns was essential.

In the summer the stony ground was baked by a scorching sun and scarcely supported the small and scattered flocks of sheep and goats that hunted for its sparse vegetation. Here, Jesus spent the forty days of his retreat and, at the eastern edge of this wilderness which plunges down into the Jordanian valley, he stood on the summit of a mighty cliff that spanned the whole valley floor. He looked towards the east, across to Syria and Egypt, for this was the place of his temptation.

Clodia and her unwilling partners reached the cave by late afternoon, desperately tired and short of water. There, they were outraged to find that the slit in the rock face to which they had been directed contained only the simplest of possessions, which included a jar of dried lentils and a single goatskin of stale water.

While her ragged band of followers quarrelled over the water, Clodia stood over the injured Simon who had been dumped unceremoniously at the back of the cave. "Well?" her voice was dangerously flat. To the prone man she was a sinister silhouette against the cave mouth.

"Draw near and cut my legs free." His voice was surprisingly strong and the request puzzled her. Without a word she slipped out her blade and bent over him, cutting the bindings. She made to straighten up but he caught her sleeve and, taking her knife, cut the splint off the shattered leg.

In the gloom she couldn't see his face, but his eyes flashed at her. She watched him carefully as he quickly cut the bindings and dragged the splint away. There was no change of expression in his eyes. She remained crouched over him, watching, puzzled and uneasy.

He reached out and took hold of her free hand, pulling it down onto his leg. In disbelief she ran her fingers down what should have been a shattered limb. The leg was whole.

Her cry of amazement was stilled as he clapped a hand across what was left of her mouth. "Send them away."

Trembling, Clodia stared incomprehensibly at the dark figure that sat at her feet. "I can't cure all of them. What will they do if you alone are made whole?"

As the implication of what he was saying sank into her brain, Clodia squatted on her heels – she could only nod in agreement.

"Four miles from here lies the village of Bethany. You can see it if you follow the path round the shoulder of the mountain. The Romans have either killed all the villagers or they have fled into hiding in these hills. There, your people will find food and water. The well is good and if they dig up the floors of the houses they will find the secret store of grain hidden by the people for such times as these...having themselves been harvested by the Romans," he ended grimly, "they will have no need of them."

The band of lepers took some persuading but the obvious shortage of water and the whip worked in the end, and in the shadows of the late afternoon the band made its way disconsolately across the mountain to the deserted village which could be glimpsed in a fold of the hills.

At this time of day threads of white smoke should have been rising as the women prepared the evening meal and the tinkle of bells from returning flocks of goats should have drifted on the still mountain air. Instead, vultures spiralled like smuts of black ash eddying from a garden bonfire, swinging lazily in the ochre haze of the last of the day's heat.

Clodia turned back from the cave's entrance, no thought or concern troubling her mind for how her little band would fare without her strong leadership. She was as indifferent to their fate as the wolf for an injured companion. Survival of self was life's all-important lesson, and she had been a willing pupil.

Ignoring her presence, Simon crouched over fragments of dried moss and was sparking a flint. Lying in readiness on the floor next to him was a roughly made torch and a straight staff of ancient dark wood. When a wisp of smoke rewarded his efforts he concentrated on blowing the tiny spark into life, gently teasing his little mound of dried mosses with a twig. He was rewarded with a sudden bright spurt as a finger of flame leapt upwards. Expertly he fed the fledgling fire, adding tiny bone dry twigs to the moss, taking care not to smother the new flame.

Clodia dropped to her haunches to squat opposite him while the task was completed.

With the fire burning strongly, she grunted her approval and only then did Simon look up. As he did so, he lit the torch and taking the staff stood up, motioning her to do the same, and without a word made his way to the back of the cave. Satisfied that he had found what he sought, he inserted the tip of his staff beneath the bottom edge of one of the boulders and with a practised heave rolled it aside to reveal a narrow passage that was a natural continuation of the cave.

He stared into the lion's mask, hideous in the torch's flickering light, its eyes glittering like chips of obsidian, suspicious, dangerous and ready to strike at the first sign of treachery. Holding Clodia's gaze, Simon spoke. "This passage leads to another cave. In it you will find a pool. Bathe and you will be clean."

Without a word Clodia turned her head and surveyed the desperately small and ominously dark entrance to the second cave. It was so narrow that she would have to enter it sideways.

Her eyes slid to the staff the man had used to lever the boulder with. Once inside the limestone passage it would be simplicity itself to wall her up forever. "You need a bath as much as I do," she said dryly, "so you can go first."

She motioned with her torch to the entrance. With a shrug Simon edged his way into the crack and after a moment's final suspicious hesitation, Clodia followed him. Even with the torch, progress through the passage was an eerie experience, the blackness so velvet and total it seemed to press down with a physical presence as though reminding them of the millions of tons of mountain above their heads.

It was cold enough to make Clodia shiver, but the walls were powder dry, bearing only the chisel marks of the original owners who had cut away enough of the projecting rock to make it possible for a single file of people to walk down the passage.

Clodia was suddenly aware that she could hear the splash of water and a few seconds later stumbled after Simon into a massive second cave, the floor of which was a huge underground lake fed by a waterfall.

Simon walked silently to the water's edge and fixed the spluttering torch between two boulders. Without a word he disrobed and dived cleanly into the black depths, surfacing at the edge of the torch's field of light, his bearded face a pale blob in the black water. Still he didn't speak.

Clodia was frightened. The oppressive weight of the soaring darkness, the black-mirrored sheet of the lake that seemed to extend forever, the echoing splash of the waterfall that sprang out of some hidden crevice, created a forbidding atmosphere – she felt as though she was trespassing.

Simon turned away from her and with a few lazy strokes disappeared into the darkness. How far, she wondered, was the other side? Did it lead to another exit?

The sudden thought of possible treachery spurred her to action and dispelled her fears. With a growl she slipped out of her clothes, but wound the whip around her naked waist before diving into the water, swimming strongly in the direction Simon had taken. To her surprise a dozen strokes carried her to the other side, which was a sheer wall of featureless rock that rose straight out of the water. Shivering slightly from the water's chill and her own fear, she trod water and looked back at the flickering torch.

Simon was standing in its light, the water streaming down his body, and he looked directly towards her. Without haste he picked up his robe. "I will leave you the torch." His voice was impersonal; it echoed around the vaulted chamber – "the torch, the torch, torch, torch, torch, torch…" and he was gone.

Clodia fought down her panic and swam as fast as she could from the opposite shore. Hauling herself out of the water with a single powerful thrust of her arms, she snatched up both the torch and her clothes before setting off at a dead run for the tunnel.

Fear clutched at her stomach, a murderous rage rising at the man's duplicity. With the skin scuffed off her elbows and knees from the mad scramble through the passage, she stumbled into the outside cave panting heavily, eyes wild, almost at the edge of hysteria.

Simon was sitting at the entrance with his back towards her, staring out across the darkening land. Clodia was trembling with anger – anger fuelled by fear. Without saying a word she spun the coils of her whip across the cave floor, back and shoulders arching for the explosion of power that would snap its iron hard strands into the man's neck.

"Woman." The authority of the voice stopped her dead. "Are you clean?"

Clodia crouched, frozen. The man made no move to turn. He remained silent. With trembling fingers she raised her hand to explore her face. With a groan she fell on her knees and rocked backwards and forwards, her forehead knocking in the dust, her mind in turmoil. The lake – the thought exploded in her head. Sobbing wildly she picked up the guttering torch and scrambled back into the tunnel. Back to the lake's surface, as black and reflective as a mirror.

The woman was forgotten. Simon stood up, raising his arms to recite the ancient evocation to the city, which, for all Hebrews, sustains their faith in one holy invisible God.

"If I have forgotten thee, oh Jerusalem,

Let my right hand forget her cunning.

If I do not remember thee

Let my tongue cleave to the roof of my mouth.

If I prefer not Jerusalem above

My chief joy."

For months he had felt the approach of an alien presence, stalked by the ancient evil that was loose in the land. He knew there was no escape and he had prayed for help to the God of his people, but in vain. Jehovah remained deaf to his cries. It seemed as if he would have to face the ultimate evil alone.

His prayer finished, Simon squatted and stirred the embers of the fire. In its sudden brightening the muscles of his heavily built torso were sculpted into shadowed relief. Above his head the narrow opening of the cave framed the early evening stars. He continued to stare across the arid land to where he knew Jerusalem lay, perched on the hills above the valleys of Kidron and Hinnom, a site that gave the city its strategic strength and made it impregnable from two sides.

He felt Clodia timidly touch his shoulder and turned to face her. She was naked except for a sheepskin robe pulled across her shoulders. In the starlight she stood taller than he, broad shouldered and wide hipped, lean and hard muscled by years of constant wandering and fighting for survival.

Slowly his eyes travelled down from her strong, sad face, no longer disfigured, to her big full breasts. An irrelevant memory of his mother flickered through his mind. He experienced the desire to suckle, to chew, to bite, to press them against his face, to lose himself in their bursting fullness, to fill his mouth with the dark aureoles of their nipples.

"Lord." Clodia fell to her knees, pressing the back of his hand to her forehead.

Simon paused, awkward, his eyes uneasy. When he spoke his voice was low, shyly hesitant. "I have lived without a woman for years. I want to be sure," he continued huskily, "that you are not offering yourself out of gratitude – or pity." This last was a growl, a rumble of anger.

At this acknowledgement of Simon's shyness, his tender consideration of her feelings, Clodia was moved by an emotion that she had thought never to experience again. She drew him away from the cave's entrance to the couch of fleeces, which lay in an angle of rock away from the draught of the entrance but close enough to the fire to get the benefit of its warmth.

When she spoke her voice was husky with emotion. "Lord, all the days of my life I want only to live in your shadow. Let me be your servant, your slave - do with me as you will but do not, I beg you, ever send me from your side."

He smiled gently and caressed Clodia's cheek before lifting her to her feet. "Woman, I have much to do and from now on my life will be filled with great danger…" He saw the panic flare in the woman's eyes, felt the muscles of her arms harden under his hands. "But," he continued, "it is written that we make this journey together" – and the sentence was completed in his head but remained unspoken, "when you will give birth to a child in whose blood will be that mysterious power that God gives to those He chooses as His special servants."

Simon trembled violently at the suddenness of his vision. Clodia, mistaking it for a surge of passion, drew him to her and offered her mouth to him. As they stood within the circle of each other's arms, she could feel his strength bending towards her and a great tenderness and feeling of wonder engulfed her.

Then Simon bowed his head and kissed her, both hands cupping her breasts, her nipples instantly hardening at his touch. She felt his tongue. He ran his lips down her neck feeling the veins palpating, nuzzling her throat, drawing the breath from her. She swayed, heavy with desire. Her skin had become hypersensitive; she could feel it rippling under his fingers. As he ran his hands down her back, a shiver passed through her sparking every nerve in her body to an arousal she had never known before.

Simon's caresses had a primitive quality – first gentle and softly smoothing, then rough and semi-fierce like a great male cat with its mate.

She shuddered with pleasure as he ran his hands over her body, probing and teasing at her sex, his fingers hooked in the bush of wildly tangled hair that curled between the cleft of her powerful thighs and climbed in silky spirals to her deeply indented navel.

Luxuriating in his touch, Clodia closed her eyes. She felt as though he had a hundred hands, a thousand fingers that touched her everywhere. Many mouths that brushed her softly all over, their velvet warmth spiced with a sudden sharpness as Simon's lips parted to sink his teeth into her breasts, the inside of her thighs, to nibble delicately at that sweep grape folded, guarded, in the lips of her own sex.

Naked and aroused Simon lay his whole weight on her. She enjoyed the heaviness of his body and tremors passed through her as she responded to his touch. Simon whispered to her in the warm dark, telling her what to do. He held her deep inside, matching the slow rhythm of his body to the caressing of his fingers. She came at once, the suddenness overwhelming her. She cried out, muscles convulsing out of control. She felt his arms around her, iron hard, protective. She fluttered like a trapped bird as he speared her savagely, driving her to orgasm after orgasm until she slumped half-fainting in his embrace.

He rested inside her and waited, the long timeless minutes sliding by as they lay in mutual harmony. Her skin was cool, her eyes shone luminescent in the embers of the dying fire. On the surface there was nothing left of the woman he had brought from the desert.

Simon could just make out her figure, her hair in wild disorder, its heavy tresses tumbling across her shoulders and down her back. She reached out a trembling hand to caress his mouth. He could feel the feathering of her breath, the ebb and flow of her life.

"A new life in a new night," she whispered.

Suddenly Simon was aware of unspoken emotions. The response was in his blood – a response stronger than life itself. As he kissed her fingertips he said huskily, "A few hours ago life was landscape bereft of hope, a desert in which all must perish. But now, I am the first man again – Adam reborn."

"Hold me," she cried. Simon pulled her close to him. Clodia's hands lay folded together against his chest. He could feel her trembling.

"We are living," he said sombrely, "at the end of an age, and this land will be the place of its death."

The fire had long since died and in the darkness of the cave he could not see her eyes blurred and drugged by the violence of her feelings, but he could hear the harsh rasp of her breath as passion rekindled.

She was compelled to touch his flesh with her mouth, with her hands, with her whole body. She rubbed against him with her breasts, enjoying the animal friction of their bodies. Then, like a great cat, she stretched out at his side kissing him softly on the lips, the eyes, the nose, as if by touch she could imprint his face on her memory forever. Her fingers were strong but light, then abruptly they would become talons that dug violently into his flesh as though to assure her of his reality.

In the depths of the night they explored each other's bodies. How the honey flowed from her.

"I was in the wilderness and you found me." It was Clodia who broke the silence.

"My life is yours – and yours mine," Simon replied. "Don't ask for more. We have the moment, no matter how uncertain the future."

As the cave lightened with the dawn, Clodia's eyes were alternately very translucent and very dark in her pale face. "We shall not die, beloved," she whispered fiercely, "for you are the favourite of your God whose favour I have been given."

Simon looked away. It was as though a weight had suddenly pressed against his heart. He knew that in the morning they would face a grim reality that would wipe away the rapture of the night. And yet, when he looked at the woman who lay at his side, he wondered. "You are right," Simon whispered in her ear. "The moment is life, the moment most keenly felt is that which is closest to eternity."

Clodia kissed him passionately. Dimly she was aware of Simon's hands lifting her. Her flesh pulsed as it drew him in until she could feel him touching the very bottom of her womb, contacting the entrance to life itself. In the final moments of union she was swept away on a storm of passion.

She felt the mingling of their seed and a wild surge of emotion so fierce as to be beyond pleasure or even pain. She clung desperately to the rock hard body of the panting man, sobbing wildly before collapsing into sleep, their bodies locked together.

3

lodia was shy with Simon and, while dying of curiosity, did not ask where they were going. For her, it was sufficient that he had decided it was time to go, and he would tell her where if he chose to do so.

"For months," Simon said, "I have had a premonition of impending danger. Two days ago that feeling was so strong that I left Jerusalem to come to this cave. The rest you know."

"To hide?" asked Clodia.

"No," he replied smiling grimly. "To collect that which was hidden," and taking out his dagger dug into the dirt packed floor. In silence Clodia watched as the hole deepened. A few minutes later Simon grunted with satisfaction as his fingers closed on a leather pouch.

Talking more to himself than to Clodia he said, "I left Jerusalem to retrieve this." He tapped the dirty bundle, "and got caught up with the Zealots who had fled into the En-Gedi, only to be overtaken by the cohorts from the legion garrisoned at Jerusalem. I was lucky to be left for dead – they normally make very certain before leaving the field."

"You were with the Romans?" Clodia was puzzled.

"I am a Roman citizen." Seeing the look of disbelief that crossed her face, Simon continued, his voice grim, "Oh yes, I am a Jew, but I am also a citizen of Rome. I learned a long time ago that, in this world, if you are not a citizen of Rome, you are less than human – at least in Roman eyes, and they are the ones with the power."

Clodia was still puzzled. "Are you a soldier then, an officer in Rome's army?"

Simon laughed. "I am a merchant and a student of Greek philosophy. At least, that's what I tell the world – particularly the Roman world, for they are greatly taken with anything Greek."

Clodia looked at him quizzically and asked dryly, "What do you really do, having persuaded Rome that you are Hellenised?"

Simon's reply was abrupt, as though he was reluctant to share such knowledge with anyone. "I do what my family was born to do." He hesitated but went on, "through the power of the magic we are given, we are appointed by God Himself to uphold His law."

If Clodia was surprised to learn Simon was a magician she gave no sign, for magic was an accepted part of not just Jewish life but of the known world. Miriam the Jewess was one of the most famous sorceresses of ancient times. She was a sister of Moses and, it was said, had been instructed by God himself.

Without further explanation Simon cut the binding of the parcel that had been hidden under the cave's floor and took out its contents. Clodia, who had expected to see something of value – for Simon had risked his life to return for it – was amazed to see that the protective leather covering contained nothing more than a metal spearhead. She was even more surprised to see that it fitted the innocent looking staff that Simon had used to lever the boulder from the entrance to the hidden cave.

Simon did not intend to carry the spear openly as he would the sword, which had appeared from yet another hiding place. When they left the sanctuary of the cave he would be armed, but the spearhead would be carefully hidden in the lining of his cloak.

Standing at the cave entrance taking a meagre breakfast of cold gruel, the early morning sun gilding the barren hills, he smiled quizzically before asking, "What is the name of the woman who will bear my son?"

Clodia laughed, blushing slightly at the thought of the previous night's passion between what were, in effect, two strangers. "My name is Clodia, my lord, and before my family disowned me and cast me out I was of noble Roman birth. The blood of Caesars flows through my veins for my mother was Procula, a granddaughter of Caesar, and she was wife to Pontius Pilate, who was governor of this land when Tiberius was Emperor."

As the bitter irony of what the woman had told him sank in, Simon bowed his head against the cave wall and rocked backwards and forwards from the waist as though at prayer, his eyes closed. His head struck the rock face with the regularity of a metronome until a trickle of blood ran between his eyes to drip unheeded from his chin. The memories he had struggled for years to suppress flooded his mind.

Pilate, the Judaean governor who had been trapped by the Sanhedrin into passing the death sentence on his brother Jesus, had been recalled to Rome only to find on his arrival that Tiberius was dead, having committed suicide when the new emperor, Caligula (Gaius Caesar), refused to restore his governorship. In time both Pilate and his wife, Claudia Procula, Caesar's granddaughter, would be canonised – Pilate by the Abyssinian church and Procula by the Greek.

Clodia watched him anxiously, bewildered that so simple a thing as revealing who her parents had been could have caused such a violent response.

"Well, at least you're a Roman – with a citizen's rights." Simon's voice was distant. Without another word he picked up one of the bundles and, without bothering to wipe the blood from his face, fled from the cave. Setting off down the mountain at a reckless pace, he leapt from crag to crag as though challenging the providence that had dealt him so hurtful a blow.

Clodia followed more carefully, but expertly, down the steep face, watchful of the dangerous scree that would avalanche if disturbed too much.

They marched across the desolation of En-Gedi for three days in almost total silence, Simon withdrawn and solitary. At night they crouched over a small fire and ate a supper of barley soup and listened to the cries of the wild beasts in the wilderness. Simon made no attempt to come near her, spending much of each night huddled in his cloak either staring at the stars or gazing moodily into the fire.

Clodia, insecure in her release from the hideous and deforming disease, frequently passed trembling fingers across her face to reassure herself that she really was cured, or during the day attempted to catch a glimpse of herself in the polished blade of her knife.

It was when they finally cleared the barren hills and were within a mile of one of the city towers that surround Jerusalem, that Clodia felt the presence of something alien.

They were in a deep gorge whose bed was a chaotic tumble of boulders, loose stones, shale and razor sharp flints. Even though it was late afternoon the heat was desiccating. It was like being inside an oven. Apart from the sound of their own laboured breathing as they struggled along its length, no other sound was heard – the silence was oppressive – menacing.

Time and again Clodia, who followed behind the sweating and grim faced Simon, would whirl to carefully check the ground they had covered. The unshakeable feeling of being stalked was growing unbearable. Something or somebody was dogging their trail and the former leper's senses, honed by years of wilderness survival, screamed a warning.

Unable to contain herself any longer she stopped and uncurled her whip. "Lord!" Her shout was both warning and command.

Simon stopped and turned, his face closed, impossible to read. "I feel it, woman. I have been hunted by it all my life – the evil who forever challenges the one God, Jehovah, whose enemy is Lucifer, the rebellious son He cast out of heaven."

Clodia, who as a child had been brought up to pay homage to a whole pantheon of gods of whom Jupiter was father of all, was bewildered by this outburst, but still very much aware of the unseen danger. "You fight with the gods?" Clodia's voice was angry, afraid, and incredulous.

"There is no God but God and the children of Israel are his chosen people." The response was automatic. Simon knelt on the ground picking at the lining of his cloak to free the spearhead he had hidden there, which he then used to carefully inscribe a nine-foot circle in the dirt, motioning the woman to stay at his side in the centre.

The searing hot air seemed to have sucked all the oxygen out of the atmosphere, making it difficult to breathe. In the failing light the shadows of the rocks assumed threatening shapes, while the sheer rock walls of the gorge seemed to press in, shutting out the sky.

In the gloom of the rapidly advancing unnatural darkness, the now terrified Clodia crouched in fear and watched the panting Simon scratching the ground with the spearhead to draw another two circles in the first, using the width of his palm to space them.

When he had done this he hurriedly inscribed in the circle the four names of God, separated by crosses. At each of the cardinal points outside the circle he drew a pentagram. Inside the eastern half he inscribed the Greek letter alpha, and in the western half omega. Then in almost total darkness he used his flint to light a small silver lamp, which he had concealed in his bundle, the oil of which was kept in a tiny flask of the same metal. As the flame spurted a shiver ran through the bed of the gorge.

Terrified at the sudden tremor Clodia would have fled but for Simon's restraining hand. The lamp with its tiny flame was placed reverently at the northern end of the circle. Ignoring the ominous clatter of loose stones rattling down from the slopes of scree loosened by the tremor, Simon carefully lit a fragment of incense and placed it in the south.

As he did so a second but more powerful quake hit the gorge loosening rock falls and boulders that crashed off the steep slopes with a thunderous roar, clouds of choking dust filling the superheated air.

The avalanching scree was the worst. It seemed as if the very walls of the gorge were falling in on them as hundreds of tons of loose stone smashed into the valley floor, silting it ten feet deep in places with shards and fragments of razor sharp rock.

At this second onslaught Clodia was too terrified to move. She crouched in a ball, hugging Simon around the knees, her face buried against his legs. Dimly she was aware of his voice. "Oh mighty living God! I worship you with the greatest reverence and submit to your holy and worthy protection in the deepest confidence. I believe with the utmost faith you are my creator, my benefactor, my support and my master, and I declare to you that I have no other desire but to belong to you in all eternity."

As Simon prayed he stood with the spearhead clutched in both of his hands held in supplication above his head. As if in response to this plea the ground was shaken by an even worse quake. It was as if the rock walls were made of jelly, bending and flexing to a power pulsing through them, the ground itself shifting, torn apart in places, swallowing up the tumble of boulders and loose stones that were now falling into what seemed to be a bottomless pit.

The noise was overwhelming – the thunder from seemingly endless avalanches, riven by the alto scream of rock being torn apart by the earthquake or boulders bursting as they split after falling hundreds of feet. The air turned black with the swirling clouds of choking dirt that billowed through the gorge. In the midst of this maelstrom, Simon's circle was an island of safety but even it couldn't keep out the cold, for suddenly the suffocating heat had given way to an unbelievably searing cold that heralded the arrival of the presence Simon had felt in the cave.

As suddenly as the tumult had started it stopped. Clodia was almost unconscious with fear. Simon covered in dirt, blinked with red-rimmed eyes into the icy darkness.

"It is the woman I want. Leave her and you will not be harmed." The voice was rasping with menace. It scraped around the protective circle like a sword blade drawn across a stone.

Clodia cried out in fear at that terrible command. "No!"

"What is she to you? She is unclean, a leper." As the voice finished speaking a light appeared, a strange murky glow seeping into the valley, a sulphurous orange that seemed to emanate from the split rocks.

Simon watched in horror as the arms clasping his legs suddenly became leprous. Trembling violently he raised his head, shouting his denial.

Inexorably, like a captive beast testing the bars of its cage, the sound of the voice filled his head. "She is unclean. Behold the face of the thing you have mingled your seed with, forever fouling the blood of the line of David."

In spite of himself, Simon was forced to look down. What he saw caused him to cry out, for the face that stared at him was no longer human.

Clodia read the disgust in his eyes and with a howl of rage would have leapt out of the protective circle to instant death, but for Simon who lunged across and grasped her by the waist, fighting fiercely to keep her inside the arena. Clodia was beside herself with despair and fought savagely to free herself from Simon's restraining arms.

It had been the reference to his bloodline that had galvanised Simon into action. It was that which his opponent really wanted. The woman was merely a vessel. It was the destruction of what the vessel contained which was its real purpose.

As he struggled with Clodia the voice rose in crescendo, screaming imprecations at both of them, goading the woman to greater efforts. It was the spearhead that saved her. It had fallen on the ground when Simon had lunged for her and in her efforts to escape she scrabbled in the dirt seeking a weapon – anything with which she could free herself – her hand closed round it.

As she swung her arm, the stubby metal blade in her fist, she was suddenly calm; the lethal swing arrested in mid-air. The trembling Simon drew her to him, his fingers closing in unison with hers around the strange talisman. "No, no, no." He shook with fear, with anger, with defiance, and with his free hand scrabbled in the dirt for his staff. With trembling fingers he fitted the spearhead and stood holding it like a wand challenging Satan.

"Give way to that which shed the holy blood, to that which has become mother to the line of David, blessed of God. I banish you in the name of the mighty Adonai, Eloim, Aeriel and Jehovah, with all my heart and with all my soul."

As Simon made his appeal he knelt holding the trembling Clodia with his left arm, his right raised heavenwards holding the spearhead aloft as drops of warm blood beaded the blade, falling onto their upturned faces.

The sound that rent the heavens following this appeal scoured the senses. It was as if the hinges of the doors of hell were screaming in protest at being closed. As the sound died a great gust of wind swept through the ravine, the unnatural phosphorous glow from the rocks was expunged and the great leaden weight, which had pressed down on them suddenly, lifted.

Clodia was the first to realise that, for the first time, they could see the natural sky, sprinkled with stars. She was sobbing bitterly as Simon tried to calm her. She drew away from him. "Lord, I am unclean again, a leper, do not touch me."

Simon enveloped her in his arms, his voice husky with emotion. "You are the mother of a child of the house of David. By the Law of Moses you are my wife, cleansed by the power of God. What you witnessed now was not reality but an illusion created by Satan. Come, we must find shelter, a place between the rocks where we can light a fire and spend the night safe from the wild beasts that roam this place."

With her spirits rising Clodia stood up. "Lord, no lion or wolf is a match for the power of the god you pray to."

Simon hid an ironic smile and replied, "Gather wood, woman, and don't boast of the God you know nothing about."

Contrite, Clodia said quickly, "Lord, I meant no disrespect but surely he is a powerful god for even the cuts on your hand where you grasped the spearhead are healed."

Simon nodded. Now was not the time to tell her that his hand had never been cut and the blood it shed was not his. He turned his face away to hide the sudden remembrance of the Roman centurion who had administered the coup de grâce to Jesus. Gaius Cassius, the middle-aged guard commander who, as the summer storm had burst overhead, had wanted the whole thing over and, standing in the stirrups of his saddle, had plunged his lance into Christ's side, driving the head of the spear up through the heaving chest into the heart.

# 4

The secret temple had been artfully concealed, positioned in the centre of the immense palace, its only entrance hidden behind a secret door. The security of the building itself was ensured by its high walls and densely wooded grounds. Slaves manned the entrance and protected its long gated drive, patrolling the extensive grounds day and night with massive wolfhounds which, if unleashed, would attack and kill all intruders.

On the special occasion of his initiation, when a candidate was permitted to enter the secret chamber for the first time, the very appearance of this carefully guarded inner sanctum never failed to strike a sudden chill of fear.

In contrast to this ruthlessly guarded privacy, dozens of public rooms were allocated as temples to the major Roman gods and always included at least a bust of the reigning emperor. The rest of the sprawling palace was taken up by sumptuous private living quarters, which boasted the most luxurious baths in the empire.

The owner of the palace was the richest man in Rome, a Greek aristocrat known only as Karkinos. He was a magician whose power of divination was legendary and whose reputation as a magus drew scholars from Egypt, Persia, Syria, and as far away as Armenia.

During the day, the nobility of Rome arrived in their closed litters to entertain or be entertained, to pay homage to the god or goddess of their choice, and have their fortunes read.

Every night the men and women of Rome's aristocracy counted themselves privileged to be invited to the events and entertainment that were made available.

Slaves of both sexes and all ages, including young children, were endlessly available in a bewildering variety of races and colours to take part in the vilest of evil rituals that were practised to gratify the appetites of the guests.

The abominations which took place in the occult and pagan rites that were performed throughout the palace's many saloons, plumbed the depths of depravity, as those who attended lost their humanity in the search for sensations which would gratify senses dulled by a surfeit of more ordinary pleasures.

Karkinos, who orchestrated this nightly orgy at the Palace Aigokerös, was a magus of world power who, in great secrecy, exercised considerable influence over the emperor. Nero had fallen under the spell of a man who acknowledged another as his sovereign – a power who regarded Nero as his puppet to be strutted across the stage of the world until his usefulness was over.

During his fourteen years reign as emperor, Nero's dormant, unnatural and savage passions were awakened by frequent visits to Karkinos's palace where, under the guise of entertainment, ancient satanic rites were enacted to destroy all that was good in him.

He became addicted to divination of all kinds, becoming morbidly concerned with every manner of means by which his future could be foretold.

It was during such occult sessions at Aigokerös that Karkinos had the opportunity to plant post-hypnotic suggestions, which could be triggered at a later date by his two most faithful disciples, Tigellinus and Poppaea.

To Tigellinus, Karkinos was a master who in turn served a power greater than Jupiter – Satan, emperor of darkness. Karkinos regarded as his mortal enemy on earth the sect of the Nazarene Jews who called themselves Christians, especially the descendants of the one they called the Christ – the elect of the Father he had rejected. They carried in their seed the supernatural power of his adversary, the God of Light.

Behind his puppets the Greek magus pulled the strings for a master who strode across a wider stage. Satan, ruler of all incarnate matter, the supreme spirit of evil, who in the Book of Job is portrayed as being amongst the Sons of God when they presented themselves before Him at stated times.

In Satan's case it is a fallen and rebellious son who, though cast out, would claim equality with the Creator in the material cosmos and challenge him for spiritual supremacy, the power of darkness locked in eternal struggle with that of Light.

Known to man under the guise of many names – Satan, the Devil, Lucifer, Ahriman and Asmodeus – he is worshipped by many as man's true God, the Antichrist, Rex Mundi, earthly ruler and heavenly brother of Jesus of Nazareth.

Karkinos was the conduit for this supernatural power, which rewarded his surrender to its service by increasing his formidable psychic powers and knowledge of magic. Through his constant rebirth as an ageless servant of Satan, he retained the collective inherited memory of a centuries old accretion of power and knowledge. At the apocalypse he would command the legions of dark angels who surround the throne of Satan, the supreme power he acknowledged as the true ruler of man's spirit.

In the meantime he had taken up residence in Rome, capital of the empire, centre of the civilised world, and had built a fabulous palace that was the envy of Caesar himself and daily drew to its doors members of the noblest and most influential families in Rome.

The secret temple in Karkinos's palace was a windowless circular room floored in black marble with an inlay of malachite prescribing a magic circle, its depthless viridian green the only note of colour in the furnishings of the entire chamber. The smooth plaster walls were black, as was the circle of high backed thrones positioned around the outer rim of the magic circle.

The altar, which stood at the centre of the circle, was a massive slab of basalt on a plinth of the same material. The domed ceiling, which vaulted over the centre of this macabre stage, was also of unrelieved black, as was the only door that pierced the northern wall.

The men who came to this coven were secret magicians, masters of the occult who had sworn allegiance to Satan and acknowledged Karkinos as their grand master.

If not summoned by him they would automatically attend the temple for worship on the last day of every month. These secret monthly meetings were always held at midnight when, dressed entirely in black hooded robes, the adepts would arrive at the palace in closed litters that were carefully checked and their occupants tested for proof of identity with secret signs, before being allowed into the high walled grounds.

The entrance to the temple itself demanded a further check, which was carried out by Karkinos, who personally verified the right of those who sought admittance.

These disciples were natural psychics who had been revealed to Karkinos when he had been in a deep trance communing with his master, Satan, and he had been ordered to suborn their souls or destroy them. Those who gave themselves to the Prince of Darkness had been trained in the ancient occult sciences, becoming alchemists and magicians who would spend their lives striving to perfect their craft through private study. Rising through the grades of their own order, their ultimate ambition was to become an adept of the highest order who, as Karcist, could be entitled to form his own coven.

When Tigellinus or Nero came to the palace they were never admitted to the temple. Both were regarded merely as tools; instruments that the grand master would use to achieve Satan's purpose.

In Nero's case it was simply a question of feeding a personality that was by nature, sensual and gullible, open to every superstition and extremely suspicious of everyone. Management of Nero was principally wrought through Poppaea, aided and abetted by Tigellinus, who between them, manipulated an already flawed character by catering to his every dark whim.

Eventually, Nero's ensnarement by this deadly trio would enable Tigellinus to attain a royal decree allowing him to wage an all-out war on those who professed to be followers of Christ and had taken to calling themselves Christians.

Meanwhile, the emperor became increasingly reliant on the divinations and horoscopes, which were cast in the heady atmosphere of séances conducted in the Greek's palace.

It was during these sessions that unsuspecting guests – including Nero – were secretly given hallucinogens in doctored wine. This laid the participants open to out-of-body experiences that could be reinforced by hypnosis and autosuggestion.

The individual will was further broken down by involving the drugged revellers in rites centred on sadistic sexual practises which frequently involved children of both sexes, the result being the destruction of all moral principles and any sense of the recognition between right and wrong.

Those who served as occult priests in Karkinos's coven had first to gain admittance to its select brotherhood. Prospective candidates had to pass stringent tests, which included the conjuration of a dark spirit before the assembled adepts of the temple and its grand master.

A successful demonstration was followed by a secret ballot whereby each adept was given two balls – one white, one black. They then passed in front of Karkinos, the coven's grand master who had the casting vote, and placed one of their balls in a container, the top of which was covered by a black cloth with a slit in it.

If a single white ball was found among the black, the applicant was immediately executed by having his throat cut and being butchered by the deacons. The victim's various organs were reserved for magic purposes, these being shared equally among the brethren of the coven, the heart going to the grand master.

Every member of the Greek magus's coven had spent years learning their craft and all had at some time left their native land to study in the secret occult societies of Egypt and Syria. In ancient times they had been taught magic by the fallen angels when, it is reputed, one of them – Amazarak – taught the secrets of sorcery to men.

Ancient cultures regarded magic equally with all other forms of learning and knowledge. For them it was a key to understanding and eventually dominating the universe. The Christian view of magic is that it is evil, since it can involve contact with evil spirits and attempts to share with God control of the cosmos. Once religion and magic were identical, the same person could serve as both priest and magician. It was the rise of Christianity that relegated magic to an inferior status, though the Witch of Endor was one of the Old Testament's most famous seers.

The foundations of magic are to be found in the astrological and numerological law of the Babylonians and the Persian traditions, later incorporated in Judaeo-Christian teachings. (The Magi who followed the star to Bethlehem were the Megui – seers, wise men, and magicians).

Chan-Zoroaster was the first sorcerer to appear after the flood, and his four sons – Cush, Mizraim, Phot and Canaan – were Lords of Magic respectively over Africa, Egypt, Arabia, and Phoenicia.

It is Canaan who is the legendary forbear of the Antichrist. The supreme adept who is constantly reborn, his powers multiplying with every new incarnation as his inherited memory is passed from birth to birth, whom Satan uses to hunt down the survivors of the Davidic line in whose genes are coded the hope of man's salvation.

In Nero's reign, Canaan reappeared on the stage of history as the Greek magus, Karkinos, Satan's principal servant on earth, an implacable adversary who challenges God himself for dominion over the soul of man.

He was destined to stalk through the dark and bloody centuries, a concupiscence of the spirit, an insidious malevolence that, linked to greed and envy, would wreak havoc among mankind. Fomenter of endless divisions of religious opinion that would result in the most savage of wars, both sides claiming divine right, and the architect of an ego that would increasingly crush the spirit of man beneath an overwhelming weight of self.

The coven Karkinos controlled was a concentration of virulent evil, a satanic force that would eventually destroy the Roman Empire and infect the development of all successive civilisations. This same evil power had caused Annanus, who had inherited the position of high priest from his father-in-law Caiaphas, to condemn Jesus's eldest brother, James, to death when he became head of the fledgling church in Jerusalem.

With him out of the way, Peter the Fisherman could be hunted down and destroyed, leaving the way clear to concentrate on the brother of Jesus they feared most – Simon. He was guardian of the greatest talisman in Christianity; the sacred spear that the Roman centurion Gaius Cassius had used to pierce the side of the dying Christ. This brother's genes were coded to carry the power of love into the future. A seed imbued with the power of redemption and retribution, mankind's hope for the future.

That Clodia had already conceived simply added urgency to the magus's work, for Satan himself had declared to Karkinos that she and Simon had to be found and destroyed. "Now," he had commanded, "is the time to raise a universal storm of hatred against all Jews" – particularly those who belonged to the Nazarene strain who must be extinguished along with Simon, Clodia and their unborn son.

At his master's command, Karkinos summoned the adepts to a special conjuration. It was midnight when the secret magicians filed silently into the sanctum, faces shadowed by the hoods of their black robes, hands hidden in the folds of their sleeves. The only light in the chamber came from a single oil lamp suspended above the altar, the flame of which was shielded by prisms of red quartz.

Prostrate on the basalt altar lay the naked body of a young girl, spread-eagled, her flesh a luminous white against the black stone. The child who had been purchased for the occasion had been selected carefully. She was a virgin of Jewish parents whose line was indisputably Davidic and had, with her parents and brothers and sisters, been sold into slavery during the first of the many Palestinian uprisings that were a prelude to the Jewish wars.

The final selection of the victim had been determined by the knowledge that the entire family, including the girl, were secret Christians and had been converted by the fisherman himself at one of his gatherings in the catacombs below Rome.

For the moment Rachel lay quiet, held by the spell of the drug she had been forced to take and which, after its administration, had been followed by hypnosis. She lay on her back, eyes open, seeing only the crimson glow of the suspended light. She felt as if she was floating warm and safe, the outer darkness comforting rather than threatening. She was unaware of the circle of hooded figures that, now seated, were almost invisible, their blackness melding into the overall gloom.

As the tapers were lit and the scent of the incense spiralled through the air, she was vaguely aware of its pleasant perfume. It reminded her of the secret prayer meetings she attended as often as she could, as she sought to learn more of the man who taught that love was more important than the law.

The dark figure that seemed to float into the edge of her field of vision gave her no cause for alarm, and the sudden cold of the chalice he placed on her belly was hardly registered by her drugged brain.

As Karkinos began the first phase of the evocation, four of the adepts, whose chairs were stationed at the cardinal points of the compass, left their seats and silently approached the altar, genuflecting to their master and acknowledging their fealty to him by kissing the ring on his left hand.

The obeisance completed, they each produced black cords concealed within the sleeves of their robes and each slipped a noose round the girl's ankles and wrists. Retaining the ends of the bindings in their left hands they stood on station with their backs to the altar facing outwards towards their brothers who, as the Grand Master started the prayer of salutation, rose to this signal and with measured tread intoned their responses.

As the prayer ended the circle was complete and the stupefied girl felt the first tremor of fear as she felt the weight of the wall of enclosing bodies pressing round her like the palisade of some dark and secret fort. The ring of fish belly white faces contemplated her without pity, the passion of the glittering eyes a result of the powerful stirrings of emotions that were roused by the prospect of an appearance of he whom they all served.

The ritual was the inductor, the means to rousing the individual psychic powers that would fuse the coven's individual subconscious into a collective emanation of psychic power. If it was directed by the Grand Master, it would have the power to extinguish the light of the sun and precipitate 'the last of days.'

Without any apparent signal being given, the only door into the chamber opened long enough to admit a large goat, an age-old symbol of Lucifer. As the animal trotted into the chamber the rank odour of its body filled the room. Its entrance was a sign for the next stage of the ritual to be enacted.

Karkinos removed the chalice and held it over the body of the girl, while the four figures stationed at her head and feet turned in unison and with a practised flip turned her over. The men at her feet drew her towards them so that she was now standing on the floor with her body bent face down on the altar.

Rachel whimpered with fear as the hold on her mind crumbled. The atmosphere in the room was becoming charged with an alien emotion, the power of which crackled through her terrified mind like static.

The robed circle continued to intone their prayer, stepping back a pace and bowing to the altar and then straightening as they stepped forward. The rhythmic bobbing of the bodies acted as a metronome in time to the cadence of their prayers – a device they had borrowed from the age-old prayer habits of the Hebrews.

The circle opened to admit the animal which, without being instructed, reared up on its hind legs and mounted the girl, enveloping her in its foul-rutting stench.

Rachel's screams, bouncing and echoing off the walls, mingled with the rising crescendo of the adepts' mantra. The virgin blood issuing from between her legs was collected in the chalice by Karkinos who raised it above the lunging goat that battered the screaming girl's buttocks with a relentless pistoning of its shaggy thighs, its yellow-green agate eyes smoky with lust.

As the animal shuddered to a halt and withdrew its steaming and bloodied member, the defiled body was remorselessly turned and dragged on its back so that the head hung over the edge of the altar.

The soiled and hurting girl struggled frenziedly but ineffectually against the cords that pinioned her hands and feet. She stared in abject, blubbering terror at the glittering steel of the sword held by the Grand Master over her head as he offered up his final prayer.

As Karkinos intoned the invocation of presence, two of the deacons circled the group counter-clockwise. One of them held the chalice for his companion, who dipped the *aspergillum* into the virgin blood, which he sprinkled on the now kneeling adepts in a profane benediction. When he reached the distraught girl's head, he knelt so that the chalice was ready to catch the blood of life, the final potentising power that would summon the beast from the void.

As the mantra concluded, the strangulated gargling caused by the girl struggling for breath was the only sound, her unsupported head flopping awkwardly over the edge of the altar, laying the innocent throat bare. As the steel sliced into the helpless flesh, the coven raised its voice in a thrice-repeated call to the power that it was trying to summon.

The sound was pierced by Rachel's bubbling scream as she became conscious long enough to realise the moment of her death and the awareness of the final seconds of a life that was pumping crimson into the proffered silver dish that so greedily captured her innocent existence.

She witnessed the coming of the Antichrist as space split. Out of the mind-numbing void of infinity, the fallen angel, challenger to God himself for the mastery of all that was matter, came to the aid of his principal servant on earth. He came in the form of an all-pervading presence that locked his mind with theirs and transported them out of the miserable confines of their earthly bodies to the Olympian summit of psychic liberation.

The dying Rachel saw the bowl containing her life being passed from bloodied lip to bloodied lip in an unholy sacrament of welcome to the son that God Himself had cast into the abyss but would not destroy, leaving him as the great mystery, the opposite force to Creation – Chaos.

As her mind fluttered like a trapped bird between consciousness and oblivion, Satan spoke to Karkinos and his followers. The voice echoed through the void, brazen as a bell, impossible to ignore, obliterating individual will. "Bind our servant Caesar closer to us and use him to destroy our enemies. For I have drawn them to Rome and delivered them into your hands, so that you may offer up their lives to me."

"Amen, Amen," chorused the kneeling coven.

The voice continued, rising in triumph, "Paul of Tarsus comes in chains to be tried by our servant Nero."

"Amen, Amen," the priests intoned.

"The Fisherman is already caught in the net cast for him. Let Peter die like his master on the cross, whom he refused when Pilate washed his hands of the one he calls the Messiah."

"Amen, Amen," moaned the intoxicated priests.

"Above all," the voice rose to a crescendo, "kill the seed in the belly of the leper, for it is endowed with the power of the Christ they crucified in my name."

As the terrified Rachel lost consciousness, the coven shrieked its hate filled response – "Amen, Amen, Hosanna to the most high." This triumphant acclamation to Satan filled the dying girl's mind, its sound echoing through the darkness of death, as oblivion finally brought its merciful release.

## 5

It was dawn when they crested the Mount of Olives.

They stood in the pale grey light, breath smoking in the cold air, huddled in cloaks banded with a black tide of dew that soaked their legs and sparkled on their hair. Both were weary from the long march but no tiredness could dispel the wonder spread out before them.

Here Solomon, son of David, had been the first to build a temple to God. In doing so he covered with a dome, the rock upon which Abraham stayed his hand in sacrificing Isaac, and instead offered up the spotless kid God provided as a replacement.

Clodia was moved by the splendour before her and she instinctively moved closer to Simon, who opened his cloak and drew her to him.

Across the Kidron Valley lay the holiest city on earth. As she gazed at it she experienced a surge of emotion that caused her to tremble at the thought of treading its streets. This was something she had not been able to do since she was a child – not just in Jerusalem but in any town or village since she had been cast out as unclean.

Simon's face was closed, giving nothing away, though his thoughts were in turmoil. For years he had avoided these hills where his brother and his Galilean followers had so often camped. Had he chosen to, he could have walked down the valley to the Garden of Gethsemane. Instead, he calmed himself by concentrating on the magnificent view of a city that had been every Jew's inspiration for four thousand years.

Across the deep ravine of the Kidron, the magnificence of Herod the Great's buildings overwhelmed the senses. The four miles of wall that topped the cliffs were pierced by a hundred towers, all built from the pure white limestone that had been dug out from beneath the city.

As the couple clung to each other and caught their breath, the first fingers of sunlight were spotlighting the tops of these snowy ramparts, reflecting the glory of the gold and silver that had been lavished on their construction.

"It's wonderful," Clodia whispered.

Simon nodded and said, more to himself than to her, "Before David coveted Zion there was a citadel here, when the last son of Jesse ousted the Jesubite and began to build." He paused while they listened to a fanfare of trumpets that suddenly sounded, as the priest who had maintained the nightlong vigil on the highest battlements four hundred and fifty feet above the valley floor, gave the signal that the dawn blood sacrifice would be made.

As the last notes of the trumpet welcoming the gift of life of a new day drew to an abrupt close, Simon continued, "The hours of the day, by Judaean custom, begin with the sun, the first hour being the first after sunrise." As he spoke, great flocks of pigeons that had been roosting on the city's roofs and domes exploded into the air like bursts of shrapnel, the white bars of their wings, a flickering dazzle in the early sunlight.

In companionable silence they watched the huge flocks rise in the cold, clean air. Some wheeled eastwards across the bare and arid grey hills of Jordan where they turned, banking steeply across the inhospitable slopes to hurtle out across the Kidron, the whirr of their flight feathers reminding Simon of the deadly thrum of the flights of arrows released by massed archers. Other flocks simply rose above the roof of the Temple like a silver and grey halo, to circle the dazzling gold that crowned its summit.

More nervous squadrons raced south to where the Kidron Valley meets the pestilence of the brooding Valley of the Hinnom, the ancient home of Dagon. This dark rocky defile was only ventured into by lepers and scavenging foxes which feasted on the refuse hurled from the walls, including the corpses of common criminals denied even the benison of a pauper's grave.

As the morning mist cleared, more and more of the city perched on the gigantic cliffs became visible and Clodia was eager for information as the rising sun lit the splendid scene.

With his staff Simon began to point out the salient features of a city he both loved and hated. Built on five hills whose sides are virtually sheer rock, all that man had to do was crown them with walls of stone to create impregnable ramparts and build inside the enclosed spaces until the city was complete.

The temple, built by Herod the Great from the finest snow-white limestone, was a square with each side a fifth of a mile long, its walls surrounded by three vast terraces.

From their vantage point they could make out the crowds beginning to move towards the city gates to access the lower arcades. "The first arcade," Simon said, squinting into the sun as he pointed with his staff, "is the outer court of the heathen." He paused to grin. "That's you, until we turn you into a good Jewish girl."

Before Clodia could reply he continued, "That's where everyone meets, but no business is done. The next court is separated by nineteen steps and is forbidden, on pain of death, to all but Jews."

"Even Romans?" Clodia giggled.

"Especially Romans," was the grim reply, but the woman was insistent.

"Can you not be a Jew and a Roman?"

"With difficulty," was the wry response.

"But what happens if you enter by accident?" Clodia persisted.

"The whole area is plastered with signs in Greek and Latin," Simon replied, "warning you to keep out and," he continued hurriedly, anticipating another question, "there are nineteen steps separating the two courts. Before you got halfway up, a hundred Jews would tear the hair from your head.

"This second court is the inner court. You can't see it properly from here because of its high walls. From there, there are twelve more steps that lead to the innermost temple; on the crown of the hill is the holy of holies where none but the High Priest may enter and even he, only once a year."

Clodia was intrigued by the intricacies of this strange religion. "But what can they do?" she asked. "Why do all these people come to this temple?"

Simon was patient. He hugged her, laughing, as he indulged her curiosity. "Before the heralds greet the dawn, the priests have left their cells, completed their ritual ablutions and dressed themselves in clean raiment. They then take up their appointed tasks. One must slay the morning sacrifice, another must lay the firing upon the altar, another must clear away the ashes, and still others must go and see to the incense, trim the lights, and replenish the shewbread. When all is ready, a lamb is led to the altar."

He paused for a moment and said, more to himself than to Clodia, "Are the singers in their places?"

Simon was staring fixedly at the temple, the sun striking the gold roofed towers crowning the purity of its snow-white walls. He was transported, he was there, and Clodia could feel the passion linking the man to the ceremony being enacted across the space that separated the hilltop from the city walls.

"Are the braziers ready? If they are," he continued, "a cymbal will sound and, slowly yielding to the pressure of many hands, the huge gate will open."

Simon paused, his fingers tightening on her shoulders. A new sound, faint but imperious, pierced the air. The sound of trumpets, but these notes came not from silver throats, they were of a wilder, coarser stock. Three times the rams' horns saluted the morning, and on the two terraces below them they could see the flash of a sudden uplifting of thousands of faces.

"At this instant the morning sacrifice is slain, its blood consecrating the temple." Simon continued, "Then the priests move in solemn procession, intoning prayers as they assemble for a reading of the commandments. Incense is burnt on the golden altar and all prostrate themselves."

"Levites conduct the ritual of the clashing of basins as a signal to the High Priest at which zither players commence the accompaniment to psalms, whose eight intervals are punctuated by trumpets, all of which causes the entire congregation to prostrate itself anew."

As they stood in silence, the clouds of low-lying mists which had shrouded the valley floor suddenly cleared to reveal a second city; this one of skins and cloths, a myriad tents and pavilions that had sprung up like exotic toadstools outside the gates that pierced the wall.

"It's a market," explained Simon. "An excellent place to get breakfast."

The rumble of her own stomach reminded Clodia how hungry she was, and she picked up her bundle and set off down a steep but clearly marked track. "Take care woman. The son you carry is of the line of David and carries the blood of kings, not goats, in his veins."

Clodia, who was used to covering any sort of terrain and was going down the mountainside with practised ease, paused to reply cheekily, "I thought he was a goatherd. Anyway, the blood of a Caesar will make up for it, for his great-great grandfather on my mother's side was Tiberius."

Simon absorbed this information with a frown and waved Clodia on, his own progress more cautious. As they made their way down the mountainside they passed the tomb of Absalom, the rebellious but much loved third son of David.

Clodia paused by the grave, instinctively drawn to it, and flashed a questioning look at Simon, who avoided her gaze. The story would have taken too long to tell and awakened too many memories.

When the couple had scrambled down the mountainside and reached the city walls, the gates were already open and the lively daily market, which they had viewed from above, seethed through the streets leading into the city.

An explosion of colours and movement, sights and sounds and scents overwhelmed Clodia's senses. The now warm air was redolent with myriad different fragrances. Spices and perfumes offered for sale mixed with the scents of fruit and flowers. Foods being cooked sizzled in hot oil, adding to this aroma, as did the pungency of man and beast in the dense crowds that packed the narrow lanes of the souk.

Seen at close range, Clodia marvelled at the hewn blocks that formed the city walls. Each was a hundred feet long and fifty feet wide and as thick again. But it was the people who caught her imagination. Every nation on earth seemed to be part of the multi-coloured tide that swept her and Simon into the city.

As the press of bodies increased, Clodia felt a sudden unease, not being used to such close proximity with other human beings. As she struggled to get back to Simon's side, a swarthy Egyptian tugged at her bundle – whether by accident or design it was impossible to tell, but the result was nearly fatal.

A space appeared like magic around Clodia who, with the speed of a striking cobra, used the knife that she kept in her sleeve to pin the offending hand to her pack. Before the man could even register the wound, he was choking on the stock whip wound around this throat, rendered totally immobile by the iron-hard knee that was buried in his back and the fingers like stone talons clutching his hair and threatening to tear his head from his shoulders.

Simon pushed his way through to the edge of the circle. "Enough." Clodia raised her face but did not release her grip. Her eyes, he thought absently, reminded him of a desert lioness. He dropped his own pack in the dust and walked over to her. Gently he touched her face. "This man is nothing to you and if you kill him we will be late for breakfast. Romans are particular about paperwork."

Under his touch Clodia shivered, the flat unfeeling stare that marks all the great hunting cats gave way and the hard muscles relaxed, allowing the almost unconscious man to slump to the ground, retching for air.

Roman soldiers attracted by the melee cleared a rough passage; the people giving way, only too anxious to avoid any kind of contact with official authority. Those who were slow were helped with a prod from a spear butt.

Clodia fully expected to be arrested by the sergeant in charge of the soldiers who, in polished body armour and a neat mail skirt, seemed positively regal against the dusty, simple clad figure of Simon. Nevertheless, he touched his helmet in salute and asked for an explanation in a deferential tone.

From the look he shot at the Egyptian, who had recovered sufficiently to struggle to his feet and was holding his bleeding hand, it was clear he regarded him as being personally responsible for the worst possible end to his watch. The thought of the report he would have to make filled him with anger. When the injured man attempted to speak, his voice hoarse from the strangulation of Clodia's whip, the sergeant waved him into silence.

"Have you had your breakfast, sergeant?"

"No sir." The Roman was surprised at the question.

"Well, neither have we. Nor, I suspect, has he." Simon nodded in the direction of the wounded Egyptian. He reached into his belt and drew out a coin, pushing it into the injured man's good hand. Picking up his bundle he smiled at the sergeant and said to the crowd in general, "Let the man go so we can all get some breakfast. Let him bathe his hand in the Pool of Hezekiah and God will decide his innocence or guilt."

A loud murmur of approval and much head wagging confirmed their agreement with this decision, and there was a scattering of raucous laughter. To Clodia's relief the crowd began to break up, eager to be about its business and when Simon pointed a fruit vendor out to her she grinned in agreement, suddenly reminded of her own hunger.

The owner of the fruit stall sat cross-legged on a carpet spread on that portion of the pavement he paid tax for, the wall at his back. Overhead hung his scant curtain while around him within hand's reach, arranged as small stools, were osier boxes full of almonds, grapes, figs and pomegranates.

As Simon and Clodia selected the fruits they would breakfast on, there came a customer that Clodia could only stare at because of his beauty. Out of the corner of his eye Simon watched Clodia's reaction with amusement.

The young man who was causing such consternation was a beautiful Greek who held his exquisitely waved hair in place with a crown of myrtle to which still clung white flowers and pale green leaves.

His expensive scarlet tunic was of the softest woollen fabric. Below the girdle of cream leather, which was clasped in front by a carefully worked buckle of shining gold, the skirt of the tunic dropped to his knees in folds heavy with embroidery. The scarf – also woollen but worked with silver and gold thread – was arranged carefully at his throat and allowed to trail casually across his back.

His arms and legs, which were exposed, were as white as ivory and of a polish impossible to achieve except through the constant application of bath oil, brushes and pincers.

At the sight of this new customer the dealer, keeping his seat, bent forward and threw up his hands until they met in front of him, palms downwards and fingers extended. The young Greek, ignoring the supplicating figure and looking at the boxes rather than at their owner, said, "What have you this morning? I am hungry."

"Fruits from Arabia, from Galilee, Caesarea, Samaria, all at your disposal my lord," was the reply.

The splendour of the young Greek in that grimy and seething market held all of Clodia's interest, until there appeared a person making his way slowly through the crowd, head bent. The man's behaviour and unusual dress made him stand out even in that cosmopolitan crowd. Munching a bunch of grapes, oblivious to the juice running down her chin, Clodia stared at him unabashed.

As he made his way slowly through the crowd the man occasionally crossed his hands upon his breast and, pulling a long face, rolled his eyes towards heaven as if he was about to break into prayer. Nowhere, except in Jerusalem, could such a character be found.

On his forehead, attached to a band which kept the mantle in place projected a leather case, square in form, with yet another similar case tied by a thong to his left arm. The borders of his robe were decorated with deep fringes and by such signs – the phylacteries – and the enlarged borders of the garment, the man proclaimed his holiness.

In response to Clodia's question, through a mouthful of pomegranate, Simon replied with a single word that left her still mystified, "Pharisee."

As they were finishing their breakfast Clodia was further surprised when a man of very noble appearance, dressed in costly garments, hailed Simon and was soon deep in conversation with him. Clodia noted that in spite of his rough dress, the stranger was treating Simon with respect.

As the two men talked, she took stock of the noble who was attended by several servants armed with short swords stuck through their sashes. With a practised eye she valued the staff the man carried and the large gold seal suspended by a cord from his neck.

Clodia noted with some amusement the nobleman's efforts to contain his curiosity as to her identity – and Simon volunteering nothing!

The meeting between them concluded, they continued to make their way across the city whose streets assailed Clodia's senses with a kaleidoscope of colours, sounds, smells and sights, all of which paled into insignificance when she arrived at Simon's villa on Mount Zion.

Of all the splendid homes that had been built for the city's wealthiest citizens, nothing surpassed the magnificence of the building that stood in acres of carefully tended walled gardens that Simon casually indicated to her, belonged to him.

The slave who admitted the couple was a Negro of enormous proportions. The pair of huge mastiffs which, though quivering with obvious delight at Simon's return, were kept in check by the training they had received and reinforced their position as gatekeepers and security guards.

The pair's arrival had been a signal for the rest of the household to materialise to greet their returning master and, under the watchful eye of the steward, they lined up to bow in deep obeisance to him.

Heading the line-up was a slight, grey haired figure of indeterminate age. From his features Clodia guessed he was a Greek.

The major domo who guarded the gate was an ex-galley slave who had been captured in battle and purchased from the oar benches, not only for his great strength but also for his exceptional fighting qualities. Kino knew more ways of killing a man with or without a weapon than Simon had ever come across in a land where zealots were forever inventing new ways of murdering people.

In Clodia, Kino was to find an admirer and willing pupil, but it was the sight of the housekeeper that took Clodia's breath away and caused such a powerful surge of emotion that it took her several minutes to recognise it. Jealousy followed rapidly by despair, which in turn was followed quickly by an assessment of how this vision of beauty could meet with an accident.

The woman who stood so demurely with lowered head to greet her returning master was a young and beautiful Jewess, the only person of Simon's household who was not a slave but in his employ.

Clodia, suddenly conscious of her filthy condition – her matted hair, her ragged clothing, her bare and calloused feet – was introduced to the woman who stood like a queen. She was dressed in a toga of fine cream linen embroidered with gold and threaded with silver; a garment that set off to perfection the apricot glow of her flawless skin.

Never in her life had Clodia seen such perfect features. Fine, delicate nostrils, soft coral lips that formed a perfect cupid's bow, and the lustrous eyes of a gazelle; widely spaced and thickly lashed, they were the indigo pools that countless Hebrew poets had eulogised since time immemorial and the mighty Solomon had immortalised in verse.

This vision of loveliness moved with the grace of a faun, the sensuousness of her slender but shapely figure subtly enhanced by the soft clinging material she wore. The crowning glory of this beauty was a cascade of hair that tumbled down her back, whose natural curls and waves were of so dense a blackness as to hold highlights of indigo, their only restraint a clasp of jewels at the nape of her neck.

Clodia registered savagely that the name of this regal figure was Miriam. As well as being mistress of the household and providing Clodia with all the practical things she would require in her new position, she would also instruct her in the customs and habits of the Hebrew people. Her enemy, Clodia bitterly decided, was to be her keeper.

Consciously she fingered the knife in her sleeve. "If," she determined bitterly "the bitch has bedded him in the past – and who could blame him? – It will be for the last time." As she trudged down a line of servants, all better dressed than she was, Clodia had to admit that this last thought owed more to bravado than reality.

She was miserably aware of how incongruous the comparison between herself and Simon's household servants was, though not by so much as a flicker of an eye did they betray whatever their feelings were.

As she reached the end of the line Simon strode into the villa and over his shoulder he ordered Hippolyte to join him in his study, and casually said to Clodia, "Miriam will look after you. Anything you need, tell her and she will get it for you. Never will the mistress of any household have a better housekeeper," and he was gone.

For a second Clodia was at a loss, then the full import of what he had said struck her. She was mistress and as such could command this household.

Dazed, she went indoors and wandered through spacious rooms floored with marble and filled with costly furniture. Through open archways she captured views of the garden and its many fountains. Throughout what seemed to be endless halls and chambers were scattered paintings and sculptures of exceptional quality in marble, bronze and wood.

In the library she gazed awe-struck at a collection of papyrus, tablets and manuscripts that covered all four walls from floor to ceiling. Everywhere were great bowls of fresh flowers and in every room the music of caged birds could be heard.

But it was the baths that simply took her breath away with their hot and cold rooms, steam rooms and rest rooms. No expense had been spared, from the mosaics that covered the floors to the tiled frescoes adorning the walls and the life-size sculptures that stood on pedestals throughout the baths.

Clodia wryly noted that they were all female, nude and beautiful, executed – though she was not to know this – by the best Greek sculptors not only of the day but from the past, as many of the works displayed were antiques of considerable rarity and value.

As she studied the figure representing a particularly nubile young girl and a satyr with decidedly erotic overtones, she became aware of Miriam standing deferentially behind her, eyes firmly on the floor with a decided blush to her cheeks.

Unaware that the girl's discomfiture came not just from this display of the female figure but a general Hebrew abhorrence of any carving or painting representing the human form, Clodia immediately attacked the girl, her voice deliberately sneering, her language of the gutter chosen to give maximum offence. "Well, there's plenty of arse on this lot. Is this how he likes them, then, or does he prefer his meat a little nearer to the bone?"

This last was delivered with a pointed stare at the young Jewess' slender form. Clodia, who had expected the girl to be discomfited by her gross remarks, was surprised and taken aback when the girl's head snapped up and she found herself staring into eyes no longer demure and shyly cast down, but appraising her with anger and no lack of confidence.

The girl's voice was strong and equally sure of itself. "Lord Simon does not discuss his likes or dislikes of anything with women. As for these, they are an abomination and an offence to the God of his fathers. The only reason you are even aware of them and I am forced to look at them is because you are in his private quarters. The bath house for women is not so adorned and if you follow me I will take you there."

"No doubt," responded Clodia, angry with herself for having betrayed her hostility of the girl so soon, "you think I need one?"

"If you do," the girl responded coolly, "the maids I assign to you will ensure you come out of it clean and, should you wish it, will provide you with sufficient clothes for your immediate needs."

"And if I don't wish it?" snarled Clodia.

"Then you had better sit down-wind of our lord who will surely find your stink offensive."

Without thinking the outraged Clodia punched the girl savagely in the solar plexus and, as the doubled up figure jack-knifed, she brought her knee up under the girl's chin and catapulted her into the cold water pool where, convulsing from the savage attack, she slowly sank to the bottom.

For a long slow minute Clodia watched the twitching figure with considerable satisfaction. It was the sudden thought that she might have done something that would displease Simon that galvanised her into action.

Dropping her bundle she dived into the water scooped up the slight figure and with a few powerful strokes reached the side of the pool. She effortlessly slung the girl out onto the pool's edge, just in time to be joined by Simon who had been summoned by a terrified maid.

"What the hell's going on?" he shouted, bending over the retching Miriam.

The dripping Clodia turned away, ignoring him. Savagely he grabbed her arm and spun her round. "Answer me, woman."

"I slipped and banged my head." The barely audible wheeze emanating from the dripping Miriam focused attention away from Clodia. "My lady, she…" Miriam finally managed to get out "…came to my aid."

Simon stared hard at both of the women. The slave girl who had alerted him to the crisis had scurried back to her quarters, wisely deciding to keep what she had seen to herself.

Helped by Simon the housekeeper struggled to her feet. Still breathing heavily she managed to say, "My lord, I will send maids to the mistress to attend to her needs. If you will excuse me, I need to change."

Doubtfully, Simon let her go. Abruptly he turned to Clodia. "Your maid will show you the women's bath. In the meantime, I have business to attend to," and he marched away. As he left he added casually, as though it was an afterthought, "Be careful of the floor. It appears to be slippery."

Clodia's return to the world of a wealthy Roman lady was via a series of baths, massages and the attention of several female slaves. They dealt expertly with the filing, shaping and polishing of her nails, the shaving of her armpits (she steadfastly refused to allow them to prune the bush that flowered with such wild profusion between her legs), and the cutting and dressing of her hair.

As the girls worked they viewed with alarm the small scratches and abrasions on Clodia's feet, lower legs, hands and forearms and the calluses on her palms and fingertips. Ingrained dirt was eased with the application of hot towels and vigorous use of sponges and soft brushes.

As the maids worked on her, seamstresses measured and stitched, cutting profligately into what looked to Clodia like cloth worth a king's ransom. When she was finally declared ready to don whatever they had created, she stood for a moment naked before a full-length mirror. The solemn figure that was reflected back at her was a stranger that caused her to catch her breath and raise an involuntary hand to her cheek.

Taller than most men she stood flat bellied with large breasts that jutted out firmly with their own unfulfilled promise. Long well-muscled legs swelled into generous thighs and wide hips.

Her waist was almost narrow enough for a man to span with a double grip. The shoulders of this Junoesque figure were as wide and firmly muscled as the arms that hung in repose at her sides.

The head carried on a surprisingly slender neck, was all Roman - proud, almost arrogant in its bearing. The face that stared back was stamped with that same pride, but a pride that had been tempered by the cruellest of circumstance, which had left its mark as an indefinable aura of haunting sadness that lay behind the watchful amber eyes.

Still not used to seeing her cleansed state, Clodia studied her new face with its strong Roman nose and full-lipped mouth, set in a long oval face with wide cheekbones and a firm jaw. The wild tangle of her hair had been subdued and coifed, its silver streaked black tresses plaited and piled on top of her head.

As the maids advanced to clothe her with the robe the seamstresses had been working on, she caught her breath at its beauty. It was made of fine blue linen with a deep, almost black, violet banding through which ran threads of silver. As she stepped into this magical creation Miriam entered the room, dismissing the well-trained servants with the slightest movement of her fingers.

With mixed feelings, not the least of which was a measure of guilt, Clodia watched the Jewess in the mirror. The girl was carrying a case, in which lay a set of jewellery made entirely of fire opals set in gold. "My lady would honour me if she wore these. They are…" she finished dryly, noticing the quick spark in the other woman's eyes. "The jewels are passed down in my family from eldest daughter to eldest daughter."

"Why do you offer them to me?" Clodia's voice was filled with suspicion; her mind was seeking the trap. In her world kindness was weakness, generosity stupidity, and mercy from an adversary an admission of failure.

"I acknowledge the woman who carries the seed of David that will be the inheritor of the wisdom and power of Solomon. This child has the blood of the prophets – of Elijah, of John, of Jesus. He will be the inheritor of the wisdom and power of the greatest of all the Magi, Solomon the King, whom God favoured above all kings, to whom he sent His angels with the secrets of all Creation, and to whom He gave power and dominion over all the earth." As the girl spoke she seemed to take on another personality.

As she listened to the declaration, Clodia could feel the hairs on her forearms and at the back of her neck rising with excitement. So had Ruth spoken to Naomi. Clodia knew in that instant that in this gentle girl she had no enemy, but the staunchest of friends. With a trembling hand she reached out to touch the dark bruise on the girl's face. "How do you know I am with child?" she asked huskily.

"Like our master, Hippolyte sometimes has the power to see into the future. Before you arrived at the gate he pronounced that the seed of David, blessed with the magical power of the blood of Solomon, had been sown, and that she who was carrying the child in whose blood that power lay, would return with our master."

For long minutes Clodia couldn't answer. The rush of emotions she felt were as strange to her as the tears she hadn't shed since being thrown out as unclean, coursed down her cheeks. When she finally managed to say something, it was barely a whisper. "I am a Roman, if not an enemy than at least an oppressor. Even your God is a stranger to me."

Miriam smiled gently, and as she took the jewels from their case and placed them at the other woman's throat and at her wrists and in her hair. She replied softly, "The God of Abraham and Moses is the Creator of All. Therefore he is the God of All. Now go, my lord awaits you. Let him see the glory that will be Israel's, for you are more than wife, more than queen, you carry the child who can never die."

# 6

As Nero came progressively under Karkinos's control, he virtually abandoned all interest in serious matters of state. He even stopped going to the Senate where all debates were either terminated or manipulated by Tigellinus. Instead, he spent his time writing bad poetry and terrible plays. Worse still, he inevitably took the leading role and so became author, leading man and producer.

Vast sums of money were lavished on these productions, no expense being spared on sets and costumes. As a theatrical entrepreneur, the Emperor's enthusiasm extended to the arena. Almost daily special pieces were enacted either under his direction or with him in a leading role. Sometimes in the more dangerous presentations he contented himself with composing the accompanying music, which frequently saw him either conducting the orchestra or rendering the solo in a slightly effeminate tenor.

These outdoor productions called for tens of thousands of wild animals to be brought to Rome by the Empire's merchant fleet on a conveyor belt system, together with an equally large numbers of slaves who would die in the set piece battles Nero decreed would be enacted. Giving the victims sufficient weapons to just prolong the spectacle livened up these tableaux, involving every kind of wild animal from elephants to the great carnivores.

The people who flocked to these circuses loved them. If they wanted to they could go to such spectacles almost daily, as their Emperor spent more and more time with his drama coach than he did with his senators.

A more serious deterioration in the Emperor's personality, however, lay in the fact that not only had he declared himself to be a god, he increasingly behaved as though he believed it.

Those who were obliged to attend his court and join him at table lived in permanent fear for their lives as the emergent sadist exercised his newly acquired omnipotence. Nothing could be denied a god. The gods were perfect; therefore they were above criticism.

Worse still, Nero enjoyed terror – other people's, that is. Nothing pleased him more than to build an atmosphere of unease either in the Senate or at a banquet, which he could manipulate by turning and twisting every phrase of his guests, until the unfortunate who had been singled out for that occasion's sport was quaking with terror.

Numberless members of the best families of Rome were invited to open their veins or face public execution; leading citizens who had momentarily fallen out of favour were ordered to throw themselves on their swords.

No wife or daughter was safe; a plea of virginity was no defence against a power which daily had a goblet of gladiators' blood for breakfast.

Caesar's favourite sport was linked to his greatest weakness – flattery of his poetic and musical renderings. He liked nothing better than to recite or play something and then invite his audience to comment.

In twisting their remarks he was at his most savage, deliberately taking what was being said the wrong way, holding the unfortunate courtier up to ridicule and pouncing on those who pandered to him by embroiling them in arguments that could lead to imprisonment, torture and frequently death.

To contradict him was to invite incredulous wrath, though rarely did anyone take that risk.

The one member of the court who did – and frequently, and got away with it – was Petronius. There was nobody in Rome his equal in oratory, or more quick-witted. Of high intelligence and courage, he regarded Nero with disgust and both Tigellinus and Poppaea with contempt. He was, though, careful not to show anything other than undisguised admiration and support for all three, while at the same time being the one man in the whole of Rome that Nero could rely on to stimulate him with his conversation.

Frequently these became verbal duels as Petronius, seemingly careless of his head, dared not only to contradict Nero but further demand that he rewrite not just verses but whole acts of the many awful plays that flowed from the royal pen.

On such occasions Petronius's enemies, who with the rest of the audience were frozen with fear, had to acknowledge the courage and skill with which such situations were managed.

What really made them grind their teeth was that the one man who didn't care about his position at court became the royal favourite. This was to the mortification of Tigellinus who, after a number of clumsy attempts to trap Petronius into saying something in Nero's presence that would irretrievably damage him, grew tired of always coming off worst and gave up. Nevertheless, the Praetorian nursed a burning hatred and an absolute determination to one day remove the independent patrician from the face of the earth.

But first Tigellinus had to wrest from Nero the right of succession and that would require two things – the Emperor's death and for himself to be declared Caesar by overwhelming popular demand. The latter would require that he controlled both the army and the Senate.

Vespasian, the most capable of Rome's generals, was safely out of the way having been despatched to fight that most difficult of wars, a religious conflict supported by terrorists who were also religious fanatics. Having murdered or caused the death of all those in the Senate who opposed him, Tigellinus was relying on Karkinos to provide him with a way of not just killing the Emperor, but for such an event to be warmly welcomed by both the people and the politicians.

It was, Tigellinus decided, becoming increasingly urgent that this should be accomplished, as Nero's jaded appetite was becoming sated and his sick mind more petulant in its demands. The Praetorian trembled lest, in a moment of pique, he found himself in the arena facing one of the monsters from Africa or simply being taken outside and beheaded by Nero's immediate personal bodyguard of Germans, half-wild blond giants who killed to order like automatons.

Tigellinus knew without doubt that Caesar's assassination would have to be accomplished outside Rome away from too many prying eyes. But first he had to get Nero out of the capital. It was at a court dinner one evening that such an opportunity presented itself.

Nero had just finished singing his latest composition and had called for comment. It was Gaius Sylvanus, one of the richest and most influential members of the Senate who responded first, his fulsome praise causing Nero to yawn and pointedly turn away, pretending some interest in the daughter of a senator who had been ordered to bring her. Much against his wife's wishes he had obeyed, for not to do so could have been construed as treason.

It was the sudden declaration by Petronius that the offering was unworthy of the Emperor that stopped all conversation dead. It caused even Karkinos, who was unfailingly invited to these occasions, to exchange a secret smile with Tigellinus who, together with more than one person in the room, thought, "At last, the man has gone too far."

"Ordinary verses that need burning." At this remark the stomachs of the diners churned with terror. Only Karkinos, hiding a secret smile, rejoiced at the response.

Since his earliest remembered years, no one, including the doting Agrippina, had spoken to Nero in such a manner. Tigellinus, having recovered from the initial shock, scowled in pretended disagreement. Nero, however, positively purred. This was in spite of the fact that his vanity was scalded with outrage. "What offends the arbiter that suggests so severe a remedy?"

"Divinity, don't believe this lot. They would lick my arse, let alone yours, before they would give you an opinion that bore even the slightest resemblance to the truth."

The cries of outrage that followed this attack delighted both Karkinos and Nero, though for different reasons. The former, because matters were going his way, and the latter, because he loved drama, and the developing situation promised to be extremely entertaining.

Ignoring the protestations Petronius, who had remained lolling against his cushions while others jumped up and down waving their arms about in anger, drawled insolently, "They know nothing, Caesar. You ask what's wrong with your verses. If you want the truth, I will give it to you." Petronius paused to sip his wine in a silence that could be felt.

Nero lay like a bejewelled orang-utan, all white flesh and ginger hair, hooded eyes as cruelly watchful as any carnivore. At his side, sleek as a black panther, lay Poppaea. She hadn't missed Karkinos hiding in the corner like an Egyptian vulture, his eyes red with pleasure as though he had just found a new corpse. The arbiter continued nonchalantly as though he was discussing the weather.

"This work is as good as Homer, Virgil, even Ovid, but it is not worthy of you. Your genius is not free to write such poor stuff. The conflagration you write of lacks descriptive power. Turn aside from the flattery of Tigellinus."

This remark whitened the Praetorian to the lips and from the assembled court came a sound compounded of sharp intakes of breath and suppressed giggles. Undeterred, Petronius popped a grape into his mouth and continued, "Had he penned this work I would have raised my glass to his genius, but your case is different, and you know why? Your mind is above his. Surely you, who are gifted by the gods, must do more. What is worthy of the greatest of us must surely be just the starting point for Caesar."

"But," and now his voice took on a mock seriousness, "you are lazy and would sooner sleep in the afternoons than spend time with your secretaries. You who have the genius to produce a work that would dazzle the world for all time, denies the time of its making."

Although the entire company was astounded at Petronius's speech, Caesar's eyes were wet with tears of happiness. "The gods have given me my small talents," he replied, "but they have favoured me with an incomparable gift, a true judge and friend, the only man who, at whatever the cost to himself, speaks the truth to my face." A few strangled gasps followed this to disguise outraged laughter which, if allowed to burst forth, would have resulted in instant execution.

A wild eyed Tigellinus ground his teeth so furiously that he broke one off, but Karkinos smiled his secret smile, delighted with the way things were going.

Nero stretched out a podgy hand, overgrown with reddish hair, and signalled a slave to bring a torch closer, holding the verses towards its flame, but Petronius seized them. "No," he cried. "Even thus they belong to mankind. If you would give me a further sign of your favour, leave them to me."

At this Nero positively simpered and while hiding a small smile behind the edge of her veil, Poppaea made a mental note to seek out this silver-tongued advocate.

"Allow me to send them round to you in a casket worthy of our friendship. I have an enamelled case from the east which you may find of some small interest." At such patronage Petronius could only bow his appreciation.

Nero paused and grew thoughtful, and none in that company was foolhardy enough to break his train of thought. When he resumed he spoke directly to the arbiter, his voice as conversational as if they were alone.

"You are right, my conflagration of Troy is an apology for a fire, but I thought it sufficient to equal Homer. A natural modesty of my talent has always inhibited my pen, but now you have opened my eyes. My spirit is released and I can soar where the gods intended, on Olympian heights of creativity."

As Nero paused for breath he was so overwhelmed by his own oratory that he leaned forward and embraced Petronius warmly before continuing, but now in a more pensive mood, "When a sculptor or a painter creates a portrait, they seek a model. I have never had a model. I have never seen a burning city. No wonder my description lacks credibility."

Petronius nodded wisely, while the rest watched round-eyed, though in not a few breasts a deep unease stirred at the direction the conversation was taking. "The great artists of the world," Petronius replied, "would recognise this."

The white mound stirred, eyes as moist as a baby seal's and voice as husky. "Dear arbiter, do you mourn the burning of Troy?"

"Not at all. I value the Iliad a hundred times over one city, no matter how great."

At these words Nero's cheeks flushed and his eyes sparkled with tears of joy. Like a child in his crib, he clapped his chubby hands with glee. "What joy to find a man who understands that for art's sake all is permitted – nay, demanded. But," and the flushed countenance took on a petulant look, the bottom lip trembling with sudden emotion, "I have never seen a burning city."

A long and thoughtful silence followed which Tigellinus broke. "Caesar." The voice was querulous, almost plaintive. "Have I not offered to burn Antium or, if you prefer, I will fire the Jewish quarter."

Nobody dared to breathe. Nero stared stonily at the Commander-in-Chief of the Praetorian, who continued gamely, "or I can build you a city in the arena and fill it with a hundred thousand slaves and burn it at your pleasure."

"Am I to look for inspiration to the burning of a toy fort?" asked Nero, casting the unhappy man a look of contempt. "Do you not," he continued scathingly, "set more value on my verses?"

Tigellinus hung his head, utterly confused, but Karkinos diverted Nero's attention from his luckless servant. "Mighty Caesar. Tigellinus is but a simple soldier, lacking the schooling in such matters so elegantly expressed by our dear Petronius. I agree that only the burning of Rome itself could possibly provide the divine inspiration a god would need."

As the now decidedly sober company digested this offering, relief came in the form of an announcement that a special entertainment was about to start. This was a signal to the ladies whose sensibilities didn't match that of a gladiator or whore to retire, for if previous occasions were anything to go by, what was about to follow would be an exhibition of the utmost lewdness or cruelty or both, enacted for their amusement.

Inwardly discomfited Tigellinus rejoiced. The suggestion to burn Rome had been made by the Emperor himself. If necessary, people could be reminded of that fact. The Praetorian didn't doubt for a minute that his true master would take full advantage of such an opportunity. Mollified he, like everybody else, turned his attention towards the next piece of entertainment that was about to be offered.

The hour was late and already they had consumed endless courses of food, washed down with the finest of wines, which had been offered and partaken of with equal profligacy. Throughout the evening most of the guests had gone outside to be sick, only to return to restart. Not a few of the older men had succumbed and lay snoring on their couches.

Knowing what was coming, most of the women had excused themselves, though a few – those with totally debased appetites – remained. These special late night shows were usually sexual, designed to cater to the basest instincts and titillate passions dulled with a surfeit of all the animal pleasures.

What was usual on these occasions was a coupling between female and animal. The more exotic the animal and the more inexperienced the woman, the better. Not infrequently virgin slaves were forced to be the unwilling partners and, as a result, the first mating such an unfortunate girl might experience would be with a donkey.

When such bacchanalia really got out of hand, it wasn't unusual for a Roman matron to offer herself or be offered as a partner. Such couplings were orchestrated by three dwarfs dressed as ringmasters, accompanied by a collection of Indian musicians whose wild strings and drums provided an intoxicating rhythm that seemed to excite whatever beast was being used to even greater efforts.

Tonight's offering was, the leader of the three dwarfs solemnly informed them, something new – something entirely different. A Parthian slave who had the longest member ever seen on a man or donkey would not only demonstrate this amazing weapon, he would challenge any of those present – male or female – to be mounted by him.

A roar of applause greeted this announcement and to a skirl of pipes, this prodigy entered the chamber accompanied by a dozen naked girl and boy slaves chosen for their youth and beauty and trained as royal prostitutes, reserved exclusively for the Emperor's guests.

The girls and boys distributed themselves among the drunken gathering, helping to divest them of their clothing, avoiding only those who they knew from experience would not welcome such attention – Karkinos, Tigellinus and Petronius among them.

The heat in the room from the various torches and braziers was tremendous and, combined with the vast quantity of wine, caused everybody to sweat copiously, so the divesting of clothing brought its own relief as well as allowing its owners freer rein to indulge their lust.

The Parthian, who was the centrepiece of this attraction, was relatively small in stature, as was the black girl who, after taking off the robe slung loosely round her shoulders, slowly and tantalisingly removed his loin cloth. Even in its resting state the man's slack penis drew gasps of surprise, envy and disbelief, depending on the disposition of the onlooker. The member lay against the man's leg like a resting snake; free of all restraint it hung its head halfway to his knee.

At a signal from one of the dwarfs the Indian musicians stopped playing and another of the dwarfs, his face blacked out and wearing a turban, ran forward with a small mat that he placed on the floor and promptly squatted on. From beneath his blouse he produced a reed pipe and parodying the snake charmers of the Indian sub-continent, and to the mirth of his audience, started to play.

It was, however, the delicate stroking of his female companion that roused this particular python. To an accompaniment of gasps, an explosive bray of uncontrolled hysterical laughter, and absolutely filthy stories which prolonged the merriment, the Parthian's one eyed snake swelled to its full glory and was offered by his charming assistant, supported on a silver platter, for their close inspection.

It was Nero himself who called for a tape and informed his guests the member was a foot long and seven inches around. It was, Tigellinus observed dryly, as big as a baby's arm with an apple in its hand!

When the inspection and the parade were over, the amateur musician gave way to one of his companions who, to a roll on the drums, announced that this mighty sword would now be sheathed and the first recipient would be the Parthian's assistant. At this all eyes swivelled disbelievingly towards the slight though shapely figure that was unconcernedly reclining on a bench, legs wide.

To a wild and savage tune that sawed at the nerve ends, the numbed audience watched in amazement as in exaggerated slowness the girl guided that monstrous shaft between her legs and inch by inch it impossibly disappeared inside her.

With the coupling completed, the music stopped as suddenly as it had started and to yet another drum roll the dwarf M.C., with his hand pointing dramatically at the fully engaged pair, offered to serve any of the Emperor's guests – male or female – who fancied their chances.

Roars of raucous laughter greeted this invitation. Nero, who had become inordinately excited by this exhibition, drew a large ruby ring from his finger and offered it to any of his guests who was willing to try.

To her husband's undying shame, the drunken wife of an eminent retired general rolled off her couch, stripped off what was left of her toga, and staggered over to the bench the slave girl had vacated.

With hoarse cries of encouragement the energetic dwarfs arranged the drunken woman and the Parthian, with elaborate delicacy, proceeded to mount her. The first thrust brought a great gasp and an effort to sit up but the dwarfs, ready for such a move, pinned her shoulders and arms. The second thrust brought a scream of pain and a sudden sobering.

Then the drum took up the beat and to its solemn cadence and the screams of his victim, the owner of that mighty spear pinned his victim like a grub to a board.

At the halfway stage the slave cast a questioning glance at Caesar who turned to Poppaea. It was her thumbs down that sealed the matron's fate, as no sooner was the signal given than all play-acting was set aside and the wiry figure bent grimly and energetically to his task.

Sinking his fingers into the matron's buttocks and curling his toes against the floor for purchase, he banged away at the unfortunate woman who fainted, her insides ruptured by the onslaught.

A pair of miniature horses garlanded with flowers managed the removal of the unconscious woman very prettily. These were galloped in and harnessed to her hair before dragging her out to a fanfare by the band.

This was a signal to the whole ensemble to engage in whatever sexual practise they so wished.

Only Karkinos, Poppaea, Tigellinus, Nero and Petronius withdrew, the last two to continue their discussion of Nero's verses and the unholy trio to plot.

## 7

With Miriam as guide and companion, Clodia delighted in exploring Jerusalem. It was she who pointed out the different races including the Galileans. They were stubborn, hardy and intensely patriotic, resentful of the occupying Romans and in the forefront of the many resistance movements that constantly skirmished with both the Roman and subservient Jewish authorities, and only came to the city's market to sell the produce of their gardens and terraces.

After a few days Clodia realised that the apparent chaos of the bazaar had an order of its own. The men and women who traded in each of the souk's narrow, crowded lanes were accustomed to come to the same spot each day. This in turn made shopping simple once one became familiar with its busy alleys.

Clodia was staggered by the endless variety of goods offered for sale. After the harshness of life as an outcast struggling for survival on what could be gleaned from rubbish dumps, such a cornucopia was overwhelming. The market gardeners from Galilee offered an abundance of lentils, beans, onions and cucumbers, brought by peasants who stood as patiently as their donkeys in a sea of swirling humanity.

In contrast to the sturdy farmers clad simply in sandals and an unbleached, undyed blanket crossed over one shoulder and girt around the waist, were the Egyptians and their camels, their owners small and lithe, their dark features, like their clothes, powdered like millers with the desert's sand. Many of them wore a faded turban and a loose unbelted sleeveless gown, which dropped from neck to knee. Their feet were bare.

Their camels, raw-boned beasts, were rough and grey with long shaggy tufts of fox coloured hair beneath their throats, necks and bellies. Restless under their loads they groaned and occasionally showed their yellowed teeth, but their owners were indifferent to these protestations. Holding the driving strap in one hand they gesticulated with the other to the boxes and bales strapped on each side of an enormous saddle, and shouted the virtues of the orchards of Hebron – grapes, dates, figs, apples and pomegranates.

After the silence of hills and desert, the noise of the city had confused and even frightened Clodia. The narrow alleys of the souk, paved with broad rough stone flags, amplified every sound – the stamp of animal hooves, the screech of unoiled axles, the groan of overloaded wagons and the rumble of their wheels. The shouts and chatter of a thousand tongues rose up in a cacophony of sound to reverberate off the solid stone walls on whose ledges perched the ubiquitous crooning pigeons which gained an easy, if perilous, living among the feet of the busy crowds.

The narrow lanes of the bazaar frequently opened out into courts. Here peasant women were dressed simply but modestly in linen frocks that extended the full length of their bodies, loosely gathered in at the waist, with a veil or wimple broad enough after covering the head to wrap round the shoulders. They squatted with their backs against the stone walls to sell the fruit of their vines from earthenware jars and leather bottles. Among these jars, rolling about regardless of the crowds but never hurt, played their naked children.

Competing with the women were men who peddled "honey of grapes, grapes from En-Gedi" from bottles strapped to their backs. When they found a customer, round came the bottle and with a horny thumb over the nozzle to control the flow, a cup was filled with a heavy red wine.

Equally as forceful as the wine vendors were the dealers in birds. Doves, ducks, the singing bulbul or nightingale and, most frequently, pigeons – all were offered from the nets, which had been used to capture them.

The peddlers of jewellery took up the best places in the courts. Clodia, who would have bought everything in sight, was gently restrained by Miriam who said deferentially, "My lady, your lord has his own jeweller, a merchant of great reputation, who will call upon you at your convenience."

Even so, Clodia couldn't resist examining the wares of men cloaked in scarlet and blue, top heavy under their prodigious white turbans and fully conscious of the power that lay in the lustre of a ribbon and the bright gleam of gold. Giggling together the two women tried on bracelets, necklaces, and rings for fingers, toes and even noses.

Clodia couldn't believe that the standing of Simon was so high that she was invited to take what she liked without the need of coin. The account would simply be presented at a later date.

The one stall Clodia firmly refused to pass by was that of a smiling Egyptian who offered for sale the rarest of oils, unguents and perfumes. When Clodia asked the price it was Miriam who stepped in to do the bartering, reminding the vendor who was paying. Too outrageous a premium would result in no further business.

A jar of spikenard caused an awkward moment. Clodia wanted to buy it for Simon. Miriam, confused and embarrassed, would only say that her master would not have it in the house, but she wouldn't say why. Sensing that behind the girl's embarrassment there could lie a serious reason, Clodia let the matter drop but stored the incident in her memory.

Outside the walls of the bazaar the street market swelled into a tented village, the booths of which formed lanes and alleys of their own that blossomed each day only to disappear with the setting of the sun like exotic flowers. It was here that household utensils, clothes, tents, ropes and animals were bought and sold.

Tugging at halters, now screaming, now coaxing, men struggled with donkeys, horses, sheep, goats and awkward camels. Every kind of animal was offered for sale except the outlawed swine.

Mingling with the crowds were off-duty Roman soldiers, powerful helmeted figures clad in breastplates and skirts of mail.

Clodia, who had been examining an armlet of carved ivory, was distracted from the trinket by the sudden appearance of a strange figure that seemed to draw either hostility or mockery from the crowd. The man's appearance was odd, but in that cosmopolitan crowd not so outrageous as to warrant special notice.

The reaction of the recipient of the crowd's attention was to studiously ignore it. Of medium height he wore a dirty and almost threadbare coarse brown robe. His uncombed hair hung in a greasy mat down his back and across his eyes.

In response to a questioning glance from Clodia, Miriam informed her that the man was a "Nazarene."

At this terse reply Clodia had pressed her, "If I am to learn more about the customs of the Jews I need a teacher who will answer questions."

Miriam blushed and bowed her head. "I am sorry my lady – I beg you to forgive me."

Clodia smiled and patted her arm. "You are forgiven. Now tell me about Nazarenes."

"They are a very pious group of Jews who consecrate themselves to God for a specific period of time, during which a Nazarene must not drink wine nor shave his head. John the Baptist, Jesus's cousin, was a Nazarene."

Clodia frowned. The answer left her none the wiser, but she had picked up that part of Jesus's family were Nazarenes – but not, apparently, Simon.

Slipping the bangle on her arm Clodia asked casually, "Were any other members of the family Nazarenes?"

Miriam nodded. "Yes, my lady. James, who was the eldest of Jesus's brothers."

"Any more?"

"After James's death there was a family meeting which the Lord Simon refused to attend because Jesus's followers were there. The purpose of the meeting was to choose who should be head of the Nazarenes now that James was dead. They chose," Miriam ended, "Simon, son of Cleophas, who is a brother of the Lord Simon's father."

Clodia, who was fascinated by what Miriam was telling her, was about to ask yet another question when a fresh incident distracted her.

If the unkempt Nazarene caused a commotion, the next person to excite the crowded street was the opposite in dress and bearing – though in this case no outright abuse was offered. There was simply a sharp intake of breath, a lift of the head and a disdainful 'tut.' There was also an immediate parting of the crowd as people withdrew from even the slightest contact.

The cause of this reaction was a man of Hebrew features and dress. His robe, richly embroidered, was belted with a red and gold sash wound around the waist several times.

His response to the hostility, which marked his passage through the crowd, was one of supreme indifference. He even smiled faintly at those who, in such rude haste to avoid touching him, stumbled or bumped a neighbour.

Miriam's response to Clodia's quizzical glance was terse enough to show her own prejudice. "He is a mongrel, an Assyrian or Samaritan. For a Jew to touch his robe is to pollute himself."

Before Clodia could say anything else, there appeared in the slow-moving stream of people a group of men whose dress and physical appearance would have stood out in any street in the Empire. In this predominantly Palestinian crowd the differences of stature and dress were so exaggerated as to be almost freakish.

As well as having unusually light blue eyes, they had such fair skins that the veins in their arms stood out like blue pencil lines. Their hair, gold in colour and the envy of every woman they passed, was cut short. Their heads, small and round, were set upon necks as thick as a normal man's thigh. Woollen tunics open at the breast, sleeveless and loosely girt, displayed bare arms and legs of such muscular development that they at once announced their calling – the arena.

In response to Clodia's lifted eyebrow, Miriam said quietly, "They are gladiators, wrestlers, boxers, swordsmen, professionals unknown in Judaea before the coming of the Romans."

"The ladies seem to like them," chuckled Clodia, who had noticed the quick shy looks passing women gave the laughing men, who were only too aware of the stir they caused.

Miriam pursed her lips in disapproval and frowned slightly, but refused to be drawn. Instead she edged Clodia away murmuring, "My lady, we are close to the Court of the Heathens, which will be of great interest to you."

Intrigued, Clodia followed the girl. They were now in the street of the Valley of the Cheesemakers, which ran through the centre of the city and up towards the Temple. On the left was the Akra or Lower City, the poorest quarter, and to the right the jutting spur of the Ophel, which had been David's city, where many of the temple priests lived.

The street they were strolling along wound round the Hill of Zion where Simon and other well-to-do citizens had their homes. Northwards, facing this eminence was the detested Roman Acropolis, the Antonia fortress, built on the hilltop, which the Maccabees had fortified two hundred years earlier when Israel rose against the heathen.

Behind, on the marshy ground to the north of the town dwelt the poorest folk. Thus he who holds the fortress commands the temple and the gates and controls the metropolis of this turbulent nation. It was from here that Roman troops kept surveillance over the temple courts.

As well as the Antonia, Herod had built a marble open-air theatre, his royal palace, and three colossal towers, which stood above the valley of the Kidron. He had named one of them Hippicus after a friend skilled in war, another Phasaelus after a brother slain in battle, and the third Miriam after his wife whom he had assassinated in a fit of jealousy.

The two women, moving with the tide of the crowd, gained the lower arcades of the temple where no business was done but where everyone met. This was the outer Court of the Heathen, placarded with inscriptions in Greek and Latin, warning unbelievers against access to the second terrace.

Nineteen steps separated the faithful from the unfaithful, and every gentile knew that to mount them was a crime punishable by death. Consequently, Romans and Greeks did not venture beyond the lower terraces where Arabs and Babylonians, frequently at war with each other and four times master of this city, likewise paused. Further than this no unbeliever could go.

Proud therefore were the Jews that the poorest and most ragged among them might climb the nineteen steps to the second terrace and stand in the inner court between high walls and tall columns. Gazing yet higher at the twelve steps that led to the innermost temple of the crown of the hill where, as all knew, was the holy of holies.

Down below in the Court of the Heathen, everything was bought and sold – flocks and herds were driven in and buying, selling and bartering went on from hour to hour. There was incense of all colours and perfumes. There was amber from Asia and frankincense from Egypt. Scrolls could be purchased and notable texts from the prophets inscribed upon parchment in Hebrew or Greek.

The various traders were challenging and shouting, hawking, spitting, cleaning their noses with their fingers, bargaining and cheating. Squatting behind small tables, the moneychangers were an essential part of this pageant, for Greek and Roman coins bearing a human effigy were not acceptable within the temple. Jews from foreign parts must change the money they brought with them, before they could pay the temple Jews or give alms to the poor.

Mendicant pilgrims stood on the steps, quiet amid the din. In Athens or Syracuse, in Morocco or Gaul, for years they had looked forward to this day when they would be able to gaze upon the home of their faith, the second temple, which had taken the place of the first, the temple richly endowed by Herod.

Praying as they went, they slowly and with ecstasy made their way upwards to the holy gates. There it is – the multi-coloured embroidered curtain, which their fathers had told them about, and there too the golden vine, emblem of fertility. At last they will be able to enter the vestibule and place amid the thousands of costly thank offerings the ones that they themselves have brought with them, the fruit of painful savings.

Seated around a pillar were half a dozen or so young men, deaf to the clamour made by the praying strangers and the chattering traders. They were listening to a learned rabbi reading from the ancient texts and expounding upon them. Here one could look down a colonnade seven hundred feet long; eighteen marble pillars, one hundred and fifty feet high, supporting the central aisle.

This avenue, and the slightly lower ones on either side, was roofed with cedar wood, as was the entrance to the still greater central court of the temple. This was the Court to the Gentiles where non-Jews of any nationality might enter. Here sat the moneychangers who Simon's brother had driven out.

Had the women been allowed to enter, across the court they would have come to a screen four and a half feet high with an opening through it from which steps led up to an inner part of the court. On this screen was a marble slab with a notice in Greek capital letters – it was in Greek so that a non-Hebrew could understand it. "Let no foreigner enter within the screen and the enclosure around the holy place. Whosoever is taken so doing will himself be the cause of the death that overtakes him."

The two women skirted the temple and crossed the bridge over the Tyropoeon Valley and found themselves in a busy market. In each of its bustling streets were craftsmen selling in front of their shops the articles made inside. To provide shade many of these narrow alleys were arched over and, although they were crowded, walking through them provided Clodia with endless pleasure as she listened to the multitude of tongues as men from all over the empire did their business.

Here, bartering with a wool merchant, was a Jew who had sailed down the Mediterranean from Spain, rubbing shoulders with another who had come from across the Euphrates and through the desert from Persia. These two were joined by a third Jew from the Nile valley in North Africa. All three listened open-mouthed to the story a fourth man, a Jew from Gaul, who told of the blue painted barbarians from the north sea islands of Britain which, eighty years earlier, had been conquered by Julius Caesar.

When Clodia and Miriam returned to the villa it was late in the day and the lamps of the household had already been lit, as well as torches at the massive oak gates that pierced the surrounding wall. The sight of Roman soldiers posted outside the gates guarding an imposing Roman standard startled the two women, who exchanged worried glances as a subdued Kino admitted them.

"What's going on?" Clodia asked in a low voice.

"The master has an important visitor, the procurator Gessius Florus no less, who has come from Caesarea to discuss with the Sanhedrin in Jerusalem the continuing rebellious nature of the Zealots, and has honoured this house."

"But why?" demand Miriam. She was more aware than Clodia of the political implications of Florus descending on the High Priest. Aware, too, of the mystery behind the procurator seeking out the Hellenised Jew whose family had been a scandal to the authority that ruled the synagogue and whose private life was more Roman than Hebrew.

The Negro guard who had admitted the two women bowed his apologies. "Alas, I don't know, my lady. The master and the steward of the house are in a private discussion with our illustrious visitor and there are Roman guards posted at the door to his chamber to ensure they are not disturbed."

Clodia dismissed the man. "Come Miriam, we must arrange a supper that not even a Roman can refuse."

Laughing, Miriam responded, "Even the mightiest solider in Caesar's army has to eat, and our table will be fit to tempt the Emperor himself. If you will excuse me, I will go to make the arrangements."

But the supper was not to be. Scarcely had the girl left her presence when Clodia's personal maid appeared, "My lady, the Lord Simon asks you to join him and his guest."

As Clodia curtsied before the man who ruled Judaea, she was conscious of only two things. First the faded brown eyes that surveyed the world from a face as seamed as a limestone crag, and second the confident voice, the voice of a man used to command.

"My apologies, Lady Clodia, but the demands of office preclude me from taking supper with you. Your husband will, however, explain in more detail the need for my immediate return to Caesarea," and he was gone, the cohort that provided his bodyguard leaving in a clatter of hooves and a blast of trumpets to clear the lane of sightseers.

Clodia looked at Simon questioningly. In the background Hippolyte hovered discreetly. Simon signalled him with a languidly raised hand. "Old friend, I need a drink. We all need a drink."

The master of the household poured the wine himself rather than summoning a slave. Even so, he doubted if what was now said would remain secret for very long. In aristocratic households the very walls seemed to have ears and gossip was the sole pleasure household slaves were able to indulge in, often at the expense of the masters they hated.

Unlike Hippolyte who was tense and nervous, Simon seemed positively relaxed. He lolled against the cushions, savouring his wine. A faintly mocking smile teased a corner of his mouth and his eyes sparkled mischievously. Clodia frowned at him.

He lifted his goblet in acknowledgement of the unanswered question and chuckled, "I told old Ironsides that the Zealots will start a civil war if he does not act quickly."

Clodia stamped her foot in exasperation. "Old Ironsides, lest you forget, just pickled five thousand Zealots in the Dead Sea and harvested most of the immediate countryside of the remaining opposition."

She stopped when Simon lifted an eyebrow at Hippolyte. "It seems the procurator has an admirer. Another glass of wine so that we can toast the invincible might of Rome."

Before Clodia could say anything, Hippolyte hurriedly interjected, holding Simon's attention on the wine he was pouring. "It is Jerusalem's fate we must consider. The various revolutionary groups forming within the city will come to pose a direct military threat to Rome. I feel that the madness will go so far as an outright declaration of war by the factions who have taken up residence in Jerusalem."

Open-mouthed Clodia turned to Simon who had got to the bottom of yet another goblet. Absentmindedly she determined to watch his drinking. While he seemed to have an immense capacity for alcohol, she was aware of the deep, often dangerous, currents of mood that it could stir up in this strange man to whom she had tied her fortune.

His face clouded over. The lightness of a few moments before had gone. As he held out his goblet for a refill he said gravely, "Hippolyte is right. We must sell this house and go to Rome."

He looked across the rim of his glass, eyes slightly out of focus with the wine he had drunk, "To prove your legitimacy as daughter of Pilate and, more importantly, granddaughter of an emperor."

He paused before going on. "If you are going to be a citizen of Rome you might as well be a powerful one."

Clodia's lips tightened but she kept her temper. "When does all this happen? When do we leave for Rome?"

"We sail in two weeks, my lady." It was Hippolyte who answered, sensing the tension building up in the room. "We will pay the procurator and sail under his protection in a fleet of military galleys that are due to leave Caesarea for Ostia, Rome's nearest port."

"In the meantime, my love," beamed Simon, his mood changing yet again, "you and Miriam enjoy Jerusalem. It will," he ended soberly, tears suddenly in his eyes, "be your last chance, for He foretold its doom."

As he sprang to his feet and strode into the garden, Clodia remained seated puzzled by the last remark. "Who," she asked of Hippolyte, "foretold its doom?"

The Greek studied the mosaic on the floor as though he had never seen it before, reluctant to answer. "Zeus," exclaimed Clodia, "getting a straight answer to anything in this place is like drawing teeth. Who in the name of Hades did he mean?"

The Greek sighed and made to leave. Before he did so, he said quietly, "His brother, Jesus."

# 8

I n spite of the underfloor channels that carried hot water, it was cold in the great hall of Aigokerös; November could be a damp, raw month and the palace's vast main salon was impossible to warm up.

So charged with emotions were the three people who currently occupied it — Karkinos, Tigellinus and Poppaea — they were indifferent to its chill.

News that Simon and Clodia had escaped his master and were intent on coming to Rome had galvanised Karkinos into action. Slaves had been hurriedly sent to summon the Prefect and the Augusta to the Greek's palace.

When they arrived the excited Karkinos wasted no time in telling them that the day of reckoning was at hand, and that they had debts of gratitude to settle.

"Our master, who claims equal power with God," they were told, "will triumph on that day as the supreme ruler of all matter, all life, all knowledge. Those who are his servants will enter into his kingdom in glory, those," Karkinos ended ominously, "who fail him will be utterly destroyed. They will be returned to the nothingness from whence they came. Obliterated."

Rigid with shock and excitement that left their mouths dry, the pair stood mute while Karkinos poured out his plans, for in planning to kill the child Clodia was carrying and seize the spear of Longinus, Karkinos intended to destroy Rome's Christians. "In death they can join their Jewish brethren who will fall with Jerusalem."

Knowing that Vespasian, the Roman General en route to Jerusalem, had orders that the city should be razed to the ground and that its entire population be either killed or sent as slaves to the Empire's mines, Tigellinus ventured a question. "What of Rome? Will it give up these Christians? Will the Emperor sign the warrant for their arrest?"

At this Karkinos, who had been slouched in a chair staring fixedly at the pair, leaped to his feet and advanced, shaking with emotion. He stopped inches from the Praetorian. "Rome" – Karkinos shot out both hands, fingers pointing – "is a trap which will close on them all."

Without taking his eyes off the Praetorian, the magus clasped his hands together and held them locked in front of him. "Peter, Paul, the Christians, the Christ's brother Simon, and," the voice rose to a scream, "the child – above all else, the child."

Genocide wasn't new to Tigellinus and being asked to commit it didn't trouble him in the slightest, but the fate of Rome being linked to that of Jerusalem, did. He asked diffidently, "Once in the city, how will we find so small a quarry in so large a trap, my lord?"

"By destroying both. Burn the cage with its captive."

The Prefect of the Praetorian Guard was not without courage. In Nero's intrigue ridden court, courage and cunning were necessities for survival, but even he, a hard ruthless soldier, felt a sudden chill at these words.

As for Poppaea, on hearing Rome's fate she became almost incoherent with fear. The Praetorian dismissed her from his mind. He had helped put one Emperor in his coffin. He could, he reasoned to himself, just as easily do the same for another.

Unable to keep still Karkinos paced up and down the marble paving of the salon. Almost trotting to keep up with him, a trembling Poppaea followed behind, plucking ineffectually at his sleeve. The thought of Rome being put to the torch in order to kill a single child terrified the Empress, who feared for her own position. "Caesar," she finally managed to stammer, "he will never sanction the destruction of the capital, not," she finished, sobbing hysterically, "simply to kill a single child."

The magician stopped in mid stride and swung round on the distraught woman, his eyes wide with sudden rage. "Caesar will do as he is told," he roared. "I will," he continued, "burn his miserable country if I have to. The destruction of the entire Roman Empire is not too high a price for the life blood of that particular child."

Not for a minute did Tigellinus doubt that Karkinos would trade the Empire for the child's life. Suddenly he was afraid, and in spite of the chill he could feel the perspiration on his forehead.

Karkinos advanced on the nervous Praetorian, his narrow and normally sallow face flushed with sudden anger. Sweat had trickled into his sparse chin beard and slicked it like an otter's pelt. Foam had collected and partly dried at the corners of his mouth and when he spoke it expanded like a tiny membrane. It fascinated the Prefect. He was unable to take his eyes off it.

The Greek came so close to him that all he was conscious of was his eyes, yellow and ringed with black, like a goat's. Empty of all human feeling. Glittering with excitement they bored into him. Suppressing a shudder and in a voice shaking with emotion, Tigellinus said, "My lord, we must plan carefully and in total secrecy."

For what seemed an eternity the Satanist faced his puppet, both men frozen into immobility. Poppaea had collapsed on her knees, clutching the magician's ankles and gabbling to herself.

An insect hummed across the room, its erratic sound sawing at the nerve ends.

The magus was the first to move. Without taking his eyes off the sweating man he embraced him with a wintry smile that pulled at the corners of his mouth. "All," he murmured into Tigellinus's ear, "will be destroyed." The voice was low, unhurried.

Holding the guard commander to his breast, the confidential murmur continued, "The Jewish scum who call themselves Christians and are followers of the half-witted fisherman…" The Greek broke off suddenly, the broad smile spreading across his face never reaching his eyes. He placed a hand against Tigellinus's cheek, continuing genially, "he can follow his master to the cross he professes to love so much."

The Praetorian, grateful for this change of mood, added eagerly in a voice that wasn't entirely steady, "His followers can keep him company. We have only to persuade Caesar that this Christian sect of Jews is a threat to Rome and he will plant a forest of crosses."

"Nero." The Greek bellowed with laughter and strode across the room, sitting down next to a table holding a bowl of fruit. Absentmindedly he picked up an apple and bit into it. "Nero," he continued through a mouthful of fruit, "will need to save his own skin when the people blame him for the destruction of Rome."

This last statement drew an agonised cry from Poppaea, who crawled across the floor, her faced puffed with weeping. With trembling fingers she clutched at the hem of the Magus's robe.

Tigellinus viewed the whimpering Empress with contempt. While he, too, viewed the Greek's plans for wholesale murder and the threat to burn Rome as highly dangerous, Poppaea's abject terror stiffened his own pride, for in the darkest recesses of his brain the seeds of succession had taken root. With Nero dead, the Empire would need a new Emperor as well as a new capital. He, he reasoned, the faithful servant, could inherit all.

His face was inscrutable as Karkinos finally acknowledged the figure at his feet. The magus bent and raised Poppaea's head, tenderly wiping her tearful face.

"Augusta," the voice that had cut like a lash was now as solicitous as a father's for a hurt child. "The throne you sit next to had murdered its own mother, poisoned its brother, and will destroy you and your son if it believes you threaten it. You are the Augusta. With Satan's help you and Tigellinus can rule this world as regents for its true master, the power we all serve."

With her lips trembling, a bewildered Poppaea stared into the magician's face. Her eyes flashed wildly. She felt sick. Breathing was difficult. From the window Tigellinus watched through narrowed eyes, every sense alert. He knew from bitter experience that when Karkinos was at his most reasonable, he was most dangerous.

Poppaea sighed and slumped with relief. "May the blessed Satan and his angels bear witness to your mercy and wisdom, my lord."

Karkinos nodded and smoothed Poppaea's hair from her flushed cheeks. As he did so he said soothingly, "I shall pray to our master for his guidance in this matter, as you and Tigellinus must pray for guidance also and seek always to do his bidding." "Let," he continued more sternly, "his will be done on earth. Let kings pay attention to upholding Satan's law, for they are his special servants by divine right."

Tigellinus bowed his head. Suddenly he was bone weary. He wanted to be out of the room, away from the presence he feared as much as he admired and served it. The Praetorian murmured suitable agreement and was on the point of asking permission to leave, when what came next froze his blood.

"In my dungeons," the magus's words fell as heavy as drops of blood, "I have imprisoned several of those Christians whom Tigellinus will question." The Greek rose and stalked across the room to face the Praetorian, his eyes hard and bright with sudden energy. Hatred surged through every fibre of his being; his voice changed to a rasp. "The last of the carpenter's spawn will be cast into the fire."

His right hand shot out and grasped Tigellinus's arm above the elbow. Through those clutching fingers he felt the depth of his master's need. "This time," the magus's voice seemed a million miles away and yet, at the same time, inside his skull, "there will be nothing left, no talisman, no cross, nothing – nothing – nothing."

Poppaea drew in her breath as the trap was sprung, but she held her tongue. She also guessed there would be no way out and if she didn't start showing some enthusiasm for Karkinos's plans, her tenure of the Augusta's throne would be cut short.

On shaky legs a grim Tigellinus bowed his way out of the salon. He had a task to perform in the dungeons at which he knew he must not fail. The Prefect, however, wasn't worried. He knew from past experience there wasn't a man or woman breathing who wouldn't, in the end, be agreeable to confessing to any crime you wished to name just to escape the hell on earth which the keepers of the Greek's dungeons were capable of producing.

## 9

For Clodia those first weeks spent in Jerusalem were an absolute joy. Under Miriam's instruction she learned the things her mother would have taught her – how to dress well, choosing styles that would show off her figure to its best advantage, and how to arrange her hair.

While the task of running a large house was something she could leave to Miriam, she was anxious to learn how it functioned, who did what, and what Simon's likes and dislikes were.

In Miriam she found an expert tutor and, as the days passed, the two women became firm friends, spending much of the day together enjoying the house and its extensive gardens as well as the city with its seemingly endless markets and street traders.

It was through Miriam that she began to learn something of the Jewish religion and the strength and passion of the belief of its followers.

The only things that occurred to mar this idyllic time were those days when one of the various underground revolutionary organisations perpetrated some outrage in the city. Then, for days afterwards, it would be tense and the army presence on the streets high. Ironically, most of these attacks were the result of Jew attacking Jew as rival organisations fought for supremacy.

Simon was as contemptuous of the men who fomented this unrest as he was of their politics. He would have nothing to do with either.

But neither was he blind to what was coming and no sooner had he returned with Clodia to Jerusalem than he was gone again, this time to the port of Caesarea where several ships that he owned were taking on cargoes.

He had been gone for several days and was due back that evening when, at Miriam's suggestion, Clodia decided to plan a special dinner for his return, and the two women spent the best part of the remainder of the day in preparation of more than just the food.

Before Clodia finally joined Simon that evening for dinner, Miriam had personally supervised her toilette and had assisted her to dress from a wardrobe that seemed to be added to daily. When she entered the candlelit room Simon was standing by an opening that led out onto a terrace. Hearing her footsteps he turned to greet her, a welcoming smile on his lips.

Suddenly shy Clodia paused on the threshold eyes down.

"I didn't know you were so beautiful." Simon's voice was husky. Clodia blushed though her heart sang. Simon crossed the room and reached out to take her hands in his. He kissed her gently and led her to a divan. A servant silently offered them wine. Simon raised his goblet and touched hers with its rim. Holding each other's eyes they drank, neither wishing to break the spell by speaking.

Simon caught his breath. The woman of the desert was at the heart of an unseen radiance and he loved her. As he watched her over the edge of his goblet it was life, he decided, that enfolded her, shaped her as a vessel for the child she would deliver. Simon trembled at the thought of the seed that, even now as it formed, could be counted as the crown and fruit.

He reached for Clodia. "In a week or so we move to Caesarea where Vespasian's main army is based."

"As my lord wishes," Clodia murmured and signalled to Miriam that she could order dinner to be served.

As the servants, with trained speed quietly brought in the food, Simon crossed the room to look out of the window. He continued, "While we wait in Caesarea for a ship we will be under the protection of the Roman army."

Clodia didn't answer. This house in Jerusalem was, to her, the ultimate in luxury. She hated to lose it. "Surely the troops in the Antonia will quell any trouble and we have our own guards."

Simon smiled mirthlessly. "Jerusalem will be utterly destroyed."

Clodia frowned and lowered her eyes. She didn't dare ask how he could make such a categorical statement.

"Clodia." She raised her eyes. It no longer mattered to her where they went. Suddenly, houses and places were unimportant.

Wordlessly but in perfect harmony, their feelings for each other welled from an endless source, an invisible light brighter than the brightest sun. Simon crossed the room and kneeling held her in his arms. He held her in wonder and felt the peace of that invisible light that flowed and flowed and yet was still. It was everywhere and nowhere.

With envy in her heart Miriam signalled the servants to stop serving dinner and leave the room and, without a word, silently left her. "The food of love," she whispered to herself – the only fare that would be sampled that night.

Simon drew Clodia close to him. He had read her thoughts.

Clodia breathed deeply. She could smell him – the perfume that he had used in the baths, the sandalwood that his clothes had been stored in, the maleness of his body. She adored him.

Quietly Simon said, "It is written. The city has offended God. Its destruction is foretold."

Clodia wisely decided to take up the matter of god or gods on another occasion. A tension had been set up in the man. She could feel it. "My heart dwells wherever your heart is, my lord. Lead and I will follow. It is sufficient that you wish it, for to hear is to obey."

Simon brushed her lips with his. "In the coming days I will tell you of a God, the only God, the Creator of the world and everything in it – of me, of you and of the child that grows in your belly." He paused to gulp at his wine, his eyes bright with passion. "Of a people, His chosen people. Of His prophets who are His word, the word that is a covenant between Him and His people."

Clodia shivered with excitement and sipped her own wine. "And what do his prophets say will happen to this city?"

"It will be thrown down, utterly destroyed." He paused. "It will be soon."

"Was this priest one of the prophets who serve your god?" The question was natural enough, for out of all the various temples erected to the many gods of Rome, its priests were often diviners, the most famous being the Oracle at Delphi.

"No, he was my brother."

Any further questioning was halted by his mouth crushing hers in an embrace she returned fiercely, her heart thudding in her chest with arousal. She felt an arm round her waist sliding down her back. Effortlessly he swept her up, his lips brushing her throat, the tip of his tongue darting in her ears, making her giggle. Without a backward glance at the food-laden table he carried her through to their bedroom.

"Rome," Simon continued, "in spite of its enormous wealth, its avarice, its self-indulgence, is gripped by a sense of insecurity and fear."

Clodia responded to his embrace, winding her fingers through his hair and nuzzling the base of his throat – but she wasn't put off by the sudden change of subject. "Why didn't they believe him?"

Simon straightened up, frowning down at the woman he had grown to love. "The last straw was at home, at Nazareth, when in the synagogue he proclaimed himself to be the promised Messiah, prophesied by Isiah, the greatest of our prophets."

He paused before continuing with a shaky laugh at the memory. "He nearly got us killed that day. The whole family had to leave town, and when we finally stopped running all he said was, "a prophet is without honour except in his own country and amongst his own kinsmen and in his own house."

Clodia raised herself on one elbow to reach for a cup of wine, which she sipped before passing it to Simon. Her interest was aroused, so rarely could she get him to discuss his family, particularly his strange brother Jesus. "What happened then?" she asked quietly.

For a moment he didn't answer, concentrating on refilling his empty wine cup. "James, Jude and Joses tried to have him put away declaring he was insane – a not unreasonable thing to do considering the blasphemy he had committed carried a mandatory death sentence. Even his sisters, Esther and Thamar agreed he had gone too far."

Clodia was intrigued. What was it Jesus taught that caused so much bitterness, so violent a reaction among the Jews?

Simon slid his hands across her shoulders to caress the tresses of silver stranded hair that cascaded across the voluptuous figure lying at his side. He smiled wistfully. "Jesus aimed what he had to say directly at men's hearts. His teaching was a rule for life. He told the people that the Kingdom of Heaven is a condition of the heart, not something above the earth."

Clodia was puzzled. "Why did that cause such a fuss?"

He didn't answer for a moment. His features had darkened and she could feel the anger that suddenly flooded through him.

"The priests hated his absolute indifference to dogma, cults, priests, theology. He taught the lunatics who followed him that the temple and the high priests were simply things and persons and that the temple had come to stand for forms and rites and dogmas instead of a rule and practice of life. He told men to live without a spiritual and religious master and to pray to God direct – and the priests didn't like that one bit."

Clodia, who had long ago given up expecting anything other than what she gained by her own efforts and regarded the endless pantheon of gods – Roman and pagan – with a resigned cynicism, was baffled by this invisible God with such a strange philosophy and even stranger followers. But she was fearful of His power. Not only having witnessed it at first hand, she was pregnant by a man who served that strange God and, moreover, was a favoured servant blessed with the power of a great magician.

Satisfied for the moment she ran her hands up inside Simon's thighs, her exploring fingers driving all further conversation away. Aroused, the man knelt between her legs, his fingers caressing her breasts through the thin material of her dress, while she loosened the cord of his undergarments to free his engorged member.

As her fingers caressed him, his breathing became deeper, his own fingers more urgent, their tips kneading her hardened nipples. "Your touch is like no other," he whispered, bending over to nibble her ear.

Clodia purred in response. In the soft amber glow of the chamber's night lamp they continued to undress each other, taking pleasure in touching each other's bodies with their lips and hands. Finally naked she lay back on the cotton sheet, her own breath ragged with mounting desire.

Simon slid into her, kneading her heavy breasts to the slow beat of his loins, which suddenly became imbued with a fierce urgency.

With a wild responsive cry Clodia arched her back, her arms wound round him, fingers digging into the muscles that ridged his bent spine. Their breathing was a hoarse rasping gasp as they were swept away on waves of emotion that rolled through their locked bodies as if they were one.

With each wave Simon pounded the soft beach of Clodia's sex with increasing force. They rode the crest of the final wave together, her head thrashing wildly from side to side, her lips parted in a scream of pleasure that corded the veins in her neck and dug her fingernails into bloody half moons in Simon's back.

As they both climaxed he shook as though he had been struck by lightning. He bore into her savagely, his legs stiffening as he held her by the hips and shuddered to his final explosion as he jetted his scalding seed into her.

With passion momentarily spent they collapsed, still locked together, and drifted off to sleep.

Clodia awoke first, slipping carefully off the bed so as not to wake the sleeping Simon. From a chest she took a gossamer shawl and draped it round her shoulders. Then she brushed the wild tangle of her hair and applied a little cosmetic to her eyes.

From a row of alabaster containers she selected a heavy seductive perfume and applied it liberally to the secret parts of her body. Her breasts and shoulders she laved in rosewater.

As she completed her toilette she was suddenly aware of Simon watching her. He lay on the bed, propped up on one arm. "You were asleep in my arms, my love," he said "and yet we were apart, for though I held you in my arms you were in another land." He smiled lazily at her as he rolled over to reach for a jug of wine that stood on a low table.

Clodia brushed his throat with her lips murmuring, "It is good that you woke for we are together again. Don't," she continued, "let's sleep any more tonight."

Simon smiled. He could still feel that which was present more than light. "How it stands behind her head," he thought, "like a halo without colour, yet as brilliant as starfire, form without shape. Her skin is suffused with it, transparent as the air itself."

Clodia was disturbed by the way Simon was looking at her. His intensity made her nervous and yet he seemed far away at the same time. "We have only a short life," she whispered. Simon would have replied but she gently placed a hand over his mouth continuing, "I am not worth much; I don't care if the age I live in is momentous or not. I want to be happy, that's all."

Simon smiled sadly. The moon was in her hair as he caressed it wordlessly. Behind her head through the open window, clouds floated like sleeping pelicans in the night sky. He kissed her fingertips. In his mind's eye were childhood memories of the scent of hay and clover, birches and willows, the river – a quiet soft flooding of the sandy places. Memories of his brother Jesus like an echo from afar.

Behind Clodia's shoulder the sky was velvet with expectation. He turned away and she suddenly noticed the small wounds on his back. Blushing slightly she picked up a perfumed flask of oil and slipped to the edge of the bed.

Feeling the weight of her body as she knelt beside him, Simon made to turn back but her hand gently restrained him. Without a word she poured a small quantity of the fragrant oil between his shoulder blades and began to massage him. He closed his eyes with pleasure as she gently worked the oil into his back.

"What is this faith that Jesus spoke so much about?" The casually asked question caused the man to chuckle.

"Now I know how Delilah got round Samson – no, don't ask me who Delilah was," he continued hurriedly. "We Jews believe that the God who created everything is unknowable, indefinable, he is the Logos – the Word – the Light. Not the light that you see by, but something far greater. It is that which is everywhere, invisible, the all-powerful force that created life and all men."

"Yes, all," he continued, raising a hand to stop the interruption he sensed was coming, "are endowed with this spirit. We are all children of God. There were those," he concluded sombrely, "who claimed Jesus was His son – a terrible blasphemy against the ineffable one."

"If I believe that, do I have faith?" Clodia asked in a small voice.

Simon rolled over and took her in his arms. "Believing that you are safe within that Ineffable Being and are delivering yourself up to It, to obey Its precepts in the way one lives, is the only way to faith – however dark life may be."

She laid her head on his shoulder. "Do you have faith?"

Only sometimes," he answered softly. "I don't know who or what Jesus was, other than that he was my brother. My faith is in my God and even then I am beset by doubt. Without Him life is nothing, without meaning, without direction, purposeless, empty."

"We Jews are taught," he went on, "that life is not given to us simply for enjoyment, nor yet that we might dream it away, nor stand about the world weeping and wailing over it."

Clodia was quiet for a moment. "I believe what you believe – what our child will become. He will honour his father and his father's God."

Simon smiled, reaching for her. How could she know of the conflict in his heart as he struggled all his life to come to terms with the God of Moses?

He slid his hand down the hill of her belly so that he could cup her furry mound and tease its wild curls. Clodia stretched like a cat, spreading her thighs in response to the probing finger which, when it entered the soft petals of her orchid, brushed against the stamen at its centre. She sighed and reached for him, stroking the sides of his legs, running her fingers into his crotch, murmuring softly into the nape of his neck.

Simon slid an arm around her waist and lifted her from the bed to sit on a low bench. Clodia giggled with pleasure at this variation and slowly lowered herself astride onto his legs. With excruciating slowness she speared herself onto his almost painfully hard penis. As she slid down that blood-swollen piston she would pause and partially withdraw but with every downstroke drove it deeper.

Simon responded by caressing her back and nuzzling her breasts, his tongue rasping her distended nipples, his teeth nibbling her to rouse her sleeping passion.

Reaching for the wine flask Clodia held it above his upturned face, spilling the blood red liquid into his mouth. When he gulped to swallow she kept pouring, letting its ruby fire splash across her breasts and run down between their bodies.

Simon's exploring tongue gathered up the scattered droplets from her smooth warm skin. She arched her back and let her hair flow across his shoulders. With her head close to his she wound her arms around him, nuzzling his throat, fluttering kisses as light as the wings of a moth across his eyes and lips. As she did so she rocked slowly and gently back and forth, holding him to the hilt.

The slide of that silken skin roused Simon to new passions. His breathing grew laboured, his chest rising and falling, as he became increasingly aroused. He stood up, cradling her buttocks in his powerful hands.

Clodia wound her legs round his waist and hung onto him by locking her hands behind his head and leaning away from him, arms fully extended. He let her hang like this for a moment before turning and laying her gently on her back on a carved, skin-draped chest, the base of her spine overhanging its edge.

Still coupled, Clodia sighed pleasurably, hooking her legs over his shoulders and sliding her hands down his back and across his buttocks. The standing man partially withdrew. In that shadowed light he could see the dripping coils of wet fur that matted Clodia's heaving belly, her powerfully muscled thighs that shivered at his slightest movement.

Savagely he drove into her by bending from the waist and scooping her upper body into his arms. Clodia screamed with pleasure, hooking her fingers into the cleft of his buttocks and pulling him into her as hard as she could. Simon was equally out of control. His legs trembled violently and his back arched like a bow as he lunged at her with great tearing shuddering gasps.

As Clodia came she sank her teeth into his shoulder and raked him from the nape of his neck to his hip and then she was clinging to him as though she was drowning, dizzy with the explosion of sensation that racked her body.

As she convulsed, Simon felt the rippling contractions of her vagina grip his swollen stem, its greedy mouth clamped around its fullness. His own passion when it was released was an explosion that drove his white-hot seed into her. Its fierce jetting was accompanied by a crescendo of thrusts against her upturned buttocks that vibrated the heavy cedar chest so hard it slid across the marble floor. Its movement caused them, still locked together, to topple off it onto the bed where they lay in a breathless tumult of arms and legs.

As they recovered they burst out laughing, holding onto each other, each reluctant to let the other go. The man didn't withdraw. Instead they lay in perfect contentment entwined in each other's arms. Even in the darkness Simon was intensely aware of Clodia's presence. He could smell her flower-like perfume. Tenderly he touched her bare shoulder and she turned in his arms to kiss his face and mouth.

"What will happen to our son?"

"He will become a great magician like Moses and serve the Lord," Simon answered gruffly.

Clodia wasn't put off. "When we were fleeing from the lake of death, you called on your God to defeat the evil that pursues us. You spoke of a child who had been chosen by God. I am afraid of these gods who command the darkness and light. I am afraid for our child."

"Evil exists because God allows it to. Why is mystery not given to men to understand. Here on earth and in the outer darkness Satan has power and that power is used against the souls of men."

Clodia shivered with fear but her voice was angry. "Why doesn't God destroy Satan?"

"God has given men the right to choose who they will follow and has chosen a people – the Hebrews – to be His representatives on earth."

"But," Clodia replied, "the Hebrews cannot agree among themselves and fight each other about religious matters. The zealots and the sicarii are everywhere."

"That's why from time to time God sends us a prophet, a messenger, to turn His people back to Him."

"And the Messiah, who is he?"

Simon sighed. "You may well ask. The Messiah is the one promised by God, the anointed one who will, at the end of days, precede the Kingdom of God and will save the race of Israel."

"If Jesus wasn't the Messiah, will our son be him?"

Simon exploded with laughter. "So much ambition and you are not even a Jewess. No," he continued. Laying a hand on her mouth before she could ask another question, "He isn't the Messiah. He and his seed are the adversaries of Satan, the Antichrist, the evil that has to be fought to the end of time."

As Clodia pondered this her eyes fell on the chest in which she knew Simon had placed the strange spearhead he had risked his life to get. He had told her of its history but she still didn't understand its potency. "What has the spear of Longinus to do with our son?"

This change of tack left him nonplussed for a moment. When he did reply it was with mock weariness. "Whatever he was, Jesus was endowed by God with great powers. Some of that power has transferred itself to the spear that gave him the stroke of mercy. Whoever has possession of that spear controls a power that can change the world."

Clodia was silent. Finally she whispered, "Is it good that the gods should give men such power? Will they not think they are become gods themselves?"

Simon took her in his arms. "Satan has already persuaded man to make that mistake and nothing can change it back."

## 10

For over an hour Nero had been reading an excruciatingly bad poem of his own composition. The entire court was frozen in rapt attention. Better to suffer the minor inconvenience of a cramped limb than to be noticed. Such unfortunates were likely to be given the honour of a leading role in one of the giant circuses, which were staged daily during the games, and frequently required the hero to die a bloody and spectacular death.

The court was more full than usual. Against the advice of her personal diviner Poppaea, knowing that Karkinos and Tigellinus would be there and afraid of missing something, had gone to the reading with her five-year-old son, Rufius.

Another reason for being in constant attendance on Nero was the fact that she was pregnant. Poppaea reasoned that, if she bore him a son, this would advance her own cause at the expense of both the magus and the leader of the Praetorian Guard. She would also be in a better position to promote the future of her son Rufius, a stepchild to whom Nero had not warmed.

For this particular reading Nero had chosen to wear a simple, unadorned white toga whose generous folds, while not hiding his ever-growing bulk, lent a certain presence. From time to time he would pause to gesture. His meaty forearms ending in fat fingered hands reminded Petronius of the dancing bears that the Macedonians were expert in training.

It was during one of these pauses, in a silence so profound that the hum of insects in the garden could be plainly heard that a long muted rasp was articulated. So unexpected was the noise, so loud in that silence, that for long seconds its cause went unidentified.

It was only when it was repeated that it was recognised and the perpetrator discovered.

Like Vespasian on a previous occasion little Rufius, bored but wise enough despite his tender years to say so, had dozed off. Unable to contain himself the poet Lucan erupted with choked laughter which, purple in the face, he had been unable to contain and in so doing marked himself down for death. Within a month he would be executed for treason. Failure to recognise Caesar's artistic genius was a capital crime.

The dancing bear stopped, his garlanded head swinging in the direction of the offending sound, his button eyes glinting redly with sudden anger. With a roar of outrage and a speed that defied his bulk, he swept up a heavy goblet and hurled it with all his strength, striking the nodding head of his stepson a savage blow. Rufius keeled over without a sound, blood streaming from a deep split over his left eyebrow.

Too late Poppaea moved to silence her son. She managed to catch his falling body before she fainted – but not before she heard Caesar shout, "I have had enough of this brood," and knew that this was virtually a death sentence. Even as she collapsed, the shocked Augusta realised that in a matter of seconds her world had disintegrated, her dreams of empire shattered by a child's snore.

When the fainting empress and the unconscious child had been borne from the court by her retinue of courtiers, Nero threw his tedious poem across the chamber, flung himself onto his throne and glowered at the assembled court, which quaked with terror at what might follow. None dared to speak for fear of calling attention to themselves and falling foul of the malevolent rage that had seized the outraged emperor.

Surprisingly, it was the old general, Vinicius, who dared break the silence. The thrown scroll had landed near the feet of his wife who was as blanched as the papyrus he bent and picked up. With a slightly trembling hand the man who had personally led the seventh legion at odds of twenty to one against the Gauls and won, advanced on the simmering white mound sprawled on the throne.

"Great Caesar, we are desolate that you should have been so rudely interrupted, but beg you not to deprive us of the beauty of your words, for without the light of your genius to illuminate our existence our days are passed in darkness. Our lives are lived in a gloom like that of your northern lands, where in winter one is robbed of the sun's golden light. For you, O Mighty Apollo, are the light of our lives, the radiance without which we cannot live."

Even Petronius was impressed by this unexpected diplomacy, coming as it did from an old soldier renowned in the army for the brevity of his speech and the earthiness of his language. The rest of the court was simply stunned by his courage and envious of his eloquence.

But the bear was not to be mollified. "Self," the voice was shrill with outrage, "Self is all you think of. What sacrifices do you make for Rome, while your Emperor suffers the torments of creation?"

Vinicius, who had campaigned for twenty years for his country and his emperor, who bore on his body the scars that witnessed the service he had rendered Rome, was nonplussed by this outburst. Unlike the shrewder courtiers who knew the depths of Caesar's vanity, his cruelty, the viciousness of a nature, which, if thwarted in the slightest way, would take pleasure in tormenting those nearest to hand, the old soldier had been brave out of ignorance.

His wife, more perceptive, had almost collapsed when he had interjected.

The noblest of Rome's aristocracy daily risked their lives in attending a court ruled by a man who could (and did) dispose of them as thoughtlessly as does a child its toy soldiers on the nursery floor. These were the most senior members of the Senate, generals and centurions of Praetorian rank, together with the thinkers and scholars of the age (among whom was no less a person than the Greek Pythagoras).

So Tigellinus held his tongue and left the field to the one man who dared speak without fear of losing his. Karkinos.

"Your enemies are not here Caesar. Here you are surrounded by those who love you, who want only to serve you." There was the slightest pause, "to help you destroy those who are so ungrateful as to bite the hand that feeds them. Is there," he finished ominously, his voice running like oil running over steel on the grindstone, "anything more ungrateful than a Jew?"

Nero frowned but was attentive. He was aware of Jews. Roman Jews paid him handsomely for citizenship. On the other hand, rebellious Jews in Palestine were causing trouble.

Encouraged by the silence Tigellinus ventured a thought on Jews. "O Mighty Caesar, Lord Karkinos is right to speak out about how ungrateful Jews are. Did not these same Jews refuse to accept Caesar as a god, and did they not throw down your standards in rebellion?"

"Vespasian will crush them like beetles." Nero's reply was abrupt. He didn't want to talk about Jews. They reminded him too much about his other frontier problems. Anyway, he wanted the attention focused on him, not on political discussion. This would involve him in abstracts. What he wanted was blood, immediate terror. Pain. Dying. These things he understood and if they were accompanied by high drama, by theatre, so much the better.

Seneca, his old tutor who, from his earliest contact with his royal pupil had seen the flawed character and tried hard to nullify it, took up where Tigellinus had left off.

"Caesar, the noble Lord Karkinos is right. You are among friends. Against the might of Rome these Jews are nothing. To even talk of them depresses us, deprives us of more worthy discussion. Your latest poem is equal to that of Homer. If not for our sakes, then for the pleasure of the gods themselves, let us continue with your reading."

For a moment Seneca almost swung it. The court held its breath. The petulant lip was no longer thrust out quite so far. This further appeal to his vanity had improved Nero's disposition.

Petronius was on the point of adding his own plea for resumption when Karkinos came back – only this time he strode boldly to centre stage, striking a pose before the throne. "Lord of the Universe, Imperator, Apollo, Radiance! You have failed in your duty as Caesar, failed as Emperor to protect Rome and her people. Failed as a god to honour the gods."

As these words rang out more than one person fainted, and two were actually physically sick.

The court, as always, was ringed with German mercenaries, Nero's personal bodyguard, who killed at his nod. Rank meant nothing to these men. Like Molossian guard dogs they were trained to obey their master without question and act immediately on his command, no matter what.

Now, like the powerful and wildly aggressive mastiffs from the Peloponnesos whose nature they shared, the guards watched, eyes shiny with expectation, the muscles of their sword arms quivering in anticipation.

Suddenly Nero was enjoying himself. No longer slouching he leaned forward, hand on chin, eyes fixed on the Greek magus. For the moment he had forgotten who Karkinos was. Instead, he thought of him merely as a man who had condemned himself to death without knowing it.

Nero's next words would be designed to bring about an awareness of that circumstance and with it fear for nothing excited the despot more than fear. Watching suffering, no matter how intense, failed to touch his emotions. Only fear did that, particularly if he was the cause.

But ranged against the supreme adept, the chief servant of Satan, the force that even Christ acknowledged as ruler of the earth, he was simply another puppet to be manipulated.

With a quiet smile the Greek unhurriedly commenced to pull the strings. "Is it not your duty, O ruler of the earth, god among men, whose presence to mortals is likened as the sun is to the moon, is it not your duty to protect yourself for your people's sake?"

There was a long pause with Karkinos playing to the gallery, only too aware of Nero's love of theatre. And loving it he was, for the emperor was now standing, eyes shining, and a slight smile on his lips, cheeks flushed with excitement as he waited for what was to come next.

"O Immortal One, O Divinity, the gods demand that you protect your artistic spirit against those who are jealous of your genius who, while living under your protection refuse to acknowledge you as a god, as they reject all Rome's gods."

"These enemies of the Empire, with their filthy habits, are even worse than the sub-human Samnites. For this scum not only refuses to acknowledge your divinity, it worships and makes sacrifice to the ghost of a common criminal executed by your procurator in Judaea."

"They celebrate him in temples raised in his honour by eating the flesh and drinking the blood of children Roman children – for these Christian Jews are given to cannibalism and in their depravity can no longer be counted as human."

If Nero was amazed at this oration there were those in the court who were completely baffled, but Tigellinus was like a wolf faced with a pen of defenceless sheep. His grin was wide and his tongue lolled with happy anticipation and admiration for his master.

Nero was captivated. "Tell me more about these Christian Jews."

At this Karkinos dropped to his knees and flung his arms up in supplication. "Divinity, beware the Jews closest to you. Even he whom you smote this evening." A gasp ran through the court. Many of those present knew that Poppaea was half Jewish and that, as a result, her son Rufius was more Jew than Roman.

Nero was stunned. He stared at the kneeling figure, his mouth hanging open. When he recovered he swept out of the room without another word, signalling Tigellinus to follow him.

That same night, as the badly injured Rufius tossed feverishly in his bed, his mother was filled with despair and knew what it was to feel the terror she had so often induced in others as she struggled to save his life. She was only too well aware that even if she were successful he would almost certainly have a fatal accident.

As midnight approached she left the child in the care of a nurse and went to the forum to visit the vestals. But on the Palatine the sentence had already been issued and Tigellinus had despatched trusted assassins, Germans who would kill anyone without question.

Armed with an imperial order, nobody dared question their right to enter the nursery where the old nurse was overcome with scarcely any effort. As they approached the cot the child awoke and without fear blinked up at them, his pupils wide with sleep his feverish smile uncertain.

His garrotting was swift, his single quavering call for his mother troubling no one, least of all his killers who casually rolled the corpse in a sheet and took it away with them. On Caesar's orders the body was taken the same night and flung into the sea with a chain wound round its feet as food for the fishes.

When Poppaea returned to the body of the dead nurse and the empty cot her screams soared through the palace and could be heard all night. It was dawn before she gave a thought to the other part Jew that she was growing in her belly. What chance, she thought dully, for this unborn son against a man who had committed matricide, fratricide and was planning to murder a nation.

## 11

With Kino in command of a hand picked coterie of household guards, Simon had formed a small caravan for the journey to Caesarea. With Clodia and Miriam at the centre together with the other women of the household, Kino brought up the rear.

They left the city taking the road south to Hebron, a route that baffled Hippolyte. "Lord," he said diffidently, "Caesarea lies to the north. Why then do we go south?"

Simon acknowledged his steward's observation with a slight smile before responding. "We are leaving not just Jerusalem but Israel, forever, and before I die I would see the tomb of my ancestor once more."

Knowing that Simon's father was buried in Nazareth, the Greek was puzzled by Simon's answer, but didn't pursue the matter although his curiosity was aroused. "After all," he said to himself, "we shall be in Hebron by nightfall so this mystery will be resolved soon enough."

They made the twenty-mile journey across the austere Judaean hills in six hours. The small town at which they arrived lay in a fold of the hills in a tiny valley that had sufficient water to support a population which earned its living as hill farmers.

Clodia was struck by a sense of restfulness that seemed to pervade the whole place, a sense of tranquillity that was more than the normal peaceful atmosphere one would expect in a remote hill town.

She sensed that this was a special place and that Simon had a particular reason for coming to it, for she was as aware as the Greek steward that it lay in exactly the opposite direction to that which they should have taken. Unlike Hippolyte she didn't question Simon as to why they had made this diversion. She decided that he would tell her if he chose to. If not, she was equally content.

In the meantime, Hippolyte, who was known to the townspeople by Simon's caravans which passed through there on there way south, had no difficulty in securing accommodation.

It was while at supper on the second day that the reason for their coming to Hebron was raised – not by Clodia, nor Hippolyte who was serving the meal, but by Simon himself, who said, "After Jerusalem, for Jews Hebron is the most special place on earth."

Clodia's interest was immediately aroused. From the moment of their arrival she had experienced an unusual sense of tranquillity and well-being. "If the place makes them feel as good as I do, I can understand why." She paused before continuing in a puzzled voice, "It is no different to twenty other hill towns and yet, there is," she mused, "an indefinable aura of peace about the place that is almost tangible."

Simon smiled and picking up an apple started to peel it, giving the small task an undeserved amount of attention. With his head bent over the fruit he said casually "Would you think it a worthy enough place to get married in?"

Hippolyte, who was in the act of refilling the wine goblets, almost spilled some at this announcement. Clodia, who had just picked up the fruit bowl, dropped it and sat frozen, staring at Simon's bowed head. She said nothing.

The silence grew so long that Simon was forced to look up. He had a mischievous smile on his face, which died when he saw the expression on the face of the woman who sat opposite him. The tears were running silently down Clodia's face, which was transfigured with joy. Faced with such transparent adoration, a naked display of feeling that held nothing back – for Clodia was without artifice – Simon put down the apple and reached across the low table to take her face in the palms of his hands.

He was no longer grinning, his expression gravely mirroring the tenderness of Clodia's open show of emotion.

"You are already my wife and carry the child of our love," he said softly, "but I ask you to be my wife bound by the law of Moses and to bring our son up to worship the God of his fathers. The one God given to us by Abraham, the God we regard as the sole creator of all, with whom we have sworn a covenant."

Barely above a whisper Clodia replied, "Lord, I have already sworn to follow you to the end of my days. Your son will be brought up to honour the God of his fathers and no other. That you honour me with your love and your name are more than I deserve."

The couple was alone for Hippolyte had tactfully withdrawn, warning the servants not to enter the room without being summoned.

"Come." Simon stood, lifting Clodia to her feet and holding her in his arms. "I have something to show you, the second reason for us coming to Hebron."

Clodia, unable to speak, wound her arm around his waist and allowed herself to be led into the courtyard of the house, which the local rabbi had placed at their disposal.

It was nearly midnight and the light from the three-quarter moon illuminated the garden as brightly as the late afternoon sun. In that clarity of silences that only the mountains have, the couple walked slowly to the end of the garden.

As they approached the gate leading into the street, Kino appeared from the lean-to next to it. In the moon's light his blue-black skin had taken on the hue of oiled ebony, his eyes and teeth flashing white as he salaamed at their approach. When he attempted to follow them into the street Simon turned him back with a friendly word, which the black giant accepted reluctantly.

They were alone in the lane, and as they walked slowly along it Clodia was content in the silence to be with the man she loved, to feel the weight of his arm across her shoulders.

"Why," she asked him softly, "is this place so special to all Jews?"

"For two thousand years," Simon replied, "this small town has been fought over and been at the centre of innumerable political disputes because it is so special."

"Yes," Clodia responded, "but why? What is it that men want that they are prepared to fight and die for?"

Simon smiled at her perceptiveness but didn't answer her directly. Instead he continued with the history lesson. "Over the centuries this town has been a Hebrew shrine, and four times it has been overrun by barbarians who have set up the false gods Molok and Astarte, but always they have been overthrown. David was anointed King here, first of Judah then of all Israel."

Clodia would have interrupted him but he put a finger on her lips and continued, "Abraham, the father of our race, bought land here after the death of his wife, Sarah, as a burying place for her and eventually himself."

They had come to the end of the lane and entered a small square, which was bounded on three sides by other buildings and on one side by the solid bulk of a mountain. In the centre of the square was a small temple.

"Here," he said, "is what draws men to Hebron, whether they are Jew or barbarian, and this is what we will never give up."

Clodia looked at him questioningly. Without a word Simon led her across the square to the entrance of the building set in the natural rock of the mountainside. He opened the door and motioned her to step inside. To Clodia's surprise oil lamps placed in niches around the walls were lit.

"This is," Simon said, "or at least, was," he continued correcting himself, "the Cave of Machpelah, purchased by Abraham together with the land immediately outside."

Clodia was too awed to speak, for in the centre of that bare, rock lined chamber were two massive stone sepulchres. Simon smiled reassuringly and, leading her to the nearest of them, took her hand and rested it reverently on top.

"Here," he said huskily, "are the mortal remains of Abraham, founder of the Jewish religion and ancestor of our race."

Shivering with a mixture of excitement and awe, tempered by a great deal of nervousness, she was led to the next tomb. "Let your belly rest against this holy stone so that Sarah his wife, blessed by God, can feel the life in your womb as she did in hers all those years ago."

Silently Clodia leaned against the cool stone. "Who," she whispered, "rests over there?"

Simon looked across the chamber at the other two sarcophagi that shared the room. "They," he answered gravely, "are the tombs of his son Isaac and his wife Rebecca. Across the square are the tombs of Abraham's grandson and his wife Leah."

With a tremulous sight Clodia allowed herself to be led outside. She stared at the small temple in the centre of the square. "Who," she asked softly, "lies here, my lord?"

"Joseph, the eleventh son of Jacob and Leah, who was sold by his brothers into slavery and became one of the officials next in rank to Pharaoh because he could interpret dreams."

"Will our son have so great a gift?"

Simon ignored the question, saying instead, "Come my love, the hour is late and tomorrow Miriam must instruct you in the wedding customs."

Clodia obediently allowed Simon to lead her back the way they had come. "Do all Jews have magical power?"

Simon chuckled at her tenacity. "No, only those touched by the finger of God or," he ended grimly, "Satan."

To stop her pursuing this line of questioning he reminded her that their stay in Hebron was to be brief. "We must leave this place in two days' time. Two of Rome's best legions, the fifth and the tenth, have arrived in Caesarea as reinforcements for Vespasian with orders that require him to pacify Palestine once and for all. Rome is sick to death of rebellious Jews."

"It seems," he continued sadly, "that Nero has decided that Jews are not only unruly and ungrateful for Roman rule, they are also ungovernable. Nero has genocide in mind."

Clodia was uncertain whether this statement was due to news that Simon had received from the many traders he came into contact with, or by divine revelation.

Seeing the look on her face he burst out laughing. "I have sent out spies to every part of Judaea," he chuckled, "who report to me daily, though the news they bring is of necessity weeks – even months – old."

"And of course," he continued, "my caravans and merchant ships bring me news, information – secrets even – for they supply the Roman armies and pick up all sorts of military information that they overhear when in a Roman port or garrison."

As a result of this network of spies and informers, Simon's knowledge of the situation in Palestine outstripped that of both the Jewish and Roman authorities.

Simon knew only too well that the country Vespasian had come to sort out once and for all was a madhouse of sectarianism as the various Hebrew peoples who lived in Palestine and its neighbouring lands all practised their own variation of Judaism.

In addition, there was a plethora of pagan gods from older religions that were still worshipped by indigenous non-Jewish populations as well as the gods of the Hellenised world imported by the conquering Romans.

Magicians, soothsayers, astronomers of all persuasions, some genuine, some simply misguided and some out and out charlatans, mushroomed as fast as the various religious cults which blossomed in this hotbed of expectation, frustration and despair. A brew of magic, mysticism and patriotism fermented strongly by the yeast of Roman occupation.

Of all Rome's subject peoples, none resented Rome's colonisation and right to rule through an empire built by force, more than the Jews. The whole of Palestine was a cauldron seething with discontent. Every town and every village had men who had begun covertly to take up arms.

As Roman law was increasingly challenged and the authority of the chief priests in Jerusalem weakened, the smouldering religious differences between the Galileans and the Samaritans burst into flames and revolutionary elements on both sides began attacking each other's villages without mercy. Sparing neither the old nor the young they burned entire communities to the ground.

Amid the flames, prophets appeared who urged the people to rise up against the Romans. As a result, Roman forces throughout the area could suddenly be faced with a howling mob that had been rallied by such a man.

Increasingly Vespasian would come to view the recalcitrant and warlike Jews of Palestine with exasperation. As the weeks passed he would have to fight for every foot of ground, the gates of virtually every village and town closed against him and their people jeering at him from their walls.

As fast as he and his son, Titus, reduced and garrisoned towns, it would seem as though all they and their legions had done was to give the Jews breathing space, for they turned their swords on each other. The Jews argued fiercely among themselves about two matters – God and State. Who were worshipping the first correctly, and no peace until they got the Romans out of Palestine!

After visiting the caves of Machpelah, Simon and Clodia only remained in Hebron long enough to be married in a simple service performed by the town's rabbi and celebrated by the few friends of Simon who lived there, plus the servants and slaves who had accompanied them from Jerusalem.

When Simon and a deliriously happy Clodia left for Caesarea, they knew from the news that Simon's informers had brought, that they would have a difficult journey, and so they decided to go across country avoiding all the major towns. That journey, which should have taken three weeks, took six months.

When Simon and Clodia arrived at Caesarea they had crossed a land on fire from end to end. God's people, saints and sinners, had risen in fury against Rome, against each other, against their neighbours and against God himself.

If the Jews thought they had suffered so far, they had reckoned without John, son of Levi of Gischala, and Simon, son of Gioras of Gesarene, who between them would be responsible for the unspeakable agony that would precede Jerusalem's destruction. That would see them deny its starving citizens the contents of its sewers and the taking of flesh from mothers who had turned cannibal and murdered their children.

It was from a premonition of this horror that Simon was fleeing. Rome was a sanctuary and Caesarea, run by Greeks for the Roman military machine, the one safe place near Palestine from which it was possible to board a Roman ship.

Their arrival in that city was immediately reported to Florus, who sent them a message of cordial welcome, but warned them not to attempt to leave for Rome until he had given them clearance.

"Why," asked Clodia, "does he want to keep us here?"

"Not us, my love, but me," Simon had replied gravely.

"Well, tell him what he wants to hear and he will let us go," Clodia answered.

Simon chuckled at her naïveté. "You don't get to be Procurator of Judaea if you are taken in so easily. No, the old fox has something in mind and until we know what it is we stay here." To which he added, grimly, "Here the Romans, for the moment, are our friends."

"And the Greeks?"

Simon laughed. "The Greeks couldn't care less which god you worship, whether you are Roman or Barbarian, only about your money – and of that we have enough to satisfy even a Greek!"

## 12

The superb harbour of Caesarea, built by Herod the Great, was a perfect setting for the personal palace he had raised on a rock in its centre. Into this safe anchorage came kings and princes, merchants of every nationality, scholars from Athens, Corinth, Rome, Alexandria and Ephesus. Men who brought the Hebraic orientalism to Palestine with Hellenistic civilisation and Roman law.

This magnificent port was embellished by a mole constructed of granite faced with limestone, and wide enough for two chariots to promenade along it, two abreast.

On the hill behind the town Herod had constructed a citadel, a palace, hippodrome and other features of Greco-Roman civilisation. It was here, in this most gracious of seaside cities, that Pontius Pilate had lived, except when he was stationed in Jerusalem at the time of the Feast, his presence being necessary to keep order.

The exceptionally fertile plain of Sharron surrounding Caesarea was another reason for the port's importance. Fifty miles in length, it skirted the base of the Mount Carmel headland, where for centuries the rains running off the Judaean Hills had irrigated the soil they brought to the valley. In the shelter of these barren hills the Vale of Sharron produced oranges, lemons, grapes, almonds, figs and olives in overwhelming abundance.

South on this same coast lay the Plain of Philistia, whose southern boundary is the desert that Joseph, Mary and the child Jesus had to cross on their way out of Egypt.

The majority of Caesarea's citizens were Greeks who owned most of the property and the surrounding farmland. Minorities, including Hebrews, had to compete with slaves for work as dockers, and only won enough to survive on. Those who farmed as tenants were only slightly better off as they toiled to earn profits for landowners to pay Roman taxes.

To Clodia's amazement Simon even had property in Caesarea, this time a seafront villa at the fashionable end of the harbour. The servants who had fled with them from Jerusalem either supplemented the skeleton staff who acted as permanent caretakers, or were sent by ship to Rome to ensure that Simon's house there would be fully staffed when they arrived.

Meanwhile, the villa in Jerusalem had been sold for a ridiculously low price, simply to get rid of it. "Better," Simon had said gravely, "to get something for it before it's burned to the ground."

Since arriving in Caesarea, Simon spent much of his time with Hippolyte, his steward, managing what seemed to Clodia to be a huge business empire based on the purchase and resale of the cargoes of ships that were still at sea and which he bought without ever seeing.

The rest of the time he was locked away in his private quarters, endlessly studying the ancient magical texts, which he valued more than the profits he made from his business enterprises.

The Roman Procurator, Gessius Florus had been fascinated by Clodia's story and had promised to provide her and Simon with letters of introduction to Caesar. Much more importantly, he offered assistance to Clodia in proving her legitimate claim to be Pilate's daughter and of noble blood – not just a citizen of Rome but a royal one who claimed Tiberius for a grandfather.

Meanwhile, the whole country was in a state of siege. No road was safe from bandits. Villages fought miniature wars with their neighbours. Towns seethed with discontent and distrust, the end of a street often marking the demarcation line of sectarian opposition.

Whole swathes of Judaea, Galilee and Samaria were simply impassable to anything less than an army. Suddenly conscious of just how badly they were outnumbered the Romans, while cracking down ruthlessly on lawlessness in the towns, kept to their garrisons. For a Roman cohort to venture into open country was to invite attack, and ambushes were constantly laid for such excursions.

The priests, particularly the Temple priests in Jerusalem, did their best to restore order. They knew only too well that civil war would destroy the nation.

They urged the various factions to draw back from outright war with Rome. In vain did they point to Vespasian's military record, to the fact that no province had ever successfully challenged Roman rule and, perhaps most ominously of all, the punishment that had been meted out to those who had tried. And that the Roman general sent against them had never lost any of the many campaigns he had fought.

By now Clodia was heavy with child and her pride in that fact was second only to the feelings she had for the man who was its father. Her years of struggling for survival as an outcast had equipped her for the long and dangerous journey to Caesarea. A journey that had been made almost entirely on foot and at night, deliberately choosing a route through wild and inhospitable terrain to avoid both Roman soldiers and Jewish revolutionaries.

On occasions, they had been trapped for weeks on end in villages that were either under attack from the inhabitants of the next village, or had themselves decided to assault their neighbours. The result was a minor war between not just neighbours but blood kin who had married outside their own village.

For Clodia, the sanctuary of Caesarea was a time of hot days with indigo evenings, of cool sea breezes and sunsets that turned the silver scimitar of Herod's magnificent harbour into pink and gold, its fringe of a thousand royal palms chocolate silhouettes stencilled along its hem.

During the six months they were to spend in Caesarea, Clodia loved nothing better than to ride with Simon in a chariot along the top of the harbour's superb breakwater at the end of a day. Sweeping around the anchorage, it was like the arm of a protective lover encircling the waist of his sweetheart.

These evenings together were precious to both of them. In companionable silence they enjoyed watching the sun spangled wavelets and the bay turning into a shield of beaten silver, on which floated the marble and white limestone confection that Herod the Great had built on a rock in the middle of the harbour.

This magnificent palace seemed to rise out of the sea like a swan about to take flight. Its crystalline limestone walls rose sheer as an ice field from the bare rock, continuing upwards in a series of vaults and arches and slender spires whose turrets and cupolas were covered in gold and mosaics of coloured glass executed in either a deep viridian green or a royal cobalt blue.

In the evening sun the whole edifice would go from silver to pink to gold to orange to blood red, and finally to charcoal as the setting sun dipped behind it before plunging into a sea flooded with fire.

In this harbour merchant vessels from the Roman world, as well as Roman warships, rode at anchor, their hulls lit by the fireflies of lanterns set by crews of every nationality. These ships trade in every known commodity, operating import/export businesses that linked the overland caravans from India, China, Arabia, Persia, Parthia and Africa to Rome.

Caesarea was Florus's headquarters and since the time of Anthony, had been a garrison town for Rome's legions. Here the procurator also lived in a waterfront villa, except when he went to Jerusalem to keep order at the time of the feast.

It was the one place of which Clodia had any childhood memory that involved her parents because Pilate, during his prefecture, had lived in the same waterfront villa. It was at a function given by the current procurator, Gessius Florus, and to which Simon and Clodia had also been invited, that after dinner conversation turned to previous occupants of the prefecture's office.

The announcement that Clodia was the daughter of one of these caused a mild sensation, and more than one guest whispered to another the difficulty she might have in proving her parentage. They were no doubt mindful of a considerable inheritance that would be hers if she could prove her claim – a thought that had crossed Florus's mind, though he was more interested in her bloodline to Tiberius and the political consequences of that, than he was concerned about mere money.

As the hour had grown late and the wine lower in the bottle, so had tongues become less guarded. It was the procurator's wife who finally dared to issue Clodia a guarded challenge. "Surely my dear," she cooed in her most honeyed tone, "there is something about this house you can remember from your childhood?"

There was a sudden silence in the room, all other conversation dying. It was as though a windlass had suddenly run down. Florus, who was on the far side of the room, turned to get a better view of Clodia, his deeply tanned face enigmatic though he knew that more than a few people in the gathering were aware of the fact that he was sponsoring her cause with Caesar.

Clodia remained silent under the sneering question. A silence that was mistaken for confusion – even worse, an admission of charlatanism.

Her eventual reply caused a glint in Florus's eye, though his weather-beaten face remained impassive. "Fortunately, I have inherited the excellent memory of my grandfather, Tiberius, and remember that this house and office belonged to my family."

Before there could be a further exchange, Simon intervened. Unsteady on his feet and spilling wine down his toga he was, nevertheless, in full command of his faculties. "Memory can be uncertain at the best of times, which these are, particularly if Rome posts you to this unhappy country."

Florus felt the barb of that remark. It was well known that he resented his office. Instead he had hankered after the legate's job in Syria. He snapped back sarcastically, "The Senate will want more than memories, good or bad, before it admits the patrimony of a claimant to the house of Tiberius."

Simon smiled coldly at this, his dark eyes as hard and bright as pebbles. He sipped his wine before replying, first wiping his mouth with the back of his hand, errant drops sparkling in his beard.

Florus watched him intently. This man fascinated him; his psychic powers, while they didn't frighten him, certainly made him uneasy. He also recognised the stubborn, rebellious nature of an independent mind. Such men made good soldiers if you tamed that spirit without breaking it.

Swaying unsteadily Simon lowered himself with the exaggerated care of a drunk to sit beside Clodia who, frowning slightly in disapproval at the amount he had imbibed, was far too sensible to remonstrate with him. "Look at me" – his voice was low, the anger had left his eyes.

Clodia stared into the dark brown eyes only inches from hers. Absentmindedly she noted how incredibly long his eyelashes were.

"Clodia."

Her mind stopped wandering and concentrated on the man she loved. His eyes were gold and brown, their dark irises holding her attention. She could feel his will, his thoughts, his very essence blending with her own mind. She let herself go; it was like sliding into a large, warm bed. She could feel his strength around her. She felt safe, secure, at peace.

Simon rose and slowly walked across to face Florus. "Clodia," his voice was firm, commanding, without being authoritarian. "What do you know about this house that is secret?" Secret! Nobody had thought about secrets. How delicious!

Even Florus was impressed. "Of course," he thought, "every house has its secrets."

Clodia, deep in a hypnotic trance, answered without turning her head, her voice drained of all emotion. "There is a hidden compartment behind the shrine to Diana in the atrium."

At this revelation, a nervous murmur ran around the room.

"How do you open it?"

Without hesitation she replied, "You rotate the statue of the goddess three times to the right and twice to the left."

The silence following this could be felt. Every mind was in the temple on the other side of the villa, wondering what would happen if you moved the statue in this way and, if such a hiding place existed, what secrets it might hold.

Simon turned away from the procurator who had paled at this revelation and walked back to touch Clodia gently on the shoulder. She blinked; looking slightly startled as though she had just awakened from sleep.

He smiled at her reassuringly. "Come," he said, "let us see what Diana guards for a granddaughter of Tiberius," and he led the startled guests out of the room, bowing to Florus and saying, "My lord, will you honour us while we consult the goddess?"

Florus heaved himself up with a wintry smile. "Yes – if only to see a Jew in the presence of a Roman god!" The hidden warning wasn't lost on Simon, who acknowledged it with a lift of the wine goblet, which seemed not only welded to his hand but never empty.

Ringed in a solemn semi-circle round the half life-size figure of bronze that represented Diana, Florus and his wife summoned some servants to assist them in rotating the figure in the prescribed manner. It would have been unthinkable for anybody else to touch so personal an item.

As the figure was put through its final rotation, a marble panel in the wall behind it sprang open to reveal a small casket, such as a lady would use as a jewel box. All eyes turned to Florus. This matter needed the seal of authority, of approval. The procurator looked questioningly at Clodia.

"It was my mother's," she whispered. He passed it to her and she took it from him with trembling hands.

"Open it, my love," Simon murmured.

Slowly she raised the lid. Inside the box was a scroll. Those who expected gold or jewels were disappointed, but not Simon or Florus, who knew instantly that whatever was written on that scroll would be beyond price.

Clodia shot a beseeching look at Simon, who pulled the scroll out and paused before unrolling it. "My lord, will you honour the granddaughter of Tiberius?" and he offered the parchment to Florus who nodded shortly and, without more ado, broke the seal and scanned it briefly before handing it, without a word, to Clodia.

He then turned to face the assembled guests. "The letter is a private one from the Lady Procula to her daughter, the daughter she was forced to abandon in the wilderness and was never to see again. It is signed, not only by her, but also bears the signature and seal of her father, the then-procurator, Pontius Pilate."

The rest of the evening was a blur of congratulations and requests for her to read the letter, which she steadfastly refused to do. Only when she was alone with Simon did she unroll her precious letter and allow her own tears to spot the vellum, adding to those shed by the writer.

When she could finally bring herself to do so, in a broken voice she read the letter out to Simon.

"To my darling daughter, Clodia, of whom I ask forgiveness. I have mourned for you every waking hour of my life. Better had I not forsaken you but gone with you into the wilderness. Not knowing what your fate has been, what pain you have suffered has been worse than death itself. Better had I shared that suffering than a tiny death each day.

"Your father has been used by the Jews to murder a man favoured by their God. In dreams I have seen His anger. This land will be bathed in blood. There is no safety in Rome for either your father or me – but our fate is no longer of any importance. Our time is over. But, darling daughter, yours is just beginning.

"I have visited the Oracle at Delphi who has prophesied that you will return to this house in glory, whole again, and carrying a child who is blessed by the God of the Jews whose Messiah they murdered.

"I leave this letter in the hope that you will find it on your return. That you are safe and well fills me with the greatest joy. My only sorrow is that I will never see you again or my grandchild.

"The final wish of both your loving parents is for your happiness and forgiveness for the wrong we did you.

Procula."

# 13

Since the murder of Rufius and Karkinos's dire warning about hidden enemies, Nero had not only refused to see Poppaea but also had shut himself off from the court. The only people who could gain admittance to his chambers were his drama coach and Tigellinus, who had been ordered to purge the senate, the court and the Praetorian guard of anyone who had a single drop of Jewish blood in their veins.

It was an exercise that Tigellinus carried out with immense enthusiasm for it gave him the perfect opportunity to remove from his path all rivals and anyone in the senate who offered even the mildest challenge to his authority. Even the neurotic Nero had a bonus, because as noble families were wiped out, he confiscated their possessions.

As the money rolled in from these murders, Tigellinus made certain that he skimmed his share off the top.

In spite of the Prefect's industry and the addition to his coffers, Nero continued to be beset by imaginary fears. He increasingly imagined plots everywhere and struck out blindly, sending hundreds of Rome's ruling class to their deaths without a single shred of evidence that they were guilty of any crime.

As the numbers murdered in this fashion mounted, even Tigellinus began to dread being summoned into the imperial presence – so an early morning command to join the Emperor for breakfast left him with a sharply reduced appetite.

"How," Nero demanded of his guard commander, "can I be free of the constant worry of assassination, of insurrection, and those who covet my throne?" The fat wet lip trembled. "How," he moaned, "can people be so ungrateful?"

Under this kind of questioning Tigellinus shifted uncomfortably. He knew from experience that one wrong word would result in a sudden explosion of hysterical bad temper. An outburst that as often as not, was fatally directed at the person nearest to hand.

The Praetorian was suddenly painfully aware that he was alone with a simmering volcano whose temperamental instability was feared throughout its court. "Perhaps, Divinity," he suggested diffidently, "Karkinos should be required to hold a private séance to divine the Emperor's enemies."

At this suggestion Nero thoughtfully sucked in his cheeks before responding. Finally, to the Praetorian's immense relief, he replied, "Arrange it, for we are beset by bad dreams and would rid ourselves of these troublesome spirits."

Karkinos was delighted with the turn of events and lost no time in arranging the séance Nero had requested.

The next day, when the Emperor arrived at the Greek's palace in a closed litter, he was ushered into the magus's private temple where the hastily convened coven awaited him. It was an experience to which he was soon bitterly regretting having exposed himself.

It was one thing to strut about and pretend to be a god, but to be faced by a force that claimed to be mightier than Jupiter himself was a horse of a very different colour.

For months he hadn't been sleeping well. More and more he dreamed of Octavia, the wife he had killed, and had attempted to block her out of his dreams by increasing the amount of opiates he was taking, washing them down with more and more wine – but to no avail.

As well as Octavia, Agrippina haunted his dreams and the spirit of his murdered mother refused to give him any peace.

To add to his troubles, voices were being raised against him in Rome, while all along the borders of the empire there was unrest and sporadic outbreaks of rebellion.

In desperation he had asked Karkinos if he could summon the spirit of his mother so that he could ask her forgiveness for her murder. The Greek had assured him that this was possible and, as a result, Nero had come to the magus's palace for the ceremony, which was now underway.

He had been placed in a circle and told, on pain of death, not to leave it, for it was a magic circle made of lead with the names of power driven into it.

Outside was a triangle made from the chains of a gibbet and fastened with nails, which had been hammered through the heads of two Christian women broken on the wheel.

Three of Karkinos's assistants stood outside the triangle at each of its three corners. In their left hands each carried a dagger, in their right a black candle made from the fat of executed criminals.

Inside the triangle more candles burned, set in black wooden candlesticks and encircled with vervain.

Along its outer edge four objects were placed, and no matter where he turned his gaze, the sweating Emperor could not avoid them. One was the head of a black dog which had been fed on human flesh for five days; the second a bat that had been ritually drowned in blood; the third the horns of a goat that had had intercourse with a virgin girl; and the fourth the skull of a parricide.

No matter which way he turned his head it was the dog that drew him. In the light of the candles its eyes, buttoned into its black fur, shone with life. Occasionally it yawned and, when it did so, he could see the tip of the spike on which it was impaled sticking through the floor of its mouth.

Nervously the Roman Emperor adjusted the silk handkerchief at his bulky neck with a hand like a fiddler crab. His fat white fingers were overgrown with coarse red hair, for he would not permit epilators to pluck this out because he feared magicians would use it to work spells against him.

Wistfully, the man who commanded thirty legions and through them most of the known world, wished he was out in the fresh air. Outside it was spring in Rome, the snow on the Alban Hills yielding to the warmth of the winds blowing from Africa. Violets and other spring flowers filled the gardens and the people enjoyed the sun's warmth filling the Forum and the Campus Martius.

Instead, he was in this poorly lit chamber, the atmosphere of which was charged with an emotion he didn't understand and which filled him with dread.

Nero's expression normally portrayed his measureless vanity, as often as not tinged with tedium and boredom – the result of an appetite sated, every whim gratified. He was now sweating profusely, though in that windowless chamber the still air held an unnatural chill.

During recent years, the imperial face had grown bullfrog wide and his lower jaw sagged under the weight of a double chin that hung like a cow's udder heavy with milk. As a result of all this extra fat his mouth, always near his nose, seemed to touch his nostrils. His small pale eyes, fringed with almost colourless lashes, were set into this pink and white face like those of a boar – restless, reflecting every mood of an unstable temperament that could become dangerous without warning.

Now those watery eyes were fixed anxiously on Karkinos, who had taken hold of the consecrated cross-handed sword and was advancing towards the northern point of the temple.

Touching Nero's brow with its point the magician said, "To thee, O Satan, be the kingdom." Frozen, Nero watched the tip of the blade swing down and touch his solar plexus. He was vaguely aware of the continuation of the mantra, "…be the kingdom." The blade touched his right shoulder, "and power," it swung to his left, "and the glory."

Karkinos turned away from the Emperor and faced the altar. Holding the point upwards he cried, "In the name of Lucifer and Beelzebub, I take in hand the sword of power for defence against the god of the Jews."

Nero's anxiety turned to astonishment as the Greek began to levitate. As he rose Karkinos declared, "May the holy archangel Lucifer protect his servants from the evil approaching from the east, for the followers of the god of the Jews are now in Rome and the seed of his most loyal servant is carried on the wind, soon to join them."

As he finished speaking the magician slowly descended. As his feet touched the stone floor the sword, which was now reversed point down, glowed with an inner light and, as Karkinos used it to draw a second circle, a line of dancing flame followed its point.

Into this circle chanting acolytes brought braziers filled with burning charcoal into which they cast hemlock, henbane and Indian hemp – all powerful narcotics. As the fumes swirled round the temple, the powdered brains of a civet cat were mixed sacrilegiously with galbanum, normally included by the Hebrew high priests in the sacred incense of Jehovah.

Standing within the circle of golden flames that danced upon the bare stone floor, Karkinos carefully placed the magic sword on the ground so that it was aimed directly at the quaking Roman, and accepted the chalice from a kneeling priest. Raising it above his head, he began the opening formula for the conjuration.

"I conjure thee, O spirit, O ruler of this world and the next, by the power of Lucifer and the legions of Hades, your servants humbly beg that we may share your presence, for your servant, Caesar, is troubled by many questions."

"I conjure you by what name the elements are overthrown, the air is shaken, the sea is turned back, the fire is quenched, the earth shudders and all of things in heaven, in earth, in hell, do tremble and are confounded. Hear thou me, for I am the angel of Ptah - Apophrasz - Ra. This is the true name, handed down by the prophets of Vril."

As he finished speaking Karkinos stepped out of the circle and flung himself flat, arms outstretched in supplication. In absolute terror Nero watched as in the flames' dancing circle a dense black shape began to form. It was as though he was staring into the darkness of heaven without stars. It grew like the mouth of some mighty cave.

In desperation the Emperor swung his head but it surrounded him, it blotted out everything. For a moment he thought he was blind. If he could, he would have fled that terrible arena, but he was held as though in chains. Tears coursed down his plump cheeks, he shivered uncontrollably as much from the terrible cold, which had suddenly engulfed him as from fear.

"What does Caesar want?" The voice that asked the question was as soft as a wavelet spending itself on a midnight shore.

Nero couldn't answer. He was dumb with terror. The silence that followed seemed to last en eternity. "Speak, for I acknowledge you as one of my children. Ask of your true father and it will be given."

The gentle voice seemed to come as though from an interminable distance, though the presence of its owner was overpowering.

The Roman Emperor was a profligate buffoon, fratricide, matricide, wife killer and mass murderer. His rule was predatory, ravenous, unrestrained in its cruelty, and rotten to the core of its being.

He sucked his cheeks and managed a tremulous response. "I am beset by my enemies," – there was a pause and Caesar burst into tears – "and I don't know what to do." This last was almost unintelligible, lost in an outburst of sobbing.

Like a circle of black crows, Karkinos and his priests stood motionless at their stations, their eyes on their master, ignoring the huddled figure of the Emperor. The magus also waited for his master and he was not disappointed.

"Destroy them." The voice was like a heavy chain being dragged across the stone floor. "Throw them into pits filled with lions, crucify them, burn them, cast your enemies into the flames."

Nero was sitting bolt upright, his eyes shining with excitement, his former tears forgotten still shining on his wet cheeks. "Fire," he whispered.

"Fire," thundered the voice, and a column of white-hot flame burst from the bare stone floor, its heat so intense the Emperor was forced to turn his head to one side to shield his face.

Oblivious to the fire Karkinos advanced on him. "O divine one, you are saved, Satan himself has come to your aid. He has delivered your enemies into your hand. O immortal one, destroy those who would destroy you, with fire."

## 14

Simon lifted the son he had named Joshua when he performed the rite of circumcision eight days after his birth, and solemnly surveyed Kino, Hippolyte and Miriam across the top of the baby's head, saying, "You three are not exactly the magi, but you can stand in for them."

Clodia, flushed with pleasure at Simon's obvious pride, still hadn't got over her overwhelming joy at having delivered a healthy male child. Even though it had been two weeks after an easy birth, she still awoke in the middle of every night before the baby cried to be fed to reassure herself that she hadn't dreamed it.

As the three adults gathered around the infant held inexpertly by Simon, Clodia was as anxious as the hovering nurse as they alternately poked the baby or offered him a finger to play with.

"Who were the magi?" Clodia asked from the couch, more to distract Simon as a prelude to getting the infant back than from any genuine interest in whatever the answer might be.

Simon stopped clucking at the child to look down at her, smiling with affection. "When his uncle was born three priests of great learning said that his birth had been foretold and that they had been guided to his birthplace by a star. They were foreigners who were not only tutored in the secrets of ancient wisdom but who had the power to foretell the future by reading the stars."

"But why did they want to see him?" asked the puzzled Clodia, her interest now genuinely awakened.

Simon paused and handed the baby back to its nurse, for his son had grown restive and was starting to protest. "The Idumaean pig, Herod, the sacrilegious plunderer of the tomb of David, feared for the throne he had stolen. He had heard that the magi had come during the census to pay homage to a Jewish king – the Messiah promised by the God of Israel and prophesied by Isiah."

By now Clodia was all attention. "What did Herod want of the magi?"

Simon strode to the window and pulled back the heavy drapes. He stared blindly into the darkness, dawn still only the faintest promise on the eastern horizon. When he replied his voice was shadowed with a long held grief.

"They came with the gifts only kings and the wisest of men are given. Myrrh for the race of Ham which represents human nature, gold for the race of Shem and to symbolise his kingship, and incense for the race of Japhet to confirm that in him was the presence of the Holy Spirit for he would be more than king – he would be priest as well."

"Which is why," he finished grimly, "there were those who would eventually claim him to be the one we Jews had waited for, for two thousand years – the priest king sent by God to deliver us from our enemies and to lead us to everlasting glory."

Simon paused. The silence in the softly lit room was laden with sudden tension. Miriam cried silently, the tears coursing down her cheeks. "And so they killed him. No crown – other than thorns – no kingdom, no subjects, for all who had cheered him and strewn flowers before him and hailed him King the week before had fled in terror for their own lives."

The last was almost a whisper, the words fluttering like falling leaves, all emotion gone – only an unutterable weariness at the remembered loss.

"And Herod?" Clodia whispered. She had left the couch to stand behind Simon, to embrace him gently and lay her cheek on his shoulder. Miriam and Hippolyte slipped out of the room, followed by the nurse carrying the sleeping Joshua.

Without turning he touched her face in acknowledgement and sighed. "The magi never told him where Jesus was. He knew that they had gone to Bethlehem, so he simply ordered his mercenaries into the town, having sealed it against anyone who might wish to leave, and killed every male child under the age of two."

A chill struck Clodia's heart. Instinctively she shot a protective glance at the baby. "How," she demanded, "did they escape?"

"Whatever else the old man may have lacked in worldliness," Simon responded in a firmer voice, "he more than made up for in intuition. When Herod's butchers arrived they were long gone, heading for Heliopolis in Egypt."

The woman was puzzled. "Why Egypt?"

Simon was patient. In her role as mother it would be important that she should be able to answer the questions for their growing son.

"The Jews have had their colonies in Egypt for centuries. Not all of Israel's children were led out of Egypt by Moses. Some stayed behind of their own accord; others returned unable to stand the harsh life of a desert nomad, perpetually driving their herds in search of pasture which at best was on marginal land that was too much trouble to fight over."

"But they weren't free." Clodia's response was more statement than question.

Simon turned, smiling, to kiss her gently on the forehead before acknowledging the fierceness of her last rejoinder. "Yes, my love, they were free and that's why we, too, must go to Rome – to stay free. The Romans are sick of rebellious Jews."

He paused. When he continued he was close to tears. "Vespasian is getting ready to march on Jerusalem. When he does he will destroy it and all Jews everywhere. The time of retribution is at hand, Jehovah will use the Romans as his instrument of chastisement for a people that has turned its back on Him for lesser gods."

Clodia shivered at this grim prediction.

Before she could say anything Simon continued in a voice hoarse with emotion, "I have been shown the desolation. The time when Jews will envy the dead, when no stone of David's city will stand upon another, when weeds will grow in the skeletons of the unburied dead and foxes will make dens where once the Holy of Holies stood, for the Temple will be no more."

Clodia tightened her arm around his shoulders. Uncertainly she asked, "As Jews, will we be safe in Rome?"

Simon laughed, freeing himself from her arms and striding to the doorway that led from the bedchamber to the garden. He opened it to sniff the air as though he would scent the coming dawn. "We are also," he chuckled dryly, "citizens of Rome," and strode out of the room, pulling his cloak around his shoulders to ward off the dawn chill.

Shivering slightly in the cold air, Clodia padded quietly out of the bedroom and leaned against him. He drew her to him without a word and she snuggled against him in companionable silence.

The day's first herald was a great searchlight of gold which pierced a deep pass in the hills that reared out of the land like the ramparts of ancient Jericho, a black silhouette that ran along the horizon as far as the eye could see. These highest ridges seemed to brush the sky itself.

Silently they watched in awe as the crest of the entire range suddenly lightened as the night sky behind the highest peaks paled to blue. The early morning sun lit more and more of the hills' black bulk. Swirling clouds gave way to reveal rocks marbled with blue and green, as bright as the sea.

As the sun vaulted higher into the morning, the sleeping land was thrown into a crystal focus that caught the shimmering dew on the spider's web stretched on the doorpost and gilded the ripening corn in sharp relief. Arms around each other's waists, they strolled into the garden.

Clodia could smell the morning – taste it. Her skin could feel the sun fingering her features. When she squeezed her eyes half closed she could capture it in her eyelashes. She broke the silence. "Lord, what must we do to protect our son?"

There was a long silence, so much so that Clodia wondered if Simon was going to reply. "Learn to trust in God. If we put our trust in Him, he will be our protection." He paused before continuing ruefully, "How can I trust God when I don't even trust myself?"

Clodia hunched her shoulders, brow furrowed in frustration, lips compressed. "What is this trust you value so highly? The gods favour those they love and are in turn loved. Are you estranged from the God of your people?"

Simon moved. He turned to her, his eyes stormy with passion. "The God of my people is love. My brothers died preaching that message. He has given me the power to heal. Like Jesus and James, I have visions of the future and can command the forces of nature, for my family is of the line of Solomon, the guardian of the sacred secrets entrusted to him by the angels themselves."

Simon paused. His voice had grown harsh. He was clearly angry. Abruptly he stood up and started to walk back to the house. His parting words were bitter. "I have prayed for a sign but the Lord leaves me in silence. I have the power but no voice to guide me, only half-remembered voices from the past when Jesus was alive and I saw what they did to him."

He stopped and turned to stare at the sky, his brows knitted. He was shaking with rage.

When he next spoke it was to shout at the indifferent heaven of the new day "Once more, for the sake of our son Joshua, I will prostrate myself before the Lord. If He hears His servant I will follow the path he chooses. If I am left in silence..." he hesitated, no doubt remembering how many of his rebellious race had argued with their God, challenging His authority over them, "then I will deny Israel and my blood line for I and my son will command men, not serve them."

A few days later Simon surprised Clodia and his household by announcing at breakfast that he was going to make a journey of his own and he was going alone. What was more, he was packed and ready to go and would start immediately the meal was over. He would be away for about a week.

Simon caught the look of worry that flashed across Clodia's face as Miriam diffidently asked him where he was going and whether it wouldn't be prudent to take along a trusted servant to ensure his safety.

He smiled benignly at her, aware of Clodia watching intently from her place at the table. "You are right Miriam, but I do not propose to be in the company of my fellow men. I am going into the hills to be alone from man – but not to be on my own. I go into the presence of God, to pray."

"But lord," Clodia could contain herself no longer. "What happens if you are attacked by bandits or wild animals?"

"Let me come with you sire, please." The eager Hippolyte joined in the rising tumult of the household's entreaties – to stay at home, to go but with servants, to at least let Hippolyte accompany him (and even Clodia if she had dared to ask).

Smiling he rose and embraced Clodia. "I go to ask the God of Israel what will become of our son. What will become of the people he chose as His own. For a man does not live by bread alone, but by every word that proceeds out of the mouth of the Lord."

Praising God and beseeching His blessing on his household, Simon left the city.

As well as the ass on which he rode, he led a heavily laden pack animal whose burden excited their curiosity, but nobody dared ask him what its contents were.

They were, in fact, secret and sacred, for Simon, as well as being a magician, was also a lifelong student of an esoteric body of Jewish mysticism. It was based on occult interpretations of the bible, consisting of ancient doctrines dealing with the mystic symbolism of star movements and how to summon the forces of good and evil.

After travelling for several days Simon entered the Judaean hills, where he unloaded his animals and hobbled them in a valley that provided them with water and an abundance of good grazing.

With his animals cared for, he returned on foot to the cave he had found for himself further up the valley. It was away from the water and the shade of vegetation that grew at its edges.

Outside the lush valley where Simon had settled his stock, the hillside was a bare dry wilderness of boulders and harsh grey sand studded with razor sharp shards of flint. During the day there would be little shade within the shallow cave but, with a ground temperature of over 50°C at midday, it was not likely to make any significant difference.

Apart from the scorpions, snakes and lizards, his only neighbours were the kites and vultures that spiralled across the barren hills assessing all possibilities.

For three days Simon sat almost motionless at the entrance to his cave. Over his head and shoulders was draped a prayer shawl. Through his fingers slipped the knotted tassels as he meditated and prayed.

In the evenings he allowed himself a cup of water from a goatskin bag he had brought with him. He ate nothing. When he slept, it was on the bare earth without any covering other than his cloak.

Snakes coiled against his sleeping body and were gone again in the morning. The solar furnace heated the air and dissolved the rocks and boulders into shimmering waves. The land was on fire – a desolate, red-hot oven that sucked the moisture out of the pores. It was as though the eyeballs were set in grit, the lids gummed themselves half closed in a protective squint and the hot dry, dusty air seared the lungs, making every breath a distinct effort.

At the end of the third day, Simon felt sufficiently purified to begin his rite, and unpacked the sacred implements of Hebrew magic – the sword and the brazier.

Hunched with concentration, the man untied the cords of the cloth in which his ritual sword was wrapped – a sword of pure metal. It had been consecrated during the hours of the sun on the seventh day under the invocation of God. Then it had been polished with the ashes of the sacred fire and moistened with the blood of a serpent.

On the hard packed dirt floor of the cave he began his preparations.

With his sacred sword he described the double magic circle, the outer circle being nine feet in circumference. Inside it, at intervals equal to the width of his palm, were drawn two other circles. In the middle circle he inscribed astrological data. In the outer circle were the names of the angels of the air who ruled the day he had chosen for his conjuration. In the inner circle he wrote the four names of God, separated by crosses.

At the edge of the cardinal points outside the circle he drew a pentagram. Inside the eastern half he wrote the Greek letter alpha and, in the western half, omega.

This done, he circled it seven times intoning, "I offer you, O mighty Yahwey, this purest incense. I offer it, O great and potent Jehovah, with all my soul and all my heart." Then, for his own protection, Simon stepped into the circle.

At the head of the pentagram he lit the magic lamp that stood on a mirrored base.

When Simon stepped into the circle he chanted, "We ask with humility that God the Almighty, entering this circle, will defend us from Satan. O Lord, in Thy most Holy name; bless our entry into this circle, for Thou art blessed forever and ever."

As he stood in the centre of the circle, his hands resting on the pommel of his sword, the light from the brazier was strong enough to gild his face but couldn't pierce the interior of the cave which was almost pitch black. With the moon not risen, there was little light outside the cave. He stood as if carved from stone, eyes closed in concentration. The use of the sword and other instruments – even the circle itself – were aids in creating a state of mental and emotional control that were designed to carry him beyond his normal self.

Simon chanted rhythmically and with increasing force, gradually building himself up into a state of frenzied intoxication. The fumes from the brazier swirled around him and, as he intoned the sacred words, he breathed them deeply into his lungs, bobbing backwards and forwards from the waist – an hypnotic pecking motion which increased in speed as he chanted.

As suddenly as he had started he stopped. His heart, which was pounding from its exertions, lurched in his chest.

A figure had appeared at the mouth of the cave. Dimly perceived at first, Simon thought it was an extra shadow or smoke curling from his brazier deceiving him. The figure, cloaked and hooded was motionless, a dark column like a post. The voice came from it – and yet did not. It had a grave, almost accusatory tone.

"Simon bar Joseph, you dare call upon the spirit of the great Elijah, you whom the Lord has blessed, call upon His favourite servant."

In fear, Simon sank to his knees and pressed his forehead into the dust. "Not for myself but for Israel, for I am afraid for her people. I am nothing, but God has blessed me and my seed and I have survived to praise the one true God and serve Him all my days."

There was a long minute of silence before the figure continued. When it did it seemed to do so from a great distance. "Then why do you not trust your future to the hand of God?"

Simon raised a haggard face. "Who are you? Are you the spirit of the great Elijah? If you are, why do you fail to understand my fear which is for all my people?"

The shadowy figure seemed to retreat for a moment before replying, "I am the messenger of Elijah, he who understands your fear and tells you to trust in the Lord."

Simon groaned and knocked his head in the dust. "The earth is filled with Romans who killed Jews indiscriminately. The City of David is doomed, the children of God are to be scattered as chaff on the threshing floor. If it is His will that they be no place of safety, then we will die praising God. If I cannot know where the road leads, then at least tell me if there is a journey to be made."

For a moment he thought the spirit had departed, it had grown so dark. "Look into the flame and the future."

The sudden command startled Simon but he obeyed, staring into the flame of the lamp. At first he could see nothing other than the bright yellow of the light, but suddenly he could see a shape forming. It was the figure of a child.

Simon was filled with terrible foreboding. The figure before him was skeletal, dressed in rags and with the eyes of a lemur. It stared at him without moving, making no gesture either of supplication or defiance. The eyes, which held his, had forgotten what it was to be young or loved or unafraid, and now they were beyond fear. They simply watched him with resignation, waiting for the next cruelty.

In horror Simon realised that the wasted troll had a Star of David tacked onto its torn coat. It was a Jew.

Behind the tiny, wasted figure was a huddle of strangely shaped buildings, above which flew a flag with a black swastika on a red and white field. Without knowing why, this scrap of humanity struck a chill in Simon's heart.

He turned his attention back to the motionless child who squatted next to a strange fence of stranded metal set with barbs. Trembling, he tried to formulate a question but before he could do so was swept past the child into the area behind it, which was a landscape of hell.

In agony Simon shrieked aloud and tore out great handfuls of his hair. He closed his eyes but couldn't shut out the pictures of more troll-like children picking over the mounds of emaciated corpses, harvesting the gold from their mouths, stripping them of their meagre rags. He watched as they helped the living adult corpses pile the dead like cords of wood, ready for the huge furnace that plumed the sky with a banner of greasy grey-black smoke.

Mercifully the picture dissolved and the wretched Simon stared in amazement at what he suddenly realised was a new Jerusalem – a Jerusalem of the future. The Temple of the Mount was unmistakable, its dome glowing in the sunlight, though many strange new buildings filled the skyline. Even stranger was the clothing of the people and the incredible machines, which seemed to run, as if by magic through the streets.

In this city the children were as golden as the sun and filled with laughter, eyes bright with confidence. They and their parents radiated happiness – and they were Jewish. As if to confirm this the Star of David, deep blue on a field of white, fluttered proudly over its rooftops.

Beyond the city the amazed Simon watched armies equipped with unbelievable weapons kill each other with concentrated hatred. He wept when he realised that the protagonists were Arab and Jew.

The final vision was so apocalyptic that he thought he was witnessing the end of the world. It was Jerusalem dissolving into a ball of fire, an incandescence so fierce as to rival the sun, which left him temporarily blind. It was later, as the fire died down; that he realised life still went on. When his vision cleared, the huge mushroom cloud building up over where the city had once stood, filled him with an unknown fear. It frightened him more than the searing fire.

Sobbing and almost fainting, the exhausted man cast himself into the dust and begged the vision to end.

"Look once more, Simon bar Joseph, and go."

With a groan he raised his head to obey the stern command. At first he could see nothing. The City of David was no more. Nothing was left except the smoking foundations of the most substantial buildings. The very stones of the city had been burned to become the dust which swelled the evil hammerhead of cloud that towered as though to heaven itself. It was impossible to tell whether it was night or day. The levelled city was a desolation of sulphurous yellow.

An excoriating black wind, howling like a thing possessed, scoured the land of every molecule of life. It flayed the earth to the bone of its very bedrock before greedily bloating into a giant mushroom of stinking, red-hot dust that finally obliterated the sun and plunged the nightmare scene into freezing blackness.

Simon had never known such darkness, or such cold. He could feel his blood crystallising. To breathe was an agony as the cold of the void seared his lungs.

Helpless, he felt his spirit being drawn into the centre of that deadly tumescence, to the very core of its existence, the seat of its terrible power where time was running backwards. Simon realised in amazement that they had returned to the place that stood at the very heart of Jerusalem, the Temple at the time of Solomon.

The parade that passed before Simon's amazed eyes was a whirling carousel that suddenly slowed and finally stopped, and he found himself witnessing the great king himself sitting on his throne and personally directing his priests in the concealment of his most precious treasures.

At the king's command a shaft had been sunk into the temple floor and a strong room had been hollowed out beneath one of the great walls. Into this men were lowering not just a vast treasure of gold and jewels, they also carried the magic mirror he used for divination and his great seal, inscribed with a spell to banish Satan.

Grimoires and other ancient manuscripts containing magic rituals were reverently carried into the temple, including handbooks on magic written by the great king himself.

It was the manner in which the last item was conveyed to this secret place that Simon was to bear witness to, and which shrivelled his soul with unimaginable fear. For, when all had departed the throne room of the mighty Solomon, some of the priests who had helped lay up the treasure, returned bearing a closely curtained ark made of black wood. They also brought with them a black he goat which they worshipped and to which they sacrificed a young child. As the evil ritual climaxed, they opened the curtains of the ark and drew out a casket of bronze.

Through mists of pain from the searing cold, Simon cried out in shock as he recognised the chief priest. It was Karkinos who triumphantly mounted the throne of Solomon in a deliberately profane act designed to add immeasurable potency to his conjuration. Reverently he placed the casket on the throne itself and, accompanied by the prayers of his acolytes, opened it by lifting not only the lid but by letting down the front to reveal the scroll of Omega, the prophesy of the end of days, entrusted to Solomon by Zarathustra.

As the scroll was exposed to view, Karkinos began his prayer to Satan and his followers worshipped the being they regarded as ruler of all incarnate matter, Rex Mundi. As the ceremony reached its climax the high priest pronounced the prophecy of 'the last of days' and the triumph of their master.

When Simon returned home Clodia's joyful cry of welcome died on her lips at the apparition, which staggered into the villa. How he had made it back she didn't know. As he stumbled towards her she saw he was out on his feet. His head was matted and filthy. His hair had been torn out in great handfuls and left his scalp a mass of angry scabs. He was covered in small bruises, cuts and abrasions where he had fallen time and again. Always lean he was down to bone and sinew and where his skin had been exposed to the elements, it was almost black.

As he lay on his bed, his heart fluttering like a trapped bird in his chest, she gently bathed his face, while Miriam ran to fetch Hippolyte.

Slowly Simon opened gummy red-rimmed eyes, from which the sight had temporarily gone. When he realised it was Clodia bending over him, his blind eyes filled with tears of love and joy. Gently she spooned a few drops of water into his blistered mouth. When he tried to speak she gently admonished him and he collapsed into sleep.

# 15

Permission to leave for Rome with a squadron of war galleys bound for the Roman port of Ostia via Corsica came as a great relief to Clodia.

Simon, having physically recovered from his experience in the hills, refused to discuss what had happened. Instead, he retreated to his private quarters where he spent most of the day pouring over his ancient manuscripts with a wine goblet never far from his hand.

Hippolyte did his best to draw his master out, but even when he put in an appearance at mealtimes Simon remained morose and withdrawn, toying with his food and relentlessly downing the heavy Syrian wine.

The Greek, who managed most of Simon's business, gave up consulting a master who was suddenly indifferent to the news of the fortunes of his caravans from India and Persia and of the cargoes of his ships that traded from Turkey, Greece, Spain and Arabia and dropped anchor at every port in the known world.

Had he wished, Simon could have summoned a ship of his own to take them to Rome, but politics demanded that he accept Florus's invitation to travel as his guest on the flagship of the convoy that had brought him reinforcements.

An invitation that was delayed for a few days because the commander's ship had suffered minor damage to its rudder during a storm experienced en route to Palestine. This had now been repaired and the ship had left the harbour for a brief sea trial and its intended passengers informed of its imminent departure.

Hippolyte had closed the house at Caesarea and arranged for their baggage and those slaves who would accompany them to

Rome to be down on the quayside under Kino's watchful eye ready for embarkation.

Waiting for the Ajax to re-enter the harbour, Simon's face brightened up. For the first time in weeks he spoke without having to be spoken to. "The Tribune can handle his ship."

To Clodia's untrained eye, the galley coming in over the breakwater seemed to be moving at a reckless speed. "It's beautiful but too fast I think."

"Faster than a man can gallop his horse," Simon replied, "manned by the most disciplined sailors in the world."

The galley, which was being brought in at racing speed to show her off, was a magnificent sight. She heeled around the breakwater and hurtled into the harbour. The vessel was one of the class called Naves Liburnicae, long and narrow, low in the water, and designed for speed and quick manoeuvre.

From its graceful bow a wave curled, sprinkling the upswept prow and the bleached deck with a sparkle of sun bright spray. The sides of the sleekly curved hull were decorated with the figures of tritons blowing shells. Below the bow, fixed to the keep and projecting forward below the waterline, was the ship's main armament, a beak shaped ram shod in iron that could split the hull of an enemy ship as cleanly as an axe head through a billet of kindling.

A decorated moulding curved back from the bows and ran the full length of the hull, continuing over the bulwarks. Below this moulding, in three rows, each covered with a cap or shield made from bulls' hides, were the holes through which the oars passed; sixty on the right, sixty on the left.

A mast, set a little forward of midship, was held by fore and back stays and shrouds fixed to rings in the inner side of the bulwarks. The tackle that was required for the management of one great sail and the yard to which it was hung was placed above the bulwark and visible from the deck.

Apart from the sailors who reefed the sail and were straddling the yardarm, only one man was to be seen by Simon's party on the mole, standing by the prow wearing his dress helmet and carrying a ceremonial shield.

The one hundred and twenty snow-white blades, polished by pumice and the constant wash of the waves, rose and fell as if moved by the same hand, driving the galley forward at about twenty knots.

So swiftly did the vessel approach; it seemed to the watchers that it must collide with the quay. The man by the prow, however, gave a hidden signal, in response to which the oars flew up, hung for a moment in the air, then slashed straight down. The water boiled and the hull shuddered in every timber.

There was another hidden gesture and again the oars rose, feathered and fell, but this time those on the right falling towards the stern pushed forward, while those on the left, dropping towards the bow, pulled backwards.

Twice the oars strained against each other, and in response the ship swung as if on a pivot before settling as lightly as a leaf broadside to them all.

This move brought the richly decorated stern into view with its carvings of dolphins and the name of the ship, Ajax, in raised gilt. Tritons embellished the rudder set at the side and the elevated platform upon which the helmsman sat, a majestic figure in full armour, his hand on the rudder rope.

In the midst of the docking manoeuvres a trumpet sounded and from the hatchways out poured the marines, javelins in hand, their armour polished for the occasion. While the fighting men paraded, the sailors scrambled up the shrouds and ran along the yard. The officers and musicians took their posts. There was no shouting, no needless noise.

As the flagship of the Roman fleet docked, a slave ran forward with a scarlet and gold carpet and the waiting chariot of the governor came forward to convey the Tribune standing in the bow to Florus's headquarters for his sailing orders.

They left in the late afternoon, the commander's boat at the point of the arrowhead formation. With the sails set to catch the stiff breeze and the sailing master setting the pace on his drum, the oarsman bent to a marching cadence whose beat was a tempo they could keep up for the two hours of their watch without difficulty.

The tribune, standing on the helmsmen's deck with his sailing orders in his hand, commenced the ritual of a new voyage, speaking to the hortator, the principal rower.

"How many oars do you have in total?"

"Two hundred and fifty oarsmen and ten supernumeraries, sir."

"Making reliefs of?"

"Eighty-four."

"And the rowing shifts?"

"Two hours, sir."

Satisfied, the tribune turned to the sailing master. "I will inspect the ship."

The officer saluted and reported the ship was ready to be summoned to battle stations. The quartermaster displayed his stores and weapons. The tribune then walked the rest of the ship. Nothing escaped his eye.

When the inspection was over the entire ship's company and her passengers gathered on the foredeck, where an altar had been placed and sprinkled with salt and barley. Before it, solemn prayers were offered to Jove, to Neptune and to all the oceanides with vows, wine was poured and incense burnt.

To Clodia's surprise Simon not only attended the service, he was familiar enough with its ritual to participate in it. When questioned he replied, "so long as the Romans don't ask me to worship a lump of stone or Caesar as a god, I will pay lip service to their superstitions," adding, "a boat is too small a world in which to have a serious difference of opinion."

Clodia, who had never been on a ship, was fascinated with it and gladly accepted the tribune's offer of a conducted tour.

He started in the central compartment, a single large cabin, sixty-five feet by twenty-five feet and lit by three broad hatches which could be closed in bad weather. Supporting the roof a row of stanchions ran from end to end.

The mast, stepped in the centre, was hooped like an umbrella stand with iron and used as a mini-arsenal. Stacked around it were javelins, spears, swords and axes. This, he informed her, was the heart of the ship, the home of all on board. Dining room, bedroom, and wardroom.

At the aft end of this great cabin, a platform was reached by several steps. Upon it the sailing master sat. In front of him was a drum on which he sounded the cadence for the oarsmen. At his right hand was a clepsydra or water clock to measure the reliefs and watches.

Above him, on a higher platform overlooking everything and surrounded by a gilded railing, the tribune had his quarters. These were furnished with a table and a cushioned couch with padded arms and with a high back. "From here," he advised Clodia, "I keep watch over my command and am," and he observed dryly, "as closely watched by them."

He described everything in view but dwelt longest on the rowers. Along the sides of the cabin, fixed to the ship's timbers, were what appeared to be three rows of benches.

A closer view showed Clodia that there were three rows of rising banks, in each of which the second bench was behind and above the first one, and the third above and behind the second. This, the tribune explained, allowed them to accommodate sixty rowers on a side. The space was sufficient for nineteen banks separated by intervals of one yard, with the twentieth bank divided so that which would have been its upper seat or bench was directly above the lower seat of the first bank.

Clodia noted that this arrangement gave every man enough room to work. The arrangement also allowed a multiplication of banks, limited only by the length of the galley. As to the rowers, those upon the first and second banks sat, and those on the third having the larger oars to work stood.

Pleased by her interest, the tribune drew her attention to the oars, which were loaded with lead in the handles and, at their point of balance, hung from pliable leather thongs. "This," he said, "makes it possible, when called for, to feather the action and gives the rowers greater control over rough waves." Each aperture for the oars was a vent through which the slave opposite received fresh air.

The only consolation a galley slave could expect in life was good food and carefully regulated work shifts. Like a valuable draught animal he was kept in prime condition. A man sentenced to the galleys was kept in chains. When he was on watch he was chained to the rowing benches below the deck. Off watch he was chained to the deck. When he died he was thrown over the side.

Later, when she asked Simon about the galley slaves, she was surprised to learn that slaves manning the oars were a recent innovation. Lying in his arms on the open deck in the warmth of the early evening he told her about an older, nobler Rome.

"When," he said, "Druilis won the first sea battle for his country, free Romans plied the oars and the glory to the rower was no less than the marines. Now prisoners of war chosen for their strength are sentenced to serve as galley slaves while they are young and strong. When the best of their years are behind them, they are sent to the Emperor's mines where they work out the last of their days."

They had been at sea for two days and nights when the sky suddenly darkened and the wind, which had been blowing constantly from the south, veered westerly without warning. But the crew was used to these summer storms and swiftly reefed the sail and set a course that would keep the lengthening waves at their stern.

"Will the storm be bad?" Clodia's question had all the innocence of one that had never been to sea, let alone experienced bad weather.

Simon kept his voice casual, not wanting to alarm her. "The summer storms end as suddenly as they start. The crew is well used to coping with them."

Clodia looked anxiously at the cradle that was shaded by an awning rigged by Miriam. Catching her glance Simon said softly, "Life and death is for God to decide."

"Yes, my beloved, but when the storm comes you must tell me what to do."

Simon smiled and nodded towards the giant Numidian who squatted next to the cradle. "Kino can swim like a fish. He will not leave your son's side until we put into Ostia."

Reassured, Clodia smiled. "And I," he bent and kissed her gently, "will not leave yours."

As their lips brushed she touched his cheek softly, indifferent to the menace of the darkening sky.

# 16

After the terrifying séance at which Karkinos had summoned the devil himself into Nero's presence, Caesar was never again to be master of his own fate.

He turned Tigellinus loose to round up the Jews who called themselves Christians. He increasingly spent more time in the salons of Aigokerös with his musicians and actors, preferring to live in the realm of make believe and escape the realities of a world that constantly reminded him of his crimes.

The Greek, satisfied that he had reeled in his prize, was ready to commit the final act designed to reduce Nero to an automaton who would destroy not just the Christians but Rome itself. The weakened and divided empire would then turn on itself to complete the destruction he was orchestrating.

But first he had to break down the last vestiges of the Emperor's will, and he intended to do that at a bacchanalia he had planned in his honour.

To assist him, the Greek summoned the members of his coven and they met in the inner chamber of their secret temple. "It is our master's wish that we bind our servant Caesar closer to him."

The members of Karkinos's inner circle, the master magicians who were the chief priests of his coven who had been called to session, nodded their agreement.

The Greek continued, "We will invite him and the court to an entertainment they will never forget." The magus paused to acknowledge the knowing smiles that greeted this announcement. "The red bear will dance to the Lord Satan's tune, but first we will have to teach him who is master."

The robed figures that had been summoned by Karkinos to his villa inclined their heads in agreement. They were there to receive instruction, not debate.

"The date is set for a week from now. Your task before then is to prepare the drugs that will destroy his will."

A murmur of agreement acknowledged the magus's command. There was a long deferential pause while the Greek stared meditatively into the middle distance. The temple in which they were meeting, sitting in a circle in their customary places around the occult altar dedicated to Lucifuge, was absolutely silent.

"Are there any questions?"

"May one be permitted to ask what is to be done with Praetorian and the whore?" This last was directed at Poppaea.

This time it was Karkinos who smiled. "Both," he said softly, "will be destroyed. But first they will know shame. They are the tools, the means by which Rome's public degradation and the humiliation will be brought about before the empire and its gods are swept away along with its Christian Jews."

A long sigh of satisfaction greeted this statement. Karkinos stood up and declared, "Go my brothers. Our hour of triumph is at hand. Great will be your reward, for you who are the true faithful will inherit the earth."

A week to the day, unable to resist the promise of an occasion that was, in the words of the invitation – "To honour the Light of the World. A poet greater than Homer, a god inspired by the gods, sent by them to walk among mortals as a mark of special favour to Rome. A reading of the Divinity's work will take place at a temple dedicated to him at the home of his greatest admirer, his servant Karkinos" – Rome's nobility flocked to the Greek magician's villa.

The scene that greeted Nero when he arrived was a pagan bacchanalia, which held echoes of a more ancient world.

Divans and tables were positioned throughout the vaulted chamber and lounging on them were men Caesar recognised as belonging to some of Rome's most aristocratic families. Some he didn't recognise, being foreigners to Rome and her provinces. They all, however, carried the unmistakable aura of power and wealth.

The low tables scattered throughout the chambers overflowed with food and wine and the male guests, who each had at least one girl to attend to his needs, chatted noisily to one another. The girls who sat with the sprawling, toga clad men, were all young and scantily clad in the costume of wood nymphs to which, for added effect, they had twined vine leaves and wild flowers in their hair.

Pine torches blazing around the walls and suspended oil lamps not only cast a warm light over the whole scene, they made the chamber hot and stuffy. In spite of this, braziers were lit and fumes rising from the incense that was frequently thrown in handfuls onto the flames, added to the closeness of the atmosphere.

As the wine flowed, faces flushed shining with perspiration. Drugs, secretly added to the wine, aroused emotions, which brought their own glitter to eyes in faces blotched and glossy with uninhibited passions.

Threading his way between the feasting tables skipped a figure in the costume of Pan playing a set of pipes. He led a bunch of Syrian musicians who tempted many of the guests to leave their couches and form a conga of wildly gyrating figures.

Nero was led to a table positioned in the place of honour – but of Karkinos there was no sign.

Two girls flanked the Emperor. One, a creamy tan, was Egyptian. The other, a Nubian, was blue black. As he settled against the silk of the cushions, one of the girls offered him wine while the other settled herself behind him to massage his shoulder and neck muscles.

The evening blurred into a kaleidoscope of rich and swirling colours, exotic foods and heavily spiced wine. The music became wilder and the dancing more lewd as the lamps burned lower and more and more people divested themselves of even the scantiest clothing.

Nero, drunk on drugs and wine, felt no embarrassment when his two charming companions, who by this time were stark naked, divested him of his toga. He lolled between the girls, his white skin contrasting in the tangle of arms and legs – café au lait and black so dense it shone with an almost iridescent sheen.

The music became even wilder. New musicians had appeared. They played instruments, which had their origins in the gypsies and wandering tribes of the Levant. A wild, swirling music of horn and brass. Over all came the great clashing of cymbals, the thunder of drums and a sound that induced madness – the drone of deep toned flutes.

Dark skinned girls with bells at their ankles picked up this savage beat as they swayed and stamped in dances that had originated at camp fire sites of the desert tribes. Light as thistledown they eluded the clumsy drunken hands of the lolling men as they dipped and swayed, the bright flash of a dark eye mocking the flushed and sweating faces leering up at them, and the nubile figures, finger cymbals clashing, spinning elusively out of reach.

As the gathering became increasingly intoxicated, more and more wine was spilled than was consumed, the result of not just the alcohol but of the drugs and stimulants which had been secretly added and which were beginning to take effect.

Never particularly discreet, the assembly shed its inhibitions along with the last vestiges of its modesty. Ignoring their lack of privacy they increasingly began to couple with each other.

Gradually the scene took on the appearance of a great gathering of aroused toads where, irrespective of gender, the animals accrete in multiple matings.

Caesar, his senses disorientated and excited with the drugged wine, was coupling wildly with the Nubian when he was assaulted from behind.

The sudden sharpness of pain in his anus pierced his dulled senses. Desperately he twisted to try and identify the cause of his discomfort, but found it difficult to change his position because of the muscular black legs clamped around his waist in a vice-like grip. The pain grew to an agony, but even by twisting his neck around he couldn't make out that it was Tigellinus, high on the hallucinogen Karkinos had slipped into his drink, who was sodomising him.

Desperately he tried to use his arms to lever himself free of the Nubian, who was clinging to him in an orgiastic frenzy of her own but, to his dismay, he found himself thwarted. In that heaving throng two of the dwarfs who had been juggling added to his predicament by seizing an arm each and, with coarse screams of laughter, urged on his assailant. A third dwarf leapt onto the Praetorian's shoulders, holding a wand and pretending to be a jockey to the grunting powerfully built soldier.

At the height of his pain and humiliation, with tears streaming down his face, his body shuddering under the quickening pile-driving thrusts, Nero felt the Praetorian's hand roughly grasp his hair and wrench his head back. Through a mist of pain, combining with the meaty paw tearing his neck back to the final colossal lunge into his torn sphincter as the monster on his back finally ejaculated, he saw his wife.

Poppaea stood in the only clear space in the room, her slender ankles only inches from his tear stained face. She was laughing at him. One arm was looped around Karkinos's waist, who bent to whisper something in her ear.

The arrival of Poppaea and the Greek magus signalled a new phase in the night's events. The hurt and humiliated Caesar, freed from his tormentor, tried to extricate himself from the press of bodies. He wanted nothing more than to leave this dreadful place but the two girls, in whose company he had taken such delight, aided by the dwarfs became his jailers. They held him captive, pinioned in the slime of his own sweat, his legs slick with blood from his outraged body.

The centre of the chamber was cleared and the members of Karkinos's coven entered. They came in procession with black candles and inverted crosses to form a circle around the Greek, who commenced to hold the Black Mass.

Titillated by this new experience, Nero forgot his pain and watched Poppaea disrobe and lie on the altar, which had been erected. Between her breasts Karkinos placed a chalice and, assisted by wizards, began the blasphemous ritual.

Fascinated. Caesar witnessed a naked babe being passed to the praying magician who, with a single practised stroke, sliced the plump infant's neck and caught the pulsating crimson to choruses of shrieks and wild ululations from the hideous congregation.

In a daze, Nero was forced to take the black satanic host. It lay as heavy as lead on his tongue. He would have refused the monstrous cup but a dwarf held his nose and, swooning for lack of air, he was forced to gag on its dreadful contents before he passed out, his system overwhelmed by the doctored wine he had been drinking all evening.

When he regained consciousness he was in bed. He had awakened in gibbering terror, sitting bolt upright and staring wildly around the moonlit room. He had screamed for his servants but none came, for he was still at the Greek's villa. Had he dreamed the whole thing? Trembling and shaking like a man with the ague, he examined his body. The stains on his legs and the dull ache in his anus were damning evidence of the night's debauch.

Groaning with the murderous pain in his head, the result of the doctored wine, he dragged himself out of bed only to double up and vomit violently. He heaved and retched until he was down on his knees with the gutting pain, which cramped his stomach like a clenching steel hand. He heaved and choked until all he could bring up was dark green bile, which dripped down his nose and ran out of his slack jaws to dribble and drip from his chin.

His head ached so abominably he could hardly bear to move it. Open or closed, Nero's field of vision was fractured by a mass of bright whirling sparks, which exploded like Catherine wheels. When he managed to get to his feet he swayed and wobbled as though mortally wounded. His efforts to walk towards the door were an uncoordinated lurch of trembling arms and legs.

Poppaea – he would find Poppaea. Forgotten was his recent displeasure with her. She would take his wounded body in her arms and soothe his tortured mind.

As he bumped his way down unfamiliar passages he became aware of the sliver of light that rimmed the bottom of a door. With a groan of relief he reached it and slumped against the cold dark wood, almost too weak to turn the handle. He was vaguely aware of a murmuring of voices. His befuddled brain grappled desperately with this latest problem as he slowly opened the door.

The light, which he had seen shining from under the edge of the door as he had shambled down the corridor, was coming from the cheerful blaze of logs burning in the fireplace. The huge couch was a tumble of snowy sheets and fat white bolsters. In the centre of it two naked figures were locked together. Poppaea's wonderful blue-black hair flowed down to shelter her own and Karkinos's dark body.

When Nero opened the door she was lying on her side, her chin on the Greek's shoulder. Her legs were drawn up and wrapped around his waist with her ankles crossed in the small of his back. Her beautiful arms hugged her lover closely to her, while her small boned delicate fingers caressed his shoulders and traced the pattern of his spine along the length of his back.

Dry mouthed, Nero stared at the couple. If Karkinos was aware of the intruder he ignored him. Poppaea, who had her eyes closed when he entered the room, slowly opened them. They were contemplative. They held his with a feline indifference, smoky with lust, cruelly mocking.

Her soft coral lips parted as she smiled at him, revealing her small, perfectly white teeth. Absently, he noticed the tip of her tongue tracing a flickering path across their neat perfection. She paused in caressing the figure in her arms and languidly beckoned the shaking Emperor to enter the room.

With a choking cry he slammed the door shut and retreated down the dark corridor. He was unaware of having reached the courtyard from where, undetected by the guards, he climbed to the parapet of the outer defensive wall. He was stark naked and pimpling with cold. Tears streamed down his face. He stared unseeingly out across the dark city, the moon hidden behind the scudding clouds.

It was a sudden clearing of the clouds and the brilliance of the full moon, which revealed to Karkinos's priests, who were standing guard, the naked, wind, whipped figure staring sightlessly into the void. Contemptuously they dragged him down and unceremoniously flung him back into his room.

Slick as a greased pig from the soaking he had had while on the walls, the ruler of the world skidded across the marble floor to lie for the rest of the night, unconscious in his own vomit.

When he awoke the next morning he was back in his own bed in his own palace. Confused, Nero questioned the startled servants, but they would only say that he had returned late at night with the Augusta.

Poppaea, summoned to appear before the trembling Emperor who still felt wretched, could only confirm what the servants and guards had already sworn to. They had both returned from the Greek's party "when the Emperor had grown weary, and Caesar had retired alone."

Holding a hand to his aching head, Nero lurched to the window to stare blindly across the garden. "What is reality and what is illusion?" he thought wearily, both inseparable in his mind.

"I must leave Rome," he whispered, more to himself than to Poppaea. "I am ill. This place is killing me; its very air is poisonous."

Poppaea sidled up to him. A sudden thought had struck her. Caesar away from Rome was vulnerable. The opportunities to engineer an accident – carry out an assassination – were infinitely more numerous than in Rome. She rested a hand on the shoulder of the hunched figure. "Why do you not take the court to Antium, my love. The sea air will do you good."

Antium – of course! Nero brightened visibly. He had always liked Antium and its sea air would do him good. "Yes," he said, "I have written some of my best work there. In Antium we shall compose our master work."

## 17

I n spite of Simon's reassurance that Kino was as much at home in water as he was on land, the changing weather conditions worried Clodia.

Suddenly the wind fell away and they were forced to row across a sea of waxen calm. Oars lowered and dipped into an unnatural quiet. The sea became still, motionless, bereft of the tiniest ripple, the slightest swell. It was like rowing through oil. It even had the colour of oil, a depth of colour rather than a sparkle, a darkening ochre as the sun, which had been absent all day, dropped below the horizon, its setting giving a little relief to the baking heat they had endured all day.

As the water became still, so did the air, the temperature inversion building the humidity level suffocatingly high. It was like being trapped inside a pressure cooker. Even to breathe was an effort.

For the galley slaves, rowing was an agony of sucking hot, damp air into labouring lungs, and being blinded by sweat which poured down the face to splash onto a torso dripping with its own perspiration. And row they did, hour after hour with heaving lungs and knotted muscles, their spines creaking with the seemingly endless strain of heaving on their heavy oars. As they rowed, they listened to the cadence of the drum beating out the time.

With Ostia in sight and the lights of its waterfront buildings assuring them of safe landfall, the cadence was stepped up, the sweating oarsmen being urged to greater efforts by an overseer who cracked a whip he rarely had to use to encourage them to greater efforts.

As daylight failed they hoisted lanterns and rowed on in a sweltering blindness – a void without form or definition. The earth had vanished and sea and sky were one. Water and air temperatures were the same, nothing moved. The flames from the torches and candles that had been lit were steady as though cut from solid crystals. The only sound was the rasp of the oarsmen's laboured breathing.

Out of the dark, the wind struck. It was as though somebody had opened the door of a giant furnace and released a great blast of searingly hot air, which caused the boats to heel alarmingly. With practised hands, the oarsmen shipped their blades and the seamen set the minimum of sail.

Their first concern was to gain sea room and head their boats into the storm to ride it out. Fortunately the gale was blowing from the north so there was no danger of them being driven on shore, but they would be blown miles off course.

With the wind came the rain and the building of heavy seas. Had there been light to see it, the dead calm would have been seen to have given way to serried ranks of closely spaced, choppy waves which battered the boats with a constant, uneven jarring. It was a particularly uncomfortable and tiring motion that forced the body to be held in permanent tenseness for the next shock.

By what should have been morning, though very little light was to be had from a sun totally obscured by cloud, the storm had intensified. This was no short-lived Mediterranean squall but an unnatural storm in the wrong sea.

The galleys had been pushed miles off course by gale force winds, which were now building waves like cliff faces and smashing down on the boats that had to be constantly baled. Tons of water was airborne every second, water driven by one hundred miles an hour winds, shrieking and moaning like some mortally wounded monster.

Salt water, ripped from the tops of waves and driven sideways through the air, slashed and battered the bodies of men in the top deck. They, with their companions in the lower decks, were rowing like furies to keep their vessels' bows into the wind, or baling with muscles on fire in their efforts to stop them from foundering.

And it rained – it rained in solid sheets of water that hammered their heads and shoulders with the pressure of a fire hose. The only sound to be heard above the demented howling of the wind was the continuous drum rolls of thunder, which they could feel reverberating in the bones of their skulls.

Every scrap of sail was stripped from their masts. Seams opened and the sea poured in greedily, eager to claim them for its own.

In the unnatural darkness, lit only occasionally by bolts of lightning, which split the sky with cracks, that left them temporarily blind and deaf, there were electric white moments in which the straining men had a glimpse of hell.

Framed in such a light, a boat could be seen pitching down vertical green-black mountainsides, slopes that went down forever into a seemingly bottomless abyss. Ahead, etched in terrible beauty was the great curved cliff of the next advancing wave, a living wall that grew as the wind sucked it out of the bowels of the sea – the cliff you had to climb before it collapsed and smashed you and your puny ship to kindling.

And so the flotilla battled through the morning. Oars were splintered and snapped, as were men's limbs as they struggled blindly in the dark with their wildly pitching crafts. Helmsmen died manning the great sweep of the tiller. Oarsmen, chained into position, died from injury and from sheer fatigue, as they made superhuman efforts against unimaginable forces. They died drowned in the bottoms of their boats into which they toppled after suffering some dreadful wound from a broken oar or a sheared spar battering its way over the side.

And still they kept going. Of the six galleys that had left Caesarea, one foundered as its seams simply opened up and let the ocean pour in. The boat sprang apart like a barrel bereft of its hoops, and the men aboard went to the bottom with a treasure of coin and precious stones worth several kings' ransoms.

The next sinking was about mid-morning. As the storm raged unabated, the wave pattern changed. Driven by the wind wave troughs became longer and deeper. It was, as it pierced the crest of one wave and was preparing to dive down the roller coaster of the next, that the second galley met its fate.

The boat was crested and hung balanced on the wave top. It was in perfect equilibrium, like a child's seesaw on which equally weighted children were astride. Oars floundered in mid air.

The helmsman braced against the tiller suddenly straightened. He stared in disbelief and pointed in mute anguish at what was bearing down on them. Numb with fatigue and pain, the Praetorian who commanded the vessel twisted round to peer through the gloom. At first it was impossible to see what had caused such alarm.

For fourteen hours they had plummeted down one terrible wave and crawled up the next one, staggering back to the surface waterlogged but still floating. Though the oarsmen were tired beyond belief, their skins cracked and bleeding in a hundred places, they had no thought of failure. Hands flayed of every centimetre of skin, bruised and swollen to twice their normal size, still firmly grasped the murderously heavy oars.

Now, as they teetered on the wave's top, their captain stared incredulously at what had so alarmed the helmsman. What he saw caused him to order his men to stop rowing. It was not an action of defeat but of acceptance.

Rising before them was what every mariner hopes he will never encounter. Sometimes called a 'five year wave,' it is a super wave that rises spontaneously when freak wind conditions occur and the monster is born.

Such waves are big enough to roll over the largest vessel completely submerging it and, if such a ship is in its path, it will be driven straight to the ocean floor. The instantaneous weight of water being so great that it precludes even the smallest piece of debris from surfacing.

To the staring tribune it was as though the entire ocean had risen up against them – a solid black wall, which seemed to touch the sky. It rolled over the galley as though it didn't exist, and swept down the Mediterranean to spend itself on the rocky coast of North Africa.

Another boat had its bottom ripped out and most of its crew drowned as it was driven off course down to Sicilia and torn to pieces on the razor sharp rocks off Panormus.

By the time the battered Ajax, the only surviving ship, finally dropped anchor in Ostia, Nero and his entire court had moved to Antium.

Clodia, grateful to have survived the storm, disembarked hoping she would never have to set foot on a ship again and, tired as she was, didn't need any persuading to make the short journey from the port to the capital.

Her spirits lifted, however, when Simon took her and Joshua to the magnificent villa that was to be their home in Rome.

## 18

Nero's absence from Rome proved to be a blessing. Not only did it give Simon time to establish Clodia's credentials for presentation to the Emperor when he returned, it also gave Clodia time to practise the manners of a Roman matron and Hippolyte schooled her in what her behaviour should be at court.

Nevertheless, Rome and the formality of Roman life subdued Clodia. The complexity of its politics and its sheer size were all overpowering. Its lack of morals scandalised her and the first time she was the recipient of unwanted advances at a dinner party, there was a comic result that could have had a more serious ending.

Simon had been deep in discussion with an influential Roman noble in a room which, as the evening progressed, had grown over hot. The guests had become noisier, drunk and more boisterous as alcohol lowered inhibitions.

To escape for a few moments Clodia had gone out onto a balcony and had been followed by a slightly drunken senator, who attempted a clumsy grope with the whispered suggestion that they retire to a bedchamber. He then made the mistake of attempting to use force to further his cause.

He had only a hazy recollection of being hurled bodily over the balcony. Fortunately, he fell into an ornamental pond. When the startled guards fished him out they assumed he had fallen over the balustrade – an assumption he decided to go along with.

"Throwing randy senators off rooftops isn't the done thing," Simon dryly observed when she told later what had really happened.

Clodia simply ignored this and confided in Miriam that, "the next old goat to shove his hand up my skirt will get more than his knuckles rapped!"

While Simon waited for Nero's return to present Clodia's claim on her father's estate and more importantly, her royal lineage, Karkinos suddenly became aware of their presence in Rome and sent a messenger to Tigellinus who had accompanied Nero and the court to Antium.

The message was, in fact, an order – an order that Simon and his family were to be taken and destroyed, the bodies of the man and woman to be thrown into the putrid pits and the child to be delivered alive to the Greek for ritual murder.

Even as a courtier left with these instructions in a leather pouch strapped to his side, a gardener in the Greek's employ, who was a secret Christian, sent a message of his own to the Apostle Paul. Although he was under house arrest in the city awaiting the outcome of his own appeal to Caesar, he was receiving converts daily in the room in which he was confined.

This messenger to the gentiles, the Jew to whom God sent visions, had revealed to him why Karkinos should react so violently to the arrival of this family of Jews from Jerusalem. Karkinos – whom he referred to in his Letters to the Corinthians as 'the great beast of Babylon' (Babylon being the code word for Rome).

Knowing Simon was a brother of the Christ he had never met filled the old man with a deep sense of reverence, and made it more urgent that he should give him a warning.

Simon's first reaction to the messenger who came asking that he visit Paul immediately was to refuse, so strong was his dislike of this new Jewish sect that claimed Jesus for its leader. It was Hippolyte who counselled him to go.

"You might," he said, "learn something to your advantage. It is well known that this light to the gentiles, who is at loggerheads with Peter and his orthodox Jews, is an intellectual who studied under Hillel and for ten years ruthlessly persecuted the emergent Christians as being guilty of blasphemy."

Simon nodded and thought about what his servant had said. He knew all about the cool intellect of Hillel's best student.

The unassailable integrity of the man who believed in the absolute purity of the sacred law of the temple that guaranteed the accused a fair and impartial trial.

Equally dispassionate in exercising this law, Paul had condemned to death thousands of Jews who had converted to Christianity as his courts found them guilty of blasphemy.

As much as anything, it was the situation of gamekeeper turned poacher that tilted the balance and Simon, in the toga of a well to do Roman, went in a litter to the slum where Paul was confined.

In mutual curiosity the two men weighed each other up. The years had not dealt kindly with the tent maker. The small, ill-shaped man, barrel chested and bandy legged with a massive hooked nose, had the hands, feet and features of a peasant. His clothing was of the poorest and was in need of attention, as was his unkempt hair and beard.

The room in which the two men sat was as stark as a prison cell. It contained a chair, a table, some writing materials and a small bench. A frameless window, which wasn't much better than a hole in the flaking wall, looked straight onto the wall of the next tenement. Even at midday it was necessary to keep a light burning.

Simon suddenly realised that the man who had single-handedly carried the essential Jewish message of Messianic hope to the gentiles had a bad squint. The evangelist read the contempt in Simon's eyes. "Sit down if you want your son to live."

The deliberately brutal choice of words was designed to shock. The drumroll of the deep bass that had mesmerised thousands brooked no argument. Reluctantly Simon accepted the proffered space on the rough bench. The apostle dropped onto the seat opposite him, resting his weight on his elbows. "My appeal to Caesar will fail. Yours will never be heard."

Simon said nothing but waited for Paul to continue. "The woman is of no importance. As for you, if you choose to refuse Christ, there is nothing I can do or say which will change that."

The old man would have continued but Simon, his face flushed with anger, interrupted him fiercely. "Renegade, speak not to me of my brother, for your grey hairs will not sanctify your blasphemy. You have turned your back on the God of Abraham and Moses and delivered His children to the Romans, and will answer to the one God for your sins."

In exasperation Paul shook his head. "The one God you speak of has sent a light into the world. The Messiah we, His people, had waited for for centuries, foretold by Isiah, has come. He was your brother, Jesus."

Simon sprang to his feet, overturning the bench with a bang loud enough to bring rushing into the room two of the young men who took it in turns to sit outside the evangelist's door to watch over him. "Call your pups off, old man, before I start breaking heads."

The Apostle waved the youths away. "There is no time for argument, nor would it be of any use. Let us…"

Before Paul could finish, Simon had left and was clattering down the grimy steps. With an oath Paul stumped to the door and bellowed after the receding back, "The power that hunted you in the Valley of Kidron is in Rome. Even now, word of your arrival is carried to its servant Tigellinus, who has been ordered to deliver the hope of the future to the altar of Satan."

At the bottom of the stairs Simon paused and looked back at the crooked silhouette framed at the head of the stairway.

"In God's name, the God we both acknowledge, the God of Moses, of Abraham, of Elijah, the Creator of All, the Unknowable, in whose ineffable name all men are brothers, Jews and Gentiles, take your son and flee. Go to Egypt, to Parthia, to Judaea – anywhere to escape the power of Karkinos who sits on the earthly throne as Satan's regent."

For a moment Simon stood motionless then, acknowledging the old man's final plea with a slight lifting of his hand, he was gone.

When he recounted to Clodia what had happened, her response was a demand that they should start packing and leave at once. She didn't particularly like what she had seen of Rome. Proving her lineage was only important in that its rank would afford her a certain amount of protection and privilege in a Roman world.

All of this paled into insignificance when she learned that the thing which had hunted them in the Valley of Kidron was not only in Rome, but that its target was her baby. Normally she accepted every decision Simon made without question, but now she argued fiercely in favour of leaving Rome without any delay.

When Simon told her that Tigellinus – even Nero himself – might issue a warrant for their arrest, her fear became anger. Simon noted wryly that the tigress of the Judaean wastes had simply acquired a veneer. Suddenly he realised that she was capable of taking Joshua and leaving Rome without either his protection or his approval. "There is nowhere to go," he said patiently.

"We can go to Syria, Parthia, even back to Judaea. I know places where nobody will find us," she replied fiercely.

"The power that sought us in Jerusalem and is now in Rome can," he replied wearily, "be everywhere. It is the great Satan, ruler of this world, the enemy God permits but will not allow into heaven where He alone rules."

Clodia's mouth tightened. "You defeated this devil once with the help of the sacred spear. Why can't you ask your God to let you kill this enemy once and for all?"

Simon inclined his head to acknowledge her argument. He attempted to put his arm around her waist, but she would not be mollified. She pulled away and stood stiff backed, still determined to flee if Simon wouldn't fight. "Perhaps," he mused softly, "that's why we are here. Jerusalem will be destroyed and God's chosen people broken and scattered to the winds."

"But we came to Rome to be safe," Clodia grated.

Simon nodded and lifted a bell to summon a servant. "Yes," he responded, almost to himself, "there is safety in Rome, but for whom? Not for those Jews who call themselves Christians, and not for those who believe in the one true God."

"We must flee – but not yet. Paul was right about one thing – we have been directed here for a purpose. What it is God will reveal in His own time. In the meantime we must go into hiding."

Clodia's lips compressed in anger. Sullenly she nodded her reluctant agreement. She had, however, quietly noted that her enemy had been named and that Karkinos, even though protected by a god, was mortal.

"Let us see," she thought to herself, "what Satan will do when his servant is minus his head."

## 19

For three days the Egyptian warrior priest had fasted and prayed, alone except for Karkinos who supervised his thrice-daily rites of purification. Finally he was ready to consecrate his life to the devil, and dressed in wolf skins, he was imbued with the power of the demon Machochias.

With his servant prepared, Karkinos presented him to Satan in a ceremony where the Egyptian dedicated his life to the special task he had been given – the murder of the infant Joshua and the theft of the sacred spear.

He had been summoned from Egypt, where he served in the temple of Isis and was a member of the Vril secret society that had cells throughout the known world. From the age of five, together with other carefully selected children, he had undergone a long and dangerous training that only one in ten survived.

Not only were these specially selected novices trained in their priestly duties, they were schooled in magic and at various stages in their development subjected to psychic attack to test their spiritual strength. Those that survived were sent to secret monasteries in the desert to be trained as assassins – a training which concentrated on teaching the art of concealment, to become expert in the use of every known conventional weapon and some that they had developed themselves.

They were also taught how to use magic to attack an opponent and were initiated into those secret arts that enabled them to control snakes and spiders, using varieties that were particularly poisonous as their allies.

Before Xilka, as he was called, was appointed priest and devotee of Karkinos, the Vril circle had put him to a final test in the temple at Karnak. Here there was a labyrinth that consisted of a series of tunnels, many of them so small that you could only get through on your hands and knees. Stripped naked, the acolyte entered the maze at midnight and, once inside, the stone block that had been removed to give him entrance was promptly put back into place and resealed.

Alone, in total darkness and absolute silence, the naked man had to attempt to find his way to the centre of the maze, which was a temple, dedicated to Satan. Having taken an amulet from the altar as proof of his success, he then had to find his way out through a passage that emerged in the Temple of Baal – a distance in a straight line of some four miles.

En route in the passages and tunnels he would encounter the guardians of Baal, poisonous snakes that could sense fear, which if detected, caused them to strike at once. Only he who believed they were truly his brothers survived an encounter with them in the dark. Equally dangerous were other tunnels protected by deadfalls and traps of poisoned spears, wire nooses and blocks of stone set on the most delicate of balances.

Blind and deaf from the total silence, the acolyte constantly had to choose which passage to take, relying on his psychic power to make the right decision. Frequently he would have to crawl around a chamber, which would offer him up to four choices, of which only one was a safe passage.

Without food or water it took the survivors on average up to three days to navigate the labyrinth of Baal. Those who emerged from this ordeal would complete their training by successfully carrying out a ritual murder, the victim being selected either by Karkinos himself or one of the twelve master magicians he controlled worldwide.

Xilka was the star pupil of the Vril. He had not only found his way through the maze in record time, but from the moment of his entry into the monastery as a child, he was found to have exceptional latent psychic ability and as a consequence was given special training to develop his gifts.

By the time he was ten he was able to control his body functions to such a degree that he could be buried for up to a month and emerge as strong and in as full command of his faculties as when he was interred.

Clairvoyant and telepathic, he developed a high degree of mind control and was able to hypnotise susceptible people over long distances by simply concentrating his mind. These exceptional psychic powers and the ability to focus a will of extraordinary power during the casting of a spell or the summoning of the powers of darkness through a conjuration had drawn him to Karkinos's attention as a wizard of exceptional promise. And had resulted in him being summoned to Rome to undertake a special task for the Greek magus.

Before leaving Egypt he demonstrated his astral powers to the priests at Karnak by shattering a pre-selected block of stone positioned a mile away.

Even his journey from Egypt to Rome had been accomplished by astral means – a feat that few of the magicians in Karkinos's own coven were capable of accomplishing, particularly over so great a distance.

The mission that he had been chosen to undertake was not just the theft of the sacred spear. He was also to attempt the kidnapping of Joshua, for Karkinos had been instructed that the blood of this particular child would be used in a sacrificial ceremony that would rock the world.

The night chosen for the attempted kidnap was overcast and pouring with unseasonable rain. Had the moon been up, its light would not have penetrated the thick clouds. In total darkness Xilka entered the grounds of Simon's villa with consummate ease by levitating over the high walls.

The mastiffs, which should have been patrolling the grounds, were either sheltering under bushes or low hanging trees. The guards, including the major domo, kept to their quarters. Only the men at the gatehouse maintained any real watchfulness.

Like a wraith, the Egyptian slipped across the lawns, taking cover between the ornamental trees. Fifty metres from the villa he stopped under a tree with a massive canopy beneath which the darkness was absolute.

Ignoring the steady drip of rain, Xilka remained motionless, studying the building. He knew from Karkinos its exact layout. Had he been asked to do so, he could have gone from room to room totally blindfolded, at a run, without bumping into a single object.

He knew to within an inch where Joshua's crib was. He also knew that his nurse slept in the room and that a guard was posted outside his door – none of which bothered the Egyptian in the slightest.

What did, was the life field whose force he had just encountered and which was radiating from the room. Unmindful of the icy rain trickling down the back of his neck, the priest focused his mind on the window of the room to which he needed access. Entering a state of self-hypnosis his spirit left his body and attempted to penetrate the child's nursery. He got as far as the balustrade and was turned back by the power within the room.

Patiently Xilka tried again. This time he moved cautiously, carefully testing and probing the invisible barrier, assessing its strength, seeking a weakness.

After twenty minutes he decided that the child was the source of this extraordinary power and that kidnapping was out of the question. He even doubted that he had the strength to reach the crib and kill the child.

His assessment complete he bowed his head and chanted the invocation to Lucifer. "Hail to Satan who gives his servants the power to crush dragons, scorpions and all thine enemies beneath thy feet. Nothing shall harm us."

As clear as a bell he heard the voice of Karkinos. "You have done well my son. The brethren have gathered and the true ruler of this world and the next will be supplicated to join us. Together we will form a power storm that will render you invincible. When you hear my voice again you are to attack. If you cannot steal the child, kill it, tear its heart out and cast its body to the dogs."

Trembling with emotion the Egyptian acknowledged his instructions and settled down to wait, his mind locked in communion with the coven, which had gathered to summon the forces of hell to their aid.

"In the name of Lucifuge, go." Like an arrow released from a crossbow, the black clad figure streaked across the lawn and gained the terrace with one elastic bound that carried him twenty feet into the air.

The guard died instantly, his body pulped by a single thought. The nurse died at the touch of his fingers before she could open her eyes. As he gained the crib the sprinting man gasped as if struck by a heavy blow. Suddenly he felt as though he was wading through treacle, his vision blurred. Desperately he shook his head.

He could hear the brethren chanting a mantra and Karkinos screaming with excitement. Behind the cacophony of sound he felt the raw power of the evil force he served. It revived his failing strength and gave him a burst of energy.

With a snarl of triumph he gripped the ancient spearhead which was hanging over the crib for protection, and snatched up the child which howled in protest at such a rude awakening – a cry which alerted the guards who patrolled inside the house.

Conscious of the enormous power drain to which his spoils were subjecting him and the urgent instructions from the mind link to leave at once, the Egyptian dipped into a pouch at his waist and cast a pair of snakes at the guards who had frozen on seeing him. They died instantly.

With his heart pounding wildly, the Egyptian hurled himself across the room and over the balcony, landing like a cat on the sodden grass. If anything it was raining even harder and the darkness was impenetrable.

Suddenly he felt unutterably weary. The mind link had started to fade and the energy field surrounding the child was gaining power. He determined to kill it while he still had the strength. Flinging the infant to the ground he tore open the shawl exposing its breast. The heavy knife, which he plucked from his belt, was capable of gutting a stag.

A sudden and unexpected sound stayed the downward sweep. The crouching Egyptian raised his head in puzzlement. What he had heard – or thought he had heard – was the neigh of a horse, the clink of a bridle, the creak of saddle leather.

He wasn't wrong. It came again, only this time it was the sound of a horse at the gallop. Desperately the priest turned his attention back to the child but he couldn't move and the sound of the invisible horse was on top of him. With eyes bulging in terror he stared towards the sound, but could see nothing.

As the pain exploded in his breast he had a millisecond of vision. Above him reared a powerful horse, its rider a Roman centurion in full armour, bearing down on a lance whose point pierced his heart. As he died the figure dissolved, turning away, the withdrawn lance trailing blood that sparkled like fire. The darkness that closed in on him was filled with a terrible sound.

Karkinos howled through his mind, red-eyed with fury. The coven was a shambles of screaming, moaning figures that were beating themselves with whatever came to hand until the blood flowed.

Never had the dying man known such cold. He was compressed by it, reduced to nothingness, a dissolving atom, a particle of waste, his being burned by the fury of his master in a cold black vacuum of nothingness that terminated in total oblivion. It ended in a death scream that echoed across the city and caused the lions in the vivarium to shatter the night's silence with answering roars that reverberated against the low flying cloud and awakened the entire city with their power and ferocity.

Clodia was out of bed and into the child's room before Simon was even awake. In her right hand hung her beloved stock whip. In her left she carried a snatched up sword. She stared in shock at the empty crib.

There was a sudden cry from the baby on the lawn and she was over the balcony, lowering herself to the ground with the aid of her whip. As she snatched up the howling child she turned the dead priest over with her foot, like a lion turning its prey over with its paw, searching for any sign of life.

When Simon and the servants finally reached her they held their lanterns high to make certain they would be identified, for the woman they found was mad with rage and, in the darkness, sword in hand, was aching for an enemy.

Simon approached her alone, calling softly to her, gentling her like a wild animal. Slowly she lowered her blade but flatly refused to give up the child, which she cuddled to her breast. Absentmindedly he picked up the spearhead, which lay on the grass, unconsciously wiping the fresh blood that whetted its blade on his cloak. "Come my love, our son is getting wet."

Clodia shuddered and suddenly burst into tears, rushing into his arms.

Quaking with shame and fear, the major domo crawled to Simon's feet. "Lord, I heard nothing."

Clodia spat at him in fury. "Turd. You will hear even less when you have been cropped."

Simon shook his head. "Kino could do nothing about this." He pointed with his toe. "Only God can defeat the devil, but this is a warning to us."

The major domo mumbled his gratitude but Clodia refused to be mollified. She ignored him totally. The man knew that at that precise moment the only thing that stood between him and death was Simon's reason. The other quaking guards stood back out of the lanterns' circle of light. The woman's fear that had turned to towering rage was seeking an outlet and, while she had lowered her sword, she hadn't relinquished it.

It was the protestations of the child, who by now was cold as well as wet that sent her scurrying to the house. Bringing Joshua and his crib into their room and lighting a hastily laid fire, Simon and Clodia tried to come to terms with what had happened.

Clodia was baffled and frightened. Her anger had been replaced by a deep anxiety as she began to grasp Simon's explanations to her that their child was threatened by a god whose power was a thousand times more terrible than that of any of the gods of Rome.

Simon was baffled. "Who," he mused to himself more than to Clodia, "drew us to this city – God or the devil?"

"If God wants us to be here," grated Clodia, "let him say so. In the meantime we are leaving as soon as it is light."

The man frowned at the fire. "Don't call upon God in anger but put your trust in Him."

Clodia bit her lip. This strange invisible God that her husband worshipped was as beyond her comprehension as Simon's strange powers. That he claimed these powers for their son was something she regarded as a mixed blessing.

His inheritance from her of the power of Rome through the bloodline of its emperors was something she felt more at home with, but the man at her side was her lord. Never for a second did she forget that he had brought her out of the pit and into the light. She loved him above her own life, even above the life of the child for whom she would have died without a second's hesitation.

Simon smiled at her gently. "Rome will follow Jerusalem. Like my people, the Romans and their empire will be swept away."

Clodia frowned. "All the more reason for us to leave" – but she was suddenly pensive. "But for where? If Rome falls, where do we go?"

"Egypt," was the immediate response.

The woman stared at him intently. "Why Egypt?"

"Because it will not be touched by either event and I am respected there. And so will our son be. He will need to go there anyway to enter the Temple of Amon to learn the ancient wisdom – the secrets of the magicians and priests who ruled behind the throne of the Pharaoh."

"And if Egypt is closed to us?"

Simon shrugged. "There is always the Essenes. They won't turn us away. They taught my brother and they remember his name to this day." This last was slightly bitter. "Trouble is," he continued gloomily, "they don't believe in sex and regard poverty and abstinence as positive virtues."

Clodia grinned wickedly. "The Essenes are obviously a last resort."

Simon burst into laughter and grabbed for her. "If we are to go on short rations," he said, running his hands down her back and caressing her buttocks, "I'd better stock up now."

Clodia purred, closing her eyes and arching her back, pressing herself against him, her hands busy burrowing beneath his clothes.

"Meanwhile we must move to less ostentatious lodgings. Before we leave for Egypt, I must know why we were drawn to Rome – otherwise we will be hunted forever by the great Satan." Though they moved within the week to a secluded villa at the southern end of the Palatine, they were too late to ward off the psychic attack launched by the Greek magus. Distraught with rage at the failure of his servant Xilka, he draped Satan's altar with a scarlet cloth and put on a black robe.

On his hand the magus placed a ruby ring. His magical instruments were made of iron and his rod of power, a naked sword. Acting alone, Karkinos placed five lights on the altar and burnt saltpetre and sulphur in his crucible.

His very being corroding with hate, he opened his throat and screamed for Geburah, Satan's arch devil, to come to his aid.

Having performed this mighty invocation he prostrated himself upon the altar as a channel through which the cosmic force of the manifestation could travel and reach out for the soul of Simon bar Joseph.

The power of the sacred spearhead kept the new whereabouts of the family hidden from Karkinos, but the conjuration performed by the Greek magician planted a demon in Simon's soul. The magus felt the evil spirit strike and fasten. Like an angler in a boat who feels the hook bite and the hidden fish take a hold, Karkinos knew he could play the mind of Simon along the invisible psychic line that now joined them.

As he felt the thrum of that magic power down his invisible rod, the Greek howled in triumph before the blood-red altar, calling up his master to witness his success.

# 20

Since fleeing to the villa on the Palatine, Simon caused the few people in Rome who came into daily contact with him to become increasingly worried about his health. Under the psychic assault launched by Karkinos, he had been seized by a deep melancholia. He not only avoided contact with people, he kept to his private rooms, admitting no one, not even Clodia.

The attack on the child had affected him profoundly and emotions suppressed since Jesus's death boiled up inside him, sending him into a deep depression.

Without knowing why, he only left the library at night to wander aimlessly through the gardens, retreating back to his quarters if Clodia tried to approach him.

The servants who took him his meals brought them back untouched, and the guard who patrolled the grounds at night reported that not only did Simon's light never go out, it was rare for a night to pass without the most terrible cries coming from the apartment. This phenomenon was causing Clodia and the servants concern, and the superstitious among them were becoming increasingly reluctant to pass beneath the tormented man's window.

The cries, which were upsetting the household, were the result of Simon suddenly awakening from a sleep made hideous by terrible nightmares.

Desperately tired he failed to sleep, knowing that inexorably they would return to torment him. To try and stay awake, as long as possible he had stopped going to bed, preferring to slump in a chair huddled in a blanket. The worst part of his torment was that as soon as he awoke, shrieking in fear from whatever had manifested itself as soon as he dozed off, he couldn't remember what it was that filled him with absolute terror.

He had come to fear the dark as much as he feared sleep, never allowing the oil in the lamp to burn out, even when he was reeling from weariness. When finally he was forced by sheer exhaustion into a chair, he positioned a strong light fully on his face so that while he was conscious, even through closed eyes, his blind world was roseate with the opaque ruby of blood seen through his eyelids.

It was the slipping, even for a few seconds, into what should have been the blessed benison of sleep's oblivion that he feared. As he slid over the edge of consciousness, even for a few seconds, whatever monster had taken residence in his mind returned to stalk him relentlessly. Every time he jolted back into trembling, sweat soaked wakefulness, his heart pounding wildly, his whole being was suffused with a feeling of unimaginable fear. His terror was made more dreadful because its cause was unknown.

Frequently Simon's awakening was so violent that he would find himself crouched in the centre of the room having sprung from the chair gibbering like a madman. Shaking from head to foot as though afflicted with palsy, eyes red-rimmed with weariness, he would thrash wildly about as though seeking his dreadful unknown opponent.

He deteriorated rapidly and soon developed a severe nervous tic, which puckered his face from the lid of his right eye to the corner of his mouth, ending with a slight but violent jerk of his whole head. It was an action not dissimilar to that of a fish trying to shake the hook from its mouth.

He spent his days not in meditation but in an almost trance like state. When not closeted in his room he sat in the garden, staring blindly into the distance.

In desperation Clodia turned to Miriam for help. The Jewess, who was only too aware of Simon's feelings about Christians, was torn by her love for her master and her fear of his anger.

It was Clodia's anguished reminder that the Christ they believed to be the Messiah sent by God himself was the brother of her tormented master that persuaded Miriam to suggest that the Apostle Peter might help.

When the old fisherman heard Miriam's story, he left the safety of the catacombs and came at once to the aid of the man whose brother he had denied in his hour of greatest need.

He found Simon sitting, as had become usual for him in the late evening, on a stone bench in a deserted part of the garden. As he drew near the seated figure it made no move to acknowledge his approach, in spite of his arrival being heralded by the crunching of the gravel path.

"Simon." The Apostle spoke gently but got no response from the ashen-faced figure slumped dejectedly, staring unseeingly at the dark yew of the opposite hedge.

Peter reached out and gripped him lightly on the shoulder. He tried again. "My son." Slowly Simon swivelled his head to stare, unfocused, into the older man's worried face. "Simon." The Apostle's voice was sharper. "We must talk."

With a shudder the younger man focused on the face floating in front of him and, with an obvious effort of will, concentrated on the Apostle who sat next to him. "Why?" The abrupt response was scarcely whispered.

"Because your cross has become too heavy. Why will you not let God help you carry it? Have you forgotten how your brother, our blessed Lord Jesus Christ, needed help to carry his cross? Why are you so proud that you will not let Him take up your burden?"

Simon dropped his head into his hands and began to sob violently. The old fisherman drew the younger man to him, holding the shaking figure in his arms as a mother would a hurt and frightened child. He waited, saying nothing, for the paroxysm of emotion to subside.

When the storm passed, Simon straightened up and Peter dried his face with the edge of his cloak, quietly resuming his questioning. "When did the demon that has entered your soul first possess you?"

There was a long pause. For a moment the fisherman thought he wasn't going to get answer. When he did it shook him to the core. "Maybe it's always been there, waiting to deliver me to my enemies, as it did Jesus and James."

Having spent his entire life fighting evil, Peter had become all too familiar with its power. While he doubted the truth of what

Simon had just said, he didn't dismiss the possibility that he was the victim of possession.

The fisherman tried again. He kept his voice very matter of fact. "Very well, which of Satan's demons has entered your heart?"

Abruptly Simon stood up. He turned away from the Apostle and stood with his arms tightly crossed, hugging his body as though fearful that some part of him would escape. When he replied, the voice held a flat certainty that increased Peter's concern a thousand fold. "I am possessed by Satan himself."

The Apostle's reaction was not to immediately reject out of hand what he had just heard, though he was greatly concerned about Simon's mental state. Privately he feared that he was on the edge of a nervous breakdown and in need of a physician, not an exorcist. Nevertheless, he hesitated before speaking. Taking a deep breath he continued, "What form does this possession take?"

Simon's reply simply added to his disquiet. "Only when I am awake can I keep Satan out of my mind. Asleep I am lost, my soul is hunted by him. In nightmares I am dead, enduring the final descent into everlasting darkness, falling forever downwards into the horror I can feel all around me but cannot see. When I awake, my nostrils are filled with an unimaginable stink but, worst of all, I cannot remember what he looks like, I have no memory of Satan's face."

As he finished speaking, Simon strode away from the Apostle towards the villa. Peter jumped to his feet and hurried after the departing figure. "Wait," he cried. "We must put a face to this nightmare or you will be lost forever."

Simon stopped dead and spun round. "And how," he ground out, "do you suppose we should go about summoning the devil?"

Before replying, the older man walked up to him and stood very close, his eyes only inches from Simon's. "In your distress you forget yourself, my son. It is not man who will bring you face to face with Satan, but faith. Only through faith in God can we not only face evil but defeat it."

This admonition was delivered in a cheerful, almost matter-of-fact tone of voice. An outward show of confidence that masked the deep concern the Apostle had for the safety of the distraught man.

Maintaining his cheerful manner, Peter continued, "If it's the devil we have to face, we won't face him alone but with God."

If Simon was surprised at this suggestion he didn't show it, and his mute acceptance convinced the apostle even more of the urgency of getting to the bottom of whatever it was that was destroying a brother of the man he believed had been the long awaited Messiah.

After gripping the younger man firmly by the arm, the old Apostle took his leave, promising to return before midnight with skilled Hebrew magicians who had been converted by him and who would assist him in the rites of exorcism. One of them would be Linus, the man who would succeed him within the year.

It was the promise of occult help, which persuaded Simon to return to the garden some hours later. As a magus himself, skilled in casting out devils, he recognised that the help he was being offered was his only chance of survival.

Towards midnight, accompanied by Peter, Linus and two other church elders who had been asked to assist him, Simon was taken to the catacombs at Ostium on the outskirts of the city.

Under Peter's instructions, the five men made their way quietly to an improvised altar where the apostle indicated that Simon was to lie prostrate, face down and arms extended, so that his whole body assumed the attitude of a cross. The four men took up the Stations of the Cross and Peter led them, beginning the exorcism with a reading from the psalms.

Simon, face down and eyes closed, lay like a dead man, with the four figures chanting over him.

As the reading drew to a close, Peter offered up a prayer to God, not only for Simon's soul but also for the safety of himself and his companions, for he was only too aware of the danger, which could result from what they were attempting. He then placed his right hand on the prostrate man and, interspersed by signs of the cross made over the body, began to read the prayers for exorcism.

"I command thee by the maker of the world, by Him who had power to send you to hell, that you depart from this servant of God, Simon bar Joseph, who returns to the bosom of Israel. I command you again, that you depart from this servant of God, Simon bar Joseph, whom Almighty God has made in His own image."

"Let the image of God command you. Resist not, submit without delay and leave this man, since it has pleased the Lord to dwell in his body. And although you know I am a sinner, do not think me unworthy, for it is God who commands you."

As Peter reached the end of his first prayer, Simon began to bray like a donkey, his whole body trembling with the force of the noise he was making.

He stopped as suddenly as he had begun and then, to the amazement of his four companions who had continued with the prayers for exorcism, he started to levitate. Still in a position of prostration his stiffened body rose twelve feet into the air. When he stopped rising, Simon began to speak in a voice that was not his own, a rasping baritone filled with menace. For ten minutes he spoke at length in a bewildering variety of languages, none of which the witnesses recognised.

It was when he switched to Greek that Peter, filled with a premonition, told his companions to stand under the floating figure with arms outstretched. It as was as well they did so, for no sooner had they taken up their positions, than Simon stopped speaking and crashed downwards. The figure that dropped into their arms was unconscious and breathing heavily.

The old fisherman looked at Linus who, in answer to the unasked question said, "I don't know. We must get him to bed and see what happens. Until he regains consciousness he must not be left alone. I will stay by his bedside and pray for his soul."

The old man nodded. "I am grateful for your efforts and will add my prayers to yours for the safety of the soul of our brother in Christ."

Throughout the night Simon lay unconscious, his condition owing more to coma than to natural sleep. The stertorous breathing had been replaced by an extreme shallowness of respiration, barely sufficient to mist the bronze mirror that an anxious Clodia, who was kneeling at the head of his bed, held in a shaking hand in front of his face to reassure herself that he still lived.

It was at three a.m., when Peter joined them in the vigil, that a change occurred, though the change was wrought not through Simon but through the aged Apostle who, on entering the room, had knelt on the opposite side of the bed to Linus.

As the old man knelt, the votive lamp, which Linus had lit and placed with a cross at the head of the bed, suddenly went out. The startled Peter, who was kneeling at the other side of the bed holding a cross, had never been so afraid in his life. He was fixed, unable to move. He was like a man experiencing a hideous dream. A man who knows he is asleep and at the end of his nightmares must awaken if he is to live, but is powerless to do so.

With the extinguishing of the light, the room temperature plummeted to a point below freezing – so cold that Clodia and the two men had difficulty in breathing air so icy it seared their lungs. Blind and helpless, held in a vice-like grip, they were suddenly aware that Simon was thrashing violently in the bed. The fact that the tormented man uttered no sound as he lunged like a hooked fish, only added to the horror.

As suddenly as they had started the wild gyrations ceased, and in the vacuum of absolute silence that followed, the aged Apostle spoke through a voice which was not his. It was a noise as terrible as its message.

The thunder of sound pouring in the dark out of the old man's mouth was so loud as to be almost impossible for Linus to decipher. It not only wakened the occupants in the caves immediately adjacent to Simon, it brought lights on in neighbouring tunnels as their startled occupants were roused by the terrible brass voice booming through the night.

Later, when Peter and Linus tried to piece together what had happened in the final terrible seconds of the exorcism, the testimony of those who had been so rudely awakened was so contradictory as to be virtually useless.

Peter himself remembered nothing. The only credible witness was Linus, and it was Peter himself who decided that the incident and its message would only be recorded in the secret gospel, "That which would only be revealed to the few, though many would be called."

What Linus thought he heard Satan say was, "The secret of the harlot who whelped the bastard Nazarene stands in my shadow, eclipsed by the last of days. The Archangel, his wings plucked out, falls into the void. The thunderbolt is frozen in the hand of Jehovah."

# 21

To Clodia's immense relief the 'cure' was instantaneous. The evil spirit that had possessed Simon's soul had been driven out by the exorcism. In a matter of days he had recovered his strength and was seriously thinking about fleeing to Egypt.

"The Lord has delivered me but hasn't sent me a sign," he confided to Hippolyte. "Perhaps," he continued pensively, "He allows Satan to destroy Rome and Karkinos is His willing servant."

Hippolyte, who was neither Jew nor Christian and had the born sceptic's view of the vast pantheon of Roman gods, ventured a quiet response, not certain if one was called for or not. "And the Christians – the fisherman's Jews and the tentmaker's gentiles who follow the cross, what of them?"

"Misguided," Simon responded wearily. "If the Messiah has been and gone," he ended waspishly, "where is his victory? Did not Isaiah prophesy his triumph when, at his coming, the faithful of Israel would be raised up and their enemies destroyed?"

The steward stayed silent at this.

"And yet," Simon continued, speaking almost to himself, "I have to admit that Rome is doomed, the empire will crumble, but the Jews will be swept away with the Romans for, even as we speak, Jerusalem is under siege and will eventually fall."

"Then should we not leave for Egypt before Rome is eclipsed by whatever fate awaits her?" asked Hippolyte.

The two men were in Simon's study. Growing restive as he wrestled with the problem of whether to go or stay, Simon stood up and walked to the window.

As he did so there was a tap on the door. Hippolyte gave permission to enter and a slave came in bearing a sealed parchment, which the steward gave, unopened to Simon. There was nothing on the outside to give any indication of the sender and the seal was simply a blob of pressed wax.

"Nero has signed the tentmaker's death warrant."

Hippolyte said nothing. He didn't doubt the accuracy of the report or question its origin. Simon still received reports from sources that he kept to himself.

"I must see him before he dies," cried Simon – though if asked why he wouldn't have been able to answer.

Hippolyte pursed his lips anxiously. "Lord, such a journey will be dangerous. Is it worth taking such a risk? Tigellinus's men are combing the city for you and the lady Clodia." He would have mentioned Joshua as well in his efforts to dissuade Simon from leaving the house, but Simon's mind had been made up.

"Ask the lady Clodia to await my return. I might just get to Paul before they take him to the killing ground."

"And then?" the steward asked.

Simon shrugged and, picking up his cloak, said, "I will be back as soon as possible; in the meantime start packing," and he was gone.

When Clodia learnt that Simon had left she was beside herself with anxiety. She greeted with relief, however, the news that they were to pack while Simon was out.

Leaving Hippolyte and Miriam to organise the household slaves she concentrated on gathering together those items which were of special value to herself. She was in the midst of re-reading her mother's letter, which she had just taken from its hiding place, when Miriam burst white faced into the room.

"My lady, the Palatine is on fire. Kino, who sent a slave to see how bad it is, reports that it is out of control and the wind is blowing the flames in our direction."

Scarcely had she finished speaking when Hippolyte appeared though, unlike the flustered girl, he had regained his composure.

Clodia looked at him questioningly. "The fire is bad, my lady. Worse still, rumour has it that it was deliberately set by Tigellinus."

At this Clodia's jaw dropped. "Why on earth would the Romans want to set a fire that could destroy their capital?"

"Tigellinus would only be obeying Nero's orders," was the grim response, "and if it suited his mood or provided a backdrop for one of his awful poems, he wouldn't think twice about putting Rome to the torch."

"Simon?"

"He is not in immediate danger, my lady." It was Miriam who responded. "The house he has gone to is on the other side of the city. It is doubtful if the people there are even aware of the size of the fire."

"But they must know about it, surely? They must see the smoke."

Hippolyte nodded. "Yes, but fires in Rome are not uncommon. They will assume that the city's fire-fighters will be working to extinguish the blaze."

"Aren't they?" Clodia asked incredulously.

"No," was the grim rejoinder. "On the contrary, what hoses are available have been sabotaged. Worse still, where bucket chains are being formed, groups of thugs appear as though out of thin air and attack them. These disappear," he concluded heavily, "equally as quickly."

"And the authorities?"

"Conveniently absent, which points the finger of suspicion even more firmly in Caesar's direction."

"Miriam, look after Joshua. Hippolyte, put Kino on the door while we go up to the roof to assess the situation."

Hippolyte bowed, a glint of satisfaction in his eyes. He had always admired the decisive character of his mistress. By the time Clodia and the Greek steward had gained the roof, the fire had worsened. Driven by a strong wind with nothing to check it, it had engulfed several streets that included a considerable number of warehouses. The contents of these – timber, cotton, oil and dried grains – were now burning furiously and a firestorm was building.

In this area of the city, streets were composed of terraced buildings, often five stories high, and the width of the streets was extremely narrow. From the roof top Clodia and Hippolyte could clearly see the banner of flame and its cap of smoke mushrooming into the sky.

Clodia pointed to the street below. It was filling with panicking people. "We must go while we can. Another ten minutes and the street will be impassable. We shall be in as much danger from those fleeing the fire as the flames themselves."

"I shall pack only the most valuable of my lord's possessions."

Clodia shook her head. "Pack nothing. Take what gold we have and clean water. They will be the only currency that will have any meaning."

Hippolyte bowed and turned to go. "And weapons." The Greek lifted his eyebrows. Clodia had her back to him. She was standing on the edge of the roof watching the advancing flames. Crowded onto the rooftops of neighbouring houses were their occupants, all pointing and anxiously discussing the fire's advance.

"Make sure that we are all armed with knives and short swords, good for close work."

The Greek, who had reached the head of the staircase, stopped. "Surely Caesar will maintain law and order. If he doesn't, the people will riot."

"The people," Clodia said quietly, "will be picked clean. With no law to hold it in check, the city's scum will rise to take full advantage of the situation."

Between them Hippolyte and Kino quickly armed the household and snatched up enough food and water to meet their immediate needs. Clodia's jewellery and what coin was in the house were firmly belted around the Numidian's waist. The precious spearhead was with Simon who had taken to carrying it hidden on his person. Finally, the infant Joshua was wrapped in a blanket, before being put into a pliant reed basket that Clodia slung across her chest, leaving her arms free.

When they finally left the house smoke was curling down the street, which was filling rapidly with people fleeing from the advancing flames. Kino formed his contingent of household guards into an arrowhead and placed Clodia, the Greek steward and the servants inside it.

Under the Numidian's command they pushed into the stream of humanity tumbling through the narrow streets and were swept along in a current of frightened and panicking people.

As the jostling crowd engulfed them, Clodia caught glimpses of what she had forecast on the roof. Helpless to assist, like a canoeist shooting rapids with no time to do anything other than observe, cameos of what was happening to that turbulent river of people flashed in front of her and then were gone.

Thieves were plunging into the crowd, cudgelling and robbing those who weren't part of a large group. Men and women of well-to-do appearance were their principal targets.

The gangs worked to a set pattern; one of the group would single out a likely victim and point him or her out to the rest, who roughly bumped through the crowd to surround their unsuspecting prey, who was simply clubbed from behind and in seconds stripped of all valuables.

The ever-increasing number of people crowding into the streets immediately threatened by the fire posed a new menace to the dazed and shocked victims of these attacks.

Left on the ground, semi-conscious, they were trampled on by the rush of people stampeding to safety, and Clodia noted helplessly that it wasn't just those who had been attacked who were threatened by this additional danger. Increasingly, other people were losing their footing and falling, never to rise again. The old and the very young were particularly vulnerable.

In that desperate flight, as Clodia and her servants struggled to keep their feet, they had reason to be grateful to Kino and his trained guards. They were like basalt boulders around which the panic-stricken river of refugees flowed. They were the rocks to which time and again they needed to cling.

A child separated from its mother was a vignette of tragedy. As the mother's straining fingers slipped from the tiny hand, the toddler lost its footing and went down between the crush of feet and the wheels of the handcarts piled high with household goods that their owners were trying to salvage.

Old people, unable to stand the crowd's buffeting, increasingly gave up the struggle and were left stranded in doorways where they sought shelter. Others crowded into the lee of upturned carts where they clung to each other for comfort.

It took Clodia and her household nearly an hour to reach the Via Altira, which opened out into Pompeii Square and allowed the torrent of people to disperse into its space like the rapids of a river spilling into the calmer wider waters of its delta.

Battered and weary beyond belief, the little group rested at the foot of the Minerva fountain. During the flight they had been overtaken by night and the sky over the eastern half of the city was illuminated by a giant sulphurous glow.

"Where to now?" Clodia asked, more to herself than to her companions. With Tigellinus hunting them she did not dare to approach any of Rome's noble families for assistance or shelter. All of the property owned by Simon – his warehouses, even his ships that rode at anchor on the Tiber or at Ostia, had guards mounted over them.

Neither did she trust Rome's Jews, even though she knew Simon supported the Temple with frequent and substantial donations.

As for the Christian Jews who roosted illegally in the city's underground cemeteries, they were beyond her comprehension with their docile acceptance of whatever indignity Rome chose to heap on them.

"We must take refuge with the Christians in the cemetery at Ostium." It was Miriam who spoke.

Clodia could scarcely believe her ears. "The Christians," she almost spat the words out, "are hiding from Caesar like rats in their holes, and when his dogs flush them out, Tigellinus beats them to death at leisure."

Miriam blushed but persisted. "They will protect Joshua in whose blood flows the blood of the Christ they worship."

Clodia, who had sprawled wearily against the fountain's base with little Joshua safe in his basket tucked between her feet, stiffened and sat bolt upright. "What do you know of these Christians? Suddenly you are an expert."

Hippolyte answered for the startled Jewess, who was almost in tears in the face of Clodia's hostility. "The girl is right, my lady. The Christians will protect us because of the child. They believe his uncle was the Messiah, the one chosen by their God to lead them to freedom, to be the salvation of their nation."

Clodia ignored him. Instead she continued to stare at the discomfited Miriam. "You," she grated with a flash of insight, "are one of them."

There was a long pause at this. Even Kino, who took no interest in the gods of Rome or the Jews, worshipping a deity of a much older origin, turned his head to see what Miriam's response would be.

"Yes, I am a Christian, my lady, and we will hide you and your son, and defend him with our lives."

At this Clodia scrambled to her feet, snatching up the startled baby. "Defend! Your lot defend against Nero?" The scorn in her voice cut like a lash. "You would be less than the dust on the boots of his Praetorians. They would have you for breakfast. Kino, we march - and now – out of this cursed city. We will find refuge in the Alban hills."

Without a second's hesitation the giant Numidian was on his feet, his guards rising without need of instruction, ready for his commands. Kino's orders were from Simon and had been explicit. This woman and her child were his absolute responsibility; in his absence Clodia's word was law. Not even Hippolyte, to whom he normally answered, could countermand him in this matter.

Nevertheless, it was the steward who intervened. "My lady, the ground beneath Rome is honeycombed with natural caves. Even without the help of the Christians they are a good hiding place." Seeing the anger in Clodia's face he finished hurriedly, "they are the first place Lord Simon will go to find you and his son."

Clodia, who was already picking up her bits and pieces paused, her mouth compressed with anger and frustration. She had momentarily forgotten Simon.

A sudden flurry of raised voices and a swirling cloud of smoke eddying into the square caused them all to turn to state towards the street they had earlier battled down. The fire was closer. The sky above it was filled with flames and it was smoke from these, which had gusted into the square.

Kino looked questioningly at his mistress. It was the point about Simon, which swayed her. She turned back to Miriam and impulsively embraced her. " To the Christians and their caves. As long as I live I will never understand you Jews, but I thank you for your protection and the love you bear my child."

"My lady, we must go." Hippolyte had been watching the ever-increasing numbers of people who were pouring into the square. Frightened, dishevelled and confused refugees, who were beginning to mill about in panicking confusion.

"Miriam, you know the way. So you lead us." Miriam nodded happily but as the group rose to move off a new and more deadly element of danger arrived in the square. From several of the other streets than ran into it, long columns of mounted Praetorians suddenly appeared under the command of a tribune who had one of Karkinos's occult priests at his side. They were wheeling to surround it, oblivious to the fire and the mob.

"We must break through," Kino said grimly. "If we push towards the street furthest from the tribune and start a panic they won't be able to hold us."

Clodia nodded her assent. As they pushed into the jostling crowd the tribune stood up in his stirrups and shouted to his men. Even Clodia felt a wave of fear flow through her as his words reached her. "Take the child alive. Tigellinus wants the child alive."

Suddenly the horsemen, there square complete, started to move forward. As well as their normal swords they were armed with clubs which, Clodia realised, were better suited to taking their quarry alive.

As they pushed into the crowd she kept close to Kino, who had abandoned the short sword he had been carrying for his great mace that had been carried by one of the household slaves wrapped in a cloak. Like a giant black buffalo cresting the grasses of the summer veldt, he pushed easily through the crowd. As he went he hummed deep in his throat the song of the warrior going to war.

Suddenly the priest pointed in their direction. In his hand he held a rod of ivory taken from an Egyptian tomb. Bellowing out orders to close in on the little group, the tribune spurred his horse into the crowd, cursing at them to give way. In a matter of seconds Clodia and her followers were surrounded and fighting for their lives. Hopelessly outnumbered, they savagely defended themselves, but even as she battled against the ever-increasing numbers of Roman cavalry, Clodia was conscious of her losses.

Hippolyte went down defending Miriam who had fallen to her knees clutching the shaft of a spear buried in her belly.

Kino and his guards sold themselves dearly. The last Clodia glimpsed of the major domo was the huge black figure with his death's head grin, bloodied from knees to chin with his own and his enemies' gore, his mighty war mace singing its song of death as it whirled around his head keeping his enemies at bay. The lances they buried in his back finally drove him to his knees.

With Joshua at her feet and a sword and dagger in either hand, Clodia fought like a woman possessed, ringed by men who saw only the prize at her feet and were overly anxious to claim it for their own. She was taking a terrible toll of her enemies but knew it was only a matter of minutes before she would be overwhelmed.

"Simon," she screamed. "Help us."

# 22

In spite of their differences, Simon had been moved by what Paul had said to him, and following his visit had regretted storming out of the house.

When he heard that the old Apostle had been sentenced to death and moved to the Mamertine he had hurried to try and see him – a dangerous undertaking because he was a wanted man himself. But, he was too late, Paul had been moved again and the guards at the Mamertine claimed they didn't know where.

After hours of fruitless searching, Simon had reluctantly given up and was hurrying home through the crowded streets when the first cry of 'fire' was raised.

The narrow road he was on suddenly became choked with people rushing towards him. Simon cursed with frustration but wasn't unduly worried, for he knew that the city had a well-organised fire fighting system.

As more and more people poured onto the street, he decided to try an alternative route along the Appian Way, but to his surprise found it was also crowded with people.

Even so, he was not unduly alarmed. In Rome's slums fires were a common occurrence, especially in the overcrowded Trans-Tiber. This area was occupied by a desperately poor and half savage population which struggled to exist in the five storey tenements that were without sanitation and running water, all having filthy entrances ankle deep in rotting garbage and subjected to the stink of overflowing latrines.

Cheek by jowl with these tenements, so tightly crowded together that the lanes between them were scarcely a metre wide, were timber sheds, warehouses, slave marts and corn mills.

As Simon battled with the passing crowds, he suddenly noticed in the surging throng the reflected glitter of the armour of a detachment of Praetorians, their helmets bobbing through the crowd like the glass floats on a fisherman's net. The more peaceful citizens called on them for protection and the wilder elements of the crowd, who were unwise enough to challenge their authority, received short shrift from the cream of Rome's army.

Above the heads of this heaving, sweating throng, that trampled over each other as they rushed aimlessly about, wheeling like shoals of fish fleeing larger predators, a cloud of smoke suddenly billowed. Pushed by the breeze down the densely packed streets it created a deadly choking fog that would eventually kill more than the actual fire.

Cursing the crowds and the fire Simon struggled to the Appian gate, but groaned when he realised that he couldn't use it to reach the city centre because its walls were glowing with heat. Worse still, people were screaming that the bridge at Porta Trigenia, opposite the Temple of Bona Dei, was burning from end to end.

Suddenly the situation had reached a crisis and Simon realised that if he wished to cross the Tiber he would have to try and find another route across the city.

Meanwhile, the rage and despair of the fleeing people were causing them to fight among themselves and increasingly Simon found he had to defend himself against mindless assaults.

The road into which he eventually turned was equally chaotic, blocked by piles of goods looted from shops and buildings and then abandoned. Wine from smashed barrels swirled round costly furniture looted from the villas of the nobility – beds, tables, chairs, chests and piles of clothing clogged the streets.

Here and there the citizens fought hand to hand in the choking smoke, their sweating bodies ruby from the glow of the fires which swept across the rooftops and burst from every window, sparks showering down like meteorites. Increasingly the drumroll of collapsing buildings would rumble like thunder, adding tons of red-hot choking dust to the clouds of smoke, turning it a sulphurous yellow.

Suddenly a new sound was added to the general uproar – one that raised the hair on the nape of Simon's neck. The vivarium had either caught fire or the smoke and sparks from the general conflagration had been carried there on the wind. Above the howls and shrieks of every kind of wild beast, the thunderous roaring of the lions was punctuated by the high screams of panicking elephants.

Cages began to creak under the pressure of beasts, which, mad with terror, were throwing themselves at the bars and gratings of their pens. Soon a new horror would be inflicted on the desperate people as every variety of wild animal broke free.

Panicked with fear lions, tigers, panthers, huge black bears from Spain, bison from the plains of Africa, elephants from India – would all plunge into the horror of the city. A catastrophe worsened by Tigellinus's incendiaries who ran through those sections of the city not yet affected, setting new fires indiscriminately.

As he struggled through the choked streets, Simon was suddenly caught by a furnace blast as the fire exploded over his head, jumping from one street to the next in spontaneous combustion. He went down on his knees, eyes bulging, as all the oxygen was sucked out of the atmosphere by the fire. A dense pall of smoke rolled out of the flames and engulfed the whole road.

Desperately he crawled into the gutter, trampled by the panicking crowd, suffocating as they ran. Sparks covered his body and his hair smouldered. As he opened his mouth to gasp for air it was filled with soot. The blood pounded in his head; even the smoke seemed as red as the tide of blood that filled his eyes.

At ground level he suddenly found a current of air and his chest heaved as his bursting lungs sucked it in. Panting like a dog he suddenly realised that his smouldering clothes had burst into flames. Desperately he rolled on the ground to put them out. As he wriggled into what he thought was a pool of muddy water, he suddenly realised it was in fact blood from a horse that had speared itself on the broken shaft of its chariot as it reared in panic.

Wearily he dragged himself to the momentary safety of some open ground outside the wall. Light from the burning city filled the sky as far as the eye could see.

A bloated moon, its appearance distorted by the superheated air, rose sullenly above the bonfire of the burning capital. Its single red eye seemed to glow malevolently on the luckless humans scurrying like ants through the piles of burning rubble that had once been its streets and squares, to finally find refuge in the city cemeteries or on the open ground outside the city where they collapsed in shock.

By nightfall the fire had reached the commercial district of the city, an area composed almost entirely of warehouses. Exploding olive oil vats started a river of flame which, as it ran burning down the gutters, fired stores of grain, seed, timber and barrels of turpentine which, when they caught, blew buildings apart so fierce was their combustion.

Clouds of sparks burst out of these exploding streets and were carried thousands of feet into the air, showering down like meteorites in miniature. The Tiber, mirroring the flames, seemed composed of molten lava so redly did it glow.

Many of the helpless people invoked the gods. Other sang hymns and thousands bitterly cursed Caesar and the gods – all to no avail. Neither blasphemy, hymns, protestations of despair or anger, had the slightest effect. Within a few hours that part of the city, beyond which lay the Campus Martius, had gone, dissolved in a sea of fire that erupted into hammerheads of flame and smoke as though Rome had suddenly been turned into a volcano.

The wind fanning this flame blew it to a super heat like a blacksmith's forge and in this now white-hot furnace the very stones began to crack.

Desperate to get home, Simon turned and headed for the other side of the city; by going round in the opposite direction he hoped he could reach the house on the Palatine where he had left Clodia and Joshua. He knew that this meant he would have to cut through the gardens of Pompeii for the fire had not yet reached that part of the city. He also knew they would be packed with desperate people fighting to get themselves and a few of their more precious possessions out of the capital.

As he battled through the crowded streets, Rome burned on; the Circus Maximus fell in. Gutted by the flames whole districts were collapsing, the sound of the falling rubble rumbling against the banked clouds of smoke.

Then the wind changed, blowing in from the sea – a shifting breeze that took the fire to the Esquiline. A fortune had gone up in flames, vanished in smoke. Slaves and freed men, rich and poor, of every nationality, stumbled dazed through the smouldering ruins or simply huddled together, eyes dulled with shock, shivering with reaction.

When the fire was finally to abate, they would be homeless refugees with only the scorched rags they stood up in between them and the threat of immediate starvation. Eventually they would form one huge camp of makeshift sheds, tents, huts and wagons, covered with ash and dust, short of water and relying on bread provided by Nero to survive.

Nearly a million people would be huddled together in the flimsiest of shelters – a mixture of slaves, freed men, merchants and street traders who had lost everything. Craftsmen of every kind – workers in stone, metal, leather – together with gladiators, deserters from the army, prostitutes, housewives, orphan children by the thousand and the helpless old.

Rumour would spread through this vast multitude that, not only had the fire been set deliberately, it had been set by Tigellinus under Nero's orders and his incendiaries had kept it going, running from street to street, district to district, setting new fires and stopping the fire brigades from functioning.

Meanwhile, the fire had reached the Via Nomentana and had been turned by a shift in the wind towards the Via Lata and the Tiber, and was sweeping towards the Palatine for a second time.

Unable to get through, Simon prayed that Clodia and Joshua had fled in time, drawing comfort from the fact that in Hippolyte and Kino, he had resourceful and trusted servants. But for the moment he had to accept that there was no way he could reach the house on the Palatine in which he and his family had taken refuge.

# 23

When the fire began, to avoid any accusations of having started it, Nero remained in Antium – but as the fire took hold, Tigellinus sent couriers to keep the former Emperor advised of its progress. Nero only moved when he received word that the flames had reached the Palatine, rushing to Rome to be certain of seeing the flames at their highest and the city's final destruction.

Accompanied by Poppaea, Nero arrived at the walls at about midnight with the whole court in attendance. Together with the nobles of the court were senators, knights, freed men, his own and the court's slaves and attendants. Thirty thousand mounted Praetorians were arranged in line of battle along the road to keep the people back.

Some cheered Nero's approach. Others hissed and shouted curses, which Tigellinus had drowned out by ordering trumpets and drums to be sounded as though for a triumphant battle march.

At the Ostian gate Nero reined in his chariot and announced, "Your Emperor joins you in your hour of need."

Without waiting for a reply he moved on to the specially prepared steps that would take him to the top of the gate. Behind him came the Augustinians and a choir of singers and musicians playing lutes and other musical instruments.

In stunned silence, from the top of the gate the court saw what the guardian of the empire had done to the seat of his authority. Even Nero stood silent at the spectacle he had ordained. Wrapped in a mantle of purple and crowned with a laurel of finely worked gold, he gazed awe-struck at his handiwork.

When his theatrical tutor silently handed him a golden lute, he lifted his eyes to the fiery heavens as though he would find there the inspiration he needed. The people, seeing him standing on the parapet of the Ostian, framed against the leaping flames and the nimbus of smoke that rose like a bloody hammerhead behind him, roared in anger.

Ignoring them Nero scanned the city. The most sacred and ancient of Rome's edifices were burning. The temples of Jupiter and Luna built by Servius Tullius, the temple of Hercules built by Evander, the house of Numa Pompilius, the sanctuary of Vesta with the penates, statues of the sanctuary's gods.

Rome's history as well as its present was burning, but Nero was not thinking of his dying capital, only about what posture to strike, and whether or not the theatrical expression he was wearing on his face was convincingly tragic. Could he now find the words to describe how momentous the catastrophe was? Words that would excite the admiration of the thousands who had somehow survived the holocaust. No matter what they had lost – wives, husbands, children, parents, and friends – he still expected applause and praise.

He hated the city and despised its citizens. He loved only his own songs and verses. At his command Rome, capital of the world, was in flames and he, lute in hand, would compose its epitaph – an epitaph that would be admired throughout all time for the magnificence of its verse. Who were Apollo or Homer compared to him? He raised his hands and striking the strings pronounced the words of Priam, "O nest of my fathers, O dear cradle!"

The assembled senators, dignitaries and Augustinians, bowed their heads reverently and assumed what they hoped were suitable expressions of rapture.

As Nero continued to sing, the choristers picked up the last verse and repeated it. Then he theatrically struck the lute for a final verse. When he finished he dropped the instrument and wrapped himself in his cloak and stood in a posed and brooding silence.

A burst of applause from his dutiful court broke the silence, but it could not drown out the enraged howling of the common people. "O gods!" said Nero. "What a night. On one side an inferno – on the other side a sea of raging people." He then struck a pose that he fondly imaged portrayed him as nobly bearing up under a great tragedy.

In the orange and yellow light the jeering mob pressed against the massed ranks of the Praetorians. A forest of upraised arms and hands carrying every kind of weapon, eyes inflamed and red with dust and heat glittered madly.

Sweating faces, distended with rage and frustration, pushed forward. Spittle flew from lips as the mob screamed and shouted. The noise was deafening, the mood ugly. A sea of people surged towards the gate and the steps of the parapet, which the Emperor was using as a podium.

The outburst of protestations increased to one long sullen roar. Poles, forks, even spears were brandished. Grasping hands reached for the reins of the Praetorian horses. "Divinity," said Tigellinus, his voice shaking slightly, "speak, O Divinity, to the people and make them promises."

Nero glared at his commander contemptuously. "Shall Caesar address scum? Let another do it in my name." He turned to the court; his lower lip thrust out petulantly. "Who will answer for Caesar?"

There was a long silence while the assembled court stared at its toes. It was Petronius who answered with a cynical smile – "I!" Without hesitation he swung into the saddle and rode to the head of the cavalcade, moving easily at a slow pace between the massed ranks of the guard and then alone, as though fording a river, urged his mount into the seething mass of people. Almost standing in the saddle, he raised his right arm in salute, in a sign that he wished to speak.

"Quiet, quiet." The cry was heard on all sides for most were curious to hear what Caesar's envoy had to say, for there was no doubt who he was. Gradually silence fell and he raised himself up on his horse.

"The city will be rebuilt. In the meantime, tonight the gardens of Lucullus, Maecenas, Karkinos, Caesar and Agrippina, will be opened to you. Tomorrow and every day thereafter wheat, wine and olives will be distributed, so that every man and woman will have their fill.

"Then Caesar will have games for you such as the world has never seen and, during these games, you shall feast at banquets and," he paused, turning to survey the mesmerised crowd, using the silence to lend weight to his words, "there will be gifts for you. It will be," he concluded, "that many will be richer than before the fire started."

As he finished speaking a great sigh went up. A few people began to cheer, but again Petronius silenced them by raising his hand. "In Caesar's name I have promised you bread and circuses. Do not cheer me, but he who cares for you as his own family."

Half a million throats roared out their approval of this bounty. As Petronius unhurriedly walked his horse back to the steps leading to the Ostian, Nero looked down onto a field of suddenly upturned faces in which a million eyes gleamed at him, reflecting the light of the fire he had started.

Petronius made his way back to the Emperor who, sweating freely, stood on the edge of the parapet striking a series of poses in acknowledgement of the crowd's adulation. He placed a hand on the arbiter's shoulder. "Tell me," he asked, "how did I look when I was singing?"

"You did justice to the spectacle and it you," Petronius replied as he turned to face the great ball of fire that now engulfed three quarters of the city he loved.

# 24

Before being captured Clodia, armed with sword and dagger, had fought like a madwoman. Standing over the screaming infant, she had taken a heavy toll of her attackers.

The guards, at first amused by her resistance, had grown angry and then determined to simply kill her out of hand. But the sergeant in charge of the cohort, who had suddenly seen the chance of a good profit from the sale to the arena of this veritable Boadicea, forbade them on pain of death to kill her.

Before they overwhelmed her, however, she had wounded several of her attackers – one had lost an eye and even the sergeant had several cuts and bruises. When they finally separated Clodia from Joshua they had to render her unconscious with an iron bar. When she came to she was chained hand and foot as well as to a neck restraint that ran to an iron ring set in the wall of the ruin where they had camped for the night.

Every jail in Rome was full and captives even swung at anchor in prison ships moored in the port of Ostia.

The centurion in charge of Clodia's group had been told to hold his prisoners in the open for one night. The next day ten thousand Christians would make room in Rome's prisons by dying in the arena, and would go on dying at this rate every day of the month long games.

To avoid losing any of his prisoners at night, and lacking the resources to chain more than a handful of his charges, the centurion had been reinforced with a troop of Persian cavalry. Having set a ring of torches around the huddled prisoners, they gave a swift

192

demonstration of their skill by bringing down a flight of pigeons that whirred overhead.

The Roman soldier who had lost an eye in the encounter with Clodia was a Parthian. While he nursed the pain of his exposed socket he also nursed thoughts of revenge.

To stop the baby screaming he had given the child to a young Jewess who, though suckling a baby of her own, had milk enough for two. In his anger and desire for revenge he had considered blinding Joshua or reaming him with a red-hot iron when Clodia recovered consciousness and could witness the operation.

A sudden groan from the chained woman and the fluttering of an eyelid warned him that Clodia was about to recover. He kicked her savagely, first in the belly and then in the breasts and, as she instinctively rolled away from his lashing feet, booted her in the kidneys. A warning growl from the centurion making his rounds, who paused long enough to intercede, caused him reluctantly to stop.

As Clodia came to he drew his knife. "Perhaps," he said, "for openers I can castrate your little bastard." Involuntarily his remaining eye met those of Clodia. In five years of campaigning against the pagans on the empire's borders, he had never seen such hatred.

Unable to hold that burning gaze he turned away. As he did so, a slight movement out of range of the torchlight caught his eye. Picking up a brand from the fire he hurled it across the rubble in its direction.

As the torch struck the ground it sent up a shower of sparks and a sudden burst of flame. In its light what he saw stuck his tongue to the roof of his mouth and fear caused his legs to suddenly shake.

Instinctively he reached for a rock to chase away the grey apparition that crouched in the jumble of burnt roof timbers and the stones of collapsed walls. As his hand closed around the stone he froze. A terrible idea suddenly sparked into life. The bat-like figure before him rose to its feet.

"Stay," he croaked. The figure paused, uncertain. He was afraid it would flee for its presence in the city was forbidden on pain of death. "There is food at the fire. I will get it." The soldier was gabbling, desperate to hold the figure's attention.

"Come," he beckoned, walking slowly backwards, hardly daring to take his eyes off the wary intruder. He reached the edge of the firelight and stooped to pick up a piece of bread, the remains of the cohort's supper. The figure fell on it and would have fled.

"Wait, there is more. See." The Parthian grabbed a cloak and began feverishly filling it with all the food he could lay his hands on. As he worked the figure came closer. Finally, it squatted, waiting patiently for its prize but alert as a desert jackal, its head turning constantly ready for flight.

With the bundle complete, the Parthian ran to the prisoner who had wet nursed Joshua and tore the child out of the woman's arms. As he scrambled back to where he had left the pile of food, he shouted to his wounded companions.

Hurriedly he explained his plan. With savage shouts of joy and agreement they approached the chained Clodia to witness her reaction to their companion's plan.

But the visitor refused to approach the camp any closer. Not even the proffered bundle of food would persuade it.

One of the soldiers, who had been wounded in the arm by Clodia, disappeared for a moment. When he returned he held triumphantly in his good hand a heavy baggage net. With congratulatory approval this was cast over Clodia and, before her neck chain was released, she was thoroughly entangled in its heavy meshes and a length of chain passed around her body.

Securely bound, the men carried her beyond the camp to the patiently waiting figure, sitting like a gnome among the rubble. They took with them torches so that Clodia could clearly see what they planned for her child.

They laid the baby on top of the food and stuck one of the blazing brands between the stones, signalling that both should be taken. Slowly, timidly, the figure advanced. When finally it stood revealed in the flickering light, the soldiers became sick with terror at the sight of the horror before them.

As it bent to scoop up the baby Joshua, Clodia shattered the night air with shriek after shriek that awoke the slumbering camp, causing the Persians to nervously notch their bow strings with their arrows.

What had once been a woman cowered under Clodia's screams, but she refused to let her prizes go. Before she hobbled off with both, Clodia witnessed a sight she had hoped never to see again outside the nightmares she couldn't lose.

The leper's hair had grown exceptionally coarse, tumbling across her humped shoulders and back like coiled wire. Her eyelids, lips, and the flesh of her cheeks, was a festering rawness in which two weeping craters, black as prune pits, were all that remained of her nose.

Numb with horror the men watched as though in a nightmare, the claws that picked up the child and drew it to the outcast's fetid breast. When the miserable figure rose to scuttle away with its bounty, its poor rags could not conceal a body ravaged by the loathsome disease.

Clodia stopped screaming and, thrashing wildly like a netted cat, started to bite the constraining net. Blood from her torn mouth poured down her chin.

The centurion, roused by her initial shriek, came upon the scene sword in hand in a furious rage at the alarm that had been spread through his hitherto peaceful camp.

The sight of the madly struggling Clodia and the Parthian who had disobeyed his orders was the last straw. Without a word he struck the man across the throat with the flat of his blade. As he reeled backwards he hit him savagely in the solar plexus with the hilt and, as he rolled gagging in the dust, called for the Persians to arrest him and re-chain Clodia to the wall.

This time he mounted an armed guard over her, though he feared she had been ruined for the arena. She seemed, he thought in bitter rage, to have been driven to madness, for even in a neck collar she fought her bonds, flaying the skin from her neck, wrists and ankles, where the metal touched her. But it was her eyes that troubled him most. Muddied and bloodshot, they were emptied of all human feeling.

## 25

To celebrate the promised games, Nero ordered several amphitheatres to be built in what was left of Rome. Scarcely had the flames been extinguished when the trunks of trees, felled on the slopes of the Atlas Mountains, were brought by sea and tied to barges that towed them up the river Tiber.

Thousands of slaves worked day and night on these stadia, which were lavishly decorated. Pillars were inlaid and ornamented with bronze and amber. The seats reserved for the nobility were decorated with tortoiseshell, ivory and mother-of-pearl.

Special irrigation channels were connected to the city's aqueducts to run ice cold water from the mountains to below the seats to keep them cool during the heat of midday.

A huge amethyst velarium was put up as an awning to shade the more aristocratic of the spectators, and urns for the burning of Arabian perfumes were placed strategically between the seats. For added comfort, slaves were stationed behind the best seats to sprinkle the court with a dew of saffron and verbena.

Two days before the games were due to start, the beasts were not fed. Instead they were teased with pieces of bloody flesh, which were offered to them outside the range of paws thrust through the bars of their cages.

As the moment drew near for the opening of the vomitorium gate the noise from the spectators was deafening. Bets were being laid all around the arena; fierce arguments broke out about the merits of this gladiator or that. Greetings were exchanged. Parties of families and friends debated the competitive ability of lions and bears to tear their victims apart. Horror stories were circulated about the Christians who, it was alleged, had not only started the fire that destroyed Rome, but were sub-humans who drank the blood of murdered children and worshipped God by eating a child's body in His honour.

"Where," people asked, "have these Christians come from?"

"From nowhere," was the answer. "They are simply Jews by another name."

Tigellinus's carefully planted agents provocateurs replied, "They have been hiding among us for years as a secret Jewish sect, for they are Jews. They are the Jews we have taken in, to whom we have given citizenship, allowed to grow rich at our expense, allowed into our government, and this is how they have repaid us."

"Death to the Christians," howled the mob. "Crucify them, burn them, throw them to the lions."

Tigellinus smiled. His dungeons were full. In fact, listening to the voices of those he rounded up who were at that moment crying in terror, he doubted whether the beasts wouldn't grow weary of killing and leave him with the chore of a simple mass execution – which was always a problem, being so boring.

In fact, the soldiers detailed to carry out this task had, in the past, been pelted with cushions. But the Praetorian knew from experience how to manage these events. Not only was it important to have spectacle in circuses that could last a month and run twelve hours a day, it was equally important to have variety.

Not wanting the people to be wearied too soon, small detachments of gladiators entered the arena under the command of men called lanistae. Unarmed and naked, these heavily muscled fighting men, their bodies gleaming with oil, paraded with garlands of flowers, which they threw to the crowds.

Many were known personally and greetings were exchanged, and some of the women and girls present blew kisses to their favourites. Then, with a final flourish, the men withdrew.

Behind the gladiators came the mastigophori, men armed with scourges whose job it would be to lash the combatants to greater efforts and seek out any sign of cowardice.

The creaking arrival of teams of mules piled high with wooden coffins signalled the importance of the spectacle, for only the most favoured would be granted this final dignity. The great majority would be fed to the big cats and the rest simply dragged out and dumped into lime pits.

After the mules, came men dressed as Charon or Mercury who were responsible for killing the wounded. They were followed by arena attendants, whose duty it was to run the circus and manage the slaves responsible for clearing litter and showing people to their seats, selling food and drink, bearing messages and policing the crowds for unruly behaviour.

When all was ready the Praetorians, glorious in their dress uniforms, marched in. Then the prefect of the city arrived with his guards. After him, in a serpentine column, the gilded litters of the praetors, ediles, consuls, senators, army officers, Patricians and beautiful women arrived. Some litters were headed by lictors bearing maces; others by bands of slaves. The common people cheered them, for their arrival meant that the spectacle would soon begin.

It only needed the arrival of Caesar, preceded by the priests of the various temples, who would be followed by the vestal virgins.

Nero, wishing to win favour with the crowd, arrived promptly. In company with the Augusta and the Augustinians, he took his place of honour in the centre of the podium, which was sheathed in gold. The lower seats were blanketed with the snow of the togas of his senators.

Next to him sat Poppaea, beautiful but remote. On both sides were the vestal virgins, powerful officials, senators of special rank, and officers of the army. In the further rows sat knights and higher up, strung like multi-coloured beads, a sea of common heads above which, from column to column, were strung garlands of flowers and sprays of laurel.

The chatter of thousands of spectators filled the air. Unless one shouted, it was difficult to make oneself heard. In spite of this, some particularly witty remark would cause a burst of laughter which, as it was repeated, would provoke merriment which rippled like a row of falling dominoes along the rows of seats.

Then with impatience came the stamping. Spasmodic at first it became like the boom of surf against a beach. The Prefect rose and raised a handkerchief. For a moment silence reigned and then as the scrap of linen floated to the ground, a great shout of anticipation went up and the Andabates opened the proceedings. These were the clowns of the arena, forced to fight in helmets with no eyepieces. Totally blind but armed with swords and spears, they slashed at random until they killed each other.

These clumsy duels were ignored by the nobility but amused the common people, who called out instructions to the groping protagonists. Frequently this 'advice' was designed to get the combatants going in the wrong direction and, as a result, small groups of fighters would collect like blind crabs, hacking and poking at each other in a desperate frenzy.

When the last of the Andabates had finally fallen, slaves would run to unceremoniously drag the corpses out and swiftly rake the bloodied sand.

With a more important contest, interest stirred among the nobility who began to place bets on the outcome. Tablets, on which had been recorded the names of favourites and the amount wagered, sped from hand to hand. Spectati – champions who had fought many times in the arena – found favour, but outsiders new to the arena had bets placed on them by those who hoped that these long shots would net them a fortune.

Everybody, including Nero, gambled and when the common people ran out of money he or she frequently bet their own freedom. These then waited with pounding hearts, and murmured prayers to the gods were frequently heard.

The bray of silver trumpets brought everyone to the silence of expectation. A quarter of a million eyes turned to the great doors that a servant of the games dressed as Charon approached and, amid the breath-held silence, struck twice with his rod.

Slowly, both halves swung open onto a gully as black as a well shaft, out of which the gladiators marched onto the dazzling white sand of the arena. Thirty thousand of the finest fighting men – Thracians, Persians, Germans and Gauls. All heavily armed they marched in their separate nations.

At the sight of them the applause exploded and was kept up throughout the entire parade as the gladiators circled the whole of that shining silver disc on which they would soon shed their life's blood. They halted before Caesar's box, bodies hardened by countless hours of training, confident of their own strength and skill, proud of their calling.

A blast from a marshal's trumpet brought the applause to a ragged halt. The gladiators extended their right arms and raised their eyes upward towards Caesar, roaring out their own salute, "Ave Caesar Imperator! Morituri te salutant!" Then they took up their assigned stations, for they were to fight as nations.

Nero lifted a languid hand in permission and the signal was given for battle to commence. The fiercely partisan audience roared their teams on in turn whistling, applauding and jeering. The gladiators in the arena fought with desperate ferocity, for only the fittest would survive.

At such close quarters, the short stabbing swords favoured by the Romans for close combat wreaked havoc. Some of the less experienced combatants tried to flee the carnage but arena overseers drove them back with leather scourges tipped with lead that could lay a man's spine bare with a single stroke.

On the sand, bloodstains formed in ever widening circles as more and more mortally wounded bodies fell and bled their lives away. The living clambered over the corpses, slipping and sliding on the blood and guts of the dead and dying. It became difficult to hold a sword or mace, so slippery had they become with sweat and blood.

In the last desperate stages of the battle, as a handful of weary survivors struggled to find each other across the mounded dead, the crowd went berserk, intoxicated with the smell and sight of so much blood and the spectacle of death in a myriad of forms. The few survivors, all severely wounded, laid down their arms and knelt trembling in the arena, arms raised in supplication. To these, the victors were given the spoils – crowns, olive wreaths and, the most precious gift of all, life.

While wagons were unceremoniously loaded with the dead, a rest period was declared. Costly perfumes were burned in vases and slaves fanned their spiralling scents with plumes of ostrich feathers imported from Africa. More slaves sprinkled saffron and rosewater.

Cold fruit juices and chilled wines were served with roast fowls, lambs' tongues, spit roasted kid, olives, fresh salads and every variety of fruit. As the Romans feasted, they raised their goblets and shouted Caesar's praise to persuade him to greater generosity.

As the spectators refreshed themselves, hundreds of dwarfs, dressed as clowns, ran around the arena throwing bundles of lottery tickets, known as tesserae, into the crowds. As these flimsy slips of paper fluttered on the slightest breeze, the common people went mad. In their desperation to get one they trampled each other, jumping over rows of seats and assaulting their neighbours without a moment's hesitation.

It was not unknown for people to die stifled to death in these desperate melees, since whoever got a lucky number might win a house with a garden, or a costly well trained slave, or a share in a cargo, or a purse of gold.

Frequently the Praetorians had to restore order during these fights for tesserae and, after doing so, would help to carry out the dead as well as those who had suffered broken limbs. Because of this violence the more wealthy people took no part in the deadly scramble for this largesse.

After a while the trumpets announced the end of the interval and people began to leave the gangways where they had gathered to stretch their legs and converse. Senators and patricians returned to their seats and the audience gradually settled down. During the interval, attendants had dug out sand so stiffened with blood as to make it muddy and replaced it with new before raking the whole surface.

The turn of the Christians was at hand. No one knew what to expect. These were the people who, they had been told, had burned Rome and destroyed its ancient heritage. They poisoned water and drank the blood of murdered children. They refused to acknowledge the gods of Rome, worshipping instead an ancient pagan god of their own who demanded they destroy all gods but him.

The hatred Tigellinus had raised against 'these enemies of Rome' had reached hysterical proportions as he fed the credulous population with a continuous stream of propaganda.

"These Christians," his agent provocateurs had put about, "are not true human beings but evil spirits who have possessed them, whose god, disguised in human form, came down from Olympus to tell them they, not Rome, were to rule the world." They continued, "This god told his followers to honour him by eating the flesh and drinking the blood of the children of his enemies."

These and other stories planted by Tigellinus's men, so terrified many of the common people that they agreed no punishment could be harsh enough to expiate such crimes. And now, thanks to Caesar their protector and benefactor, they were about to witness that punishment.

As if a portent of what was to follow, the sun had reached its zenith and its light, shining through the amethyst velarium, filled the amphitheatre with an ominous light. Suddenly the crowd became sullen, the atmosphere of the arena changed. No stranger to fear or cruelty, it had stood witness to countless acts of barbarism, murder so commonplace as to pass unrecognised. For human or animal, the arena was simply a place to die – in terror, despairingly, with skill, courage, cowardice, heroism, they were all commonplace.

But now a new presence had pervaded the arena. A hush had fallen and a sudden chill was felt. The beast had arrived. Every person experienced its sudden arrival but failed to name it, for they had no conception of evil. Satan claimed them without consent.

As the old man dressed as Charon appeared and walked slowly across the arena, the silence was solid. Hate was so universal, it was almost visible. It crackled like static electricity along the silent serried heads. In the dense silence Charon struck twice on the same door through which the gladiators had entered.

The iron portcullis opened like the jaws of some fabled beast and from its dark throat spewed out the prisoners who were driven from the gloom of their confinement into the blood-red light.

In minutes the arena was populated by thousands of bewildered and terrified people – men, women and children of all ages. Many had been stitched into the skins of goats and sheep. Others huddled together and fell to their knees in prayer, and then the audience began to call on Caesar to give the order for the lions to be let loose. All around the arena the appeal gathered strength.

"The lions, let out the lions!" – which suited Nero very well for, after blaming the fire on the Christians, he could now be seen to be punishing them most severely. He therefore gave the sign for the gate to be opened and the lions, which had been starved, were driven out into the arena after being tormented by their keepers rattling the bars of their cages and poking them with red hot irons.

The first to catch sight of these tawny monsters was a young man on the edge of the bunched mass of people. He was a baker who had kept a busy shop on the narrow lane leading to the Aquae Salviae. As he stumbled into the amphitheatre his only thoughts were for his wife and children who had been separated from him while they were being prepared for the arena.

His two youngest children, girls of three and six, had been sewn into faun skins, while his son of nine had been stitched into a goatskin. His wife had been stripped and costumed as a wood nymph in a dress made of stitched leaves. A garland of roses had been wound in her hair. The man, reduced to a loincloth, had been given a short spear and a small round shield with which to defend himself and his family.

Nothing, however, had prepared him for the sight of a full-grown male lion from the Atlas. The massive bulk of rippling, sand coloured muscle was carried on powerful legs that ended in pads twice the size of his hands. A huge black mane surrounded the great shaggy head, covering the beast's throat and chest and running down its tawny belly.

Propelled by a hot iron applied to its flank, it charged into the arena with a roar that shattered the air and reverberated around the stands. It plunged into the blinding sunlight, stopping stiff legged, sand spraying from its pugs with their half distended claws, its topaz eyes smoky with rage.

At the sight and smell of that great mass of people, its mane rose, its nostrils flared and its tail flicked nervously from flank to flank. The baker stared in abject terror at this great carnivore that was crouched, baring its huge teeth, scarcely thirty feet from where he stood.

As he watched, others of its kind came bounding out of the mouth of the vomitorium. Some had never been in the arena before and, hungry as they were, bunched warily, roaring and coughing, lifting their massive heads to stretch their huge jaws and displaying – much to the delight of the spectators – the full extent of their great teeth.

There were almost fifty lions in the arena and over a hundred more still to be released before the first attack took place. The huge shaggy beasts crouched snarling and spitting in a rough semi-circle around the laagered Christians.

The entry of an experienced lioness, which had participated in this spectacle many times, saw the first attack. She came out of the vomitorium, ears back, in a series of great elastic bounds that took her across the arena, striking into the dense mass of people who scattered like a herd of antelope on the plains of Africa, wheeling in panic first one way and then the other.

As they ran, the old started to fall and once down never regained their feet. Children were separated from desperate parents, who screamed in anguish as sweating fingers lost their grip in the crush and tiny hands slipped away.

As the panicked crowd milled first in one direction and then another, the circle of irritated and excited lions crouching along the periphery charged this strange herd. The youngest of the baker's children, Lydia, trembling and crying in her faun skin, broke away from her mother and ran to her father who was manfully standing between them and the male lion that had been the first to emerge.

The sudden movement of the child triggered the beast's charge. Its ears went back, it gathered itself on its haunches, huge paws splayed to give it maximum grip, and gave out a short barking roar before launching itself in a gigantic leap that halved the distance between them. Barely had it touched down when it seemed to compress itself like a bronze spring to be suddenly released, its massive head and jaws blocking out the sky, its eyes blazing with the concentration of the kill.

The baker and his puny javelin were brushed aside, his neck broken with a single stroke from a heavily muscled foreleg as thick as his thigh that ended with five razor sharp claws that sheared his face off with a single stroke.

Mercifully, the child who had run to him and was clinging to his leg died equally as quickly. The huge jaws that engulfed her bit her through almost as a reflex action, a dog-like shake of the head ensuring that her spinal cord was severed like a tailor snapping his thread.

With the death of her husband and her child imprinted on her mind, the frenzied wife was swept away with a crowd, which bellowed like cattle in their terror. Faeces ran down legs from bowels involuntarily emptied.

The audience was wild with excitement. They scrambled from their seats to go to the lower passages for a better view. Suddenly, from the vivarium, rose the demented roaring of hundreds of hungry lions, which roused by the smell of blood and the sounds of their companions, were hurling themselves at the gratings. Nero, hearing the thunder of these captives, nodded at the Prefect and gave the signal for their release.

From the highest row in the amphitheatre, where he had stationed himself to bear witness and to bless those who were to die, Peter looked down in agony at this fresh influx of maddened beasts. The dreadful spectacle became an orgy of blood.

Lions were everywhere. Having secured a portion of body they sought a place to eat it, but there wasn't a yard of space in the entire amphitheatre that wasn't occupied. Soon the coats of the lions were stiff with blood. Sated they lay in crimson heaps.

The people, satisfied at last, turned to Caesar for their next entertainment, but first the arena had to be cleared. After driving the now bloated lion's back into the tunnels, which led to their quarters, the huge task of clearing up began.

Expert teams brought in wagons on which they flung the dead and dying for dumping in the putrid pits.

Knowing that inevitably they would come across survivors, usually children clamped to the bodies of their dead parents, they brought with them specially trained dogs. Huge yellow Molossians from the Peloponnesos, pied dogs from the Pyrenees, and hounds from Hybernica, flushed out these shocked and trembling mites, who provided for the common people a mini-entertainment of their own as they were run down and torn to pieces.

The arrival of the dogs was a signal for Nero and the court to retire to refresh themselves for the next event.

In the meantime, two thousand slaves toiled to repair the arena. Armed with spades, cartloads of clean sand, wheelbarrows and baskets, they followed behind the wagons clearing the bodies and digging out the worst of the blood soaked sand over which a thick new layer was dredged before being raked and rolled firm.

That done, cupids scampered in to the music of flutes and sprinkled baskets of rose petals and other flowers across its entire surface.

The sensors were ignited and the velarium removed for the sun had almost set. With the onset of evening there would be a new spectacle, for Nero had promised them he would not rest until he had destroyed Rome's enemies.

While the court restored itself, the spectators took the opportunity to refresh themselves and attend to the needs of nature. For those who remained in their seats, vendors did a good trade in food and drink. Men stood in the aisles and discussed the relative ferocity of lions versus tigers and, with too much wine taken, silly brawls were not infrequent.

Having failed to find Clodia, Simon had gone to the arena in case she had been consigned there. Throughout this appalling day he had crouched high up in the stadium in a fury of red-eyed concentration. Now, with his head aching abominably, he braced himself for what was to follow, hopeful that if Clodia was to be driven into that pit of death he could save her.

Twice during the day Peter had tried to comfort him but had been angrily rebuffed.

Knowing that it would be at least three hours before Nero would appear to start the evening games the Apostle, who was suffering from his own private agony, had spent the entire day blessing those who died. He bore witness with them, repenting his failure to acknowledge Christ in his hour of need.

Now he accepted the burden of having to certify the death of countless thousands of those who believed in him and were attesting to their faith by laying down their lives. The faithful who were dying were a reminder to Peter that he had failed when put to the same test.

"Why don't you rest – put your trust in Christ. This life is of no importance. Your family will be safe in the Lord's hands."

Simon raised his trembling head, his eyes bloodshot in a paper white face. So severe was his migraine he had just been sick; vomit and bile dripped from his chin. "God has nothing to do with this. That you bless the poor bastards down there in my brother's name and ask them to endure this evil obscenity in his name, is blasphemy."

"My brother was a dreamer, a half-wit who hadn't enough sense to say no to being nailed to a tree." These last words were whispered. Simon was shaking with anger, tears streaming down his face.

Peter made one more attempt. "Ask God for His peace…" but he got no further.

Simon rose in fury. Only a few faces turned towards them – violent quarrels among spectators were common. "If," he shouted, his pale face suddenly red with fury, "you love Jesus so much why don't you join the poor bastards down there?"

The old fisherman fell back on his seat, his face ashen, sweat beading his face. In silent protest he raised his hands which were shaking as though with palsy. How many times had he argued with the elders of the fledgling church that he should stop hiding from the authorities and preach openly?

Yes, the Romans would take him, but "is it," a tiny voice whispered in his heart, "another way of saying no, a repeat of the denial you made all those years ago?"

Hasty words, once spoken, forever beyond recall – forever bitterly regretted. The old man pulled his robe over his head and rocked in his misery. His companions glared furiously at Simon, who retreated with his own despair to another part of the arena to maintain his vigil.

# 26

The girl's moaning terror was ignored by the sweating men. In fact they scarcely registered it. It was only when she loosed off a burbling scream that echoed off the vaulted ceiling that they were reminded she was human.

The noise the girl was making was, however, an irritation they were prepared for, and was dealt with by one of the men seizing her face and popping her jaws by a swift and expert press from his thumb and forefinger. As her jaws gaped he jammed a short piece of wood between her teeth and bound them closed with a strip of canvas, which he passed beneath her chin and over the top of her head.

This done, the two men, who worked as a team – one of a hundred such pairs labouring in the passages and chambers beneath the Circus Maximus – continued their work.

Victims who were judged young enough and pretty enough to be worth raping were set aside, for there was a ready market for such merchandise among the day labourers and artisans who could purchase the right to violate such persons for less than a goblet of the cheapest wine. The oversupply resulted from the sheer weight of numbers of Christian Jews that Tigellinus's men were rounding up and sending for processing.

The men who were engaged in dealing with this incoming human tide were sated with pleasures of the flesh, and while occasionally reserving a young male or female prisoner for themselves, they augmented their poor wages by acting as panders. Not that the prisoners to be used in this way were allowed to be

208

removed from the cellars. Instead, smaller cells or the holding cages for wild beasts were set aside for these assignations.

Providing that the prisoner was returned alive, the hirer could do what he liked and frequently did. Freed from all restraint such lessees unleashed on their helpless victims hours of unspeakable torture and degradation as they acted out the fantasy of a diseased and degenerate mind.

Every jail in Rome was full to bursting, as prisoners were not expected to be held in them for more than forty-eight hours before being driven to the arena. They were neither fed nor watered; instead they were jammed into dungeons and cells and packed so closely that not only were they forced to stand, but those that suffocated to death were held upright by their companions.

After a few hours of such confinement in unlit, low ceilinged underground cells that were without windows, even breathing became difficult. The smell was appalling as people were forced to relieve themselves where they stood and became smeared with excrement.

Eventual transference to the Circus was done at night to avoid offending the sensibilities of the civilian population. It was one thing to watch a man die in the arena, insulated from his agony by the palisade that divided the audience from the participants. It was quite another to have him rub shoulders with you as he and his family were driven like dung-spattered cattle, lowing in their misery, tongues lolling from parched mouths, eyes bulging with terror, through avenues and squares frequented during the day by normal people, not enemies of the state.

They were 'sub-humans' who, it was alleged, practised strange magical rites, which involved the ritual murder of Roman children kidnapped especially for that purpose. Worse still, the arresting soldiers informed them, they refused to acknowledge Caesar as a god, spat upon all of Rome's gods and had desecrated the temples of Jupiter, Apollo and Diana.

They called themselves Christians, these miscreant servants of an evil god who was the enemy of the rule of law and order that Roman conquest had bestowed upon the world. These strange people with their evil and secret rites wished to destroy Rome and her gods. Instead they were to be destroyed and the citizens of Rome would be protected by her gods through their favourite, the man who was himself more than a man, a veritable demi-god, Caesar.

Nero would use Tigellinus to 'rubbish' this scum, this pestilence, this foul and loathsome threat, this filth, and tear it limb from limb, devour it, cut it down, burn it – yes, above all, burn it. Reduce it to nothingness. To ashes that can be flung into the drains, emptied into the sewers, swept into the Tiber, cast to the four winds.

A process which could be made spectacularly and entertainingly visible to citizens in the arenas where the deaths of thousands needed to be orchestrated with as much variety as possible, if brutal murder wasn't to be boring.

Games held at night proved to be as novel an introduction as the means of illumination. It was Nero himself who thought of the method and it was the job of the men who toiled in the cellars of the Maximus to provide it.

With the girl silenced, her naked body was smeared with pitch. She was then bandaged tightly like a mummy in sheets of material that had been soaked in a mixture of resin, wax, oil and pungent aromatics. The job done, the bound body was tossed aside to be collected by a team of porters, volunteers from the incoming prisoners who were willing to postpone their own demise for as long as possible, hoping against hope that somehow escape would be possible.

In the meantime, like worker ants, hands, arms and chests black and sticky from contact with their burden, they harvested the sausage shaped bundles and carried them away. They stacked their prizes in the dimly lit tunnels like the chrysalises of a giant insect. Row upon row, layer upon layer of helplessly bound terrified human beings of all ages and sexes, their skin a layer of pain from the irritation of the chemicals in the bindings, to say nothing of the pain due to the circulation being restricted by their tightness.

As they lay, corded like the faggots they were to become, some subsided into oblivion, silent, withdrawn, and shocked into an anaesthetising torpor from which, mercifully, they would never recover. Those few who hadn't had their jaws bound called out softly in the gloom. These strong spirits offered words of consolation and comfort.

Others hoarsely protested their innocence and vehemently denied having anything to do with either this so-called Christ or any of his followers upon whose heads they called down curses. Finally, they either shut up from weariness or were silenced by the porters who grew fearful that such a cacophony would irritate those who toiled at the preparation tables.

Throughout the day hordes of slaves erected posts – thousands of posts. They lined the Apennine Way and the principal streets leading to the Circus Maximus, to the Hippodrome, and every avenue and pathway in the hundreds of acres of gardens that surrounded the royal palace.

The grounds of all public buildings, temples to Roman gods, villas of the rich and wellborn, including that of Karkinos, sprouted these denuded trees. The outer rim of the Circus had a triple row of amputated trunks and in the centre of the arena a veritable forest was planted.

The posts in the middle of the amphitheatre were cut to different lengths and cleverly positioned, with the tallest in the centre. The effect was that of a mountain studded with branchless trees.

To these and the countless thousands erected in the streets and gardens were brought the results of those who toiled below the Circus.

Strange fruits that were tied to their trunks in readiness for the night, when still more teams of well drilled mounted workmen would, each holding a burning torch, at a given signal from Tigellinus gallop madly down the rows assigned to him. It was Tigellinus's proud boast that before Caesar would have time to walk down the steps of the palace and get into his state carriage, every human candle would be lit and would burn brightly for the duration of the evening's entertainment.

The awful smell of burning flesh would be masked by the aromatics, which had been thoughtfully included in the bindings. As a result, when ignited they gave off a heavy cloying smell, an incense-like perfume that lingered in the nostrils for days. In fact for months the whole of Rome, even the surrounding countryside, would appear to be swathed in a permanent fog with a sweet sickly smell that caught in the back of the throat.

While it went unnoticed by Nero, and nobody at court dared to complain, it caused many to feel queasy and go off their food.

That Clodia had survived incarceration in the Mamertine and transportation to the dungeons of the Maximus was due entirely to her constitution and her absolute determination to survive. Against the strongest men she had won the fight for space, for a place near the door where there was the faintest eddy of fresh air.

Plastered with filth, her clothes reduced to rags, she stood out in her batch of prisoners. It wasn't just her height, it was her stance, the set of her shoulders and the smouldering anger in her eyes. This was the Clodia of the lepers, as dangerous as a tiger, contained, watchful, waiting.

To have attacked the guards would have been as easy as killing two or three of them before she in turn was killed, but survival and revenge were all that mattered. To survive long enough to kill Tigellinus, Karkinos, even Caesar himself, though she had less interest in the magician and his royal puppet than she had in the Praetorian guard commander.

During her captivity she had shut her mind against the fate of her child and of Simon. To stop herself even thinking about them she muttered Tigellinus's name over and over like a mantra. To do otherwise was to be overwhelmed with misery in an agony of fear over the fate of the two human beings that she loved above all else. Tears would not free her, neither would brute force, so she schooled herself to wait for that moment of weakness, the half chance that must surely come her way.

She wasted no time in praying to the gods – Roman or Christian – for the simple reason it never occurred to her to do so. Her years in the wilderness had taught her to rely on nobody other than herself.

The batch of prisoners she was with had been herded into a cage that was normally used for housing lions. Even the smell of the prisoners she was with couldn't mask the eye watering acrid pungency of its former occupants. Through its bars she witnessed the horror that awaited her and her companions. For the first time since her capture she felt a wave of absolute despair, for she knew once bound in that winding sheet of death, no escape was possible.

"Wash that one off." It was the largest of the three roughly dressed day labourers, who was also their spokesman, who was pointing at her. As Clodia was dragged out of the cage to be doused with several buckets of water, she was the subject of their lewd jokes, while as the few miserable coins were handed to her captors as payment, she was cleaned up.

From their stained clothing Clodia knew that the trio worked in a slaughterhouse and normally would have been unable to afford the lowest grade of prostitute. She guessed that at least one of them would be diseased.

"Right, take her away. You can use the cell at the end of the corridor. When you've finished, dump her for wrapping over there." The porter casually indicated the end table where a pair of tar-spattered Gauls were binding the elderly wife of a prominent Roman senator who had been denounced as a Christian and had refused to recant.

The smaller of the three men replied, "You can wrap what's left of her for Nero himself, mate," and nudged the nearer of his two companions in the ribs and grabbed Clodia by the arm. The porter shrugged and turned away. He had seen children reduced to dog meat by these three, who were regular customers. He knew that for the woman, whichever way it was, death was going to be a long time coming, and when it did it would be as a welcome friend.

Clodia was virtually frog-marched to a cell and, once inside, what was left of her dress was torn off and flung to the ground while her temporary owners surveyed their prize. They were in no hurry. Clearly they had participated in such recreational afternoons before and had come prepared.

The shortest of the three was obviously the quarter master, for from beneath his cloak he produced a gallon skin of cheap wine and went on to conjure up a wheel of barley bread and a flask of olive oil.

More ominously, the member of the trio who up to this point had contributed nothing to the party, made amends by producing from underneath his blood-encrusted smock, a leather tawse, the split ends of its strap stiff with old blood. He laid this down and beside it a rusted grater normally used for rasping the hair from the back of scalded pigs.

Worst of all was the last item, which he drew out with a leery grin and dangled in front of Clodia's face. It was a leather phallus ringed with a spiked collar, a miniature of those fitted to the necks of fighting bull mastiffs.

Slowly Clodia got to her feet. Sliding her back against the wall, she kept her face and shoulders down, the picture of dejection.

"Big bitch, isn't she?" It was the quartermaster who spoke.

"She's got a lot you could swing on," giggled the man who had paid.

"Yeah, one on each if you're teeth are up to it cocker," grinned the largest of the butchers, flicking out a hand like a spade, the claws of his filthy callused fingers casually snapping at the woman's breasts.

Clodia feigned terror, squeezing out of the way, sliding along the wall that had the room's only source of light – a flickering torch held onto the wall by a crude iron bracket. Clodia had noticed that in the corner, directly below it, were a latrine bucket and an oaken stool. The wink of light from the bucket's interior told her that it was not empty.

Crab fingers grunted disbelievingly when his fingers closed on nothing. With a blink of astonishment he charged across the cell with a few quick strides, fists cocked. Septimus liked to hit things. In the slaughterhouse, if enough bets could be made, he would pitch himself against a luckless sheep or donkey, demonstrating how with one blow he could render the dumb beast senseless.

Not that he intended knocking Clodia out. He much preferred to use women's breasts as a punch bag, excited by the screams of agony such onslaughts brought on.

His clumsy swinging punch missed a target that simply slipped inside it. The agonising pain that exploded in his head was from an iron-hard foot kicking him with savage ferocity full in the crotch. The darkness that blocked out his vision was not the result of the blow but the torch being plucked from the wall and plunging the room into total darkness as it sizzled pungently out.

The speed at which this happened left the other two men momentarily paralysed. The quartermaster was the first to recover. As he turned to go for the door his head was crushed like an eggshell as the heavy oak stool met the back of it, powered by an overhead swing from an arm he never saw.

As the man went down, the paymaster, gibbering with fright tripped over his body. Neither he nor the weeping Septimus could believe this was happening. In the space of a few seconds an idyllic afternoon had been turned into a nightmare. They were locked in a pitch-dark room with a madwoman who had the strength of an Amazon and the eyes of a cat.

The paymaster reached into his belt where he carried one of the tools of his trade, a foot-long razor sharp knife. Holding this in front of him he got to his knees and shuffled along the floor to get his back to the wall.

Septimus, similarly armed, was sliding across the floor, his blade extended. His objective was the door, the bottom edge of which he could faintly see. He was the first to die. It was as though the woman could see in the dark. His knife arm was broken as though it was a stick of celery. Then his own blade was used to gut him.

In total darkness the terrified paymaster listened to the wild threshing that came from the floor. He wondered if he should fling himself in its direction to stab at anything that came to hand. Suddenly screams exploded like shards of broken glass, rising to an impossibly high pitch. As quickly as they had started they finished, and something warm and wet was flung against his face and draped itself across his chest. As a man who spent his days plucking lights and livers, he recognised the feel of what was slithering down his face.

With a shriek he leapt for the door. He was howling for the guard who was too far away to hear him. Instead he met a raging Isis, racked by inconsolable grief, goaded into an irresistible rage. Before drowning him in the latrine bucket she disarmed him and drove his own knife so savagely into his spine that he felt the blade snap off at the hilt.

With the last of her assailants dead, the carmined figure opened the door of the cell to the merest crack. Clodia was loose but not free.

*At least*, she thought, *I am armed and will die cleanly in combat and not shamefully on a pyre.*

A creaking sound heralded the approach of a cart laden with faggots. In the gloom of the tunnel it looked like the wagon of the angel of death itself, its cargo some nightmare pupation of a hybrid species of man and insect. In their tarred swaddling with only their heads stuck out, they were like the offspring of a hideous mutation.

The muleteer who drove this cargo wore a hooded cape and a rag tied around his nose and mouth to lessen the stink. As a free man who competed with the slaves of Rome in the struggle to stay alive, he had to take whatever work was available. "Beggars," he decided bitterly, "can't be choosers."

He never saw the knife that thudded into his chest. Before he died, though, he heard its song as it whistled through the air. The fiend that tore the clothes off his back was the last thing his dying brain registered. It was as though Hecate herself had come to claim him for her own.

With the muleteer's corpse tossed into the cellar to keep the dead butchers company, Clodia shrouded herself in his verminous cloak and bound her face with the phlegm stained rag she had stripped from his jaws.

In the bottom of the wagon seat she found an old-fashioned plaited leather whip. Experimentally she flicked it out across the mules' backs. It uncoiled through the air like a cobra, its sinuous length stretching out a satisfactory twelve feet. Like a fisherman, she spun it back, snapping her wrist in a cast that cracked the air two feet in front of the lead mule's startled nose and galvanised the beast into action.

As the wagon rumbled out of the labyrinth below the Circus, her thoughts were not on the collective misery at her back but on the face that hung before her red-rimmed eyes. Tigellinus!

The whip exploded experimentally in the air. It bit the tiniest tuft of hair from the lead mule's shoulder. She recoiled it, satisfied. She intended flaying the skin from the Praetorian inch by inch and then working her way down to the bone. If any of Simon's teaching had touched her it was the law handed down from Abraham – "Eye for eye, tooth for tooth, hand for hand, foot for foot."

## 27

When he wasn't keeping a vigil at the games, Simon scoured what was left of the city seeking news of Clodia and the baby.

After disguising himself he had even bribed his way into Rome's prisons. Among these was the Esquiline, formed in a hurry from the cellars of houses demolished to try and stop the fire. While conditions inside were bad, they were nothing by comparison to the old Tullianum near the capital, which shared with the Mamertine a reputation for being worse than Hades itself. Corpses from both were cast into lime filled holes referred to as 'the putrid pits.'

Even to enter Rome's prisons was to risk death, for with overcrowding had come the spectre of disease. But at the cost of considerable amounts of gold, Simon persuaded the guards to admit him and let him search.

First the Esquiline, but without success. He then bribed his way into the Mamertine. Once through the great iron doors he entered a long passage whose walls and roof were formed from blocks of cut stone that seemed as solid as the limestone hills from which they had been hewn.

At the end of the passage lay a rambling, vaulted cellar, which was connected by tunnels and stone staircases to even deeper chambers, dimly lit by smoking lamps that were nothing more than a shallow dish of oil and a wick. Here the air was difficult to breathe; it was so fetid from the chained bodies that were packed into its dungeons.

The lucky ones were simply in leg irons and these huddled on the ground, their elbows on their knees, their heads in their hands. Others were made to lie on their sides in a foetal position and forced to hug the back of the neighbour to whom they were joined with neck irons.

Only children were left unchained – not for humanitarian reasons, but so that they could carry water to the adults who would have died in that pestilence without it.

No food was supplied on the grounds that, within a week, the prisoners would die in the arena anyway.

When the stone benches were full, prisoners were hung like corncobs from the walls in chains run through iron rings bolted to the solid stone. Groans and soft cries of despair, of pain, of fear, carried through the air, a constant counterpoint to the sound of weeping. The more enduring cursed their captors and the jailers for lack of attention.

Fearfully Simon surveyed this gloomy hell. He despaired of being able to pick out an individual case. The mounded grey chrysalises that lined the benches or hung from the walls, or huddled like frightened rats in clusters on the floor, were indistinguishable as individuals in that poor light. Here and there faces showed, palely gleaming, as did the flash of red-rimmed eyes – but that was all.

In the end he had to light a lamp and inspect every one of those pale, terrified faces. Some slept fitfully, others turned their heads away, eyes blinded by the sudden light. Others were dead and simply stared sightless, blue lips parted in a mirthless grin.

And still that prison was less fearful than the old Tullianum, which he got into by taking a job as a corpse bearer, work that only slaves or men forced by the direst need would take. From Simon's point of view this terrible job had the benefit of taking him from prison to prison, collecting the bodies of those who had died from disease, heart failure, starvation, or had been beaten to death without reason by a sadistic guard.

Frequently when people died in the lower level of the city's jails, their deaths only came to light when the rotting bodies began to smell. These corpses, and the infection they spread, was the reason for the corpse bearers who were employed to take the dead and cast them into huge lime pits dug specially for the job.

Before a body could be taken out of the prison as dead, it had to be certified as such by the head jailer who was required to apply a heated iron to the face. If any sign of life prevailed he would then sever the spinal cord with a chisel driven into the nape of the neck.

The job of the men who ran the overfull prisons had been reduced to simply separating the living they sent to the arena to die, from the dead that went straight into the putrid pits for decomposition. Those who went to the arena either ended up as food for the lions, or food for the worms in the same common graves as their companions.

In his role as a corpse bearer Simon not only searched Rome's prisons, he scoured what was left of the city for news. In particular he concentrated on the skein of slums which unravelled around the Mamertine and which, since the fire, had been choked with a frustrated and snarling humanity which fought for what little space was left in that meanest part of the city.

Before the destruction wrought by the fire, the most backward of the Empire's subjects would not have envied Rome's poor. They eked out a bare existence in these squalid, unsanitary hovels that had been compressed between the docks and the miles of warehousing and mills that made up Rome's commercial district.

Ironically, this area of the city produced the one thing that kept the poor from outright rebellion – flour. Here were located all the huge underground mills which day and night ground the wheat which was brought to Rome from her provinces as tribute and issued by Caesar as a citizen's right. Juvenal, the Roman moralist, recorded the ordinary people's view of this bounty as the "bread and the blood of the arena are all that the Roman mob demand from life."

In a society where slaves outnumbered freemen, they made it impossible for the ordinary man to sell his labour at anything other than starvation rate. The free issue of grain just about held the desperately poor Roman proletariat in check.

To be consigned to the mills that produced this munificence was regarded as worse than being sent to the Tullianum. Prisoners in the Tullianum were frequently overcrowded, the food was appalling, and not even clean water was available in sufficient quantities.

The guards were brutal and what they didn't steal from the prisoner, the prisoners stole from each other.

Murder was frequent as, like rats in a cage, the condemned men savagely fought each other to establish supremacy of even that dunghill.

Men consigned to the mills had no opportunity to fight because they were chained to thick wooden spars, which operated massive capstans that turned the mill wheels. They were only released from their chains when they died, which was between one and three years from being incarcerated.

They died from the cumulative effect of lung diseases and being continuously beaten with thick bamboo rods. Canes were used rather than whips, which could tear a man's, flesh open. The men wielding the rods were trustees, who also controlled the issue of the prisoners' meagre rations.

What was freely available was water, because without it a man would have been dead within days from the great clouds of hot, searing dust and chaff that swirled like a dense fog through the underground mill house. It was this corrosive dust that burned away the eyelids and so inflamed the eyes that a most painful blindness was as inevitable as the choking emphysema that gradually silted lungs, making every wheezing breath a desperate, agonised struggle.

The mills' condemned worked naked in almost total darkness, choking and gasping in the hot, powder filled air, eyes swollen and festering before finally popping and cratering into weeping pits.

Only the slaves who burrowed for minerals in a variety of mines throughout the Empire were condemned to die in this way, as they too were chained to their workplace, frequently blinded to reduce their chances of escape, and routinely beaten to make them work. Again it was the trusty overseers who, to escape the worst of these barbarities, managed the mines and were the only prisoners ever allowed to come to the surface.

For the rest, being sent underground was permanent unless by some miracle you outlived your sentence. To do this required an exceptional will to live, allied to an almost inhumanly strong constitution and the ruthless exploitation of your fellow workers, whose meagre rations you had to steal if you were to survive.

Having spent yet another fruitless day searching for Clodia and Joshua, Simon, dizzy from lack of sleep, was making his way to the arena where he kept a vigil for part of the time.

As he went past the heavily guarded main gate of the Tullianum, it opened to allow a cohort to come out with an officer and a manacled prisoner who was held securely in the middle of the squad which marched off at a determined pace, using shields and spear buts to carve a passage through the clogged street. Their prisoner was so small that he was almost hidden by his burly guards.

Though Simon only caught a glimpse of him, he became aware of the fact that a number of Jews were endeavouring to keep pace with the prisoner and his escort. They were heading in the direction of the Aquae Salviae, a piece of waste ground outside the city where executions were held. This was a fearsome place that could at times be a veritable forest of crudely made crosses hung with men and women suffering the lingering torture of a method of dying which the Romans had perfected. It was the slowest and most painful way of killing another human being, excelling against the ingenuities imported from Egypt and Syria.

The execution squad was so commonplace that Simon would not normally have given it a second glance. In any event, the urgency of his own errand was such that he had no time to spend on the unfortunate who was being dragged away to what was no doubt going to be a very brutal death.

It was catching sight of an extremely wealthy and influential Jew in the prisoner's would-be retinue of followers that roused his curiosity. Grumbling to himself he started to force a passage through the traffic of donkeys, people, carts and goats, that struggled bleating through the filthy lane.

When he eventually caught up with the squad, it was at the city gate that opened onto the killing ground. Apart from the soldiers assigned to this duty and any relatives of the condemned, the only other people who would use this particular gate would be those who were too poor to bury their dead. They came to throw their corpses into a ravine where it was known eaters of carrion came regularly and in numbers to feed at a never empty table.

As the brief exchange at the gate took place Simon was in time to catch up with the group and, for the first time, got a proper look at the prisoner.

The man was short, barely five feet tall. He was also old. His almost bald, tanned bare head was speckled with liver spots and a full white beard testified to his age.

His clothes were virtually rags – nobody spends time in the Tullianum and stays either clean or fully clad – but he had managed to retain his cloak that was of plain material and a pair of cheap sandals that were strapped to the peasant's feet, broad soled and big toed.

A massive hooked nose that was almost a parody, giving the pinched and wizened face a bird-like quality dominated the face, deeply lined and streaked with dirt.

It was Paul.

It was the eyes that caused Simon to catch his breath. As blue as a summer's sky, alert as a hawk's and indifferent to his captors, to the people who had followed his escort – to Simon himself.

Simon had seen men die before, and die badly. He had seen Christian fanatics die singing with joy as they were ripped to pieces in the arena, had witnessed men die deranged, totally dehumanised, subjected to torture so evil that the applicators were taken over by the monster they had unleashed to destroy their victims.

The squad trudged out of the gate onto the small piece of bone-strewn wasteland that ended in a steep, rocky ravine – a gloomy, brooding place that supported nothing but the eaters of filth. With bored practised skill the soldiers formed a rough circle, strapped their prisoner to a post and routinely scourged him with bone tipped whips that drew blood and nipped bits of flesh out of the trembling back.

The prisoner was then dragged to a lump of stone that had served them in the past as an impromptu block, for Paul was a citizen of Rome and would be executed honourably by decapitation, the crucifix being reserved for criminals and non-Romans sentenced to death for whatever reason. A Roman citizen, for example, could sentence any one of his slaves to death without explanation and his manner of dying was entirely up to his master.

Sallus used to keep a pool filled with fish, which he fed with slaves who had displeased him. As a wealthy Roman, he counted his slaves in hundreds – a stock which could be replenished by simply sending his steward to the daily market. Feeding his pets in this way was a mere trifle to one of the richest men in Rome.

Not daring to interfere, Simon stood close to the small group of followers who were openly weeping. They wept for Paul of Tarsus, the man who believed that God had appeared to him in a personal vision and not only confirmed Jesus to be the Messiah, but had gone on to claim that the promise of salvation was given to the Gentiles as well the Jews. Salvation even to the men who were about to cut off his head – the Romans.

Having been stripped to the waist the Apostle asked permission to take leave of his friends.

Simon struggled to maintain his composure. He could feel his headache getting worse. Why, he wondered, had he bothered to digress on this fool's errand? This fanatical man was, he thought bitterly, the last but one. After him, Peter, and then they would all be dead. All, including Jesus, the one they had come to regard as the long awaited Messiah.

Simon bowed his head. His brother James, he remembered sadly, had also gone, stoned to death by his own people at the instigation of the same man who had had their brother nailed up.

These Christians, as they called themselves had, for the moment, he thought grimly, taken over from the Jews as humanity's scapegoat. With every passing day they were being singled out for destruction, as Nero and Tigellinus thought up new ways for the Christians to die.

Simon wanted to leave. There was nothing keeping him, nothing he could do. Only the sudden appearance of a reprieve signal from Nero himself would stop the proceedings and any attempt at interference would be treason and resisted by the force of arms.

The old man spoke softly to his followers. It was, Simon noted in amazement, he who was doing the calming and comforting.

It was almost mid-morning, the sun hard and bright in a cloudless sky, the sound of the town going noisily about its business coming plainly over the wall. From across the hills the faint tinkle of bells from a scattered flock trembled on the warm air. The sword blade resting lightly on the stained stone sent dazzling heliographs that made Simon's headache even worse.

Paul knelt, arms still chained behind his back, his beard fluttering slightly in the breeze. Calmly he surveyed them. His captors stared back at him indifferently, anxious to get on with it and be back in the barracks for lunch.

The tearful knot of civilians waited in appalled disbelief for the unthinkable to happen. Wound like a spring the executioner, sword grasped firmly in both hands, waited for the captain's order. Simon felt sick. It was all so ordinary, so matter-of-fact. In seconds Paul would be dead and the goats across the valley would go on scrambling for another meagre mouthful of leaves.

He would return to his neglected errand, and the city would slow for its afternoon siesta. The man who was about to swing the death dealing sword would, even before nightfall, need reminding of the man he had killed in the morning, and by the end of the week would have forgotten him completely.

The old Apostle finished offering up his personal prayer to a Jesus that neither Simon nor the Roman soldiers could comprehend though, Simon thought sullenly, the collection of degenerate blasphemous Christian Jews who mutter and skitter like sheep in the slaughterhouse pen, claim to.

For a second Paul caught Simon's eye.

In a daze Simon read the message they held for him. The man about to die was filled with compassion for him. Without any hesitation Paul closed his eyes and bowed his neck. His final words were to God whom he called upon to forgive his executioners.

The head rolled in the dirt, the still beating heart pumping furiously. Soaking the ground was the life-blood of a man who, single-handedly, had carried what he believed to be a message from the God of the Hebrews to the Gentiles, of His promise of a new covenant with all mankind, not just the Jews. The promise of eternal life. Victory over death, victory over the degradation of life on earth. Freedom from fear, from hate.

In a daze Simon watched as the guard commander signalled one of the soldiers to hand the head to one of the civilians who had come to bear witness. Absentmindedly Simon wondered what bribe had been arranged for this consideration.

Sick at heart he turned to leave when he felt a pull on his sleeve. It was a young Hebrew boy who bobbed his head respectfully before saying, "Lord, if you would spare a moment, my father would like to speak with you."

Simon squinted through his headache at the group of Jews who, having collected there, were attempting to bargain for the rest of the body. "Who is your father?" he asked grudgingly, not wanting to become involved, desiring only to get out of this terrible place.

The boy didn't answer him directly. Instead he pointed to the best dressed of the group. "He is the physician, the tall man." The note of pride was not difficult to detect.

With the briefest of nods Simon made his way across to the group. "Well?" He was deliberately rude, his perfunctory greeting on such an occasion, even for a Roman, offensive.

The man whom he addressed gave no indication that he was put out by the lack of manners. He simply responded quietly but equally brusquely and to the point. "Paul's dying words were that we are to help you. Even more, he commands that we help you at any cost. His last words to us were that we should tell the fisherman of your search and ask him to help you."

There was a long pause, the eyes of the small group curiously assessing the stranger to whom Paul had entrusted their lives.

Simon was staggered at what the man had said. He knew only too well that Tigellinus was turning Rome upside down to find Peter, and would pay any sum in gold for knowledge of his whereabouts.

With Paul dead, the final target would be Peter. His crucifixion would loose the devil himself to wreak total havoc inside and outside the fledgling church.

"Who are you?"

"I am a physician. I am known among my friends as Luke. More to the point, who are you, Roman, who commands such respect from Paul of Tarsus?"

Simon stared at Luke's face. Long seconds passed before he answered, before turning abruptly away. "I am Flavius Simon bar Joseph, citizen of Rome, and a Judaean who worships the God of Abraham and Moses, and brother of the man you call the Christ."

The last was overheard by a number of Jews present who surged forward to see who was making such an astounding claim. They were stayed by the outstretched arm of Luke who, surveying Simon's departing back, remembered happier days in Galilee and a man who had changed his life forever.

## 28

That Caesar himself should appear for the mass burning of thousands of Christians to be staged in the grounds of the Imperial Palace persuaded Simon to mingle with spectators in the faint chance of learning something that would help him to locate Clodia and the baby.

In the purpling dusk the first of the evening's crowds had begun to meander into Caesar's gardens. Dressed in their best clothes with garlands of flowers in their hair, they strolled casually along the rubble strewn avenues, chatting and smiling, calling out greetings as they recognised friends.

Many, having started to celebrate early, were drunk. Shouts of "Semaxii! Sarmentii!" rang out excitedly as they passed the newly planted pitch soaked posts, each with its swaddled and terrified victim bound to it with chains to stop it falling prematurely as it burned on its perch.

Seemingly inured to suffering, even death itself, Roman citizens enjoyed murder when presented as a spectacle. They were used to seeing people burned on pillars but never before had anyone seen such numbers.

Under Karkinos's control, Nero was not only anxious to destroy the Christians as quickly as possible, he wanted to do it in such a way that it would discredit them forever. The manner of their dying was to be an act of shame, an exhibition of the death reserved for the worst of the Empire's common criminals and enemies of the state.

"Speed," Simon thought grimly, "will also be necessary," because in the overcrowded prisons infection had already set in and was spreading with alarming rapidity. The spectre of epidemic was rising and the authorities knew it would not confine itself to the city's overcrowded jails.

As the festive crowd sauntered through the royal gardens, it marvelled at the preparations. Lining each side of the paths which wound their way through the parks and lawns that fringed the edges of the lakes, were posts smeared with pitch to which were chained the oil soaked Christians.

From viewing points within the gardens, Simon saw that the huge lawns had been crammed with bodies, while others, strung along the roads and paths extended as far as the eye could see.

This dark plantation reminded the distraught man of the harbour at Ostia. When the Roman fleet was in port it was a veritable forest of masts, overlapping trunks and yards that latticed the harbour to the horizon. Hung from this dark forest, the number of cocooned bodies, each decorated with myrtle, ivy and garlands of flowers, surpassed the crowd's wildest expectations.

Panic rose in Simon's breast. Scarcely aware of what he was doing, he started to run from post to post, anxiously peering up at each victim. As he trotted desperately among the terrified Jews, many of whom called out to their God, he shared their despair and added his own supplication.

Once the crowd's initial delight and surprise had subsided, they took to examining the helpless Jews pinioned to these rough masts. Their curiosity was aroused but not their pity. That children cried out to their parents, or husbands to wives, fathers to their sons and daughters, to their old parents, caused not the slightest concern.

As dusk turned into darkness and the first stars appeared, every street and avenue surrounding the royal gardens that had escaped the fire was packed with spectators. Near each condemned person a slave was stationed, for Nero was determined that on this occasion every single pyre would be lit at the same moment.

"You have," Karkinos had said, "to re-enact the burning of Rome if you are to achieve Satan's promised glory." Only this time it would be his enemies who burned, not the remains of the city.

At Nero's command Tigellinus gave the order for the trumpets to sound. As the notes soared out over the stricken city, every slave stood ready. As the last note died away, two hundred and fifty thousand torches were plunged simultaneously into the mass of pitch and turpentine soaked straw that was at the base of every post. Combustion was immediate.

Dry mouthed Simon watched the candles of flame leap upward to ignite the swaddling that held each victim. For the second time Rome was on fire and night turned into day.

Individual screams of terror and shrieks of pain blended into one siren howl that raised the hair of the staring Romans. As the stink of burnt flesh began to drift on the evening breeze, slaves ran between the rosy crosses sprinkling aloes and myrrh that had been prepared in readiness.

Through the leaping flames the blackened faces of the roasting Christians could be seen distorting in their dreadful agony, teeth bared as the pain caused them to shriek themselves hoarse.

Parents suffered the double agony of their own pain and fear and that of their children who, out of their minds with terror, screamed continuously, throats open wide as fledglings waiting to be fed, eyes rolled into the backs of their heads.

Down the avenue of burning bodies Simon suddenly saw Karkinos's black chariot, drawn by four black horses, rolling in stately procession wheel to wheel with his servant Nero.

In contrast to the magician's sombre cortege, four perfectly matched white Arabs drew the Emperor's magnificent gold and silver quadriga. Ten thousand horses had been rejected in the choosing of these four animals, whose harnesses of brilliant red and gold leather were encrusted with every sort of precious stone.

Nero himself was dressed in his favourite colour – a colour he reserved entirely for himself – amethyst.

Behind his and Karkinos's chariots came the court in magnificent array – senators, knights, consuls and tribunes. Through their ranks ran bacchantes, naked except for garlands in their hair. They went from chariot to chariot with pitchers of wine, accompanied by musicians dressed as satyrs playing citharas, flutes and horns, who entertained the noble maidens of Rome's leading citizens who, half drunk and half naked, flirted shamelessly with the common people.

Around Nero's quadriga ran Greek boys who shook tambourines ornamented with ribbons. Others beat drums and slaves scattered flowers in the path of the advancing cortege. As the glittering court progressed they cheered Caesar and hailed him "Divinity."

Keeping Karkinos and Tigellinus near him, Nero drove his horses himself, reining them to a walk to better appreciate the cheers of the crowd. Completely hemmed in Simon watched in helpless rage as Nero proudly stood on his chariot's gold platform, totally surrounded by a sea of people who knelt at his feet in homage.

In the blood-red of the fire his snow-white horses had taken on a rosy hue, while his golden chariot seemed to blaze with a light of its own so brilliantly did it shine in the fire's flame. Beaming with delight he drew the horses to a halt and held his meaty arms aloft. At last he felt like a deity, a veritable god, mighty as Mars – more brilliant than Apollo.

Seeing that smile, Karkinos knew that the Empire of Rome belonged to his master and that the possessed Emperor's usefulness was spent. With Rome's jails virtually empty and their occupants either dead or dying, Caesar's purpose was over. Soon it would be time for Satan's puppet to leave life's stage.

Meanwhile, the Emperor had paused to examine a victim and in turn the court stopped to see what it was about the poor wretch that had caught Caesar's attention.

To the shouts and plaudits of the mob he stepped down from his quadriga, handing the reins to the driver who had stood deferentially aside when his master had elected to play at being charioteer.

As Caesar alighted, Tigellinus firmly at his side with a dozen hand picked Praetorians, the court surrounded him. With Karkinos on his other side, he waddled down the broad avenue. In his hand he carried a monocle ground from amethyst. From time to time he would pause to use it, peering short-sightedly at the poor wretch writhing in agony above him.

Sometimes he would address the victim directly, but more frequently he threw sarcastic remarks at the suffering person, to the delight of the crowds who urged him to even greater excesses.

As Nero made his stately progress he could occasionally hear shouts of "Ahenobarbus! Ahenobarbus! Where did you put that beard?

Did Rome catch fire from it?" And of Poppaea, whom they detested, the commonest insult they hurled at her as she passed was "Flavacoma" – whore.

Nero didn't mind about the beard so much, for he had long ago shaved it off, but what he did mind were those hidden in the crowd who shouted "Matricide! Nero – murderer – where is Octavia? Surrender the purple."

The fear of rebellion was like a nightmare for the Roman aristocracy and nobody worried more about such a possibility than Nero. His spies were everywhere and they, in turn, were spied upon by those in the employ of Tigellinus and Karkinos.

Rumours of hundreds of thousands of malcontents merely waiting for a chance to seize arms and strike at their oppressors had circulated since the time of Spartacus. Now, after the fire, thousands of homeless people were squatting not only in Caesar's gardens but also in those that had belonged to Domitius and Agrippina.

Thousands more were camped along the Campus Martico huddled in portals, games courts, summerhouses and the buildings that had housed specimen wild beasts which had either escaped or been barbecued by the hungry mob before supplies had started to come in from the neighbouring port of Ostia.

Here vessels were arriving so frequently it became possible to walk as on a bridge over ships, boats and barges from one side of the harbour to the other.

To keep the mob happy, wheat was being distributed for free, while slaves who worked in relays around the clock unloaded vast quantities of wine, olives and nuts.

Sheep and cattle were driven to the city's abattoirs every day from the pastures of the Alban Hills and gradually from more outlying districts as herds were butchered and eaten. Wretches who, before the fire, had slept in the gutters of the city's worst slums and starved to death had, for the first time in their lives, enough to eat.

As a result of Caesar's bounty, the danger of famine was averted, but not that of robbery and murder. Squatting among the city's ruins, the worst of its criminal element proclaimed themselves to be admirers of Caesar and cheered him wherever he appeared.

But, the rule of law could no longer be enforced and public order crumbled along with public safety. Every night there were battles and murders and faction fights and gang warfare raged. Women were ambushed and frequently kidnapped – not for ransom but for violating in the most abominable way.

At the Porta Mugionis, where there was a halting place for the herds driven from Campania, battles were fought in which hundreds died. Every morning the banks of the Tiber were strewn with dead bodies cast like flotsam along both shores. As no one burned these corpses they decayed rapidly and the stench was appalling. Sickness broke out on the camping ground and pestilence threatened.

To placate the indignation of the city's law-abiding citizens, Nero proclaimed that a new Rome would be built renamed Necropolis. In the meantime he would entertain the people with games and circuses such as the world had never seen before, and the bounty promised in his name by Petronius would flow endlessly.

# 29

Emerging into the crowded street Clodia was momentarily confused. All her thoughts had been directed towards escape. Escape and revenge.

As the wagon rumbled out of the gate and away from captivity she was suddenly at a loss as to her next move. Drawing the mules to a halt she twisted anxiously on the wagon's rough seat, but the gate had closed reassuringly behind her.

"Help us." The suddenness of the voice made her jump, as did its close proximity. Incongruously it came from a head scarcely a foot from her own. Startled, she found herself staring into the face of one of the Semaxii that was her cargo.

"Please… in God's name, help us. Help us! In Christ's name help my child." Softly the pitiful cries rose from all parts of the wagon as more and more victims added their urgent pleas.

Clodia frowned. A number of people in the crowded street were beginning to take an interest in her load. The public was used to seeing people being burnt to death having been prepared in this particular manner, but only occasionally came into contact with the victims being transported. Theirs was the interest of the spectator at a zoo seeing a specimen for the first time outside its cage.

Ignoring the cries and groans behind her, Clodia picked up her whip and got her mules moving. She was uncomfortably close to the dungeons of the Circus Maximus.

Her plan was to find a quiet backwater and simply dump the wagon and its contents, old habits of self-preservation automatically reasserting themselves.

"Help us and our friends will help you."

Clodia ignored the voice at her shoulder and concentrated on driving. By now she had edged the wagon out of the web of narrow streets surrounding the amphitheatre and was making swift progress down one of the broad avenues that led to the Via Salaria and the Nomentana Gate. What she would do when she got there, if she was challenged by the guard, she was uncertain about. She was, however, determined not to be retaken alive.

"Turn left through the gate, say you are taking us on the ring road to the other side of the city," said the owner of the voice immediately behind her left shoulder.

Clodia didn't respond but when the guard who had waved her down asked what her destination was, she took the anonymous advice and said the other side of the capital.

"Skirt the cemetery at Ostrianum." The voice was urgent. "There is a side road at the far corner of the cemetery where you can get out of sight in the woods which cover the hill."

Sweating with anxiety Clodia cracked her whip and urged the mules to a trot, the wagon swaying wildly on the road's uneven surface. As she rumbled through the gate she turned left because the road to the right was blocked with a refugee camp that had sprouted on the open ground outside the walls and overflowed into the road. To her relief the road she was on was almost free of traffic and the number of people squatting along its length was thinning the further she got out of the city.

She glimpsed the wooded hillside before she saw the narrow track leading through a corner of the cemetery. On a sudden impulse she swung the wagon off the road. The mules, which had been driven hard, were tiring and, in spite of the whip that cracked around their ears, slowed to a walk.

The track leading into the woods was deserted and Clodia was contemplating leaping off the wagon when the wood came into view. Its trunks and shrubby undergrowth offered a temporary sanctuary and was, she reasoned, as good a place as any to abandon the wagon.

Hauling on the reins she pulled the cart off the track, standing for balance in the well of the seat as it tipped and bucked across the rough ground.

Under the woodland canopy the forest floor was surprisingly level and the wheels ran almost silently over the springy swarf of dead leaves. Within minutes she had penetrated far enough into the trees to be completely hidden from the view of any casual passer-by.

As the wagon rocked to a halt she coiled the whip and jumped down, head turning from side to side as she anxiously peered through the surrounding trees.

"In Jesus's name, help us." Clodia's brow knitted. Reluctantly she turned towards the sound of the voice. This time it had come from a child. Clodia's heart lurched at the sight of the tiny head protruding from its prison bonds of tarred swaddling.

The child who had claimed her attention was barely three. As his eyes met Clodia's his bottom lip trembled. "Please, lady, help my mama," and she thought of Joshua and how soon he would have been a child like this. With an oath she snatched up her stolen knife and attacked the child's bindings.

It took her an hour to free those that still lived and she would not have managed that if one of the strongest survivors hadn't slipped away for help. This was fortunately at hand, for many Christians had fled to the caves that honeycombed Ostrianum, which had been used for years as a natural cemetery by the less well-to-do Romans.

With reaction setting in Clodia was suddenly weary and allowed herself to be led, with the surviving escapees, into this underground refuge. To her amazement it seemed to run for miles, and even with her unerring sense of direction she doubted she could have found her way out unaided, so many twists and turns did they take before coming to rest in a natural chamber.

Tired as she was, she was surprised at the number of people who had crowded into the cave's sanctuary. Shrewdly she noted that this large, apparently disorganised mass of people was, in fact, well ordered and managed by a group of young men who brought food and water and found resting places for the escapees, many of whom were trembling badly as shock set in.

Gratefully Clodia accepted the water one of these handed to her. As she sipped she became aware of a sudden rustle of excitement rippling through the crowded cavern. Nervously she gripped the arm of the youth that had brought her the water. "What's happening?" she snapped.

"He is with us."

"Who," she demanded angrily, "is he?"

As if in answer to her question the cause of the excitement came into view. It was an old man, leaning on a staff, making his way slowly through the people who crowded round him, anxious to touch him as though by doing so they could capture some of the massive calm that seemed to surround him like an invisible but tangible aura.

Clodia was suddenly aware that he was looking at her. One of the women who had been a prisoner on her wagon was pointing her out. The man with the staff peered through the gloom, the only light coming from torches stuck into crevices along the cave walls. Clodia stiffened as he came towards her, the crowd parting to let him through.

Impassively he surveyed the tense woman. "The Lord Jesus Christ has sent you to us, daughter. In his name we shall give thanks to God for His instrument of salvation."

Clodia nodded tersely and would have turned away but for his next remark. "What is it you seek, child, that fills your heart with so much sorrow?"

Clodia could barely bring herself to speak. When she did it was in a whisper. "I seek the man who is the brother of the man you know as Jesus."

Those near enough to hear what she said turned in amazement at what they heard and repeated it to their neighbours. Within seconds the whole cave had the news. The old man's eyes widened and he involuntarily held out his arms.

"And," she finished, suddenly bursting into tears, "our son."

Leaning against the man's breast, in the shelter of his comforting arms, Clodia recounted her story and when she growled out her hatred of Tigellinus he shushed her, patting her back as though she was a child. When she was calmer he held her at arm's length. Smiling slightly he said, "Your husband scours Rome for you and daily goes to the arena, fearing that you have been taken by Tigellinus as a Christian."

Clodia gave a great shout of joy – "I must go to him" – and would have dashed away.

Peter restrained her. "We will get word to him and arrange a meeting outside Rome. Any attempt by you to go to the arena would only result in both of you being arrested."

Clodia started to protest but the old Apostle laid a hand on her shoulder, continuing, "Tigellinus has men everywhere. He must know that Simon is coming to the Circus Maximus almost daily. He leaves him alone," he added gently, "because Karkinos tells him to – for he is the bait for your recapture." His voice saddened. "Many will die tonight and I must be with them when the end comes. In the meantime, rest. You are safe here."

Almost fainting with relief, Clodia allowed herself to be shown to a simple couch. No sooner had she slumped on it than she fell asleep.

## 30

"Insurrection?" Caesar whispered the word, eyes wide with disbelief.

A grey faced Tigellinus and three of the Praetorian's most senior officers were each knelt on one knee, heads bent, in front of the seated Emperor.

To his left, in a cloud of her own courtiers, the heavily pregnant Poppaea froze like a cheetah into a hunting stillness.

"Insurrection?" This time it was bellowed as the white mountain moved. Nero rose to his feet, shaking with rage. Saliva flew from his lips, his jaws worked, he was incoherent with anger.

With sweat streaming down his ashen face Tigellinus continued with his report. "Galba with the sixth, the ninth and the eleventh legions who have declared him Caesar, is marching on Rome."

"Crush him. You have the Praetorian." The outraged Nero was shambling up and down the room, his head swinging from side to side. Had he ever seen one, Tigellinus would have been reminded of a polar bear. The little red eyes suddenly fixed on the luckless Praetorian commander. "We can count on the Praetorian?"

"To the death."

"It may come to that sooner than you think," snapped Nero viciously. "Why is Galba doing this to me?" The bottom lip trembled and a fat tear ran down the white cheeks. Nero shivered uncontrollably. Unconsciously he lifted the hem of his toga and put it in his mouth, sucking on it noisily.

"Vespasian." Nero's arm shot out and he clutched his guard commander's arm. "Recall Vespasian and his legions from Palestine."

Tigellinus swallowed and tried to answer, but failed – the words simply wouldn't come out. One of his officers came to his aid though even his voice faltered. "Vespasian's troops will take three months to reach Rome, Divinity."

Nero screamed at this news. He tugged at the neck of his tunic, ripping it along the seam. Foam collected at the corners of his mouth. "You," he pointed a shaking finger at Tigellinus, "are supposed to protect me, to lay down your life for me."

"Majesty, the Praetorian are loyal, I swear it."

Nero charged across the room to stand inches from the quaking guard commander. "Where is the army? Rome has fourteen divisions to defend her."

"They stand aside, Divinity, to see which way the gods will declare."

"Stand aside – gods?" Nero was apoplectic. "I am a god, how dare they not worship me. Why would they desert me?"

Tigellinus could find no answer to this.

"Karkinos." Nero's voice rose in triumph. "Send for the magus – through him we will summon legions from Hades, soldiers who are immortal. Galba and every man who fights under him will be crucified. Go!"

Shaking with reaction, the Praetorian officers and their commander backed out of the room. Left alone but for a silent, still Poppaea, whom he had either forgotten or was ignoring, the gross white figure lumbered up and down the room. Poppaea lay impassively on her side, a bejewelled hand resting possessively on the mound of her belly.

"Perhaps," she said softly, "now is the time to declare our unborn son your heir."

The sweating Emperor froze in mid stride, the button eyes focusing short-sightedly on the reclining Poppaea. Without warning his foot lashed out. She screamed in agony as the toe of the heavy sandal buried itself in her belly. Grunting with the effort, the big man savagely booted her again. At last he had found something on which to vent his anger and frustration.

"If," he panted between kicks, "your bastard" – kick – "wants" – kick – "to wear" – kick – "the purple, he had better put in an appearance."

In helpless horror the Augusta's servants watched as blood suddenly coursed down the legs of the semi-conscious Empress. At the sight of blood Nero beamed at the broken figure rolling at his feet, moaning in agony. Before leaving the chamber he turned the twitching Poppaea over with his toe and jumped on her from a small stool.

## 31

W hen the girl touched the shoulder of the sleeping Clodia, she awoke instantly. There was no preliminary stretching or yawning, a gathering together of thoughts. As the fingertips touched her shoulder she was awake, eyes open, watchful, hostile.

Even as the girl blinked and started back in some confusion, Clodia was on her feet in a single sinuous movement.

"Yes?" The voice was as cold as the eyes that looked past her, flicking from side to side, taking in every detail of the surroundings.

The girl was suddenly reminded of one of the great cats that she had seen being transported in a wheeled cage from the docks on its way to the arena. "I am taking you to Lavinum, a fishing village near Ostia."

Clodia, who by now was gathering up her belongings, replied abruptly. "You are taking me nowhere. I have things to do which are no concern of these people." She nodded towards the nearest of the many groups crowded into the cavern.

"Your man will be waiting for you at Lavinum." The speaker, a heavily built, middle aged peasant, was helping to distribute water which he carried in buckets suspended from a wooden yoke across his shoulders.

The distance between Clodia and the water bearer seemed to dissolve. One second she was ten feet from him and the next less than ten inches.

"And death will be waiting for you if he isn't." Clodia breathed the words into his face, trembling from head to toe with emotion. She was like a runner straining at the block, compressed like a wound spring.

The man bent to release himself from his burden. In the flickering torchlight the flash of an eye, the sudden exposure of bared teeth, marked the two faces, barely inches apart.

"Peter has asked – no, ordained – that it should be, and it will." The man's voice was flat. He made no effort to conceal his dislike for her, and he certainly wasn't afraid of her. In spite of his recent conversion to Christianity he was scandalised at her half-naked appearance and the fact that she bore arms like a man.

Clodia searched his face, hardly daring to hope, terrified of a trap. The man picked up his buckets. "The girl and her companions will take you to the village. Daily they bring fish to Rome's markets and they pass backwards and forwards without notice."

Clodia glanced inquiringly at the girl who nodded in eager confirmation. Clodia's heart soared.

"When," she gasped, "do we leave?"

It was the girl who replied in a soft, nervous voice. "The women who will take the empty boxes back to the village leave in a few minutes."

Suddenly Clodia was aware of the small group of people who had gathered in a loose half circle round her and the girl. Swiftly she scanned their faces and relaxed. She had nothing to fear, she thought, from this flotsam of battered humanity. Ignoring the noose of bruised faces, she scooped up her few belongings and gave the girl a sharp push on the shoulder.

"Let's go."

One of the onlooker's spoke, extending a nervous hand, which rested lightly on her arm.

"To whom should we give thanks for our lives?"

Clodia was puzzled by the question; she was also totally disinterested in it. Pushing the cowed girl ahead of her she shouldered her way through the frail knot of people and made for the entrance.

The girl looked at Clodia's face and murmured, "They were the people you freed. They came to thank you."

"Lead me to my husband and the debt will be repaid," she responded abruptly.

## 32

The village was a string of net festooned huts on each side of a lightly wooded ravine with a stream running along the bottom. The day's fishing over, the villagers' boats were pulled up onto the sharply sloping beach at the end of this secluded canyon.

It was early evening and in the simple stone huts lamps were being lit. From the beach they glowed like a row of lanterns strung unevenly through the trees.

Clodia had been told to wait on the beach. Always suspicious, she had checked the upturned boats and had even climbed the low sand hills before settling down to wait. She was glad of the fading light – darkness was neutral and if under its cover she faced a sudden attack it would, she reasoned, be easier for a single person to avoid capture.

A flicker of movement at the seaward end of the headland caught her attention. A small boat, its sail set to assist the rowers, had rounded the point. She crouched between the fishing boats, eyes slitted against the setting sun as the boat bounced across the bars of bright water. Apart from the breeze rustling through the marram grass and the waves skirling across the foreshore, it was reassuringly quiet.

The villagers had sworn that nobody could approach the beach either from the headland or the canyon without them knowing and a warning diversion had been planned for such an eventuality.

Against the fierce brightness of the sunset the boat and its occupants were a fuzzy arrowhead, silhouetted against the darkening sky, the oarsmen bobbing rhythmically as they bent to their blades.

As the craft came inshore the dark figure in the prow, the banner of his wind blown cloak lifting from his shoulders, vaulted into the waist deep swirling waters, pushing the boat out so that it could stand off.

"Simon." The cry torn from her throat was as harsh as the scream of the skimming gulls.

The man spun round, legs spread against the lift of the waves' roll. Clodia charged across the sand. Halfway down the steeply shelving beach she fell, but rolled and was up, pounding through the shallow water. She screamed his name, the sound smothered by the wind.

Simon, hip deep in the surging water, opened his arms and struggled, churning, towards the running figure. As he waded onto dry land Clodia, without slackening speed, leapt straight into his arms and knocked him flat on his back. As he opened his mouth to say something the next wave rolled over them both. Spluttering and coughing he struggled to his feet with Clodia clamped to him.

Her arms were wound round his chest and her legs round his hips as though welded there. With her face buried in the angle of his neck and shoulder, she growled his name over and over.

With his unwieldy burden Simon was knocked down twice by incoming waves, with Clodia oblivious to the threat of drowning. He eventually struggled doggedly out of the surf to collapse on the dark sand, where Clodia told him about the deaths of Miriam and Kino and others that had formed their household and finally, breaking down in tears, of the loss of their son.

Later, huddled together in the shelter of one of the upturned boats, she spoke of Tigellinus in a voice that raised the hairs on the back of Simon's neck.

He shushed her like a child and said, "Galba has risen. Nero has insurrection along the borders of his empire, and Vespasian's legions have declared him Imperator. Soon the Empire will have a new master." Simon continued, "and Tigellinus, together with all the other puppets, will be swept from the stage."

Clodia raised her head from his shoulder. "And this Galba, whose tune will he dance to?"

Simon hugged her to him and she responded by burrowing into his side like a puppy. "To Karkinos." The harshness of his voice caused her to stiffen. She had forgotten about the Greek magician. "Karkinos," Simon continued grimly, "will have it all, and even as I speak Roman legions march on Jerusalem."

Wordlessly, Clodia stared questioningly into the bleak face. Simon continued, staring as blind as Homer across the wind black sea, "Jerusalem will be gone forever, its walls crushed beneath the hooves of the great beast of Babylon, its tormented people swept from its burning stones and cast into the void. Scattered like chaff on the wind of desolation."

"But," Clodia croaked, "your God is greater than Satan. Will he not save His people?"

Simon hung his head. By now it was pitch dark and it was only by feeling the movement of his body that Clodia was aware of his sudden dejection. For long minutes he didn't reply. So long as the silence she thought he wasn't going to speak. A long sigh escaped him. When he finally spoke it was in a whisper so soft she had to hold an ear to his lips to catch what he said. "We have forsaken our God so he chastises us."

"But what kind of god destroys his own people?"

"We destroy ourselves. He gives us the choice – to follow the Light or the great Satan, the Prince of Darkness, ruler of this world and all matter."

Clodia was baffled. "But Satan," she shouted angrily, "is winning. After Jerusalem, Rome. After Rome, the Empire. Your people," she continued, "are destroyed, the Christians annihilated before they even get going. And our child is dead," she ended hoarsely, her body suddenly racked by the tremors of her tears.

"Joshua is lost but not dead."

Clodia tore herself free from his embrace. "Lord, do you forget what I was, what he has become, what tit he has sucked at?" The question was hissed at him in the darkness.

Simon stood up in the gloom. He could scarcely see Clodia who was crouched face down on all fours. "You forget too quickly, woman, the power that cleansed you." He paused and Clodia remained frozen, silent. "He is kept safe by that power which he has in his blood. The Light of the World is hidden from his enemy by the hand of God."

"He lives?" Clodia sprang up. He could feel the tension in the quivering body next to his. Gently he took her face between his palms. In the dark she could just make out his features. "Yes, my love. Covered by the wings of the Archangel Gabriel, protected by the power of the prophets, by the spirit of Elijah, of Moses and Isiah, he is waiting for us."

Clodia was speechless with joy. Simon bent and busied himself with the simple lamp that he had brought ashore and had waited patiently for it to dry out. She knelt beside him, shielding the spark from the flint from the gusting wind. "Was..." Clodia's voice was husky, "was the one they call the Christ, the promised one?"

The flame caught suddenly, a tiny nest of brightness. Carefully Simon blew on it, teasing out the fluff of the tinder to catch the flame. As it caught he leaned back on his heels, feeding it minute scraps of material. In the flicker of that tiny light she could see his eyes; they were like obsidian.

"I don't know," he replied, his voice breaking with emotion.

Clodia waited, frozen. She trembled as a tear suddenly welled and rolled down Simon's shadowed face. Its wetness splashed her hands, warm as blood. She swallowed, terrified of asking the next question.

Simon stood up holding the now burning lamp beneath his cloak and showed its light to the sea. The answering twinkle told Clodia that the boat in which he had come ashore was standing to. She shrugged off the crowding questions. Her child was waiting to be found, her man was by her side. She hugged him joyfully.

With arms locked about each other they went down to meet the boat. At the water's edge he turned to face her. "The boat will take you to a ship waiting further out."

Before he could say anything else Clodia grabbed both of his arms. "You are sending me away?" She dropped to her knees. "Lord, kill me." Like magic a blade appeared in her hand, its point drawing blood at her throat, "but do not send me from your side."

The boat scraped on the sand and a dark figure leaped over the side to hold it steady. Simon knelt to face her, his hand closing over hers, drawing the knifepoint away. "The ship will take you south to our child."

"Come with me, lord. Why do you stay? Let Galba have what is left of Rome and her Empire."

"Karkinos." Clodia shivered at the sound of the beast's name; its very sound invoked in her a nameless dread. "First I must face the great beast or he will hunt our son forever."

She moaned and clung to him more fiercely.

"My lord, the wind is rising, we must go." It was the boatman who spoke.

Simon shook her. "Faith," he said, "have faith in the power of the one God."

Clodia's fingers slackened. Dully she let her arms drop to her sides. He lifted her into the boat, which lifted under an incoming wave and rocked wildly. "Go," he commanded.

Without wasting breath the dark figure struggling to keep the boat steady pushed off the beach and scrambled inside. With a few powerful strokes the oarsmen pulled her through the undertow.

Clodia crawled to the stern. The man on the beach was barely discernible. "I love you," she screamed.

The boat dipped and he was gone; when it rose he was further away. A momentary, fragmentary figure lost in the dark shadows of the upturned hulls on the beach.

"Wait for me in Herculaneum." The thin voice pendulumed fretfully on the wind.

Weeping bitterly, Clodia sank to her knees in the pitching boat. As they came alongside a larger vessel she shrugged off the helping hands and scrambled up the nets and over the side. As she gained the deck the moon broke through the clouds and she instinctively turned her face heavenwards. "Jesus," she whispered "help him."

# 33

While a few people had camped in the gardens of Aigokerös, most shunned the grounds of the Greek magician's palace and nobody dared approach any of its buildings.

It was midday when Simon, carrying the sacred spear, slipped unchallenged through its gates and made his way quietly to a shrubby area close to the main building. Standing beneath the canopy of a large bush he scanned the area for signs of life.

A bee droned by. He watched its erratic flight across the shrub's honey rich blossoms. It was late in the season and as the insect hovered among the flower heads, petals broke off and fluttered down to join a pink and white drift among the looping roots.

Simon shivered, though not with cold. The silence was oppressive. He could feel the presence of an alien force, a field of energy that shimmered like the mesh of an invisible web as he approached it. Sweating profusely he warily entered one of the outer courts – but it was deserted, as was every other room that he explored.

Even when he penetrated the Greek's personal apartments he found nothing. Nothing had been disturbed or was out of place. The fruit on the table was as fresh as though it had been picked within the hour.

Carefully he began a search for the temple's hidden entrance. In one of the apartment's walls he found a hairline crack masked by a decorative moulding. Running the tips of his fingers over the moulding he sought a hidden lock.

Suddenly he had difficulty in breathing. It was as though a band had tightened around his chest. Gasping for air he raised the spear, intending to force it into the crack. Before he could do so, the door flew open with a bang that caused his heart to thump.

It was dark inside except for a faint glow – a pulse of energy coming from somewhere inside the vault. Simon knew that this was the temple of Satan and that the altar to the great beast lay within. He stood just inside the doorway, his chin slightly raised, every sense alert.

"We are like the blind combatants – the Andabates – you and I, struggling to find each other through a dark eternity."

Simon swallowed at the sound of the voice. He recognised its owner instantly. "If you have sought me, Greek, then give me your hand so that never again will you lose me." As Simon spoke, he slipped into the room. Balancing his spear in his right hand, he groped into the darkness with his left. He felt the door close behind him.

The voice chuckled. "So anxious for combat when the war is over." The source of the voice was impossible to place. It seemed to flow around the room. The energy field, though, was constant. It dimly lit a huge basalt slab, an altar on which lay Karkinos's sacred sword. Simon caught its reflection as he turned cautiously towards the glow.

"You will never find the child." Simon's probing statement drew a grating reply.

"I have all eternity to complete that hunt. The game I seek now is here – you are my quarry."

"Liar," Simon shouted, angered at the casual and belittling reference to his son. "This," and with a sudden lunge he placed the spear point on the stone floor, "is what you seek," and before the voice could reply he drew a fiery circle around himself, flames springing up from its tip as it traced its protective arc.

"Jew," Karkinos thundered. "You dare challenge my power with your miserable dart?"

The altar glowed, a swelling of intense cosmic light. Simon crouched in his circle, one hand shielding his eyes from that terrible radiance. Through the latticework of his fingers he squinted as the sight of the magus rising majestically on its tumescence. Sword in hand, clothed in gold and silver armour and crowned with a casque set with precious stones, the awesome figure stood challengingly on the jet black of the altar, laved in starfire brighter than the brightest sun.

"Behold, Simon bar Joseph, and weep for your son, for the days are coming in which they shall say to the mountains 'fall on us', and to the hills 'cover us'." As he spoke, Karkinos swept his sword above his head. In a burst of blinding light it sheared the walls of the building, exploding them apart.

Within his circle Simon watched the temple disintegrate in a fire that burned stone. As the roof and walls dissolved in flames, he was dismayed to see that not only had Karkinos's garden caught fire but so had the neighbouring buildings and streets.

They were completely surrounded by fire. The magus sprang fearlessly into the heart of the flames declaring, "Satan, the ruler of this and future worlds, will destroy the father who cast him out of Heaven. Simon bar Joseph worship Satan, the true son of God, and in his service great will be your glory."

The walls of the temple had gone and the trees in the park were exploding in spontaneous conflagration.

"Karkinos," Simon shouted. "Nero is doomed. Rome, the great beast of Babylon is in ashes. But death has not finished, magus, he is close at hand and will not depart until one of us joins him."

Karkinos mocked Simon. "You speak of death. I speak of oblivion. Your God is dying and he and all that believe in him will be returned to nothingness. Creation itself will cease to exist."

Simon swallowed hard. "God the Creator of All," he replied defiantly, "the known and the unknown, of that which is the spirit and that which is flesh. His existence denies nothingness. To be excluded forever from God's presence, denied His love, that is nothingness, oblivion, true death."

"And what," asked Karkinos slyly, "of Satan? That which you call evil not only exists, it prospers. Proof is all around you. Man has chosen to live by the sword."

Before Simon could reply, the Greek continued mockingly, "This God, this Jehovah you Jews are forever whining to created me. He created Satan." The sarcastic banter of the Greek's voice suddenly changed to a harsh challenging tone. "Without your so-called God's consent, how can Evil exist?"

There was the briefest of pauses. In its silence Simon could feel doubt creeping into his heart.

"Satan," Karkinos continued, making no effort to conceal the triumph in his voice, "was created by your God, for without his consent how can the dark force you call Evil exist?"

"God created consciousness in man," responded Simon. "This divine gift sets him above every living thing in His creation. It gives man an understanding of choice, an understanding of good and evil and the freewill to follow either. Satan exists so that man can exercise that choice."

"And," interrupted Karkinos jubilantly, "man has chosen Satan, for only those who are strong enough to take what they want by force can live as free men."

"You deceive yourself Karkinos, as Satan deceives you. Man can never uncover the mystery that is God. In the beginning everything, including Evil and its servant Satan, was His creation. Everything is God's creation because only God is eternal – ever was – ever will be."

"And at the end of time," the magus asked, "who will rule everything?"

"You speak of beginnings and ends as though time existed outside man's consciousness," said Simon, watching his adversary carefully, relying on his instincts to tell him when to cast the spear he balanced in his right hand.

Before Karkinos could reply, he continued, "This time you speak of is man's invention to mark his days and measure his life. For the eternal God, who has always existed, there is only the present. Past and future are concepts man uses to frame his mortality. Satan, and those who choose to serve him, must eventually cease to exist because they are not eternal."

"A clever argument, worthy of the Greek philosophers," Karkinos growled, twisting his head as though Simon's words were arrows to be avoided.

Before he could continue, Simon seized that momentary lapse of concentration. Rocking back on his heels he was beyond fear. Incoherent with rage he sprang from his circle. Like an ancient Greek athlete the heavily muscled body was wound like a spring, the bent right arm gathering power for the classic javelin throw.

As the Spear of Longinus flew from Simon's fingers, the magus raised his glittering sword to deflect the missile hurtling like a comet towards him.

Blinded, Simon hid his face in the crook of his arm.

Dissolving into a whirlpool of cosmic energy, the magus mocked him, "I must leave you. I have an appointment with your son."

Simon raised his head. The roof had gone. The walls and gardens was a lake of fire. The streets across the park were sheets of flame, which showed the ribs of burnt out buildings.

Pausing only to recover the spear, Simon scrambled through the burning timbers and flung himself onto the cinder-encrusted lawn. It was almost impossible to breathe in the superheated air. Earth and sky were an inverted molten bowl. There was no horizon – no up, no down.

The Palace of Aigokerös had gone. Advancing walls of flame surrounded him. There was no question of escape, there was simply nowhere to go.

Resigned to his death Simon dropped to his knees, head bowed. His clothes and hair were smouldering. "Jehovah," he prayed, "into Thy hands I commend my spirit."

"Simon." The familiar voice was achingly remembered.

"Jesus," he whispered, raising his smoking head. His heart lurched for, impossibly untouched by the fire, a familiar figure was walking towards him, hands outstretched.

## 34

From the open flap of his campaign tent Galba could see Rome. A pall of smoke hung over the city, unable to disperse in the early morning stillness. Of the fourteen districts of Rome there remained only four. Fire had destroyed all the others.

Amidst the ashes an immense space was visible from the Tiber to the Esquiline – grey, gloomy, dead. In this space could be seen rows of chimneys like columns over graves in a cemetery. Among them large crowds of people moved about in the daytime, some seeking for precious objects, others for the bones of those dear to them. At night, dogs howled above the ashes and ruins of former dwellings.

All the bounty and aid Caesar dispensed did not stop the people complaining. Only the gangs of criminals and homeless poor, who could eat, drink and rob, were contented. People who had lost all their property and their nearest relatives were not won over by the opening of gardens, the distribution of bread or the promises of gifts and games.

As Galba breakfasted, the routine bustle of the Roman military machine reassembling itself for a new day's business went on all around. His senior officers, whom he had just finished briefing, stood about him enjoying the comradeship of a simple meal – crusty bread, cheese, olives and anchovies and young red wine cut with fresh spring water.

The young tribune who had led out a dawn scouting party swung down from his horse and fussily adjusted his uniform before reporting, "The road to the city is clear of everything except normal early morning market traffic, sir."

"And the surrounding countryside?"

"No troops, sir, though large numbers of refugees from the fire are camped in the groves and cemeteries close to the walls and along the line of the streams that feed the Tiber."

One of Galba's senior officers interjected, "could you see how much damage yesterday's latest outbreak did?"

The tribune turned and replied, "Yes sir. We rode up to the gates themselves, which were manned by reserve troops. We could have entered the city, had we wished. The fire seems to have been contained. So much of the western side of the city had already gone, its burned out streets acted as a firebreak."

"And the people?" It was Galba who spoke.

"Either in a state of shock, sir, or running wild," was the reply.

Galba nodded. "We must," he said, more to himself than to his officers, "question one of them as soon as possible, preferably an educated man whose report will assist us in planning our strategy." He paused and then went on briskly, "Dismissed, gentlemen. We march at once."

The group saluted, murmuring and nodding agreement, and started to break up.

"Sir." The young scout was diffident.

"Yes?" Galba said shortly, anxious to get moving while the tide was flowing in his favour.

"We found a man outside the walls. He was lying exhausted in a ditch. From his dress he is a Roman citizen of some substance."

The Roman general's eyes flashed with interest. "Where is this man now?"

"With the master-at-arms, sir, who has orders to tend to his needs."

Galba smiled, indicating with a wave of his hand that his staff officers should wait. "Bring him before us," he ordered.

The centurion saluted and hurried away, returning almost immediately with his captive.

Galba thoughtfully surveyed the man who stood before him. He noticed with some curiosity that though a civilian he was using a Roman spear to support himself. "You are somewhat singed," the soldier said dryly.

The figure leaning on the spear made no reply.

With a practised eye Galba noted that the man's injuries were superficial – minor burns to face and arms, a few cuts and bruises. He was, though, clearly exhausted. His clothes, though filthy, were those of a man of rank. The haggard face gave nothing away; the deeply sunken eyes that stared back of him were carefully blank of all expression.

"Who are you?" For a moment the Roman general thought he wasn't going to get an answer.

When he did the voice was hoarse. "Simon bar Joseph, a Jew and a citizen of Rome, sir."

"A Jew maybe" – Galba's voice took on a more menacing tone. "Or a criminal perhaps. One of the scum who take advantage of the lack of order and steal whatever comes to hand, including the toga you are wearing."

"My captains at Ostia will vouch for me. If," he concluded, coughing, "the man who stole the Empire has not sold them and their ships to pay for his games."

"Sir, I know this man. At first, because of his condition, I wasn't sure, but he is who he claims to be." It was one of the centurions who spoke. "I saw him in Egypt some years ago. He was with the Pro-Consul and they were finalising the contract to ship the grain harvest."

With this the Roman general visibly relaxed. "We must learn more, and quickly, for we march within the hour."

Seeing the unkempt figure sway slightly, not yet recovered from the exhaustion of his ordeal, Galba ordered that a stool be brought which Simon gratefully accepted. For over an hour, in a voice strained and hoarse from the smoke he had inhaled, Simon recounted the savage debauchery of Nero and Tigellinus. He made no mention of Karkinos, for what he was would have been beyond Galba's comprehension.

When he had finished, the Roman general gave orders to break camp, offering Simon a place at his side so that he might "return to face the tyrant and accuse him of the murder of his people."

Simon shook his head and said, "Sir, you have an empire to take. I have a family to find. Release one of my ships to me that I may travel to Herculaneum more quickly."

"If that's what you want."

"It is, sir, and with all my heart."

"So be it."

As the orders were given for the legions to form up in marching order, a scribe wrote out the order releasing the ship Simon had requested. An order Galba personally signed and fixed with seals denoting his rank and authority.

As the legions wound through the Alban Hills, they marched to the pipes and drums of a ceremonial band. Galba was to enter the Rome Nero had fled and be welcomed with garlands and branches of myrtle and tears of gratitude from its terrified citizens.

From the back of the horse given to him, Simon watched them go before turning to make for Ostia. From the crest of the hills he could catch the faint sea smell, pick up the smallest sliver of silver between the rolling hills. Wordlessly he kicked his mount into a trot and then into a gallop.

The wind pulled at his cloak and flung it like a flag over his shoulder. He stood in the saddle, the horse moving strongly under him. Across his back was slung a Roman spear.

In Herculaneum was Clodia. Together they would find Joshua whose name means – salvation.

## 35

When Simon's ship docked at Herculaneum he was met
by the harbourmaster, who had picked up from the
pennants at the masthead, that the owner of the fleet
was on board. Before the ship entered the harbour he relayed this
information to the merchant Rabbi Judah ben Isaac who had placed
a house, the Villa Keos, at Clodia's disposal with enough servants to
ensure that her temporary household could be properly maintained.

Like Simon, ben Isaac was one of those immensely wealthy Jews
who traded not just across the Roman world but also into lands
which Rome's legions hadn't penetrated.

Ben Isaac's first instinct had been to send a servant to advise
Clodia of Simon's imminent arrival, but then he decided against it.
Since her arrival in the city, she had been withdrawn and distant,
politely refusing all his invitations to dine.

In vain he had offered to show her the city; he had even made
a day boat available to her so that she could explore the beautiful
coastline – but to no avail. Clodia had been a recluse. The only
person she saw was a weapons instructor, a man who trained the
gladiators who fought in the city's famous arena.

That she should spend any of her time practising any form of
martial arts scandalised the straight-laced Jews of Herculaneum
who learned what was going on at the Villa Keos from her servants.
Angrily they had demanded that their rabbi – Judah ben Isaac –
withdraw his support of a woman whose actions would have
scandalised even a pagan Roman household.

Ben Isaac had refused but he questioned the gladiatorial instructor,
Paetus Soranus. It was he who spent up to two hours every morning

instructing Clodia in the use of not just the sword but also javelin throwing and the intricate art of the retiarius, which requires its exponent to deploy a net and a trident against an opponent.

To his amazement he learned that Soranus held a very high opinion of his pupil's skill, and would have bet on her to more than hold her own in the arena against hardened professionals, had she wished to test herself.

The rabbi had digested this information before asking, "Why does she train so hard to acquire the skills of war? Surely she cannot be thinking of entering the arena as an amateur? Her position in society would be lost forever."

Soranus had hesitated before replying. When he did his voice was deliberately impersonal. "This is no ordinary woman. She has already killed – and several times."

Ben Isaac had gasped aloud at this revelation. "How can you know that?" he finally got out.

"When you have killed as many men as I have, and trained as many more to do the same," Soranus had responded grimly, "you know."

Ben Isaac had pulled his beard and remained silent for long moments. "Who is her enemy?" he had asked shrewdly, speaking more to himself than his companion.

"Whoever has her child," had been the equally softly spoken answer.

So the rabbi had decided it would be better if he prepared Simon for what awaited him at the Villa Keos. When the ship came alongside Simon was over the rail before the plank could be run out and embraced his old friend. "Where is she?" he demanded.

Ben Isaac smiled, relieved to see that Simon appeared to have recovered from the chaos of Rome, for news of what had happened to the capital was being brought to Herculaneum almost daily by a constant stream of refugees who had fled the burning city.

"Soon enough, old friend, but we have much to talk about – arrangements to make – some," he ended delicately, "that would be best concealed from your wife."

Simon looked sharply at the old merchant. He trusted this man's judgement above most.

"Would it not be best," ben Isaac continued softly, "to plan how we might get news of the child without involving your wife…" There was a long pause. Simon considered this thoughtfully. He had a sudden memory of Clodia on the beach.

"Get on with it, man," he answered gruffly, hardly daring to trust his voice.

The old Jew pursed his lips and squinted in the bright sunlight. When he spoke his voice was flat, devoid of all emotion. "By now the child will be a leper."

Simon blanched but the rabbi was remorseless. Grasping Simon by the arm he continued grimly, "Even if you could find the child, think what you will go through in the process, what your wife will suffer, as you trail from colony to colony, and what horror might finally await you." The old man sighed, "Leave the matter in God's hands."

Simon shook his head in contradiction. "Send messengers to every known leper colony to ask of my son. Those who serve me in this way will be paid whatever they ask."

Ben Isaac inclined his head and touched the fingers of his right hand to his forehead in acknowledgement of his friend's decision.

Simon clapped a hand to the old man's shoulder. "Send word to me old friend, but secretly, so that I can have time to prepare Clodia for whatever lies ahead," and with that he was gone, leaping into the chariot that the merchant had had the foresight to arrange.

Simon's unannounced arrival at the Vila Keos caused joyous pandemonium, and for only the second time since she had been handed over as a child to the lepers of Judaea, Clodia wept.

Without speaking Simon wrapped his arms around her and let her cry herself out. When she finally stopped sobbing he said gently, "There are very few lepers in Italy and their places of refuge are known. We will find Joshua, I promise you."

Clodia sighed and snuggled close to him. She felt ashamed of her unspoken doubts. In spite of her own cure, her ingrained fear of the loathsome disease was something she couldn't shake off. But she kept her thoughts to herself and hugged her man fiercely. "I love you," she said, in a voice shaking with emotion.

Simon hugged her back and said gently, "To the end of my days you are my heart, my life, my love. Never again while I live shall you leave my side."

That night as Clodia lay in his arms, Simon told her of the struggle with Karkinos and his deliverance from the fire.

For the first time since Joshua had been taken from her, Clodia dared to believe her son would be safe and that he would be returned to her. "Will," she whispered to Simon, "will Jesus help him as he helped you?"

Simon didn't answer immediately and, as the silence lengthened, Clodia thought she wasn't going to get a response. Then, gently stroking her hair, he murmured quietly, "Joshua doesn't need Jesus's help – he has God's."

## 36

S haking his shoulder, Clodia awakened Simon. As he gathered his sleep-befuddled thoughts she whispered urgently to him, "We have a visitor."

As Simon struggled to sit up he cocked his head but could hear nothing. Without wasting any more time Clodia got out of bed, pulled a robe around her shoulders and walked across the room to draw aside the heavy window drapes. As the moonlight flooded in, Simon noticed she had picked up a short sword, which she concealed in the folds of her robe.

He was just about to tell her she was hearing things when there was a gentle tapping on the bedroom door. This was followed by the deferential voice of one of the servants. "My lord, there is a man downstairs who claims he is in your employ and must speak with you at once."

In response to Clodia's questioning look, Simon frowned and shook his head. "Who is he?" he asked the servant who had remained standing discreetly outside the door.

"He refuses to say, my lord, but he says he has word of your son."

Before Simon could even blink Clodia had the door open and was down the corridor at a dead run.

"Wait." But Simon's call was ineffectual. Sighing, he slung a cloak around his shoulders and followed the departing woman.

Simon recognised the man as one of those that ben Isaac had found who, for gold, would scour the haunts of Rome's lepers. The man was standing in the atrium under the distrustful scrutiny of the household's steward and was ignoring the barrage of questions Clodia was hurling at him.

Simon put a restraining arm around her shoulders, shushing her gently. When she was finally quiet he spoke directly to their visitor, wishing with all his heart Clodia was elsewhere but knowing it would be fruitless to try and persuade her to leave.

In the poor light of the hurriedly lit lamps there was nothing in the appearance of the man who had disturbed their sleep to inspire their confidence. It wasn't his run-down appearance or travel stained clothes that caused Simon's disquiet but rather his countenance, for he had a sly and knowing face, the demeanour of the born fixer.

"What do you have to tell us?" asked Simon evenly.

The man grinned patronisingly and bobbed his head, knuckling his forelock. "I have news of the child you seek, my lord."

Keeping his arm around Clodia and his voice under control, Simon said, "Give us your news and be assured of our gratitude."

The man shifted from one foot to the other. "I've had a long hard ride, my lord, and there is much to tell."

Clodia would have interjected but Simon spoke first. "While we talk you can take food and wine, after which you can rest," and without waiting for a response led the way into one of the villas salons where a slave was ordered to bring refreshments.

"What is your name?" Clodia asked abruptly.

"Theasides of Attica," was the response. "Freedman of Rome," he added proudly, before flopping into a chair.

"Where is my child?" Clodia couldn't hold herself back any longer.

"Well, my lady, that's a difficult question." At this point the slave returned with a board generously laden with cold meats, followed by a companion carrying a pitcher of water and several goblets. Without being asked the man picked up a chicken and tore it in half.

"One that you are in a position to answer?" This last from Simon was in a deceptively soft voice.

The man buried his face in a chicken leg. "Yes," was the muffled reply. "If the price is right."

With a howl of rage Clodia lunged across the table, the point of her sword underneath the startled man's chin before Simon could make a move. "How about your life, scum. Is that high enough?"

Red in the face and spluttering pieces of chicken, the man shouted back, "Kill me and you will never see your brat again." In spite of the sword point remorselessly digging into his throat the Greek wasn't cowed. "He," the man pointed at Simon, "promised that the one who found the kid could name his own reward. He promised it on the grave of his father, on the altar of his god." The man was coughing, a piece of chicken stuck in his throat. "Well, where is it? I want it in my hands before I tell you anything."

Simon reached out and pulled the sword away. "The man is right, I did make that promise."

Clodia was about to protest, but he silenced her with a gesture. Simon stared at the man, his eyes expressionless, "But be warned – if your information is false, death will come as a friend."

The man grinned, his tongue hanging out. Simon was reminded of the guard dogs that he used to keep in Jerusalem.

"Lie and your life is mine." Clodia's voice was harsh with menace. The man's grin faded when his eyes met hers.

"I promise you, my lady, I do not lie," he muttered, suddenly conciliatory, "but I am a poor man and I have risked my life to bring you this news." This last was a positive whine.

"A letter of credit for one million sestertia in gold and a ship to carry you to any part of the Empire." Simon's offer caused the man's eyes to widen with greed.

He licked his lips. "I don't know anything about letters of credit," he finally managed to get out.

"If I give you the money in gold, you will be dead before you get ten miles," Simon replied dryly.

The man gulped. He knew Simon was right. "What I want," he said hoarsely, "is a farm, well stocked, and," he ended defiantly, "with a good house and slaves to work the land."

Simon could feel Clodia beginning to simmer. "In the morning before we leave," Simon said – "for you will lead us," he continued – "I will assign to you the deeds of such a farm on the island of Kythnos where I own an estate. Included with the farm are the slaves who work it, the household servants, all the crops and draught animals."

Dazed at his good fortune the Greek could only nod his agreement. "Now," growled Clodia, "tell us what you know or the only earth you will get will be the grave you dig."

With a less than steady hand Theasides poured some wine and hurriedly gulped it before replying. "There is a colony of lepers in the Alban Hills. They live in a desolate ravine. They have taken sanctuary there for as long as can be remembered. The cliff caves," he continued, "provide them with shelter and they scavenge what they can from Rome's rubbish dumps."

As he swigged his wine, a restless movement from Clodia prompted him to continue without delay. "An unblemished baby was recently brought to the colony by one of the female lepers." The man hesitated.

"And?" This was from Simon.

The Greek moved away from Clodia, sensing that what he had to say next might bring a reaction that could be directed against him. "The lepers mate among themselves. They," he shuddered, "sometimes have children."

"No, no, no. In all the names of the gods, no." Clodia's anguished screams raised the hairs on Simon's neck. He held the howling woman to him.

"What else, man?" he shouted. "What has this to do with our child?"

It was Clodia, suddenly calm, in a voice devoid of all feeling, which answered, "Such a woman is his wet nurse."

Simon stared at Theasides, who nodded in confirmation. Simon swallowed hard but had to ask, "Has the child contracted the disease?"

The Greek shook his head and muttered, "I don't know, my lord. I only know what I know because I gave Gallus Psellus, the leader of the clan, many things. Money," he ended sombrely, "is of no use to people who cannot find anybody to take it from them."

"At first light you will lead us to this Gallus Psellus." Simon's voice was firm.

Theasides shook his head. "I have told you all there is to know and where to find the child. Our bargain is complete." The words died on his lips as his eyes met Clodia's.

Simon ignored this. He issued a stream of instructions to the steward who ran his temporary household, a competent Thracian who assured Simon that by daybreak a small caravan would be equipped and ready to leave.

Simon even considered making part of the journey by sea, returning to the port of Ostia, but he finally decided against it, uncertain how Galba was faring in his march on Rome. "Better," he said to Clodia, "to go overland and swing around the city. The area the lepers live in is a desolate piece of wasteland well outside the city limits."

Clodia was in agreement, confident that she could take their small party across any kind of terrain with the utmost stealth, should it prove necessary.

They left at first light, Rabbi Judah ben Isaac coming to see them off. Their reluctant guide's feelings were somewhat mollified by the thick bundle of deeds now strapped around his middle, Simon having kept his promise to assign him the property he had spoken of the night before.

"Go with God." The old rabbi lifted his hand in farewell.

They were mounted on horses that ben Isaac had provided, and slung in panniers on their backs were the stores they would need, not just for the journey but with additional quantities which they hoped would gain the outcasts' confidence.

Simon lifted his hand to acknowledge the salute and the benediction, and without any further exchange led them out of the courtyard.

Clodia had estimated it would take them three weeks to reach their destination. During this time Theasides would be watched day and night. She had already detached four of the armed mercenaries who formed part of their escort to guard the Greek, with orders that if the man attempted to sneak out of the camp they were not to kill him, only incapacitate him. Before he died, she told them, she had questions of her own that she would need answered.

The bright-eyed Syrian mercenaries, under the command of Miletus, a Spartan gladiator who had won his freedom from the arena as an undefeated champion, grinned happily at their orders and hoped that the Greek would be foolish enough to try and evade them. Not that it was likely; Syrian cruelty to their prisoners of war was legendary.

## 37

Three weeks to the day after leaving Herculaneum, Simon and his party reached the desolate country to the north west of Rome. Theasides led them into a narrow ravine that ended in a cul-de-sac that widened into a natural amphitheatre. Its steeply rising walls were pock marked with caves which were connected by a series of narrow paths formed from the ledges that latticed the bare, angular rock faces.

On the floor of this arena was a rough circle of stone benches that surrounded the embers of a fire that was still warm enough to give off faint tendrils of smoke.

These and the buzzards that eddied like specks of soot in the window of blue sky that opened above their heads, were the only signs of life.

As they clattered to a halt, the noise of their arrival echoed off the stone walls and they unconsciously lowered their voices. They could all feel the presence of life in the intense silence of that lonely place.

Reluctant to dismount they stood in their stirrups to relieve their aching backs and cricked their necks as they twisted to scan the ramparts of the natural fortress they had entered.

Clodia was the first to speak. When she did so, it was barely above a whisper. "Lord, we are being watched."

Simon nodded imperceptibly to acknowledge Clodia's warning. He turned to Miletus and said in a deliberately loud voice, "Have the provisions unloaded and stacked near the fire."

Miletus, who had also felt the unseen presence of hidden watchers, summoned the baggage master who had seen and felt nothing, though Miletus's men, their senses honed by battle, could feel the atmosphere of the place and were uneasy. The porters hurried to obey orders, anxious to move out of the confines of the canyon into more open country.

As the men busied themselves, Clodia kneed her mount level with Simon's. A flutter of movement on one of the ledges had caught her eye. "They are above us," she whispered.

"I know," was the quiet rejoinder.

Miletus, who had overheard Clodia's whispered comment, made a play of inspecting his horse's hoof. As he did so he said quietly, "The watchers are the afflicted who live in this place."

As he finished speaking a figure suddenly appeared at the mouth of one of the higher caves. Even at that distance, its appearance was a grisly reminder of the terrible fate of those who contracted the feared disease of leprosy.

The creature howled in hate at the figures below, its voice ricocheting madly from wall to wall.

The porters, who had almost finished their task, dropped the last of the bundles and ran for their horses that were skittering nervously under that raw sound.

"Steady," Simon said, as he raised his hand to shade his eyes. "We bring you food and blankets," he shouted. "The first of what could be much more."

The figure on the high ledge moved out of the cave mouth to get a better view of the supplies that had been piled around the fire. "What do you want?" The question floated down, the voice suspicious.

"To talk." It was Clodia who answered.

"Talk? Talk?" The apparition on the ledge suddenly burst out laughing. At least, that was what those on the valley floor decided that the gargling sound was. The figure turned its head from side to side and peered upwards. As it did so it called out, "Brothers and sisters, where are you? Have you no manners? You have guests – they want to talk to you."

There was a pause, punctuated by another peal of manic laughter. "Perhaps they'll stay for dinner."

In response to the leper's command there was a rustling sound. It reminded Simon of bats leaving a cave at dusk, a flapping of countless thousands of leather wings.

"Oh God." The involuntary exclamation came from a white-faced Clodia who was gripping her saddle pommel with hands that were knuckle-white in an effort to keep herself from fleeing in panic.

Miletus had drawn his sword and threatened to kill the first porter who made any attempt to mount a horse, even though his own stomach was turning at the sight of the monsters who were appearing to crowd the cliff's ledges. Wrapped in filthy rags the lepers scrambled out of the caves in which they had been hiding. They hopped and crawled out of their sanctuary to squat in uneven rows, staring impassively at the laagered party below.

For long seconds there wasn't a sound as the two groups stared at each other. It was broken by the sound of a rock bouncing sharply in front of Simon's horse. Another and another followed it as the lepers on the ledges followed the lead they had been given. A cry of pain from one of the porters as one of the stones found its mark was enough to cause them to break ranks. Even Miletus's drawn sword couldn't keep them under control.

In wild disarray they turned and ran, retreating the way they had come to the catcalls and jeers of their assailants, who hurled a final volley at their retreating backs.

Simon and Clodia, with Miletus and his mercenaries, had no option but to follow their fleeing porters. When they were out of range, and breath, the stampeding porters stopped to regroup.

Miletus was in a towering rage and would have dealt out summary justice on the spot. He was all for executing one in three there and then as a Roman example of how cowardice should be treated.

"These men are porters, not soldiers," Simon reminded him. "Anyway, their task is complete."

The ex-gladiator frowned, doubtful of this decision. Simon smiled and thumped him on the shoulder. "Get them to set up camp here for the lady Clodia and me and then take them home."

Miletus shook his head in disbelief. "You and the mistress cannot stay here alone, lord, with," and he shuddered faintly before continuing, "with this filth. They will kill you for the clothes you stand up in."

"For revenge," hissed Clodia. "For being whole and not like them, for the pleasure of your pain to match theirs."

Simon put his arm around her shoulders before saying, "Do you forget why we came here? Go if you wish, no blame would be attached to you. Wait for me in Herculaneum, but I must talk with these people."

Clodia bridled at this suggestion. "You mistake me, my lord. I will not leave this place until we have what we came for." She continued grimly, "If it is here, but," she finished sombrely, "Miletus is right, when it is dark they will come for us."

"Then we must be ready for them," Simon replied quietly. Miletus asked to be allowed to remain. Simon admired him for his courage, but the mercenary didn't press it. Secretly he was relieved to be returning with his men and the porters. Brave as a lion in battle, Miletus couldn't cope with the horrors that lived in the canyon's caves.

Before he and his men took their leave, they erected a tent and would have dug a trench around it six feet deep and twelve feet wide had they been allowed to, but Simon restrained them.

Shaking his head in sorrow, Miletus ordered the porters to hobble the horses they would leave behind and stack sufficient stores for the return journey, which he doubted Simon and Clodia would ever make.

It was early afternoon when he and his mercenaries departed with the porters. They were anxious to put some distance between themselves and the lepers before they made camp.

With the rest of the party gone, Simon said, "Shall we see if they are still there?"

Clodia nodded and picked up a sword. She already had a knife tucked into the strands of the whip wound round her waist.

"One sword against so many will not help you. To carry it is a sign you are afraid."

Clodia dropped the sword and, with a ghost of a smile, said, "Our fear has put them in this place. Now they can judge us as we did them."

Simon nodded and picked up the spear of Longinus. He released the spearhead and hid it under his tunic. Staff in hand he smiled, "Let's go."

The terraces, which earlier had been filled to bursting point, were empty. The pile of stores they had stacked around the campfire had gone.

Simon raised his head to face the cave he assumed was that of the leader. "I am the merchant Simon bar Joseph, citizen of Rome and a Jew of the House of David, and this is my wife Clodia, the granddaughter of Tiberius." He paused but there was no response. "We will not leave this place until we have what we came for." His voice, echoing off the rock face caused a slippage of pebbles to clatter down.

"We will wait for you at our camp."

Standing at his side Clodia scanned the cliffs. "They are up there," she whispered. "They can hear you."

Simon continued, "You can kill us, but you cannot make us leave. But if we die you will not get the food that I have pledged by the God of Abraham and Moses to give you." The man deliberately paused. He swung his head, scanning the soaring pockmarked walls. "A wagonload of supplies every month, for as long as there are lepers in this place, pledged by me and my seed in the name of the one God."

As he turned to go Clodia couldn't help herself. From the wells of dark and terrible memories she shouted a message of her own. "Come to our fire in peace or come prepared to fight, for we will not die alone. If the end is to be in this place – so be it, by whatever gods you want to swear by."

Without another word and forgetting herself for a moment, she marched out of the ravine ahead of Simon, who followed with a faint bitter smile at his headstrong wife.

When they got back to their camp darkness fell swiftly, the high cliffs suddenly shuttering out the setting sun.

## 38

Arattle of loose gravel warned Simon and Clodia, who were sitting by their lighted campfire, that they had a visitor. Without undue haste Simon picked up a brand and holding it above his head stood up, stepping towards the sound saying, "Welcome to our fire. Come, sit with us."

The figure that materialised out of the dark was a reminder that raised the hair on Simon's head of the fate of those who became the diseased outcasts of a society that forbade you, on pain of death, ever to return.

Draped in a torn blanket and propped on crutches, the grotesque figure of what had once been human spoke to them, its voice a husky rasp, the words slurred and difficult to follow. "If you are so anxious for the company of lepers you are invited by our leader to join us for supper." Without waiting for a reply the figure turned and hopped back the way it had come, its progress in the dark marked by the occasional rattle of disturbed pebbles.

Without hesitation Simon stood up. Clodia swallowed hard but, without protest, joined him. In silence they followed the barely discernible figure hopping and fluttering across the uneven floor of the ravine.

Rounding a bend they could see that the flames of the fire had been rekindled. Around it were crowded the lepers of the ledges. Taking hold of Clodia's hand, Simon stepped boldly through the circle of now crowded stone benches. Across the other side of the fire, one of these was occupied exclusively by what had once been a man of giant physique. From what was left of his face Simon guessed he was Roman.

Clodia suddenly stopped shivering. Inexplicable fear fell away from her. She let go of Simon's hand and stood easily at his side. He felt the change in her demeanour and marvelled, for the hideousness of the fresco of figures that surrounded them exceeded even the wildest imaginings of poet or painter who, down the ages, had attempted to describe the underworld of Hades.

"You promise much, Jew. Why shouldn't we take what we now have rather than wait for what you promise on account?" The voice of the leader rumbled out of a cavernous chest.

Observing the man's physique Clodia was not surprised that, for the moment, he held power.

"Who are you?" Simon asked, ignoring the other's question.

The man leaned forward, the heavy sheepskin draped across his shoulder slipping down his back. "I was Gallus Psellus, citizen of Rome, and now I am your executioner. That is," he ended grimly, "when my children have had their fill of you both. She," he continued with a flick of his eyes in Clodia's direction, "will suit my tastes and when I and my brothers have had our fill she will be one of us, I can promise you."

The response to this was raucous shouts of approval, punctuated by wild whoops and short shrill outbursts of barking laughter. Clodia suddenly noticed that many of the figures were carrying clubs.

As Psellus finished speaking, the squatting lepers scrambled to their feet, the noose of figures suddenly tightening around the couple.

"Every day you burrow like pigs in the middens of the towns and villages for that which even dogs refuse to eat." It was Clodia who spoke. "This man has brought you the kind of food you haven't tasted for years, has sworn by his God to go on bringing it for as long as you are here – why?" Clodia advanced to the edge of the fire. She turned her back on Psellus. "Why? Before you kill us and lose what Simon bar Joseph has promised – you who are less than dogs – ask yourselves why."

The menacing circle paused, momentarily confused. Behind them, blind to reason, Psellus roared his hatred. "The woman is mine for tonight. Tomorrow she is yours." Simon tightened the grip on his staff.

"Wait," the voice came from the darkness above their heads. It was a woman's voice. "They have the power of the child. They bring you more than bread or blood. That which made me clean is within your presence."

As the voice stopped silence followed, broken only by the sound of the fire spitting and popping as it burned.

Psellus stood up. As he did so they realised a leg had gone, and had been replaced by a timber peg. As he swung round the fire they could see that the disease had ravaged the left side of his body. A leather shaft ending in a double-edged blade had replaced the man's left arm to the elbow. Half of his face was a corrugated ruin of swollen distorted flesh that looked as though it had erupted like lava from the top of his skull, and flowed down the hillside of his head to cool and settle by chance.

"Is what she says true?" Psellus's voice was hard with contained emotion, not daring to show any expectation of hope, not wanting to expose himself to even a flicker of disappointment.

Simon swallowed. The atmosphere was explosive. In every breast in that dark throng, the deep dormant spirit of hope was released. It rose like a bubble from the mud of despair to break softly, awakening that which was no more than an aching memory. Hope.

"I have felt that power. My wife was made whole by it, my child is protected by it." Simon's voice echoed off the cliff walls.

Inches from Simon's face, Psellus stared deep into his eyes as though there he might discern the truth of what was said. "Cure me."

The man's guttural cry was flung across the fire-bright circle. "And me – and me. Cure me, in the name of all the gods."

"Cure me." The agonised plea echoed off the canyon walls, supplicating, demanding wails, pitiful, tremulous, angrily pleading, all blended together.

"Cure me." It rose to an hysterical scream. Hands reached out, arm stumps were thrust forward. Ruined faces of those crawling in the dust pushed forward. In a terrible microsecond of memory there flashed in front of Simon's eyes a picture of Jesus and those who had crowded to him for a cure.

In sudden fright Clodia clung to Simon, who raised his arms and shouted for silence. Gradually order was restored and the crowd fell expectantly quiet.

Psellus had retreated to his bench where he lounged, a sardonic gleam in his one good eye. "They are waiting," he growled softly.

Simon took a deep breath. "No man can command God. No man can demand His power."

"What will this God of yours do?" The bitter question came from the shadowed circle of ruined faces.

"Give you His love in this life and the next, a place in His kingdom where you will be whole and clean forever."

A wild burst of raucous laughter greeted this reply. "At least" spluttered Psellus, "he promises the next life will be better." The leader of the lepers suddenly jumped to his feet. "Who," he howled, lurching powerfully round the circle, "who wants more life? More of this shit? Is this, or any other god's kingdom, worth living in?"

The cries of anger, despair and hate that this evoked crackled through the night.

"Then die now." It was Clodia who spoke. The challenge silenced the querulous mob. "Borrow my blade." She held out the knife she had plucked from her waist. "He who is tired of this life can escape it now, in this very instant." She paused and when she continued her voice was sombre but no one doubted her resolve. "If there is one among you who would go but cannot make the stroke, let your neighbour do it for you. If," she raised her voice, "your neighbour won't help you, I will."

This offer was considered in a thoughtful silence. It was Psellus who broke it. "The faithful followers of this god of love are here to do you a favour. They'll cut your throat if you want them to. Just line up on the left!"

Howls of delight went up at this sally and on all sides figures shambled about offering their throats to each other in a macabre parody of mass suicide.

"Die or live – live or die – there are no other choices." It was Simon who spoke, or rather shouted, above the noisy crowd.

"Not even Psellus can offer you an alternative. If you choose to live I cannot cure you but I can feed you, I can clothe you, I can love you. Yes," he continued with a roar, "love you – all of you – for that is the power God shares with you, the power that will lead even you out of the darkness and into the light. Choose, but choose now – life or death."

"And if we choose to kill you and live?" Psellus mocked them from his bench.

"Then," said Clodia, "you will have chosen a living death, for what time you have left in this world will continue as it is now – in fear, despair, pain and misery."

As she spoke Simon trembled at her words. He started at her in amazement. "I have come for the child and I will not leave without him. The power that protects him has sent Simon bar Joseph to you, to raise you from the pit to the light. The choice is yours. Make it – make it tonight," – she paused – "for tomorrow I will seek my son with the sword."

She allowed this to sink in before continuing, "I have no fear of leaving this life behind, for without my child I am already dead."

In silence the pair pushed their way out of the stilled circle and returned wearily to their tiny camp.

## 39

Exhausted, Simon and Clodia dragged themselves into their tent to collapse into sleep, barely remembering to pull the blankets across themselves.

Clodia was the first to awake. Lying in the shelter of Simon's arms she frowned. Something had disturbed her. She stared at the roof of the tent. Through the tiniest of pinholes she could see a dazzle of light. It was morning. Outside she could hear a blackbird singing. As she turned her head to listen Simon woke and blinked at her sleepily.

The sound that had disturbed Clodia came again. With a shout she lunged for the tent's entrance. As she did so she almost brought the whole lot down as she cannoned into the central post. Simon, scarcely awake, flailed to rise, getting tangled as he did so in the rumpled blanket and, as he struggled to his knees, getting kicked in the chest by Clodia who was scrabbling desperately for the entrance.

As she tore open the flap Simon was dazzled by the sudden sun. Clodia's scream brought him through the flap on his hands and knees, panic rising in his throat. He stopped dead at the entrance.

Clodia was kneeling, tears streaming down her face. In front of her in a basket lay the smiling Joshua, chuckling happily at the row of crudely made bobbins strung across the top as a plaything.

With shaking hands Clodia picked up the gurgling infant. With trembling fingers she undid the cloth in which he was wrapped and examined him inch by inch. "Clean," she whispered in a wondering voice. She raised her tear-stained face to Simon who, smiling with joy, held out his arms. "Clean!" she shouted, and leapt into the man's embrace, the baby protesting at such rough treatment.

As they clung to each other Simon suddenly stiffened and looked over Clodia's head. She turned to see what it was that had caught his attention. It was a woman. She had been hiding behind some loose boulders and had come into the open. She stood motionless a hundred feet away. With the sun at her back she was nothing more than a silhouette.

Simon motioned her to approach. The figure bobbed its head in response, and came slowly towards them. The first thing that struck both Simon and Clodia was that she had no visible signs of leprosy.

"Who are you?" asked Simon.

"I am Ruth, the daughter of a Jewess, the woman to whom the Romans gave your child."

"But," said Clodia, and stopped.

The woman smiled gently. "Yes," she said. "I was a leper. Now I am clean – as is the woman who suckled your baby."

Clodia could only gaze at her in wonder. "Why did they let you return Joshua to us?"

The woman smiled. "He is the living proof of the God they don't understand, the God of love of whom you spoke." The woman paused. When she continued her voice held a challenging note. "Your caravans will bring them the food you promised?"

Simon nodded. Clodia, always sensitive to atmosphere, interjected, "As a Jewess you, of all the others, should not doubt my husband will keep his promise."

Simon smiled. "They don't doubt the arrival of the food I have pledged. They hunger for that which I promised that has no price."

Clodia, holding the baby, stared first at the woman and then at the man. "The Word, you promised them the Word."

Ruth nodded in agreement and turned to make her way back up the canyon, not waiting to see if they would follow. Stopping only long enough for Simon to snatch up the precious spear, they hurried after their guide.

With little Joshua in the crook of her arm Clodia fell into step beside Simon. She looked up at him mischievously out of the corner of her eye. "Lord," she asked innocently, "when you tell them about Abraham and Moses, will you tell them about Jesus?"

Simon laughed.

The camp was in sight. Every ledge was filled. In the centre of its arena stood Psellus, his ruined face grave, watchful, and suspicious. As the couple approached he would have stepped back to avoid contact, but he was caught in Simon's embrace. A gasp went up from the watchers on the ledges.

Clodia sat silently on one of the benches, Joshua on her lap.

Simon raised his head and slowly turned to scan the canyon walls. Ranged along the latticework of ledges that seamed the cliff faces like cicatrices of ancient scars were perched pathetic bundles of what had once been humans.

Tier after tier of these squatting figures had dragged themselves from their caves into the unforgiving brightness of the early morning sun. Those that couldn't walk had hopped or crawled; a few had been carried. Others who were helpless and friendless lay dying in dark corners, but even they struggled to raise themselves up to listen, for the rumour that had packed the ledges had reached even their neglected couches.

Hope had entered hell.

Squinting against the sun Simon returned the silent stare of the fragments of humanity who met his gaze. From beneath the rags pulled over their bare heads, their shadowed eyes struggled to hide the tiny flame of hope that might show, as though to even admit its existence would render it stillborn.

Simon signalled Clodia to hand Joshua to him. With the child in the crook of one arm he raised the Spear of Longinus in his free hand and began to speak.

Slowly at first but with increasing power, he spoke of the God he had struggled against all his life, of the brother he had misunderstood. Of the Father who loved them, who had sent Jesus into the world as a light that reached even the pit into which they had been cast.

That the Kingdom of Heaven would be established in men's hearts and not in a place above the earth. That the resurrection of Jesus was the triumph of life over death. That He would sustain them in this life and be with them in the next.

# Appendix
## The Evidence

*Encyclopaedia Britannica*, under **James**: One of the Lord's brethren.

The Bible: In **Matthew 22:47** and **Mark 6:3** we read of James who, together with Joses, Judas and Simon was a 'brother' of the Lord. The **Epithanian** view is that Jesus's brothers and sisters were born **after** the birth of Jesus.

The **Helvidian** theory as propounded by **Helvidius** and apparently accepted by **Tertullian**, makes James a brother of the Lord, as truly as Mary was his mother. This seems to be more in keeping with the Gospels (see W. Patrick, *James, the Brother of the Lord*, 1906, p.5).

James, the brother of Jesus who became leader of the Church in Jerusalem. *The Lion Handbook of the Bible*, p.666, James 1:3 (Lion Publishing). He was traditionally the author of the Epistle of the New Testament, which bears his name (see Epistle of James).

According to **Hegesippus** (see Eus H.E. II 23) he was a Nazarite and because of his eminent righteousness was called 'Just' and 'Oblias.'

So great was his influence with the people that he was appealed to by the scribes and Pharisees for a true (as they hoped) and unfavourable judgement about the Messiahship of Christ. But from a pinnacle of the temple he made public confession of his faith and was seized by the temple priests, hurled to the ground and murdered. A detailed account of this event is covered on p. 99–100

280

under the heading 'The Martyrdom of James, The Lord's Brother' in **Eusabius's** *The History of the Church*, published by Penguin Classics in 1965, translation by G. A. Williamson. This was immediately before the Roman Siege.

**Josephus** (Antiq. XX 911) tells that it was by the order of **Ananus** the high priest that James was put to death. **Josephus's** narrative gives the idea of some sort of judicial examination, for he says that James and some others were brought before an assembly of judges, by whom they were condemned and delivered to be stoned to death.

**Josephus** is also cited by **Eusabius** (H.E. II 23) to the effect that the miseries of the siege of Jerusalem, which was led by **Vespasian**, were due to divine vengeance for the murder of James. According to **Eusabius** (H.E. VII 19), his Episcopal chair was still shown at Jerusalem.

In addition to the above, see articles under the heading 'James' in the *Hastings Dictionary of the Bible* (Mayor) and *Dictionary of Christ and the Gospels* (Fulford), and the *Encyclopaedia Biblica* (O. Cone).

See also the introduction to the *Commentaries on the Epistle of James* by Mayor and Knowling.

See also *Jesus: The Evidence* by Ian Wilson, p.61, 109, 138, 148–51, 173, 196; brothers and sisters p.149, 151, 170.

In the third century **Origen** expressed astonishment that **Josephus**, while disbelieving that Jesus was the Messiah, should have spoken so warmly about his brother (**Mark 6:1–6**). Jesus went to his home town of Nazareth and they said, "Where did this man get all this? This is the carpenter, surely, the son of Mary, the brother of James and Joses and Judas and Simon, and are not his sisters here with us?" They would not accept him and he could work no miracles there.

St Paul also corroborates the existence of James as the brother of Christ in **Galatians 1:20** on making a trip to Jerusalem. "I saw only James, the brother of the Lord."

Also:
*Westminster Dictionary of the Bible* by John D. Davis, revised and rewritten by Henry Snyder Gehman, published by Collins (1944), p.280–81.

*The Moffat Concordance* by Dr. James Moffat, published by Hodder and Stoughton (1950), p.252, Gal. 1:19.

*The Life of Christ* by Frederic W. Farrar, DD, FRS, published by Cassell Petter and Galpin, p.74–5.

*A Dictionary of Christian Biography and Literature* edited by Henry Wace, DD, Dean of Canterbury and William C Piercy, MA, Dean and Chaplain of Whitelands College SW, published by John Murray (1911). See p. 436 an account by **Hegesippus** of James the brother of Jesus being brought before Ananus the high priest and the assembled judges of the Sanhedrin, accused of blasphemy and stoned to death.

*The History of the Church: From Christ to Constantine* by Eusebius, edited by Andrew Louth and translated by G. A Williamson. Introduction p. 9, James, the Lord's brother was the Bishop of Jerusalem.

**Eusabius** succeeded Marcellus as Bishop of Rome AD309, born AD260, native of Caesaraea and Bishop of Caesaraea, intimate friend of the Roman Emperor Constantine. Eusabius wrote the only surviving record of the Christian Church during its crucial first 300 years, including the proceedings at Nicaea.

**Helvidius** a western writer (AD383) who put forward opinions on anthropological subjects opposed to the generally accepted teachings of the church in his day.

**Tertullian** AD150–220/40. A Roman who became a Christian theologian. He founded the Church in Africa. Prolific writer of theological works.

**Hegesippus,** commonly known as the father of Church history. Date of birth not known. Wrote much of the Church's history *prior* to AD167. Only fragments of his history survive.

**Orignes** AD185–AD251. Theologian of prodigious output.